GIVING HER NO TIME TO REACT, HE TOOK HER HAND IN HIS AND TUGGED HER TO HIM

Appearing dazed and bewildered, Kat did not resist. He pulled her inexorably closer, until their breaths mingled. She inhaled deeply and her breasts rose, brushing his chest with tantalizing effect. Air whooshed from his lungs as though he were drowning.

He released her hand, but before she could escape, Alex cradled her head in his hands and slowly dipped his head. She stood still as a stunned doe surprised by an unwelcome intruder. But the intruder was unrepentant and took blatant advantage of her lapse.

Alex inhaled Kat's jasmine-and-spice scent as he swooped down, his eyes intent on the absolution her lips bespoke. Finally, his mouth made contact, barely brushing the corner of her bottom lip, a teasing caress that made him groan with the need of a deeper communion.

He repeated the reverent gesture on the other side of her mouth. "This is to seal our bargain, of course," he said in a deep husky timbre, then covered her mouth with his.

BOOK YOUR PLACE ON OUR WEBSITE AND MAKE THE READING CONNECTION!

We've created a customized website just for our very special readers, where you can get the inside scoop on everything that's going on with Zebra, Pinnacle and Kensington books.

When you come online, you'll have the exciting opportunity to:

- View covers of upcoming books
- Read sample chapters
- Learn about our future publishing schedule (listed by publication month *and author*)
- Find out when your favorite authors will be visiting a city near you
- Search for and order backlist books from our online catalog
- Check out author bios and background information
- Send e-mail to your favorite authors
- Meet the Kensington staff online
- Join us in weekly chats with authors, readers and other guests
- Get writing guidelines
- AND MUCH MORE!

**Visit our website at
http://www.kensingtonbooks.com**

Vow of *Seduction*

ANGELA JOHNSON

ZEBRA BOOKS
Kensington Publishing Corp.

http://www.kensingtonbooks.com

ZEBRA BOOKS are published by

Kensington Publishing Corp.
119 West 40th Street
New York, NY 10018

All Kensington titles, imprints, and distributed lines are available at special quantity discounts for bulk purchases for sales
promotion, premiums, fund-raising, educational, or institu-
tional use.

Special book excerpts or customized printings can also be created to fit specific needs. For details, write or phone the office
of the Kensington Special Sales Manager: Attn. Special Sales
Department. Kensington Publishing Corp., 119 West 40th
Street, New York, NY 10018. Phone: 1-800-221-2647.

Zebra and the Z logo Reg. U.S. Pat. & TM Off.

ISBN-13: 978-1-4201-0857-6
ISBN-10: 1-4201-0857-3

First Printing: October 2009
10 9 8 7 6 5 4 3 2 1

Printed in the United States of America

I dedicate this book to Joe Cowdin—
my hero, my love, my inspiration

For believing in me before I believed in myself

Acknowledgments

I owe a debt of gratitude to many people for making this book possible. Thank you to Kansas Writers Inc. for their unwavering support and encouragement; to my wonderful and talented critique partners—Tammy Ard, Anne Barringer, Morgan Chilson, Tish Glasson, Lori Martin, and Shayne Sawyer—for molding me into a better writer; to Morgan for her much appreciated work on the final edit of *Vow of Seduction*.

Many thanks to Chris Hubbell, my tech guru who rescued me on many occasions; and to Leann and Shayne for lending a hand, or two, when needed.

I'd also like to thank Marj Murray and the Interlibrary Loan Department at Washburn University for their assistance in my researching endeavors.

Lastly, I thank Hilary Sares for giving me this amazing opportunity, and Megan Records, for making the transition between editors a seamless process.

Prologue

In the year of our Lord 1267
Montclair Estate, Kent, England

Lady Katherine of Montclair squeezed her thighs tightly around Hunter's sleek body and rode him hard. Sunlight speared the oak forest canopy, dappling them with heat. Leaning over Hunter, she whispered loving words into his ear and stroked her hand down the taut length of his neck and powerful shoulders. In response, his flanks flexed beneath her, thrusting harder, faster. Her heart pounded sharply and excitement pulsed in her blood.

For her, there was naught more exhilarating than the raw sensation of her steed's muscled loins pumping between her thighs as she rode at full gallop.

Her nose pressed to Hunter's neck, Lady Katherine, or Kat as she stubbornly insisted, inhaled deeply of the sharp tang of heated horseflesh. A bead of perspiration trickled down between her small breasts. And her short black hair, captured at her nape by a leather band, came free and stuck to her moist skin.

Wearing green hose and a knee-length tunic, with her cropped hair and a quiver of arrows across her back, she looked like a lad instead of a girl age ten and four.

Without warning, Hunter slowed his pace, his ears pricked forward. A sharp tickle rose on the back of Kat's neck, chilling the dampness there. She tugged on the reins and pulled the black to an abrupt stop.

The shady woods were eerily quiet. "Aye, I sense it, too, Hunter. But what?"

Her head cocked, she peered through the leafy screen shielding the glen up ahead and listened for possible signs of danger. The wind sighed. Smells of rich loamy earth and sun-warmed leaves permeated the air.

The sudden clang of steel upon steel rang out. Her heart jolted. Hunter whinnied. "Quiet, boy," she crooned, patting his silky black neck while the sounds of battle echoed through the trees.

Kat removed her longbow from the saddle, slung a long, slender leg over her horse's rump, and slid softly to the moss-covered ground.

She crept towards the clearing as quiet as a snail. Her blood pumped hard and fast. Her hand caressed her well-oiled yew bow, a ritual that never failed to calm her galloping nerves. Caution ruled until she ascertained the identity of the intruders on Montclair lands. Danger abounded from thieves and rogues intent on mischief.

Stopping next to a stunted oak, Kat peered into the glade and gasped. Upon seeing the carnage in the once peaceful glen, she nearly dropped her bow from nerveless fingers. Near the large pond in the center of the clearing, two men lay dead, one with blood gushing from his neck, his head severed from his body. Two more men fought with swords in a violent dance of death.

Her heart about to burst in terror, Kat could not move. For the shorter of the combatants was Alex de Beaumont, her intended husband. But long training side by side her father's men-at-arms had taught her to fight through her fear. She took a deep breath, and then exhaled. A sudden calm descended upon her. A silent, fervent prayer upon her lips, she withdrew an arrow from her quiver and nocked the feathered end, then waited for a clear shot.

Alex was at a disadvantage, wearing only his sherte, blood oozing from a shallow slash across his thigh. His shoulder-length black hair was wet and slicked back off his forehead. He must have just emerged from the pond when these brigands attacked him. The man he fought was dressed all in black and wore a gambeson, a padded knee-length leather tunic. A great hulking brute, he had a crooked nose and deep-lined forehead.

When the ruffian lunged at Alex, Kat tensed. But Alex, using his smaller, more agile body to his advantage, sidestepped to the right and shoved the larger man as he stumbled past.

The brute roared, turned with surprising speed, and charged again. Alex swung his sword up at the last moment to meet the other's violent downward stroke. Their swords crashed to the hilts, sparks flew. Struggling against one another, their eyes glittered with malice.

Sweat trailed down Kat's temples. She waited, her arms tense with restraint.

Then in rapid succession, the dark outlaw shoved Alex hard, Alex staggered back, and as he did, his sword came up and slashed the bastard's cheek open. Blood spurted and the man howled in pain and surprise.

Unfortunately, Alex tripped over the foot of one of the dead men sprawled in the grass and fell down. His head slammed into the ground, his sword hand smashed against a boulder, and he lost his grip. The hilt clattered against the rock and out of his reach.

The dark fiend, his face contorted in rage, loomed over Alex and raised his sword high for a killing thrust. Alex cursed; in one smooth motion, Kat drew her bowstring, sighted her target, and released her missile.

Hissing through the air, the arrow thumped into flesh, finding its mark. The outlaw, shock palpable on his face, blood dripping from his cheek wound, looked down at the arrow protruding from his shoulder.

Another arrow nocked and ready to be drawn, Kat ordered in a gruff voice, "Drop your sword and back away from him, or my next arrow will sever your gullet."

The stranger, his black gaze cold and merciless, spouted inanely, "You're naught but a lad."

Kat grunted. "A lad I may be," she said. Bitterness twisted her lips. Though not a lad, neither was she a lady, meek and mild. Never had she felt comfortable in the role to which the Church and society dictated she conform. She followed her own path the way she thought best for her. Kat continued, "But this *lad* has the upper hand. Now do as I say." She dared not look at Alex.

The villain scowled, the wicked slash on his cheek like a big gaping smile. He seemed to gauge his chances, unwilling to accept defeat, before he finally dropped his sword to the ground and stepped back several paces.

In a flash of white, Alex jumped to his feet with his sword in hand, but he stumbled in his haste. His attacker seized the moment of confusion and fled, charging for the trees.

Nay, the knave shall not escape my net so easily, she thought.

Kat turned and sighted her target. But at the last moment, with a wicked smile, she lowered her aim and released her missile. Just before he reached the woods, the man howled in pain and clutched his right buttock. Limping, he ran into the trees, an arrow embedded in his shoulder and another in the vulnerable flesh of his nether cheek.

"Mayhap you shall think *twice* next time before attacking me and mine!" Kat hollered after him. Her hands shook in belated reaction.

Not wanting to reveal how afeared she had been, Kat turned to greet Alex, a huge grin on her face.

He, on the other hand, glared at her, his hands clenched at his sides. "You little fool, you could've been killed." His gaze skimmed over her, his full lips twisted in contempt. "Any other young lady of breeding would have had the good sense to run for her life and leave the battle to men. How could I have forgotten you don't have the sense God gave a ewe?"

Kat fumed at the injustice of his diatribe. If she were a man—which she was not, unfortunately—Alex would be thanking her for saving his life, instead of scolding her like an errant child.

She raised her hand up in a swift motion. "Enough. If I were any other *lady,* you would be dead right now. How is that for sense?" she asked, not hiding her disgust.

Alex's face reddened in fury, or embarrassment perhaps. In several quick strides he towered over her like some ancient monolith, grabbed her arms in a vise-like grip, and yanked her up against his chest, eye to eye. Defiant, she glared into his startlingly blue gaze, unnerved by the strange sensation of her small breasts cushioned against his hard chest.

His eyes bore into her and an angry tic flared in his cheek. "How arrogant you are, Lady Katherine. I have escaped worse predicaments before and would have done so again. I had no need of your interference. And I certainly don't need to be *rescued* by a skinny waif of a girl!"

"Oh," she cried out, "you ungrateful wretch." She squirmed against him in an attempt to escape his painful grip, but he held firm. "And I'm not a little girl anymore, Alex, but a woman full-grown."

The irritating man quirked his black eyebrow in disbelief, sorely pricking her vaunted pride. *I shall show him,* Kat thought. She arched her back and rubbed her breasts against his hard body. "See you, I have breasts."

Shock glazed his deep blue eyes and he staggered back, releasing her.

Kat cupped her small breasts and lifted them, just in case he needed solid proof. "Here. Look at them."

Alex looked down at her chest with a penetrating stare. Tingling heat suffused her and an odd sensation fluttered in the pit of her stomach. Her anger soon gave way to confusion and she dropped her hands. She glared up at him in challenge, not that he noticed.

His sun-bronzed hand covered her breast and then squeezed. Heat speared through the fabric and into the soft flesh cupped in his palm. Kat inhaled, stunned.

"So, Kit-Kat, underneath all that armor you hide behind, you have breasts," Alex said, his expression bemused. "Though hardly full-grown, as you say."

The old endearment that rolled off his tongue warmed Kat briefly—he had not called her thus in eons—but his insult rankled.

Kat lashed out. "I'm not a kitten, so you may stop stroking me like one!"

Alex cursed and dropped his hand as if burned. His face turning red, he blustered, "Get your horse while I dress. 'Tis growing late, we should leave anon. Why your father allows you to roam the woods alone is beyond baffling. Were I him, I would have tanned your arse long ago." So said, Alex turned his back on her, clearly expecting compliance.

At his condescending words, all the anxiety and fear for her ailing father she had managed to suppress over the past weeks threatened to overwhelm her. It was too much. White-hot fury erupted inside her, consuming her, and she launched herself at Alex.

Pounding her fists against his back, she screamed, "You arrogant sod, how dare you criticize my father. He is the kindest, most honorable man I know and you have no right to judge him. He is worth a hundred of you!"

Alex turned around, grabbed her flailing arms, and pulled her to his chest. "Easy now, Kit-Kat. I meant no offense. Your father is the best man I know. Forgive me."

His compassionate understanding opened a rift in the solid façade she had built to hide her fear from Montclair's people, and she began to sob in his arms. He stiffened, and then clutched her tighter. Never once had she let him see her cry, for she only showed the world the side of her that was strong, brave, and confident.

Now, she wrapped her arms around his neck and clung to him, her face buried against the comforting warmth of his chest and steady beating heart.

Alex rubbed his hands up and down her back, murmuring words of comfort. "Easy, love, don't cry. Everything is going to be fine. You'll see. Your father is strong. Easy, now," he continued in this vein until her sobs quieted to hiccoughing sighs.

When she calmed at last, she breathed in the pleasurable scent of his sandalwood soap and masculine sweat. His chest rose and fell beneath her ear, the beat of his heart a stirring melody. With each deep inhalation of his breath, his muscled strength brushed her young breasts. That odd feeling in her gut stirred again.

She drew away, awkward and embarrassed, blaming her unusual emotional display for the disturbing sensations. Kat quickly turned her back to him, wiping away her tears with her fists.

A warm touch on her shoulder startled her.

"Come, your father no doubt is wondering where you have disappeared to," Alex said gently. "I'll send someone back later to get the two remaining brigands and make arrangements for their burial. But I need to dress first." He pointed to the rock where his clothes were folded and started towards it.

Strands of her hair hung in her eyes, and with an impatient swipe of her arm, she shoved them off her face and started after him. "Alex. Wait. When did you return home? And what brings you to Montclair? I thought you with Lord Edward," she said, her voice riddled with anxiety.

Alex turned to her, his expression wary. "Aye, I was. But your father sent word that he wanted to see me."

Kat shivered with premonition, knowing he was not being completely forthcoming. "And? Papa must have given you a reason for requesting your presence. I would hear it now."

"Come, I'll explain on the way."

"Nay." Kat drew up before Alex's six-foot frame. Tall for a woman, the top of her head reached his chin. "I would hear all of it before another moment passes."

When he looked as though he would refuse, she clutched his arm to her. Her gray eyes beseeched him. "Prithee, Alex. You must tell me. I cannot bear another moment not knowing."

Alex tensed, his biceps straining beneath her touch. "Very well," he said, his lips turning down in a grimace. Then he looked away, pausing, before he continued in a rush, "Lord Montclair asked me to return with all due haste, on account of his ailing health. He wishes to formalize our betrothal." He turned, his eyes dark as midnight, his jaw clenched tight. "It shall be done this day, with our marriage to take place three years hence."

His chill voice did not bode well for their future. Stricken, though she proudly did not reveal a quiver of distress, Kat went to retrieve Hunter.

Chapter 1

Westminster Palace, nine years later
In the year of our Lord 1276
Fourth year in the reign of King Edward I

Today was her wedding day. Kat stumbled on the flagstone floor. She clutched her cousin Sir Rand Montague's arm tighter, quickly recovering her step. Afraid she would lose her composure should she look upon the capricious faces of the courtiers gathered in the chapel, her gaze sought her groom. Sir Luc de Joinville stood near the priest before the gilded rood screen. His smile eager and blond hair burnished bronze beneath the candlelit coronas hanging from the vaulted ceiling, Luc was handsome beyond belief.

He wore a dark green surcoate or over-tunic embroidered with gold leaves around the neck and calf-length hem. It was cinched in at the waist with a jeweled belt that emphasized his narrow hips and broad shoulders.

Hot and intimate, his gaze slid down her body and back up, meeting her eyes once more. Awe, pride, and masculine appreciation glowed in his golden eyes, the green flecks brilliant in the light. Then he flashed a smile at her, his teeth straight and white.

She raised her chin a notch higher and continued walking down the nave of the smaller, more intimate palace chapel of St. John. Breaking protocol, Luc strode forward, taking the few remaining steps between them, and commandeered her gloved hand. Without causing a tug of war, Rand could do naught but release her. Sir Luc led her back before the scowling priest, his strong clasp warm through her calfskin glove.

Shocked gasps and smothered giggles of the court were drowned out by King Edward's booming laughter. "Father, I believe the groom is most anxious to see the ceremony completed so he might enjoy his lovely new bride. Let us proceed with alacrity, not unseemly but succinct. Shall we?"

Posed as a question, it was a command nevertheless. The disgruntled priest nodded, cleared his throat, and began the rite with the blessings of the ring.

At Edward's ribald comment, a flush crept up Kat's neck. She was unsure what the night would bring. Although Sir Luc's kisses had been pleasant, they lacked the fire and excitement her body craved. But it was unfair to condemn Luc for her inadequacies. He loved her and that was more important than any temporary sexual gratification she might achieve. Lust was fleeting, as her first husband, Alex, had so readily proved.

"If anything is contrary to the law of God why this couple may not marry, let him now speak, or else hereafter forever hold his peace."

Kat held her breath in the pause and even Sir Luc tensed beside her.

With her marriage to Sir Luc, she was one step closer to achieving her dream of having a child. Ever since her mother died giving birth to a precious male heir when Kat was five years old, she had longed to be loved for who she was. She believed having a child of her own to love and cherish would replace the emptiness she felt inside and give her life meaning. But, deep down, she feared someone or something might shatter the peace and happiness she sensed was so near.

When no one voiced dissent, Kat willed her racing heartbeat to slow. The priest continued with the ceremony.

The churchman turned to Sir Luc and asked him, "Sir Luc de Joinville, do you want this woman?"

Sir Luc, his gaze boldly holding hers, replied in a deep, clear voice, "Aye."

"Do you wish to serve her in faith of God as your own, in health and infirmity, as a Christian man should serve his wife?"

"Aye."

The priest turned to Kat. The heat and musky smell of incense was overpowering as perspiration trickled down her cleavage. "Lady Katherine de Beaumont, do you want this man?"

Kat did not hesitate. "Aye," she replied to both questions. She had no qualms about her decision to marry Sir Luc. Indeed, Luc's devotion to her and no other, along with his desire to have children, would assure their lasting happiness. He would never abandon her, as had every other person she had ever cared about.

Next, the priest inquired, "Who giveth this woman in Holy Matrimony to this man?"

Rand stepped forward and took her right hand—her palm was damp inside her glove. "I do, Sir Rand Montague." Giving her hand an encouraging squeeze, he placed it in the priest's hands.

The doors at the back of the chapel crashed open, shattering the reverent silence. Kat cried out and spun around, even as the whole court turned to gape at the madman who charged inside.

Wearing a dirty, tattered hooded cloak, the intruder paused just beyond the threshold. Though the voluminous hood concealed the man's face except for the untamed black beard he sported, Kat sensed his penetrating stare upon her. A curl of fear rose up her spine. Feeling trapped, hunted, she did not move or even breathe. Then the man surged forward.

"Guards, seize him," Edward shouted.

The frozen guards posted at the door belatedly charged forward and grabbed the cloaked intruder by the arms.

He struggled in their grip, hauling the men forward with the strength of his fury. Men and women tripped over each other as they scrambled to get away from the resulting scuffle. Beside Kat, Luc wrapped a strong arm around her and drew her close. Rand charged down the nave to aid the guards.

"Release me," roared a deep, vibrating voice. "I demand to see King Edward."

A shiver of awareness raised the hairs on her arms; the voice was strangely familiar. Before she could place to whom it belonged, Rand approached the stranger, who immediately stopped struggling. The air laden with a hushed expectancy, a brief exchange of words ensued between Rand and the intruder. Then suddenly, the two men embraced, slapping each other on the back and laughing as the confused and muttering crowd watched on.

Kat, meanwhile, felt a murmur of unease—an instinctual response she had learned to heed after the debacle of her first marriage.

The king, his face livid, brushed past her and Sir Luc and strode down the nave towards Rand. "What is the meaning of this? Who dares to invade the sanctity of the Lord's house and disrupt these proceedings? I could have you brought up on charges of treason," he thundered.

Kat wanted to know the answer to that question, too. But Queen Eleanor and her ladies-in-waiting—Kat's sister-in-law, Rose, among them—crowded past and blocked her view of the king. Luc's arm tightened around her shoulders and she looked up. His smile gone, unease dimmed his eyes to tarnished gold.

He quickly composed his features. With a brief, reassuring smile, he held his arm out to her. "Shall we join the king and see who this knave is who interrupted our wedding? He has caused quite an uproar and I would see our marriage concluded forthwith."

A growing sense of dread rippled through Kat. To Luc, she nodded and threaded her arm through his. "We are in agreement. Knave, indeed."

He laughed, his gaze once more bright with anticipation, and led her towards those gathered around King Edward. When they drew near several courtiers looked back at them. Their expressions were very disturbing—stunned and maliciously gleeful at the same time. Then the crowd parted before them like a herd of titillated sheep. Kat faltered, full-blown trepidation dogging her steps.

Standing beside King Edward, the cloaked stranger turned as Kat approached on Luc's arm. Almost as tall as the king, the man removed the hood of his dirt-begrimed cloak. The first thing she noticed was his long, shaggy black hair and beard. He should have looked completely out of place among the richly garbed court. But his bearing was as proud, arrogant, and unapologetic as that of the noblest noble. Then his penetrating gaze locked on hers.

Kat froze in disbelief, while her blood slowed and thickened as though time reversed. Her gaze was snared by the blue, blue eyes of a dead man. But a fierce inner light glowing within them belied his state. Blazing heat speared her core.

"Alex," she breathed. She would recognize his distinctive eyes anywhere, no matter how different he looked, for she had dreamed of those eyes for six long years. Suddenly, her heart jolted with joy—Alex was alive! He had not died in the attack four years ago while on Crusade.

Vaguely, she realized Luc went rigid beside her. Alex shifted his gaze to Luc, glowering at his arm around her shoulders. Alex took a threatening step forward, his voice chill. "Unhand my wife, Sir Luc. Now."

Kat stiffened at Alex's command, the full implications of his return registering at last. Alex was *alive.* She was no longer a widow, apparently had never been one, and she could not marry Sir Luc. Her euphoria plummeted as quickly as it came upon her.

Nay, I am dreaming, this cannot be true. Her vision blurred. Everything was happening too fast, her thoughts were a jumble. She could not think or move or feel.

Then the king motioned to her, breaking the expectant silence. "Come, Cousin, your husband has returned to you after six years, four of which he spent in captivity when we all believed him dead. Will you not greet him like a good, dutiful wife?"

Someone nudged Kat from behind. Rose, she thought, Alex's sister, and she stumbled forward. Frantic, she turned back to Luc. Her heart thundering, her eyes beseeched him. Luc reached out to her, as though he intended to pull her back, his face twisted with anguish and disbelief.

From behind her, a rough hand clutched hers and drew her around, not ungentle. Kat was surprised at the uncertainty flickering in Alex's eyes, though his voice was sure and steady when he spoke. "Greetings, wife." Alex pulled her to him and bussed her cheek, his beard scratching her tender skin, before he whispered into her ear so none but her could hear, "I have missed you, Kit-Kat."

Kat flinched away. Finally, his combined touch and careless words woke her from her stupor. A flash of pure rage struck her like a bolt of lightning. She slapped him with all her strength, his head pivoting to the side from the impact.

His shoulders tensed. Then slowly, Alex turned his face back to her. The vulnerability she glimpsed earlier in his eyes was gone. Cold menace crystallized his blue depths, promising retribution. She shivered, but ire overrode caution.

"I give you good greeting, husband," she said with biting mockery. "The likes of which you so richly deserve."

Alex, his face rigid with anger, kept his back to Kat while the last of the guests filed out of the chapel. His temper was a fierce beast he fought to keep silent, lest it rage out of control. He was not fit company for civilized folk anymore. Prison strips a man of moral compunction, down to the basest of primal instincts; survival at all costs.

And Kat was his salvation, though he felt unworthy of such a prize.

Tasting the tang of blood, he pressed his tongue against the split skin where his teeth had cut his inner cheek when Kat slapped him.

With difficulty, he drew his gaze back to her. She was more beautiful than the day he married her—with her long slender nose, high cheekbones, almond-shaped gray eyes, and full ruby lips wet, as though she had recently licked them. She wore a barbette and fillet headdress—the barbette a linen band going under the chin and pinned on top of her head and the fillet a crown of stiffened linen. Beneath the headdress, her luxurious straight black hair hung down to her waist, glinting with blue streaks where candlelight struck.

He continued his perusal. Her dark blue gown fell in graceful folds over her girdle and to the floor. Underneath her light blue cloak, lined with the same dark silk as her gown, he noticed her body was fuller, curvier than he remembered, her breasts in particular. He wanted to test them, weigh and measure them with his calloused hands, then taste their soft fullness with his lips and tongue. But her eyes, the ever-changing silver orbs that fascinated him, no longer looked at him with adoration.

He touched his throbbing cheek, then spoke, his voice rough from disuse. "I grant I deserved that, but never show me such disrespect again."

Her gaze incredulous, Kat pushed away from the column she was leaning against. She crossed her arms under her heaving chest and glared at him. "Is there any reason why I should respect you after what you did to me? A man who abandoned his wife like a heartless coward?" her voice rose sharply. "I deserved more than that pathetic note you left me."

He could not deny her accusation.

Though he had resigned himself to his marriage all those years ago, in his heart he never accepted it. So when Edward, not yet king of England, announced his Crusade, Alex jumped at the chance to escape his marriage. Like a coward, he slunk away in the wee hours of the morning, his bride of less than a day sleeping blissfully unaware in their marriage bed.

But Alex was not the same man. He had suffered trials and torture such that ordinary men could never conceive of, and survived where others had not. The shrill screams and pitiful cries of the men who died in the bowels of the fortress still echoed in Alex's dreams at night.

Too late, he had realized that Kat was like no other woman he had ever met. That he had thrown away something unique and precious: her love. But how was he going to convince his wife to give him a chance to prove he was a changed man?

Kat watched Alex throw back his shoulders. His chest muscles flexed like a sleek black leopard beneath his faded surcoate, then he approached with long determined strides. Feeling as though she had awakened a sleeping beast, apprehension fluttered in her chest.

Alex stopped a foot away and raised her chin with his knuckle. His blue gaze seared her as he proclaimed, "You're still my wife. Surely you have not forgotten the night I claimed you. When my body became one with yours, my name upon your lips as you cried out in ecstasy. I assure you, I have not forgotten one blissful moment of it." His voice ended on a husky whisper. His breath a warm caress on her lips.

She had not forgotten one blissful moment, either. Never forgot his touch, his taste, his musky scent. Nay, she would never forget. Memory was a powerful curse.

Kat gasped, appalled. "We're in the Lord's house, Alex. Have you no shame?"

He smiled without humor, his gaze bitter. "Nay, Kat. There is little shame left in a man who has experienced the humiliating debasement of slavery." His voice was different, deeper and almost raw.

Alex ran his thumb over her lower lip. She thawed as warmth spread through her, her lip tingling. She batted his hand away and moved to lean against one of the side altars to distance herself from him.

"What happened to you, Alex? That night after you were attacked and you disappeared, we waited months for a ransom demand. Then they discovered your body buried in a shallow grave and the authorities declared you dead. Obviously it wasn't you. So where were you all this time?"

A palpable wave of violence emanated from his body like heat off molten coals in a blacksmith's forge. "I was in hell, Kat. A Saracen hell," he gritted out and paced away from her.

Kat thought that was all he was going to say. But his face in shadow, he continued in a low, tortured voice. "While on a mission for Edward, I was ambushed outside of our encampment one night. I received a blow to the head that knocked me out. I woke up several days later in one of Baybars's Mamluk prisons."

"Why did we receive no ransom demand?" she murmured.

"Stripped of my raiment, the prison officials neither cared nor believed that I was a landed knight, capable of raising a ransom. So there I rotted for four endless years, until I found a way to escape. I fled to the nearest harbor and caught ship." He swung his head back to her, his face in the light once more. His gaze burned like blue flame into hers. "And all I could think of on the long journey home was returning to you. But when I returned to Briand Castle and the succor of my family, I learned instead you were marrying another man." His voice grew deeper, colder. "Sir Luc de Joinville, of all men."

Kat raised her chin at his malevolent tone. "Sir Luc is a good man and he loves me. Which is more than I can say for you!" She welcomed the return of her anger, remembering Alex was captured in the Holy Land because he selfishly abandoned her to go adventuring. He did not deserve her sympathy.

He crossed his arms over his chest, his expression belligerent. "Did he tell you we became good friends along the journey to the Holy Land? How he saved my life during a raid by Mamluk warriors?" he asked cynically.

Her eyes widened in shock. Luc had told her about his unlikely friendship with Alex, but he never spoke of saving Alex's life. Kat remembered how Alex, at their wedding celebration, had accused her of flirting with Sir Luc and nearly came to blows with the man. "He saved your life? How?"

He waved her question away. "It matters not now. Just tell me this. Do you love him, Kat?"

His intense gaze held hers. He waited for her answer, the look in his eyes almost haunted. Surely it was just a flicker of the candlelight in his eyes, for they became blank and unreadable the next moment.

Her chin raised a notch. "And if I do? What matters it to you? You don't love me."

He grabbed her arms, his fingers digging into her flesh, bruising her. "Answer me!" He bit out each word slowly. "Do . . . you . . . love . . . him?"

Kat wanted to hurt Alex the way he had hurt her when he abandoned her. So she stared directly into his eyes and lied. "Aye, I love him. More than I ever loved you! I love him so much, I would die for him." She knew it was a mistake before the last words rolled off her tongue.

His features froze into a hard mask and he crushed her against him. Then his mouth swooped down and claimed her lips in a fierce kiss. She beat her hands against his chest, but he pressed her closer, trapping them. His mouth molded to hers like hot marble, while his hands clutched her buttocks and pulled her flush against his loins. She tried to resist, but he ground his erect shaft against her long-deprived flesh. Shivery heat slithered over her body. She whimpered, her hips flexing without volition.

Alex groaned at her response. His lips eased their pressure and his tongue entered her slackened mouth. Though his beard chafed her skin, the exquisite slide of his tongue along her inner lips, the roof of her mouth, the flesh of her tongue, made up for any discomfort. It had been too long since she had felt this amazing rush of excitement, the blood pounding in her veins in tempo with her heartbeat.

As suddenly as the kiss began, it was over. Alex raised his

head, still clutching her tightly. "I would lay odds Sir Luc never made you respond like that when he kissed you," he practically growled. "That he never made you moan and writhe against him in abandon."

Heat suffused her cheeks. "You arrogant bastard. You would lose that bet."

A light flared in his eyes and he clutched her face. His fingers threaded through the hair at the nape of her neck and he yanked her head back. Her scalp tingled. "You are a liar. You may care for Sir Luc, but you still want me. And I could make you fall in love with me again, given a chance."

She laughed, the sound bitter and full of rancor. "You are deluded. I shall never give you a second chance to break my heart. I hate you!"

He flinched and Kat reveled that she could inflict some small measure of pain to this heartless man. She had naively given her love and trust to him, and he had rejected it in a most callous way. She would never forgive him. Ever. Then he surprised her when he clutched her face in his palms and kissed her tenderly on the forehead.

His eyes, filled with bitter regret, held hers. "I have wounded you and I am deeply sorry for that. When we married, I was a proud and selfish young fool. I convinced myself that I had to go on Edward's Crusade because I had made a vow to do so. I did not tell you my plans because I knew you would be devastated, and I wished to avoid a confrontation. But I have regretted my decision every day since," Alex's voice was soft and melodious, compelling her to weaken and forgive him. "I know it will take time to regain your trust, but I would like us to start anew as husband—"

"You know naught, Alex," Kat interrupted vehemently, "and you never have." She shoved him with surprising strength and broke his hold. The back of her thighs bumped into the side altar and she gripped the polished wood in her hands to hold herself up. "But I will tell you what I know and what you should have known. I know my *husband* wedded me, bedded me, and then abandoned me mere hours later to go on Crusade. I know you thought only of yourself and cared not how your sudden departure would affect me. I *know* you are a cold, heartless bastard because long ago you gave your heart to a woman who does not deserve your love! *That I never had a chance to gain even a small piece of your heart for myself!"* She sucked in a deep breath in an attempt to check her tumultuous emotions. She had not intended to reveal to him the wretched pain she carried inside.

"That may have been true then, Kat, but I have changed. And I do care for you. More than you know," Alex implored.

But he does not love you, the insidious thought echoed within her aching heart.

Pain shot through her cramped fingers. Kat released her tight grip on the altar and brushed back a sliver of hair from her moist temple. "I don't care how you feel, Alex. You betrayed me and shattered my trust in you. Don't think you can tell me a few pretty lies so you can crawl back into my bed. The only thing I promise is to be civil to you in public."

Kat spun and marched away, heading for the chapel door.

"Kat, wait. *Prithee?"*

The agonized rasp tugged at her heart and drew her to a reluctant stop. Her temples pounding, she turned back, and as she did, Kat thought she saw a look akin to desperation flash in his eyes. She scoffed at the ridiculous notion. Alex cared for no one but himself.

"I know I have hurt you terribly, Kat," he said, his voice gruff and surprisingly sincere. "While in prison I had much time to reflect on my past transgressions and I bitterly regret abandoning you. But I have suffered, too." As he spoke, Alex drew steadily closer. "Whether you believe it or not, I spent four agonizing years in prison dreaming about you. I vowed that one day I would return to claim you. I know I do not deserve a second chance, but I am going to do everything in my power to earn your forgiveness and win you back."

Kat stood as still as a stone statue, unable to move, the intensity of his blue eyes holding her spellbound. They reflected the flames of a hundred flickering candles. He hovered so close the heat of his body melted into her skin.

Kat stiffened and drew back. With distance her good sense returned, along with her anger. How dare he presume that his wishes mattered to her! Did the fool still believe her a gullible, lovesick young girl easily persuaded by empty words?

Her voice full of conviction, she said, "There is no power on earth that can change the way I feel about you, Alex. I despise you for what you did. You may as well be the rushes beneath my feet; I would sooner step on you as look at you."

Alex inhaled deeply. "I'm a patient man, Kat. That is another thing captivity taught me." Unsmiling, his eyes filled with grim determination. "One day you will love me again. I shall not cease until you do. I vow it."

Chapter 2

Standing in a shallow wooden tub, Alex poured a bucket of water over his head to rinse out his hair, which he had scrubbed with some foul-smelling soap to remove any vermin he may have picked up in prison. He raised his arms and squeezed the excess dampness from his hair, then accepted the linen towel his friend Rand handed him. He rubbed his skin till it tingled, then stepped from the tub and wrapped the damp linen around his hips.

The wooden bench Rand sat on creaked as he leaned back against the bathing room wall. "I don't understand. How is it you are alive? We searched—I searched for many moons to find any trace of you, any word that you were alive. We even offered a reward for information regarding your disappearance. A man finally showed us your grave. I saw your body, what I thought was you, anyway. The face was unrecognizable, but the body was dressed in your clothes and could have been your double in every other aspect."

Alex felt a blow to his stomach and took several deep breaths to control his rising fury at this latest evidence that his imprisonment had not been accidental, but been a well-planned scheme to get rid of him. While in prison, he had garnered some information that revealed there was a traitor in their midst, that the attack on him and his subsequent captivity was plotted by one of their own. And now he knew someone had gone to great lengths to make sure everyone thought he was dead. Rand had been his best friend since their days fostering with Rand's grandfather, Earl Richard of Cornwall. But Alex did not want to discuss his suspicions with him until he had a chance to confide in King Edward.

It took effort to control his anger, but he relaxed his tense shoulders and explained matter-of-factly, "I don't remember much, really. I had wandered a short distance from camp for a bit of solitude, wanting to think without distraction. I must've been very preoccupied, because I did not hear my attacker approach. What I do recall is feeling pain explode in my head, and next I woke in the bowels of a Saracen fortress." Alex began to dry his hair with another towel.

Rand blanched and then dropped his gaze. A moment later, he looked up, eyes glimmering with guilt. "I should have been there to protect you. We made a vow to protect each other with our lives, but I failed you. Can you ever forgive me?" His voice ragged, tortured.

Alex braced his hand on Rand's shoulder and squeezed once. "You're not responsible for my capture and imprisonment, Rand. Nor do I blame you. But if you need my forgiveness, you have it."

"But I was—"

"Nay, Rand. My stay in prison is in the past, where it belongs. I managed to escape and now all I long for is to begin my life anew as a free man." *And see that the traitor responsible for my captivity pays with his life,* Alex thought, jaw clenched tight.

Rand nodded, his shoulders shuddering. Then his gaze cleared, and leaning forward, Rand rested his forearms on his thighs, probing, "How *did* you manage to finally escape?"

Alex waved away his question and reached for the pair of hose on top of a pile of clothing next to Rand. Rand had pilfered the garments from his own wardrobe for Alex to wear until he could make other arrangements. Alex had rushed from

Briand Castle to Westminster the moment he learned of Kat's marriage and therefore had naught but the clothes on his back. Rags, really.

His hose tied, Alex pulled on a linen sherte and an unadorned calf-length blue tunic over that. "There will be plenty of time for me to answer all your questions later, Rand. Right now, I have more important matters on my mind, and I don't want to keep my wife waiting any longer."

Rand's eyes widened, incredulous. "Your wife? Now you claim Kat your wife?" He shook his blond head pityingly. "You may bet Kat shall disagree with your claim. Indeed, you are going to have an uphill battle trying to convince her of that. After I returned from Crusade, she did not speak to me for a whole year because I kept my silence about your intentions."

He did not delude himself into thinking it would be easy. Indeed, frustration gnawed at him. Alex rolled his shoulders, trying to ease the painful knot at the base of his neck. With his abandonment, he had destroyed all trust between him and Kat. If he was to succeed in his endeavor, he had to prove to Kat that he could be trusted. And he could. Alex would rather tear out his own heart than hurt her again.

But he had no idea how to begin without losing all pride in the process. He did not think she would be satisfied until he crawled to her on his hands and knees and begged her forgiveness. And even then she would just laugh in his face.

Rand stood up and paced away, shoving his hand through his shoulder-length hair. "As you may imagine, it was quite a shock when you barged into the chapel. 'Tis still hard to grasp you were never dead, but held in a Saracen prison all this time."

Alex gritted his teeth, seething with jealousy. "Not nearly as shocking as returning home to learn I was considered dead and my wife about to become a bigamist, not to mention an adulteress."

Rand dropped his gaze, cleared his throat and looked everywhere but at him. When his eyes alighted on a stool, he reached for it and plunked it down before him. "Sit. I shall remove that foul-looking beard so you do not frighten the ladies." Then he retrieved a small leather case on a table by the bathing room door.

Alex was not fooled. Rand was hiding something. "Very well." Alex sat and Rand draped a towel over his shoulders. "But afterward, I want to know what I said to make you as skittish as a virgin bride."

Rand's eyes widened, then dropped once again to the task at hand, neither confirming nor denying his accusation. At the first scrape of the razor on his neck, Alex flinched and the blade nicked his skin. A bead of blood rolled down his neck.

"Be still. Do you want me to slit your throat?" Though Rand's voice was stern, his eyes were sympathetic.

Alex relaxed and looked away, hating that he had revealed so much. Any sign of weakness and his enemy would gain the upper hand. For now the man responsible for his imprisonment was unaware Alex had evidence his attack was no random act. And he intended to keep it that way. He needed to keep a cool head and remember he was no longer at the mercy of his cutthroat captors. His slavery was a thing of the past, not his future.

When he finished, Rand grunted in satisfaction, removed the towel, and handed him a mirror. Alex hesitated, not knowing what he would see reflected back. He had not seen his image since before his capture and who knew what imprisonment had wrought on the outer surface?

Rand turned away, placing his shaving items in the bag. When he raised the mirror to his face, Alex blinked, startled by the stranger staring back at him. His face was leaner than he remembered, sharper, his cheekbones jutting out in stark relief. Grooves edged his unsmiling lips, which were compressed into an uncompromising, almost grim mien. The scar on his chin gave him the appearance of a man dangerous to cross. Where once his eyes had sparkled with mischief, now the blue glittered coldly with determination, and creases etched the corners.

Alex stood and thrust the mirror at Rand, then turned and strapped on his borrowed sword and scabbard. "Now, I would hear what you are keeping from me," he demanded. When he faced Rand again, he thought he had prepared himself for the worst, but how wrong he was.

My wife is an adulterous whore.

His temples throbbed, blood roared in his ears. Alex stood on the threshold of the banquet hall, searching for his wife. His initial shock had turned to icy rage. He stood rigid, afraid he would shatter into a thousand pieces, or smash someone into a thousand pieces as the horrible implication reverberated inside his head.

To have come so far, only to learn . . .

Rand's words replayed in his head.

"Mind you, they are simply rumors. I will never believe it of Kat. But I believe it best you be forewarned, for you will no doubt hear them yourself."

Alex stiffened. "Just spit it out, man."

Rand paced. "When you abandoned Kat so soon after the wedding, rumors spread that you spurned her because she was no chaste virgin. Your violent argument with Sir Luc at the wedding celebrations contributed greatly to this misconception. Then Sir Luc paid his respects to Kat after your declared death and the rumors were born again. He began to court her assiduously over a year ago when she arrived at court. Now, court gossip is that Sir Luc and Kat are lovers. Though neither has indicated such in word or deed."

Rand turned to Alex, righteous ire flaring in his gray-green gaze. "Foul lies, all. But for the life of me I do not know how the rumors started."

Now, violent thoughts whirled in Alex's head. Kat was a passionate woman. Luc was a charming and handsome man. Kat had believed him dead, leaving no obstacle to keep her chaste. What were the odds Rand was wrong?

Alex felt a sharp tightening in his chest, the pain wrenching. He was a cuckolded husband. No matter that Kat thought him dead, he still could not help feeling betrayed. While he had been rotting away in prison, dreaming of the day he would return to Kat, she had been lying in Sir Luc's arms. His body shook with the violence of his thoughts. Kat was his and his alone.

His gaze moved across the swirling sea of brightly colored, silk-clad lords and ladies, their smiling countenances counterpoint to his turbulent emotions. When he spotted Kat at last, his jaw clenched tight. Next to her stood his rival and once friend, Sir Luc de Joinville. The man's very elegance and golden handsomeness irked Alex. Sir Luc leaned close to her and whispered in her ear. Kat sipped from her chalice and nodded without looking at Luc, and then Luc moved away and into the crowd. A rush of fury pumped swift and hot through his veins.

Alex charged across the room, the crowd scrambling to get out of his way. At the commotion, Kat glanced up and their eyes locked. Her silver eyes widened, but she never wavered as he came closer and towered over her. Alex had no idea what he intended to do until he swooped her up into his arms.

Fear flashed in her eyes, though quickly doused. Satisfaction rippled through him. She said not a word as he marched out of the dining hall, no doubt not wishing to create more of a scene. At that moment, he could care less. Leaving behind a stunned silence, he exited the chamber and headed for the privacy of the rooms reserved for the Beaumont family.

Kat, her jaw clenched, did not struggle or speak as Alex carried her up the spiral stairs. Controlled fury emanated from his embrace, his muscles seemed hewn of granite and his glare as cold. It was not fear that kept her silent, nay, she was incensed at his brutish tactics, but the numerous servants they passed with their mouths gaping or snickering behind their hands was untenable. She would not risk her dignity further with open conflict.

Alex carried her into her chambers. "Damn you, Alex, put me down."

Alex released her and she darted away. The door slammed shut; she jumped, startled. She did not understand why *he* was so angry. Alex had humiliated her before the court, carrying her off like prized booty.

She massaged her aching temples and moved to the table along the right wall opposite the fireplace. The fire beckoned her, but another pleasure equal to the fire's warmth waited on the table. Two goblets and a full flagon of wine sat on a tray. She filled one of the cups, quietly thanking her devoted servant Jenny for her thoroughness. She stared into her cup, absorbed by the pale rosy hue of the claret, then took a drink, swallowing half the contents.

The warm yeasty liquid slid smoothly down her throat, in sharp contrast to the cold voice that reached out from the room's shadows like icy tentacles. "Aye. I am damned indeed."

Kat well remembered that deep husky voice, but a new and dangerous current flowed under its pleasant surface. She shivered. Taking a deep breath for composure, she searched the darkness where Alex stood. She saw the tip of his boots first as he stepped from the shadows and into the area lit by the fire. Next, her gaze rose up his long muscular thighs, which flexed beneath his tunic. He appeared leaner through the hips and waist, broader of chest and shoulder. His whole body was superb in form and shape.

Cynically, she wondered why his imprisonment seemed to have had no adverse effect upon his muscles. They appeared strong and healthy, not weakened from years of confinement, as one would expect. Finally, she came face to face with her sneaky, conniving, worthless husband. Shaved now, his face was leaner, carved with masculine lines honed from hardship.

She glared back at him scornfully. "So, the prodigal husband has returned at last."

The bastard. He was still as handsome as the devil; more so, since the scar on his chin added a dangerous quality to the strength and character of his face, which appealed to her reckless side. But it was his gaze blazing with heat that caught her attention. It was the only indication of the anger she sensed he held tightly in check.

Alex flushed, but his eyes hardened. "You know I had not intended such an extended visit to the Holy Land, but my captors were insistent," he said, his voice caustic.

Kat slammed her chalice down on the table and laughed bitterly. "Do I know? I say I do not know you at all. Mayhap all this time you have been enjoying the hospitality of one of those harems I have heard so much about, slaking your lust and unwilling to return to your unwanted wife."

"Are you calling me a liar?" he asked softly, his voice a cold caress.

But she did not heed the warning and shrugged. "Nay. I think of you more as a treacherous bastard."

Alex lurched forward two steps and grabbed her arms in a fierce grip. His fingers bit into her skin. She gasped in pain, while her head jolted back with the motion. "And you, my beautiful wife, are naught but an adulterous bitch!"

Kat jerked, all the breath squeezed from her lungs. So, Alex had heard the rumors that she and Luc were lovers. How ironic that the rumors had begun because Alex had abandoned her the day after their wedding. The nasty rumors had destroyed her reputation, leaving her open to all manner of degrading advances. Now, after keeping her resentment bottled inside for too long, his unfair accusation gave her leave to retaliate.

"Aye, Sir Luc is my lover. I am not ashamed to admit it. He is a magnificent lover. I revel in every moment spent in his bed."

Alex dropped her arms as though stung. His face a mask of rage, he drew back his hand to slap her. She glared at him, daring him.

With a roar of outrage, he picked up the stool near his feet and smashed it against the wall. The legs shattered and, reflexes quick, Kat lunged aside as a sliver of wood bounced off the wall and nearly struck her in the head.

The ensuing silence was deafening. A spark popped in the

fire, the orange glow illuminating Alex's face. He looked appalled, drawn and disconsolate. She smiled, cold and defiant. Good. She meant to hurt him as he had hurt her. He deserved to suffer for a long time.

Alex, meanwhile, stared blindly into the fire, ashamed at his violent outburst. "Kat, I—" When he touched her cheek, she flinched, and he dropped his hand.

"Don't touch me. I loathe you." The venom in her voice left him in no doubt of that.

Alex collapsed wearily onto the cushioned settle, a long high-backed bench situated before the fire, and dropped his head into his hands. How suddenly the night had gone from bad to worse. Deep inside, he had hoped when he confronted her she would deny the accusation. But she proudly boasted of her adulterous actions without one bit of remorse.

Sad and defeated, Alex despaired. With sudden insight, he realized a secret part of him he never acknowledged had depended upon the constancy of Kat's devotion. He felt lost without it now. "Why did you do it, Kat? Was this your way to punish me for leaving you?"

Kat's laughter echoed scornfully. "What a conceited man you are, Alex. The fact is I do not give a damn about you. As to your question, I am an experienced woman now, you saw to that. You were dead. Luc and I desired one another, and we acted upon that desire."

Alex rose lithely to his feet. He pulled her into his arms and forced her flush against his body. Her breasts cushioned against his chest, her scent enveloping him, she smelled like some exotic spice with a touch of the floral, jasmine, mayhap. He grew hard, his flesh rising against her softness. "As you can tell, I am not dead. Nor am I a complacent husband. From now on the only bed you will be sleeping in is mine."

She pulled out of his arms, her eyes narrowed with contempt. "We may still be married, but I will never share your bed again."

Then she spun on her heel and entered the bedchamber. Alex moved before the hearth to stare into the flames. He was deep in thought when she returned. In her arms were a straw mattress, woolen blankets, and a pillow.

"Here are some blankets. You may sleep in the antechamber until you find other accommodations tomorrow."

Alex threaded his fingers through his hair, sweeping it off his forehead. "Answer me one question?"

She placed the bedding on the settle and nodded reluctantly.

"Rand mentioned that when I left to go on Crusade, people thought I had spurned you because you were not a virgin. I don't understand. How could this be? The proof of your virginity was on our bridal sheets. I made sure our marriage could not be contested, knowing I would be away for some years."

"You need not remind me of that night," she choked out, bitterness tainting her words. "I remember how you forced me to consummate our marriage."

Kat stood straight and proud as she glared at him, her stormy gray eyes condemning. She was beautiful in her wrath. Her clear smooth skin glimmered golden in the firelight. Her long, straight hair tumbled over her shoulders. Through the black silk screen, her breasts peeped out like twin melons, lushly abundant and full. He wanted nothing more than to pluck the sweet flesh to readiness, to suck and plunder her breasts with his lips and tongue.

"I may have tied you to the bed when you refused me, but there was no force involved. You climaxed sweetly in my arms several times that night."

She raised her chin in defiance. "So that makes it all right? You know I wanted no part of a marriage based on duty."

"Neither of us had a choice. I made a vow to honor and protect you and that meant a consummated marriage. And you swore an oath to your father before his death to marry me because he wanted to insure your protection from grasping usurpers."

"That was before I realized you were the man I saw rutting with that slut Doris in the stables the day before our wedding."

Alex gnashed his teeth in frustration. "Must we go over this again? Aye, I bedded Doris. But I had not seen you in three years, Kat, and—more to the point—you and I were not yet wed. I broke no vows to you."

Kat scoffed. "And after we married? Surely you do not claim you have been a faithful husband these last six years."

Red crept up his cheekbones, his voice gruff. "I have lain with no woman since the night we wed. No woman but you, that is."

Her mouth dropped open. Then she snapped it shut and her eyes narrowed to disbelieving slits. "I don't believe you."

He stiffened. "Believe it or not. But it's true."

"Whether true or not, that does not absolve you of your actions that night. You tied me to the bed, by God—"

"After you nearly unmanned me! My duty aside, your father entrusted me with your welfare and so I took whatever means necessary to ensure your compliance."

"How dare you! My father would never condone what you did."

"Can you honestly tell me I harmed you in any manner, that you did not enjoy every moment of our joining? Because I remember vividly you writhing beneath me when you climaxed."

Her eyes glowed with ire. "Enough. That is not the point—"

"Nay. There is no point in discussing this anymore, Kat, 'tis in the past and cannot be undone. And I no longer feel as I did then about our marriage. Now, will you tell me what happened after my departure?"

She looked away and stared into the flames, brooding. Alex went to the table.

He picked up Kat's chalice, refilled it and poured another for himself. Then he returned to Kat and handed her the wine. She scrupulously avoided touching his hand and sat down on the cushioned settle.

Alex watched as she drank, her gaze never wavering from his. His wife had ever been challenging. She licked her lips before beginning. "When I woke to discover you had gone on Crusade, leaving only a note behind, in my anger I destroyed the evidence of my deflowering." She shrugged nonchalantly as if to prove how indifferent she was to her actions now. "Had you not left, I never would have destroyed the blood-ied sheet, it would have been hung for all to see, and my status as a chaste wife would have been confirmed."

Her silver gaze glittered with contempt. "But when you scuttled away directly after the wedding and no proof of my virginity could be displayed, vile rumors started to spread. People claimed you discarded me because I was no virgin. Or worse, that you were so repulsed by me you could not bring yourself to consummate our union."

Alex paced away. A sense of powerlessness, such that he had not felt since his imprisonment, rose up to choke him. He clutched the goblet until his knuckles whitened. Then he re-leased a long shuddering breath. He had been a thoughtless fool. Not once had he ever considered how his hasty depar-ture would be interpreted or that Kat would be harmed by such cruel speculation.

Kat had every right to be furious with him. Had he remained behind and not run away like a coward afraid of his burgeon-ing feelings, the rumors never would have been born. Though he took a healthy swig of his claret, it tasted as dry as dirt.

He spun around, placed the chalice on the small table by the hearth and knelt before Kat, taking her hands in his. The flames flickered across her face, the red glow highlighting her long slender nose and high cheekbones, her full blush lips. "Forsooth, I had no idea the damage my departure would in-flict upon your reputation. I was selfish and thoughtless. But I swear to you that I shall do everything in my power to make up for the hurt I have caused you."

Shivery heat shot up Kat's arms.

Troubled, she jumped up and paced away. When he touched her, her body responded counter to her mind and heart. Kat momentarily forgot the heartache she had suffered because of his betrayal, and merely felt.

But passion alone did not make a marriage. She learned that lesson the painful way. Kat had loved him once, but his abandonment destroyed some vital essence of her being and crushed her dreams. She would not allow Alex to turn her into one of those pathetic women who pined away because they foolishly fell in love with a man incapable of loving them.

"You can no longer hurt me, Alex. Indeed, I want naught to do with you. This conversation is over. I bid you goodnight."

As she entered the bedchamber, his voice reached out to her, soft though determined. "Sleep well, Kat."

Chapter 3

Alex moved to the table and refilled his chalice. He drank deeply until he drained the cup. Though Kat refused to share her bed, he had no intention of lodging anywhere else. Why give up such comfortable quarters? They were still man and wife and naught could change that. Besides, not to mention the gossip it would cause, how could he seduce his wife if they slept in distant chambers? But he had no desire to disabuse her of her assumption yet and argue with Kat again.

After Alex prepared his pallet by the fire, he stripped naked and slid beneath the blankets. He was so weary. All that had happened today was too overwhelming. Fear that he would arrive too late to stop the wedding was all that had kept him upright on his horse on the long journey. Then he turned into a rabid beast when he saw Kat and Luc standing so happy before the priest.

Alex's head sank deep into the soft pillow, every ounce of his strength slowly ebbing away. The scent of lavender teased his nostrils. A long, deep groan of pleasure erupted from his chest. He had not felt this clean and comfortable in six miserable years. Since he had left Kat in June, the year of our Lord twelve hundred and seventy.

After leaving Kat, Alex had gathered his troops and made his way to Portsmouth, where Edward's fleet was preparing to set sail for France. Edward's departure was delayed, but on the twentieth of August the English crusaders crossed to France, traveled inland down to the Mediterranean seaport of Aigues-Mortes, and then sailed for Tunis. There Edward was to meet up with another crusader force led by King Louis of France. But when Edward arrived in North Africa, Louis was dead, struck down by disease that had spread rampantly through the crusader ranks in Tunis.

At this turn of events, France pulled out, but Edward was determined to carry on. Finally, in the spring of the next year, Edward and a thousand crusaders landed in Acre. The fighting, little more than raids and counter raids, lasted for about a year and achieved no major victories. When King Hugh, nominal king of Jerusalem, signed a treaty with the Mamluk Sultan, Baybars, ending hostilities for ten years and ten months, Lord Edward was appalled. But there was little he could do with so few troops at his disposal.

Before returning to England, Edward had sent Alex with a small contingent of men on an embassy to Tripoli. They made camp at a watering hole on the second night of their journey, and it was there Alex was ambushed. He had been unprepared, restless and preoccupied with thoughts of Kat, measuring the time until he could hold her again.

It seemed little had changed, he thought in frustration. Alex shoved the heels of his hands against his eyes as images of Kat entwined naked with Luc tortured him. He swore he would obliterate every memory she ever had of the man, no matter the cost to his soul.

She is mine.

Naught could keep him from the peace and devotion he desperately craved. With Kat he had felt alive and challenged, yet humbled by her unswerving devotion. But he had discovered the truth only after he deserted her. And with that single, despicable, self-absorbed act he would regret for the rest of his life, he had destroyed any feelings she had for him.

Sighing in misery, Alex turned on his side and pulled his

blanket up. Mayhap by the morrow, a plan would have come to him on how to go about wooing his wife, to convince her to give him a second chance. But what if he could not persuade her? Suddenly, the sensation of drowning was overwhelming. Sinking deeper and deeper, he gasped for breath. Perspiration broke out on his temples.

If he did not win Kat, he would slowly be deprived of air until he was well and dead. Leaving him prey to the demons that haunted his dreams.

A fierce cry startled Kat from a deep sleep. Drowsy and disoriented, she sat up and blindly reached for the dagger under her pillow. Her hair tumbled over her face. She shoved it back and stared into the darkness. The guttural cry came again from the antechamber, followed by the hissing sound of a steel sword being withdrawn from its scabbard.

That was when she suddenly remembered Alex was sleeping in the other room. Or had been sleeping. Kat pulled the blankets up to her neck, wondering what Alex could possibly be doing when all honest men were fast asleep? She wiggled her toes, and jiggled her legs, but unable to contain her curiosity, she pulled the bedclothes aside and slid off the bed. She crept quietly to the curtained archway and peered into the other room.

Kat gasped. Alex knelt completely unclothed amid his disheveled pallet brandishing his drawn sword. The fire shimmered golden light over his smooth muscular chest and the indentions down his taut stomach. His powerful hips and thighs flexed as he got to his feet. Unable to keep her eyes from going to his groin, she stared wide-eyed, then flushing with embarrassment, quickly raised her gaze back to his face.

But he was not looking at her. His eyes were oddly vacant, even as they darted around the room as if he expected an attack from imaginary foes.

"Alex, what are you doing?"

When he did not respond, Kat slowly approached him. "Alex," she said more loudly, sternly.

Alex turned towards her with his sword extended. She jumped back when the tip nearly sliced her stomach, her heart leaping into her throat. "Don't come any closer," he swore, his voice sounding as though slurred with sleep. "I demand you release me. I have told you numerous times I have the means to pay ransom."

Shock held her immobile as she tried to make sense of his strange behavior. Obviously he was not cognizant. He was trapped in a nightmare that held him as surely as the Saracen fortress once had. She wondered what had happened to Alex that he would be reduced to fighting demons in his sleep?

Her heart contracted at his fear. But Alex was a proud man and would despise her pity.

Desperate to do something to wake him, she ran back to her room. When she returned, she tossed the water in her basin at his head. It was a direct hit. Alex roared in outrage, shaking his doused head. Kat gasped as water splattered her thin chemise and face.

He took a menacing step towards her, his furious gaze raking her face. "What the hell did you do that for, Kat?"

"I had to do something to wake you." She motioned vaguely to his bared body, the sword dangling in his hand. Her gaze purposely avoided his groin area.

Frowning, he looked down. "Jesu," he swore. His sword clattered to the floor. He raised his gaze to her, fear replacing his anger. "My God, Kat. Did I hurt you?" He stepped forward with his arms outstretched, then jerked to a halt. A shutter fell over his eyes and his arms dropped to his side.

Kat sat the basin down on the small table by the fire. "I am fine, Alex. But I'm concerned about you. What just happened here?"

Not looking at her, Alex shrugged. "'Twas naught but a waking dream," he said, his voice gruff. "I had too much wine after little sleep. You need not be worried."

Then Alex's gaze moved to her breasts. His eyes darkened. Midnight flame engulfed her. "Mayhap I spoke too soon," his voice a hoarse caress.

Kat followed his gaze. Gilded by the firelight, the dark crests of her breasts were visible through the flimsy fabric. She swore and crossed her arms over her chest.

Alex moved her arms down. "You have beautiful breasts, Kat. You need not shield them from me."

Disgusted that he would turn her concern into something lurid, Kat turned her back on him and moved towards her chamber. "I'm going to bed. I suggest you do the same."

"Is that an invitation?" his voice wickedly amused.

At the threshold, she turned around and glared at him. Dark and ruggedly handsome, he stood naked and bold as Adam, the flesh between his legs stiff and stretching skyward. He was a large man; his tumescent shaft, long and thick, sprouted from a nest of curly black hair. Her stomach quivered in primal reaction, but she ignored it.

"Don't hold your breath or you will choke on it." Then she yanked the curtain closed on his grinning face.

Stomping to her chest, Kat tugged her wet chemise off over her head and tossed it to the floor. She found a clean, dry chemise and changed into it. Normally she slept bare, however, while Alex resided in the next room, she felt more comfortable sleeping in a shift. She knew it was a rather flimsy shield, but protecting herself came naturally to her. Her instincts warned that Alex would be ruthless in his pursuit of her.

Kat crawled back into bed and was surprised when she heard the outer portal open and then shut. When she went to peer into the antechamber, Alex was gone. No longer tired, she pulled on her chamber robe and moved to the window alcove overlooking a small private garden, wondering what Alex meant to do at this time of night. Then she inwardly berated herself for even caring. The man betrayed her, humiliated her, and rejected the only thing that she as a woman was truly free to gift a man. Her heart.

What did she care where he went or slept? Or with whom he slept? The notion that Alex remained celibate these last six years was laughable. His prowess with women was as renowned as his skills on the battlefield.

Kat curled up on the cushioned window seat, opened the shutters and looked up at the midnight sky. A soft breeze blew; wisps of hair hanging loose from her braid fluttered and caressed her cheeks. The deep blue of the night was the exact same hue of Alex's eyes when they darkened with lust. She recalled the way he had stared at her breasts, his desire unconcealed.

Desire, not love, she hastened to remind herself. To believe otherwise would be foolhardy. His betrayal still seethed in the deepest, darkest corner of her heart, buried with all the pain and humiliation she experienced when Alex rejected her love.

Still, she remembered his earlier tormented words. *I know I have hurt you terribly, Kat . . . But I have suffered, too. Whether you believe it or not, I spent four agonizing years in prison dreaming about you.* Indeed, he had suffered. When Alex was held in the grip of his nightmare, Kat had seen the welts caused by severe whippings crisscrossing his back. Scars she knew he did not carry on their wedding night. Nor could she forget the pain etched on his face when he thought he was back in his captor's hands.

Now he had returned to claim her. But no matter his internal and external wounds, she could not weaken.

When Alex deserted her, she vowed to keep what remained of her heart inviolate. If she relented and accepted him into her bed, eventually he would become bored with her. He would discard her again without a thought. Nay. She tugged her robe tighter around her. Love was a weakness Alex would manipulate to his satisfaction and that way lay destruction. She would never survive the pain of betrayal a second time.

A sound in the garden below caught her attention. Peering out the window, she looked down. Moonlight shown on a bare patch of grass and revealed a man clutching his sword with both hands. Kat frowned. Alex swung his sword madly at invisible foes, chasing away the night creatures that rustled in the darkened sanctuary.

Exhausted and sweaty, Alex quietly entered the antechamber. It was not yet dawn and he did not want to wake Kat and burden her with his darkness anymore than he had. He was ashamed of his weakness. And he had nearly endangered Kat because of it. Only once before did he wake in such a state—mostly his demons were harmless to none but him. It was the blasted wine. In future he would have to be more careful. This time he'd deftly distracted Kat from asking more prying questions.

Alex tugged his tunic and sherte off. With his linen sherte he wiped the sweat from his face and chest. Some good came from his exertions, though. While exorcizing his demons in the garden with mindless physical activity, it freed up his thoughts to work out a solution to his dilemma.

Six years ago, he acted selfishly by not telling Kat of his plans to go on Crusade. She was his wife and had had a right to know of his decision. Though he could not have forsaken his vow to take up the cross, he could have given her a choice to accompany him to the Holy Land or stay behind at Montclair.

In order to redeem his selfish act, he must make a huge sacrifice in exchange. And in the process he could regain a measure of control. This time Kat would have a choice. It was a risky proposition, but naught worth having should come without struggle, lest a man not appreciate what he had until he lost it. Unfortunately, he learned that lesson too late.

Chapter 4

A gaunt, dark-robed clerk ushered Alex into the king's private receiving room later that morning. Curious, Alex glanced around.

"The king will be with you shortly, my lord." The clerk bowed and exited out a small hidden side door on a painted wall that depicted a map of the world.

The room was long and narrow, but its high ceiling, gold-leafed beams, and painted walls gave it a sense of grandeur. Below the painted map on the west wall of the chamber were a table and two chairs. The narrow, shorter wall opposite the entrance had a cold fireplace, above which hung a portrait of Queen Eleanor sitting on a bench reading a book in her rose-drenched garden.

Alex strode to one of the rare, stained-glass east windows and opened the casement. Locking his hands behind his back, he stared unseeing into the garden as soothing sunshine warmed his face. And pondered the wisdom of the plan he'd concocted to win Kat's heart. His abandonment left Kat scarred in ways he could not imagine, and he did not know if she could ever forgive him. But he had to try. Without Kat, he had naught left.

He would succeed. He must succeed.

"Alex."

Alex started at the great booming voice and turned from the window to greet his monarch. King Edward closed the door where the clerk had exited earlier and strode into the room. Known as Edward Longshanks because of his great height, the king stood a few inches taller than Alex. They met in the center of the room.

"Sire." Alex bowed deeply and then rose at the king's command.

Edward's golden hair shone in the sunlight, and his smile broadened as he clasped Alex's shoulders heartily.

"'Tis good to see you hale and whole." Edward surveyed him critically with his probing blue gaze. "Prison seems to have had no adverse effect upon you."

Alex's mouth quirked. "Do not believe everything you see. My sojourn with the Saracens was no picnic, though I did meet many English guests to keep me company during my visit," he finished dryly.

"Indeed. The Saracens are renowned for their hospitality," Edward rejoined ironically. Then his mien swiftly turned serious, his gaze stern with rebuke. "You were missed last eve. I expected your presence at the feast."

Alex's own smile turned grim as he confessed, "I'm afraid once Rand made known to me of certain rumors, my anger got the better of me." He did not elaborate. The king no doubt was aware of all that went on at his court.

Edward smiled slyly. "Aye. That was quite a spectacle I witnessed." He moved to the table along the wall. "The queen has done what she can to quell the rumors at court, but I'm afraid naught may be done when gossipmongers converse in private."

On the table waited a flagon of wine and two chalices.

"Come. Let us toast to your miraculous return."

A close companion of Edward since the Barons' War, Alex was unsure how to act now that Edward was king. Edward sat in the larger, more elaborate chair and filled his chalice with wine from the flagon. Eased by the informality, Alex followed suit.

King Edward raised his goblet in a toast. "To England and your safe return."

Alex raised his chalice and then drank deeply. The claret was smooth and sweet, but with a slight bite to it.

Edward lowered his wine, leaned back and rested his forearm on the table. "Now. Tell me how it came about that you ended up in a Saracen dungeon. I understand you were accosted not far from camp on the second night of your journey. When your men discovered you missing in the morning, they searched for you and found a pool of blood where you were attacked."

Gathering his thoughts, Alex set his cup on the table and linked his fingers together on his stomach. "Aye. It was late and I had wandered away from camp before retiring. Someone attacked me from behind and as I turned, a hard blow to my head knocked me out. I woke several days later in the oubliette of a fortress in Syria with my skull pounding and two Frankish prisoners for companions."

"Why did we not receive a ransom demand?"

"My attackers stole everything of value that would identify me as a knight. And when I tried to explain I could pay ransom, I was ignored. The guard came twice a day to drop food down the oubliette, but he never spoke or answered my demands. For a month I was held in the pit with no contact with anyone other than the two prisoners. Then I was removed to a dungeon cell."

Alex had tried to forget that dismal time without success—the unending misery and gnawing hunger had clawed at his innards until he had prayed for a quick death. There was never enough food to feed one man, let alone three. It was a cruel game played by the captain of the prison guard to provide sustenance enough for one man and see who had the strongest instinct for survival.

Alex shared the portion he secured with one of the Frankish soldiers who was wounded and unable to fend for himself. But as Alex grew weaker and the Frank did not improve, he realized they would both die if he continued sharing. Having alone survived, Alex still agonized over the death of those two men, for he as good as killed them himself. They had not died honorably in battle like warriors should, but were treated like savage beasts and slowly starved to death.

The king leaned forward abruptly in his chair, drawing Alex's thoughts back from the past. "Once released from the oubliette, what did you do then?"

Alex reached for his chalice and took a long, soothing draught of wine before he answered. "You may be sure I tried again to convince my captors of my ability to pay ransom. But my entreaties were not appreciated, and the guards had a unique way of silencing recalcitrant prisoners." Uncomfortable revealing even a hint of the torture he endured, Alex shifted against the back of his chair. The hard wood chafed the welts lacing his back.

From a distance, Alex heard the king say, "And yet you are here. Returned to us, like Joseph, the lost son of Israel reunited with his family after years of slavery."

A guttural laugh escaped Alex. The similarities between their experiences *were* eerie. Alex, too, was betrayed, tossed down a pit and sold into slavery in Egypt, or rather Egyptian-held Syria. But unlike Joseph, he was not so forgiving. Years of his life were stolen from him, years he could have spent in Kat's arms. Nay, Alex lived for revenge. And he would receive satisfaction if it killed him.

Alex loosened a white-knuckled grip from his chalice and replied, "Aye. 'Tis a miracle you see me before you, alive and well."

Then Alex went on to tell Edward how he escaped and made it back to England, paying passage on a merchant ship with the two horses he stole when he fled.

"'Tis an amazing journey you have had, Alex," said Edward. "But something troubles me. This attack that landed you in a Mamluk dungeon is very odd. If the men who attacked you were enemy soldiers, you would be dead now. It was too dangerous for them to encroach upon the camp simply to capture a prisoner. And if they were simple thieves, they would have killed you or left you where you lay. But instead they captured you, carted you hundreds of miles away, and sold you into slavery. It sounds to me like this attack was personal."

A vein in Alex's temple throbbed. "Aye, Sire. I've come to the same conclusion," he said, his voice low and lethal. He refilled his goblet.

The king's eyes lit with keen interest as he leaned forward in his chair again. "You have a powerful enemy, my friend. Whoever it is, he wants you dead, and not a quick, merciful death, but a slow, agonizing one. Do you know who might have a grudge against you?"

Alex shrugged, but he saw the king was not fooled.

"Come, man, I know you must have some idea who the culprit is."

"I made many enemies, as you well know, when I helped subdue the rebels after the Barons' War. It could be any one of them." Alex paused.

King Edward's chair creaked. Not given to idleness, he rose from his chair and moved to the wall of windows. "Aye. Many lost their ancestral homes or paid steep compensation to regain their confiscated lands. But we have peace in the land now, and many former rebels I consider friends." As he gazed down on the scenery below he asked, "Do you have any proof or clues? Did you perchance get a look at your attackers' faces?"

Alex rose from his chair and sat on the edge of the table, crossing his arms. "It happened very quickly, but I did see the face of the man who struck the blow to my head. He was dark skinned, with a distinctive scar on his left cheek."

"And was he known to you?"

"As a matter of fact, we met on one occasion. Though I don't know his name. And the circumstances were quite similar. He and two others ambushed me on my wife's estate several years before Kat and I married. I killed his two minions, but he escaped."

Alex smiled in remembrance at Kat's brave interference.

He was so angry with her then, but looking back, he could not help feeling an odd sort of pride at her fearless defense of him. Alex did not explain to Edward that he was responsible for the man's disfigurement.

Alex continued. "The first time the man whom I have come to call Scarface attacked me, he bragged he was hired to kill me. The incident occurred only a year after all the rebels were subdued. But when there was no other attempt on my life, I thought that the end of it. Until he attacked me again."

Edward turned, his gaze intense. After pondering Alex's words, he began pacing as he spoke. "So you believe one of the defeated barons hired this Scarface to kill you. When it failed, he waited for you to become complacent and looked for an opportune moment to dispose of you, and in such a way your death would not be examined closely. He wanted no suspicion to be raised as to the cause of your death. 'Tis absolutely diabolical, if so."

Alex said naught, his jaw clenched. A black mist rose before his eyes, blinding him with rage. His entire body locked as he controlled the desire to grab the table and toss it aside like kindling. King Edward's quick, analytical mind had sorted out the bare facts and rearranged them to form a coherent puzzle.

Edward paced back to the table and refilled his chalice. "What do you intend to do now? You saw the face of your attacker, yet you don't know his identity or his whereabouts."

Alex expelled his breath slowly and met Edward's perceptive gaze. "The night I was attacked, the only weapon I carried was my dagger. If you remember, it was a very distinctive weapon, passed down through generations of Beaumont eldest sons."

"Aye. I remember the Beaumont dagger. The Saxon heiress your great-great-great-grandfather married had it commissioned upon the birth of their first son. She gifted it to her husband as a gesture of peace. Early Briton in design, was it not?"

"You do not err. In prison, I met an English knight by the

name of Sir Richard of Ludlow. He told me that before his capture he witnessed a man with Scarface's description selling the Beaumont dagger to an English traveling merchant. The merchant trader resides here in London, and I plan to seek him out as soon as I can. From him I will secure the mercenary's name and where I can find him."

"And when you find this Scarface, he will lead you to the man who hired him."

Alex would not rest until the perpetrator was either dead or rotting in gaol. "That's my belief. And with Parliament coming up, I reason the man behind the plot will be here soon at Westminster, if he is not already."

"Then it's imperative that no one suspects you know your incarceration was deliberate and not a random act."

"I've told no one but you of my suspicions, Sire."

King Edward returned to the window and his inspection outside, sipping his wine. Slowly, as if in deep thought, he asked, "And what about my cousin, your lady wife? Do you intend to tell her?"

"Nay. I don't want Kat involved. The danger is too great. I have a cunning enemy who I doubt will be happy to see me returned from the dead, and the fewer who know, the better."

Besides, his wife was stubborn and willful and loyal to a fault. Despite how she felt about him, he believed Kat would insist on helping discover the traitor. In a misguided attempt to help, there was no telling what mischief she would stir up. Like the day Scarface attacked Alex at Montclair. Heedless of the peril, Kat had charged into the battle. She was not harmed that day, but the next time she put herself in the way of danger she might not be so lucky.

Alex picked up his chalice and drained the last of his wine. Nay. It was best for all concerned that Kat remain ignorant. Although he did not like the deception, the alternative could only lead to disaster. He would go to any lengths to protect Kat from harm.

The king spoke over his shoulder, "'Tis for the best." Then

he turned and leaned against the window embrasure. "I hear your father is on the mend."

Alex left the table and joined Edward by the window. "His leg is finally healed enough that he can start walking on it again. But it will be longer before he is able to travel. He has asked me to stand proxy for him at council."

"Good, I will need Briand support if I am to find a way to pay the debt accrued by my Crusade." With the mention of Parliament, and no doubt the reminder of the difficult task of raising taxes, the king concluded the interview. "'Tis good to have you home at last, Alex. Let me know what you discover from our merchant friend. I intend to support you in this endeavor."

Dismissed, Alex bowed. "Thank you, Sire." Seeing Edward's facile mind was already on other weighty topics, Alex left the chamber.

Alex exited the palace and entered the garden, the sky overhead full of fast-moving clouds interspersed with sunshine. It was the shortest route to the river landing, where he planned to catch a watercraft and travel down the Thames to London. When he woke that morning, Kat had already left their apartments, so he'd been unable to speak to her of the decision he came to in the early morning hours. Alex decided he might as well use the opportunity to find the merchant who bought the Beaumont dagger from Scarface.

Gravel crunching beneath his scuffed boots, he followed the path to the left skirting the fountain at the center of the garden. He was intent on avoiding the well-populated areas and any who might detain him.

His stride swift, Alex passed a birdbath and exited the garden through the tall wooden gate near the river. The briny smell of the tidal water wafted upon an easterly breeze across his right cheek. A peasant whistling a jaunty tune pushed a wheelbarrow of firewood down a path towards the palace kitchens.

Green lawn scattered with white daisies and deep blue periwinkles spread out before him almost to the riverbank, where tall grasses and willow trees grew. Further north, a row of houses backed onto the west bank of the river, their small garden plots bright with blooms.

A flash of movement caught Alex's eye, drawing his gaze to a willow tree up ahead beyond the river stairs. The tree trunk grew not straight up, but angled out over the river, so the long, silvery-green leaves stretched their fingers towards the water's edge. He peered into the shadows beneath the verdant canopy and spotted a swath of blue cloth. Recognizing the long, elegant lines of his wife's body, his heart beat faster. She was propped against the willow trunk, unaware of lurking danger.

Alex slowly approached, then pushed aside her leafy concealment and stepped into her hidden bower. Hearing him, her head snapped around. Their gazes collided; hers widened in consternation. She tried to bolt, but he caught her arm and pushed her back against the tree. She narrowed her eyes on his hand, which still gripped her arm, and he released her.

He met her softly veiled gray eyes, her nearness, her jasmine fragrance a provocative distraction. Today her exquisite face was framed by the veil and circlet she wore, and her hair hung unbound down her back. He longed to sift his fingers through the cool, silky blue-black tresses he remembered so vividly in his dreams. His member tightened and swelled.

Kat stared at Alex, dismayed. The air in the confined space thickened and her heart pumped with agitation. His midnight eyes darkened with an inner light, his smile ripe with satisfaction. She gathered her courage and raised her chin, defiant. "What do you want, Alex?"

"We need to talk." He looked around the shadowy interior and returned his gaze to her. "Here seems as private as any other place."

"This may surprise you," she said sarcastically, "but I have no wish to speak to you, in private or otherwise."

His jaw clenched and the scar on his chin whitened. Then Alex pressed his body closer, the scent of sweet wine on his breath. "Oh, I believe you will want to hear what I wish to discuss."

Instead of responding, she raised an eyebrow in question. As she waited for him to explain, the heat of his body and alluring sandalwood scent pressed in on Kat, creating an intimacy she diligently ignored.

Suddenly appearing uncertain, Alex shrugged his broad shoulders. "I've been thinking a lot about us and our marriage. And I have come to a decision at last."

Kat stared at Alex, flabbergasted. A crack sounded in the tree limbs above, breaking the stunned silence. A leaf-covered branch plummeted into the river with a splash, then drifted downstream with the current. "You have made a decision?" she said stunned. "Concerning you and me? You must be jesting. It was your decision that got us into this mess! Did you not learn a thing when you abandoned this marriage and destroyed any chance for it to prosper?"

A stabbing pain in her heart, Kat turned her head aside and bit her lip. Her dreams were small and had not changed since she was a woman of marriageable age. She wanted to marry a man who would love her unconditionally and give her children to love and adore. She had thought Alex was that man, till the day he abandoned her without an explanation and crushed her vulnerable heart. Alex would never understand the extent to which his desertion still hurt her.

Alex reached out with one finger, pressed it against her clenched jaw and drew her face back to his. His gaze held tenderness and regret. Despite her pain, a soft, fluttery sensation curled low in her stomach.

Alex shook his head. "Forgive me. I didn't express myself very well. What I meant to say is I wish to make you an offer. You may accept it or reject it. But this time the decision shall be yours. If you choose to accept my offer, I promise to abide by your decision no matter the outcome."

Kat had difficulty understanding what Alex meant. He was giving her a choice? What choice?

"What are you talking about, Alex? What sort of offer are you proposing? And why do you think I would be interested?"

"Because I know you well, Kat. You are unable to resist a challenge. And what I'm proposing is a marriage bargain. At the end of which, you will have the ultimate decision whether we reconcile or not."

"What are you saying, Alex? That you wish to end our marriage now?"

Kat's heart skipped several beats as dismay filled her. Nay, not dismay, it was just that he had piqued her interest and she did not want to get too excited in case she misunderstood what he was proposing.

Alex closed the distance between them. "Nay, never." He caught her hand and pressed it against his chest. His gaze held hers. "Do you feel how fiercely my heart is beating?"

His heart thrummed beneath her fingertips and his blue gaze narrowed to pinpoints of light.

"You are the only woman who makes my heart race uncontrollably. The only woman I want or will ever need."

I will not believe it.

Kat stepped back and Alex's arm dropped to his side. "You make no sense, Alex. One moment you are swearing you will not relent until you win me back. The next you say it is my decision if we reconcile or not. What exactly are you proposing?"

Alex braced his left hand on his sword hilt. "Do you remember our wedding night?"

How can I forget?

Alex's eyes glittered in remembrance. "That night you asked me if all I cared about was duty and honor. I didn't understand what you wanted from me then, but now I do. I have changed, Kat. I, too, want more than a marriage based on duty. I care about you and I want you in my life. All I ask is that you give me a chance to prove it and win back your trust."

Kat could not believe what she was hearing. Alex deluded

himself if he thought there was anything he could do to earn her trust back. The pain of his betrayal resided deep in her heart like a burning coal. "I'm afraid you are six years too late, Alex," she said, her voice cold and disdainful. "You made it clear when you left that you did not want me for your wife. Well, you will have to live with that decision, because I certainly don't want you for my husband now." Her breast heaving, Kat turned and pushed the hanging branches aside to leave, but his next words stopped her.

"Do you not wish to hear my offer? The marriage bargain I would propose?"

She looked at him over her shoulder, her eyes narrowed in contempt. "There is not one word you can say I would have the slightest interest in hearing, Alex."

He smiled, but it did not reach his eyes. "Annulment."

Except that word.

Chapter 5

Kat whirled around, her gray eyes narrowed with suspicion. Alex was pleased to catch her speechless. He had barely choked out the word, and his stomach roiled with nausea. But it was too late to turn back now.

"If this is your idea of a jest, Alex, I don't find it amusing," she said finally, scowling.

"Nay. I have never been more serious. I shall seek an annulment with the Pope, if you agree to abide by certain conditions."

"Even if it were possible—"

"'Tis definitely possible. We could get our marriage annulled on grounds of non-consummation due to impotency or frigidity. The fact that our bloody bridal sheet was never displayed gave me the idea. It would give credence to the claim, should you be willing to testify that we never consummated our marriage."

Sunlight dappled her bold straight nose and cheekbones like gold dust. "You have my attention. What are these conditions you mentioned?"

"Firstly, you shall give me three months to court you and prove my worthiness. Secondly, you must spend time in my company, at my pleasure, whenever you are free from your duties to Queen Eleanor. And lastly, but most importantly, you will not find ways to avoid me and will seriously consider my suit."

Kat crossed her arms under her breasts, the feathery leaves swaying behind her. "And how do I benefit from this bargain, should I choose to accept?"

"At the end of three months, if you still wish to end our marriage, I will seek an annulment with the Pope. As long as you don't contest it, the annulment should be granted. Not only would your dowry estate, Montclair, return to you, but you could also marry again in one year . . . if that is your wish." Alex bit his tongue, tasting blood.

"You would do that for me, Alex? Declare yourself impotent? Why?" Distrust shadowed her almond-shaped eyes.

"I have told you why. I want you, Kat. But I want all of you, body, heart, and soul. I shall not settle for less. This time you will have a choice whether you want me as husband or not."

It was a risky gamble. Alex knew Kat would use all the tricks at her disposal to keep distance between them. As lady to Queen Eleanor, Kat could immerse herself in doing the queen's bidding and ignore him completely. He could woo her as relentlessly as he wished, but with an absent bride, success would be highly unlikely. And more importantly, perhaps, courtship of a hostile Kat was not in his best interests. *Or conducive to my good health.*

"But you would never be able to remarry or sire an heir for Briand." Alex longed to smooth the worry lines from her forehead as she gazed uncertainly up at him, her exotic flowery scent a potent allure.

"My brother, Brian, is growing into a fine young man. Should it come to that, he can sire heirs for Briand."

A shout from the river reminded Alex of his mission.

"Come, walk with me to the river stairs." Giving her no opportunity to decline, he took her hand and put it in the crook of his elbow, then led her out from under the concealing willow. "You need time to think about my offer, and I have business in London town. You can give me your decision when I return."

A breeze from the southeast blew in from the river and caught strands of Kat's hair. They wrapped around his neck like a possessive lover, undulating around him softly, arousing him with their scent and silky texture. But Kat remained oblivious of her runaway hair and his ultimate torture. Then quite suddenly, another breeze unwound the silken tie from his neck.

Disappointed and relieved at the same time, Alex looked down at the woman beside him as they strolled along the river in silence. His gut clenched at the sight of her loveliness. Though young, she exuded an innate sensuality that beckoned him like a houri to take her and claim her as his. But by his very bargain, he might lose the right to do so. He just prayed his gamble would succeed.

Kat, meanwhile, was still reeling from Alex's unexpected proposal. She relaxed her grip on his arm. The muscles of his upper arm were surprisingly big and firm. Without volition, Kat squeezed the bulging flesh, testing it. His muscles flexed in reaction, and although he did not stop walking, he raised an inquiring brow in askance.

Kat blushed with embarrassment, cursing her momentary weakness. She covered up her mortification with a comment. "You say you spent four years in a Saracen prison before you escaped. Yet you appear strong of limb and muscle. I find it odd, is all."

Alex pulled her to an abrupt stop. Surprised, Kat swung her gaze to him. Staring down at her, his blue gaze grew heated and his sensual lips curved in a wicked grin. The combination singed her blood and sent butterflies scurrying to life in her belly.

"'Strong of limb and muscle' you say." His voice deepened. "As you have explored for yourself, you know my arms are strong, but how can you be positive all of me is as well?

Unless . . . Would you care to examine the rest of my muscles as you did my arm? Just to be certain?"

Kat's lips pinched tight at his irreverent wit. "Fine. Answer me not. 'Tis of no import to me."

Alex straightened and started walking again. When he spoke his voice was devoid of emotion. "The fortress where I was held was a work camp. We toiled away every day, hauling heavy stone blocks quarried from a defensive ditch around the castle walls."

Kat saw the river landing up ahead even as she marveled at the horrors Alex must have suffered, the frustration he no doubt had felt knowing he had the means to obtain his release but unable to convince his Saracen gaolers. The experience had changed him, made him harder, more ruthless, no longer the charming, carefree young man she married.

Her ears heated as outrage consumed her. She hoped the bastard who had sent Alex to a living hell was dead!

"Do you know who attacked you?"

Alex tensed beside her, but then immediately relaxed. "Nay. I didn't see who knocked me out. I have learned it happened the same night an assassin stabbed Edward with a poisoned dagger. I think it most likely the two incidents were related."

Willow trees and tall grasses lined the west bank along the river landing. A flat-bottomed barge, rowed by several men, came alongside the embankment and bumped up against the stone stairs. The pole man stepped out, moored the boat, and then waited near the landing to carry his passenger down the Thames. Kat inwardly breathed a sigh of relief, glad that Alex would depart shortly and free her of his troubling presence for the rest of the day.

The pungent odor of the river wafted on the mild breeze. A section of her hair that had come free fluttered across her face, tickling her cheek. Kat pushed the wisp of hair behind her ear and stopped.

"I shall bid you good day, Alex."

He turned to her. His big warm hands clasped hers gently. A calloused thumb stroked her fingers. Then suddenly, Alex's right hand tightened on hers. Clutching her fingers, he raised her left hand and stared down at it in an oddly tense silence. "Where is your wedding ring?" he asked, his eyes dark with anger.

Kat tugged her hand to free it. "What concern is it of yours?" she snapped.

Alex tugged back. "Because you are my wife!"

She kept her voice lowered and hissed. "Nay. You never wanted me for your *wife*. You made your wishes clear on that score the day you left me. I took off the ring then and have not worn it since." Kat raised her chin defiantly. "I saw no reason to be shackled by a symbol that proclaimed me your wife when you had no intention of fulfilling your vows."

Alex tugged again and unprepared, Kat stumbled against him, her arms caught against his hard chest. "But there you are wrong, wife. I aim to fulfill my vows, *in every way,*" his voice rumbled in a seductive purr. He pulled their bodies flush before his lips swooped down on hers.

His kiss was not forceful or demanding, otherwise she could have resisted his advance. Instead, his soft lips molded hers in a gentle caress, coaxing her lips apart. Her mouth melted and he took stealthy advantage. His tongue entered the warm cave of her mouth, giving Kat a brief taste of wine and honey, before retreating.

One large hand branded her left bottom cheek. He thrust the hot, hard ridge of his shaft against her stomach, a silent warning, and a relentless promise. Wet heat pooled between her thighs, drawing a moan from her lips. Then it was over. Alex stepped back, his hands holding her upright. Kat stared down; her fingers clutched his azure tunic, crumpling the material.

Gasping, she released him. "How dare you! I did not give you leave to trespass upon my person," she accused Alex, though her anger was turned inward at her own weakness.

Alex stiffened. "I beg to differ. You cannot trespass upon the willing, madame."

After bowing mockingly, Alex turned and made his way to the waiting craft. He jumped in the boat and called out before it moved away from the stairs. "Think about that, my wife, while I'm gone this day. I shall return in time to change for supper."

When Alex's barge pushed away from the bank, Kat turned and flounced away from the river. She had no idea where she headed, walking willy-nilly as she replayed every word of their conversation in her head.

Kat groaned. She had behaved like a wanton, melting in his arms with just one brush of his sensual lips. She could no longer lie to herself. A traitorous part of her still yearned for his touch. Her heart raced with fear. If she were not very careful, Alex might succeed at slowly chipping away at her resolve to resist him. She did not doubt that he would besiege her until she surrendered her heart and soul, leaving only a ruined shell behind.

Deep in thought, her brow puckered in concentration, she did not at first hear the muffled curses and shouts. A boy's cry pierced the air.

Kat looked around, bewildered. She stood in the middle of Lousmede, surrounded by a sea of grass and cuckoo flowers, their pale lilac petals bobbing in the breeze. Behind her to the southeast lay Westminster Palace, up ahead was an abandoned apple orchard not far from the leper hospital of St. James.

She cocked her head. A sharp cry pierced her heart, followed by answering shouts and laughter coming from the orchard. She reacted without thinking. Hoisting the wet hem of her tunics to her knees, she crashed into the trees towards the sound of that pitiful wail.

The orchard was deserted, its neglect revealed by the weeds and green shoots of new growth allowed to grow wild along with the rotten apples littering the ground. It appeared forlorn as nature's bounty fought to grab hold and reclaim this forgotten, once fruitful Eden. Dashing down several rows of trees, Kat veered to the left when she spotted a splash of color in the otherwise barren orchard.

A small boy about seven summers old was perched in a tree, trying bravely to cling onto the limb as a rotten apple pelted him. His dark head peeped out amid the flowering branches. Four boys of varying ages, all older than the lad, stood below harassing him. They were all dressed in the king's livery.

The oldest boy, about twelve, blond-haired and apparently the leader, hollered, "Come on down, Matthew. If I have to come up and drag you down—" he left his sentence hanging, making his threat that much more ominous.

The others jeered and called him a coward. But the lad ignored them and sat in stoic silence.

Kat hated bullies, no matter their age. When a child, she had been taunted and scorned for being different one too many times. The black-haired lad in the tree, smaller and outnumbered, had no way to defend himself.

She moved stealthily closer until she had a view of the whole scene. Upon closer inspection, she recognized the blond-haired leader, knew who his father was. In this case, it was indeed true that the proverbial apple never fell far from the tree. Lord Calvert, the boy's father, was a minor baron from the north, a petty and cruel man.

The older bully, his threats exhausted, began to climb up the tree. Kat reacted without forethought. She removed the dagger from inside her boot in one smooth movement—metal hissed as the blade scraped the sheath. With his arms and legs wrapped around the tree, the blond boy shimmied up and reached for the lower branch. A thud sounded in the ensuing silence, the embedded blade quivering in the branch just inches above the lad's outstretched hand.

Crying out, he lost his grip and plummeted to the earth. He hit the ground with a loud thump, and a wail issued from his lips. His comrades yelped startled exclamations, turning to find the source of danger. Into this chaos, Kat strode boldly to the lad lying on the ground. The other boys scattered, their fallen friend left to fend for himself.

Kat removed the dagger from the tree. She looked up and met Matthew's wide-eyed gaze. "'Tis safe to come down, Matthew. No one can hurt you now."

"You are a girl!" the boy's voice floated down to her.

Kat laughed and returned her trusty blade to her boot. "Aye, the good Lord saw fit to make me so."

He swiped an arm across his nose and swallowed. "But how did you learn to throw a blade like that?"

"I would tell you, but it is difficult to converse with one in a tree. 'Tis hard on the neck, you see."

A black lock of hair fell on Matthew's forehead as his gaze shifted to the boy moaning at her feet. Then he turned and clambered down the tree like a monkey Kat had seen in the royal menagerie at the Tower of London.

"Who are you?" he asked when he reached the ground.

"I am Lady Katherine de Beaumont. But you may call me Kat. All my special friends do."

He smudged his toe in the dirt under the tree and looked up at her shyly. "I thank you, Kat. And I am Matthew of Oxford."

Kat smiled at him, and then knelt beside the injured boy to check his arm for broken bones. He cringed and tried to scuttle away. "I do not intend to harm you. Now let me see your wrist so I can determine the extent of your injury."

Not waiting for his assent, Kat grabbed hold of his arm and gently probed the wrist in question. As she thought, there were no broken bones, only a swollenness that indicated a mild sprain.

Looking into the boy's sullen black eyes, Kat admonished him. "You are most fortunate. 'Tis only sprained. I would recommend you find more honorable activities to pass your time in future. A word of advice—there is always going to be someone bigger and stronger than you. Let this be a lesson to you, although I doubt you will pay me heed. Now go, you are no doubt neglecting your duties."

The blond boy scrambled to his feet, scowling as he backed away. "I shall tell my father of your deeds this day. He is bigger than even *you*. He will make you pay for daring to harm me," he spouted boastfully, then threw a hate-filled glance at Matthew and fled.

Matthew looked at her with a worried frown. "He is trouble. Can his father really harm you?"

"Don't worry, Matthew. His father is a cowardly bully, just like him. And I can take care of myself. Besides, my husband is a powerful man and Lord Calvert would not dare cross him."

"Would you teach me to throw a knife like you do?"

The sudden change in topic was understandable given the circumstances. He wished to be able to protect himself, so he would feel less vulnerable. Kat sympathized with his ambition, but he was a bit young to be wielding such a dangerous object. Still, there was a way she could help him and give him a safe haven from those who would torment him.

"You are too young yet. Knifes are very dangerous and should be used with great care. Some day, when you are older, you will be trained as a squire and will learn all there is to know about handling weapons. But there is something I would like to show you instead."

"What is it?" Matthew asked, his warm brown eyes intrigued.

"I cannot say. 'Tis something you must see for yourself."

His eyes sparkled with excitement and he nodded his acceptance. Kat turned back towards the river with Matthew. When his small hand slipped trustingly into hers, Kat's soft heart thumped with happiness. She longed to have children of her own someday. It was the main reason she had decided to accept Luc's offer of marriage.

Whether boys or girls, she would love them equally. Though her parents had loved her, their endless attempts to sire a male heir, despite numerous miscarriages, finally resulted in her mother's death. Because her mother preferred death to accepting the female child she bore her husband, Kat had felt inadequate and unworthy of love.

That was why Alex's rejection had been so hurtful. Was it wrong to want to be loved unconditionally?

Children were loving and trusting, their needs so simple, and their love unconditional. She had much love to give. And with a child to love and to love her in return, she would finally have the acceptance she desperately craved.

"This is the stable," Matthew said in surprise.

"Aye. There is a friend of mine I want you to meet."

They entered the large stable, the wide-aisled structure cool in the shadows. The familiar smells of saddle leather, hay, and horses that Kat loved filled her nostrils while her eyes adjusted to the dimmed interior. Thirty stalls lined each side of the long pillared building, only a third of them with occupants. Apparently, the king was out hunting with his court, one of his favorite pastimes.

A familiar whinny drew Kat down the aisle to an occupied stall. Behind her, Kat heard Matthew whisper in awe, "He's a beauty."

Opening the wooden door to the stall, Kat chuckled. "*He* is a *she,* and her name is Lightning." Patting her palfrey's muzzle affectionately, Kat crooned, "Aye, my lovely lady, you are without compare. And please forgive Matthew, he meant no offense by mistaking you for a male." The mare was steel gray with a black mane and tail, but in the sunshine she took on a silvery hue.

Matthew hovered outside the stall, his eyes filled with awe and a little trepidation. "Is this *your* horse?"

"Aye, and my best friend. Come on in, Matthew. Grab that stool as you do."

When Matthew hesitated, Kat coaxed him in a soothing voice she used to calm her mare. "Lightning is a very special horse. Gentle, too. She was a bride gift from my father-in-law. You need not fear her."

"I'm not afraid," he said quickly, and bravely entered to stand beside her.

She took the stool from his hand and set it on the hay-covered floor. Lightning bent her head and nudged Kat with her nose. Matthew laughed, an infectious giggle that warmed her heart.

"Climb up on the stool, Matthew, so you can reach her." He obeyed immediately and Kat showed him how Lightning liked to be petted.

Matthew had a charming dimple in his left cheek when he smiled. "She is so warm and soft," he said, stroking the gray mare's chest. His eyes sparkled and Kat was glad she had helped him forget his cares for a while.

"Whenever I am troubled, Matthew, or need to get away from my worries, I come here. Just being with Lightning makes me feel better straight away."

"You are lucky to have such a friend," Matthew whispered, his face averted.

The statement verified what Kat had already suspected, and she blinked back the tears welling in her eyes. She well remembered the loneliness of her own childhood. Children were sometimes cruel and, as a child, she was teased and tortured for her mannish behavior. She was stronger for it, but that did not make the hurt any less.

"I want you to consider Lightning your friend, too. You may come and visit her in her stall whenever you want, whenever you need to be alone. Do you understand what I mean, Matthew?"

His brown eyes grew wide and filled with understanding. "I would like that above all things."

"Good." At that moment, Lightning whinnied and shook her head. Kat patted her in acknowledgement, lavishing her with attention. Beside the mare, Matthew wrapped his small arms around the warm horseflesh and laid his cheek along Lightning's neck.

Kat had not lied to Matthew earlier. Whenever distressed, she sought the company of her horse. And Alex's return certainly qualified as distressing. She had a very important decision to make whether to accept the devil's bargain.

After removing a curry brush from the back wall, she showed Matthew how to groom the gray mare. As she did, her troubles seemed to slough away like horsehair from Lightning's back. A sense of peace filled her. Even so, quietly and insidiously, one thought resounded in the back of her mind: *'tis merely the calm before the storm.*

Chapter 6

A rumble sounded in the distance as Alex walked the narrow cobbled streets of Cheapside. He stared up into the sky between the overhanging buildings and spotted dark clouds moving in from the east. He hoped the weather would remain clear. Alex had been searching every weapons and antiquities dealer in London for hours.

The wind picked up with the coming of rain clouds just when Alex spotted the shop he felt sure was the one he sought. The last shop owner he spoke to told him about it. The merchant who owned it traveled to the Near East regularly in search of his commodity—ancient weapons of the once powerful Romans. But he had fallen on hard times a few years past. The thatched roof was thin in several spots, and the sign above the door was worn and nearly illegible.

The rusty door hinges screeched viciously as Alex entered the shop. Dust covered the nearly empty open-shelf counters that lined the perimeter of the room. A wooden structure holding a rusted suit of Roman armor stood like a lonely sentinel in a back corner.

From behind a curtained door at the back of the shop, a middle-aged man emerged. Bald, with a fringe of gray hair around his head, the shop owner's facial features were nondescript and weathered, most likely from years in the hot

Eastern sun. The man greeted him pleasantly enough, but Alex quickly measured the pudgy man's shifty character. His eyes were dark and close set, and flitted away from Alex's measuring look.

"I am Torcere. How may I serve you?"

"I'm looking for a dagger, preferably Briton in decoration. I want something old and unique. 'Tis a gift for my father and must be special."

Torcere, obviously believing he had a ripe plum in his midst, bowed obsequiously and motioned Alex to a counter in back. "Of course, of course, come this way. Though I specialize in Roman artifacts, I do have a small collection of daggers reminiscent of the early Britons. I'm sure one of them will meet your requirements," he said with a nervous twitch of his head. He unlocked a door behind the counter and pulled out a long oak box. Inside the felt-lined interior lay a collection of carved ornamental daggers, but none were of jeweled enamel.

Alex scoffed, assuming the arrogant attitude of a rich nobleman unimpressed. "These are for peasants. I want something fit for a king. I see I have been misled. Pity, I will have to go elsewhere."

Alex turned and headed for the entrance.

"Nay. Prithee, do not leave." The little man scuttled quickly around Alex and blocked his way to the door. "I have the very thing you seek, my lord, a dagger old and jeweled and beyond compare. 'Tis in my private collection, but I would be willing to sell it to you for a fair price."

Scowling, Alex nodded as if reluctant. "Very well, but you had better not waste my time. I'm not a patient man."

Torcere nodded, bowing. "Aye, my lord, I understand. If you will just wait here, I must get the dagger from the back room. I promise you shall not be sorry." He turned, not quite hiding his sly, greedy grin before he entered the back room.

Waiting only a moment, Alex shoved the curtain aside and stepped into the room behind Torcere. The dark, airless room consisted of a worktable, bench and a heavy ironbound chest against the back wall. Torcere had knelt down and inserted a complicated set of keys into the chest's barrel padlock.

The shop owner spun around, stark fear etched on his face. "Mi—Milord."

Alex waved him to continue and sat down at the table. Torcere hesitated, but greed won out, for he turned back to the chest and inserted a second, then third key. The latch opened at the third click, and the shady merchant raised the lid and withdrew a plain ebony box.

Alex held his breath, his body tense with anticipation. *Could this be it?* he wondered. *Could my search for the Beaumont dagger be over at last?* Torcere set the box on the table before him. It seemed an eternity before the man opened it and revealed the contents. Then shock quickly followed. The exquisite dagger, its leather sheath ornamented with silver mounts that had raised double spirals inlaid with garnet enamel, glowed in the flickering candlelight emanating from the table.

Alex stood and slowly released his breath. His hand shaking, he picked the dagger up. The cool metal felt perfect in his hand as he unsheathed the blade. Alex examined it with reverence, caressing the beloved surface like a long-lost lover. He brushed his thumb over the steel blade, and traced the familiar Latin inscription he recognized by touch alone. *Ad mortem fidelis* it read—faithful till death.

"I believe you are right. This *is* just the dagger I have been looking for," Alex said. In a flat, emotionless voice, he added, "Where did you acquire a blade of this craftsmanship?"

The merchant was nervous and twitchy by nature, so the threat in Alex's question was not missed. The shop owner's legs quaked and he slid into the other chair to keep from falling. His eyes darted to the dagger as Alex ran a caressing finger along the sharp, lethal blade.

Torcere gulped. "In the Near East."

"I must needs be more specific, I see." Alex moved to stand over Torcere, a threatening presence with the unsheathed dagger in his right hand.

Torcere, fidgeting with the sleeve of his tattered tunic, looked up abruptly.

"Give me the name of the thieving mercenary you bought this dagger from."

The merchant cowered. "How did you—?" Eyes dilated by fear flicked to the dagger.

"His name. I shall not ask again." Alex stared coldly at the repugnant little man.

Torcere stuttered out a name incoherently. Gathering his composure, he repeated in a strained whisper, "Sir Hugo Krieger."

Alex's knees went weak in profound relief, yet his heart raced. *Praise God, I have a name at last.* But he steeled his elation.

Alex sheathed the dagger and then tucked the distinctive weapon inside his boot. Until he caught the traitor, no one must know he had it in his possession. He tossed several gold coins onto the table. The fear faded from Torcere's eyes and they began to glitter with avarice as he stared at the coins.

"I want to know everything you know about this Hugo Krieger. Absolutely everything. Leave no detail out."

Refreshing herself before supper, Kat stood before the washstand and brushed her hair. "I wonder where Jenny is?" she murmured beneath her breath.

"You have beautiful hair." The deep male voice rumbled under her skin like a shivery caress.

Startled, she stopped in mid-stroke and looked up. Alex leaned against the curtained-archway between the bedchamber and antechamber. His arms were crossed over his chest and one booted ankle rested over the other. His admission surprised her, but she kept her expression bland. The quickening sensation in the pit of her stomach was not pleasure at his compliment.

"You're back," she said inanely.

"Aye, I am back." His blue gaze seared her meaningfully.

Kat looked away, her cheeks reddening. "I'm late. The queen required my presence in the royal chambers and I have no idea where Jenny has disappeared. She was on her way up here when I spoke to her a moment ago."

"I sent her away."

Kat whirled around and planted her hands on her hips. "You did what? Jenny is my servant. You had no right to order her to leave."

"She didn't seem to mind. I am quite capable of assisting you with any of your needs should you require my services." His hot gaze raked down her body and then settled on her breasts, the carnal undertone of his words blatantly evident.

Her nipples pebbled and Kat gasped. "Your arrogance is exceeded only by your conceit. You may be sure that I shall never have need of your 'services,' now or in future."

Alex's face was shaved smooth and his black hair hung loose to his shoulders. Over a purple tunic embroidered with gold leaves on the rounded neck, he wore a dark green calf-length surcoate. Kat instantly regretted her choice of gown. She wore a green tunic embroidered with delicate green leaves, and over it she wore a purple surcoate with tight cuffs.

Alex shoved away from the doorway, his eyes bright with laughter. Something fluttered in her stomach. Kat, annoyed at her reaction, gathered her wild mane over her shoulder and plaited it in a quick, simple style.

It was still somewhat of a shock to find him alive. Had it only been yesterday when Alex burst into the chapel and stopped her wedding to Luc? When he destroyed her last chance at finding peace and happiness? And the family she desperately craved?

Kat opened the pearl-inlaid casket that held her valuables and found a jeweled snood. She pinned the net in place and then chose a silver filigree brooch.

"Allow me," Alex whispered. From behind her, he plucked the brooch from her hands. Hot breath poured over her bared neck. Their eyes met in the mirror hanging above the washstand. For several beats of her heart, his gaze snared hers, desire blazing within the dark depths.

Then he raised his hands to her shoulders and turned her to him. His fingers slid down inside her bodice, skimming the upper slope of her breasts. Kat sucked in her breath. Her heart thumped erratically. Light strokes teased and tantalized her flesh as he lifted the fabric away from her chest and pinned the brooch to her tunic.

No matter how much she told herself she hated Alex, the tug of attraction was as strong as ever. The few times Luc had kissed her were pleasant, but never had she felt for him this breathless eagerness to press her body against his and indulge her senses.

Her reaction was all the more reason to accept Alex's marriage proposal. After she fulfilled her part of the bargain, she would be free to start her life anew with a man who truly loved her.

The pin fastened, Alex stepped back.

Kat released her pent-up breath. "Thank you, my lord."

Alex smiled down at Kat, his breath short and erratic. "It was my pleasure. Have you given any thought to my proposal?"

"I have thought of little else all day."

He leaned back a little. "Have you decided to accept my offer, then? Will you allow me to court you for three months and prove my worthiness?"

"Nay. I shall grant you but a fortnight. If you have not convinced me in that time, you never will."

"Nay. A fortnight is not sufficient. I shall agree to two months, but no less."

A stubborn glint flared in her eyes. "One month and no more."

Alex slid a finger down her jaw. "As you wish. One month." He calculated the days. "Upon the feast day of St. Barnabas, shall we say? But I have a final condition or else I shall remove my offer altogether."

Her eyes narrowed, but she nodded. "Very well. What is this condition?"

"I insist that I sleep in these chambers during the duration of our bargain."

Kat stiffened. "I will not sleep—"

"You may have the bedchamber to yourself. The pallet in the antechamber will suffice for me. I shall not enter your domain unless you invite me."

"That will *never* happen. You are—"

Alex placed his finger across her lips. She shifted, her thigh brushing his knee and a quiver raced through him. "Do we have an agreement?"

She hesitated, biting the corner of her plump lower lip. Emotions flickered in her gaze—fear, doubt, indecision.

She nodded. "We have an agreement."

Giving her no time to react, he took her hand in his and tugged her to him.

Appearing dazed and bewildered, Kat did not resist. He pulled her inexorably closer, until their breaths mingled. She inhaled deeply and her breasts rose, brushing his chest with tantalizing effect. Air whooshed from his lungs as though he were drowning.

He released her hand, but before she could escape, Alex cradled her head in his hands and slowly dipped his head. She stood still as a stunned doe surprised by an unwelcome intruder. But the intruder was unrepentant and took blatant advantage of her lapse.

Alex inhaled Kat's jasmine-and-spice scent as he swooped down, his eyes intent on the absolution her lips bespoke. Finally, his mouth made contact, barely brushing the corner of her bottom lip, a teasing caress that made him groan with the need of a deeper communion.

He repeated the reverent gesture on the other side of her mouth. "This is to seal our bargain, of course," he said in a deep husky timbre, then covered her mouth with his.

Her soft lips trembled, the plump flesh tasting sweet and

vulnerable. But it was not nearly enough. For too long, Alex had dreamed of this moment. During the long years of his imprisonment, when he was filthy, freezing, and hungry, he had despaired of ever seeing Kat again, and only memories of their incredible wedding night had kept him alive. Alex intended to seize every moment now that he was back.

His mouth increased the pressure and her lips parted on a sigh. He welcomed the opening as his tongue stole inside and captured hers. His cock flared with heat and hardened stiff as a pike. Kat raised her arms, her hands brushing against his chest to finally settle like an awkward butterfly on forbidden territory. He sighed with satisfaction.

Kat shoved his chest with surprising strength and he bellowed in surprise. He stumbled over the carpet on the floor and nearly fell. Instead, he steadied himself on the washstand and glared at Kat.

"What was that for?" Alex demanded.

"*That* was to conclude our bargain, of course," Kat said, her face cool and composed, although her eyes glittered with anger as she crossed her arms over her chest.

"You have an odd way of doing it," he grumbled.

"Indeed. But rather effective I think," she said with an arrogant smile.

Alex laughed despite himself. "*Very* effective," he said ruefully.

The smile lingered on his face. It had been a long time since he had laughed. Years, really, and he was a bit rusty. Though he could not remember when he last laughed, he did remember that Kat had always had an uncanny way of making him do so, especially at himself.

Alex chuckled again at the befuddled look on her face. Apparently, it was not the reaction she had been expecting. Alex seized on the revelation like a drowning man seizes a rope tossed to him; perhaps it was a good idea to keep her slightly unbalanced. He had only a month to convince her he wanted to be a husband, to create a family with her. That she could trust him to cleave only unto her. And he had his own parents' loving marriage as an example to guide him.

But because of his abandonment, he had seriously damaged her ability to trust him. By keeping her slightly unsteady and off balance, he might be able to slip under her guard long enough to prove to her he was trustworthy. And with trust, hopefully, would come love.

Kat moved to the chest at the foot of the bed, opened the lid and pulled out a braided girdle.

Though she did not trust him, Alex knew she still wanted him, still desired him. The explosive passion they felt for one another in the days leading up to their wedding, and on the night they consummated their vows, had not burned out in the intervening years. He had seen it tonight in her glittering eyes, sensed it shimmer along her trembling flesh, and tasted it on her wine-sweetened lips. Every breath, touch, and taste proclaimed her need.

The same need that echoed resoundingly within him.

"Why are you staring at me like that?" Kat asked, knotting the long end of the girdle at her waist after buckling it.

Startled, unaware of what his face might have revealed, Alex asked, "Like what?"

"Like . . . oh, never mind," she said, veiling the expression in her eyes with a sweep of her eyelids. She stepped away from him abruptly, changing the subject. "So is everything settled? Do we have a bargain?"

"Almost." Alex went into the other room to fetch his sword Rand had brought back from Crusade after Alex's capture. Kat followed him, her boldly arched eyebrow raised in inquiry. Alex withdrew the sword from its scabbard. The scrape of steel reverberated throughout the quiet room. He held the beautiful but lethal weapon up for his inspection; firelight glinted off the silver blade and the ruby embedded in the pommel glowed with an ethereal light.

Holding the grip, Alex pointed the blade to the heavens. His eyes never leaving her gaze, he vowed, "With everything that I am, I will earn your forgiveness and prove to you I am worthy of being your husband, as God intended. But if on the feast of St. Barnabas, you still wish to revoke our marriage, I vow to declare our marriage unconsummated and see our marriage annulled. I swear to this before God almighty."

Alex handed Kat the sword, hilt first. She clutched the grip expertly before her chest and copying his actions, she said, "I vow before God almighty, to be amenable to your courtship, I will not find ways to sabotage your efforts, and will seriously consider making ours a true marriage. At the end of the month, you will have my answer, whether aye or nay. This I vow, with all my heart."

Alex took the sword from Kat, their hands touching briefly. "Our bargain is sealed. 'Tis too late should you wish to turn back now."

Kat smoothed her hands down her skirts, her voice carefully neutral. "We are in agreement, then. I shall hold you to our bargain as well."

"Aye. Come the feast of St. Barnabas, you shall have a choice. And I pray you choose me." He held his left arm out. "We should proceed to dinner. We do not wish to be late."

After a slight hesitation, Kat placed her hand on his arm, the enormity of her decision like a sudden weight on her shoulders. His muscles flexed at her touch, strong and vital. Warmth radiated into her hand, up the length of her arm. Alex looked down at their joined flesh, and smiled, a wolfish smile that did little to reassure.

She would not change a thing, though. Indeed, Alex was a fool if he believed he could persuade her to give him a second chance. When the month was over, she would be free to fulfill her dream of marrying a man who truly loved her and start a family of her own.

She could not wait to return home where she felt needed and respected. The people of Montclair depended upon her for their livelihood, and she missed the fertile fields and rolling meadows of the river valley where her home resided.

Luc was a good man. He respected her knowledge of estate management and had no desire to challenge her authority in the running of Montclair. On the other hand, she did not doubt that Alex would claim his right of lordship and run things the way he saw fit. Arrogant and controlling, he would not deign to consult her or ask her opinion, despite the fact she had made Montclair even more prosperous in the six years since he left.

Snaring her gaze, the dark blue depths of his eyes challenged her. "Let the battle begin," he said, and then led her out of their chambers, leaving her to ponder his cryptic words.

Chapter 7

Alex and Kat entered White Hall, a lesser hall used for everyday use. Colorful tapestries adorned the walls and voices raised in conversation echoed off the vaulted ceiling. They had barely taken a step into the long, spacious room when a man stopped in front of Alex.

Alex recognized Lord William Calvert immediately. The baron was no more than medium height, but was built like a bull, his broad chest all muscle. He wore his blond hair short and his lips were etched in a perpetual scowl, giving him the appearance of a petulant child.

Beside Alex, Kat stiffened.

"Lord Calvert." Alex did not smile. He had never liked the man, personally. And Lord Calvert despised him in return.

In the last days of the Barons' War, Lord Calvert had refused to surrender. Alex had been with the troops sent to lay siege to the baron's castle and capture him. The siege lasted three months, but just before the Royalist forces razed the castle, Alex spied two men fleeing the stronghold in peasant garb. Their furtive behavior alerted Alex and he gave chase. He soon discovered that it was none other than Lord Calvert and his heir, who was about the same age as Alex. They had fought and were soon captured, but in the process, Alex had fatally wounded Lord Calvert's son.

Lord Calvert smiled. "Sir Alex. I am so glad to see you safely returned to us. You were sorely missed by all who know you." His words and smile were obviously insincere.

Alex responded in kind. "You honor me with your heartfelt words, Calvert."

The baron's lips pulled down in a sneer. "That aside, your wife owes me an apology. And my son, too," he said snidely.

Surprised, Alex turned to Kat, who glared at Lord Calvert with contempt. "Your son is a coward and a bully, Lord Calvert. I owe neither him, nor you, an apology."

Calvert reddened and his chest puffed up at the insult. Alex wondered what event had precipitated such an outburst.

"You assaulted my son without provocation and broke his wrist. I demand recompense."

"I didn't touch your son. He fell from a tree. And he did not break his wrist, he merely sprained it."

Calvert sputtered. "He fell from a tree because you threw a dagger at him!"

At his belligerent tone, heads turned, drawing unwanted attention. Alex had long thought Calvert a blundering fool, but wondered now if he had underestimated the man. After all, the baron had sworn to avenge his son's death.

About to send the baron on his way, Kat retorted before Alex could. Her chin shot up at an obstinate angle. "I did not throw the dagger at him. I'm a very skilled marksman and threw the dagger above him as a deterrent. Your son meant to attack a boy half his size who had climbed up into a tree to seek refuge from his tormentors. I don't apologize to bullies. Now, be gone from my sight."

Calvert, his face a bright shade of vermilion, took a threatening step forward and hissed. "No woman talks to me that way. I am a baron of this realm and demand respect." His furious gaze swung to Alex. "Have you no control over your woman?"

Alex swore, his hand on his sword in warning. "You insult my wife. She is free to speak her mind as she likes. As to the apology you say she owes you, I agree . . ." Kat gasped and

Lord Calvert smiled smugly, until Alex's next words registered, "with my wife. If Kat says she saw your son bullying another boy, I believe her. And a father who condones such behavior in his son deserves no respect. I suggest you leave as my lady wife bid you."

The baron's brown eyes narrowed menacingly. "Your wife is no lady. She is a shameless whore!"

Alex reached out in a flash of rage, clutched Lord Calvert's neck in his fist and shoved him against the wall. His face carved with fury, Alex squeezed his fingers tighter around the baron's throat. Calvert gasped for breath, both his hands clawing at Alex's hand. The baron's face grew redder and redder. Rand pushed through the crowd and came to his side.

"Alex, Edward forgave your outburst in the chapel, but he will not condone murder. Think what you do."

Reason returned at the sound of Rand's voice. Alex relaxed his grip on the baron's throat, but did not release him. The older man gulped in a deep breath.

"Apologize to my wife." Alex's voice sliced through the room. "Now. Unless you wish to settle this matter at Tothill Fields."

Calvert shook his head, his lips compressed. The apology clearly galled him. "I apologize, Lady Katherine. Forgive my insult."

Kat raised her jaw in stiff affront. "I accept your apology," she replied, her voice cool.

Alex released the man and stepped back. The blond baron walked away, his back stiff with wounded pride. Alex decided it would be prudent to keep a close watch on the disgruntled baron. Calvert could very well be the traitor Alex sought.

Frowning, his gaze sought Kat. Eyes of silver shone with surprise and satisfaction. "Are you all right, Kat?"

"Aye. Lord Calvert is a braggart and a fool. His foul insults can't harm me."

Alex agreed. Not for the first time, Lord Calvert had revealed himself to be a coward. Like the day he scuttled away from his besieged castle in disguise, leaving his retainers to the mercy of the conquering Royalist forces. Nay. The baron would not fight him honorably in the open, man to man. He would hide in the shadows, like a black beetle, plotting Alex's death behind the scenes, hiring any scoundrel to do what he was too cowardly to do. As he had hired Scarface to do? Alex wondered. Was Lord Calvert the traitor he sought?

Indeed, the first threat to his life was shortly after the death of the man's older son. Lord Calvert also had gone on Crusade, giving him both motive and opportunity to see Alex dead. Aye, the baron bore watching for the nonce.

The dining hall was overly warm with the press of over a hundred men and women seated at cloth-covered tables, talking and laughing while they dined on an abundance of food and wine. Alex, meanwhile, was disturbingly aware of Kat sitting next to him on the raised dais. The clinking of silver tableware and drinking chalices added its own melody to the cacophony, but she remained stubbornly silent and unresponsive to his overtures.

It was just as well, for King Edward sat in the chair to his left and seemed inclined to have conversation with him. He wanted Alex to describe the fortifications of the former Crusader castle where Alex had been held.

The king was speaking again. "I want to learn all I can, for I intend to build more castles throughout my lands, with the latest and most modern techniques in castle construction. And I plan to begin by building a line of defense to protect southern Wales."

That caught Alex's complete attention. "That is a very ambitious and daring project, Sire. Our neighbors to the west will not like it."

Edward chuckled. "Aye. Llewelyn will be furious." Then he sobered. "But I don't trust him. The Prince of Wales will not be content for long holding only the northern lands of Wales.

And my spies report that Llewelyn has decided to ignore my summons to do homage for his principality. Again."

"Do you fear hostilities will break out between England and Wales again, Sire?"

Kat's voice startled Alex. He turned to his wife and stared, incredulous that she would pose such a bold question.

Instead of taking offense, Edward laughed. "Fear? I am afraid of naught, Cousin. But I would prefer to complete this business of putting the kingdom's affairs in order before I begin fighting any new wars.

"My cousin is a rare woman—her interest in worldly affairs and such," Edward said as if Kat were invisible, a hint of disapproval in his voice.

Kat stiffened beside Alex. He laid a warning hand on her thigh and spoke up before she said something in anger. "Kat *is* a unique woman. But I'm a man of unusual tastes, and I enjoy the challenge."

The king laughed heartily, while Alex's remark earned him a sharp pinch from his wife. Pain shot up his inner thigh and he jerked. He removed his hand from her leg and rubbed his own injured limb.

Alex turned to her. "Was that necessary?" he said in an undertone, loud enough for Kat alone to hear.

"No more than your insulting comment. If that is your idea of courtship, I would rethink your strategy. Unless you *want* to lose our wager?"

Alex watched, fascinated, as Kat's unusual eyes sparked bright as lightning, and then darkened to the color of a thundercloud. His breath hitched. When angry, Kat was an extraordinarily beautiful woman.

"Wager?" Alex replied. "I consider it more in the nature of a promissory note. When the note comes due, I promise you will never regret your decision to become my wife in truth." His voice dropped huskily at the last.

An image of Kat lying naked in bed filled his head—her long-limbed body arched towards him in entreaty as he kissed and licked a slow, moist trail up her inner thigh. The image appeared so real his flesh hardened.

Kat must have read the desire in his eyes, for she reached blindly for the cup of wine they shared and took several deep draughts. He dropped his eyes to her throat when she swallowed, entranced by the sensual movement of the tendons in her neck.

With every deep breath, he inhaled her intoxicating scent, a mysterious blend of spices, jasmine, and Kat. It seduced his senses. He grew light-headed. The trestle table covering his actions, he tugged the suddenly tight linen braies away from his straining flesh.

Desperate for any distraction, Alex took a deep draught of the wine.

Released from Alex's penetrating gaze, Kat blinked in confusion. Heat suffused her. She felt dazed, her senses scattered, as though she were awakening from some deep, enchanted spell. King Edward chose that moment to stand before the court; Kat breathed an audible sigh of relief.

Edward raised his chalice and rapped the table for attention. "Join me in a toast." The noise in the hall ceased to a roaring silence. "It was a happy day for England when one of her bravest and most loyal knights returned to her shores upon his escape from a Saracen dungeon. To Sir Alex, a man of honor and conviction who has served me most faithfully. Welcome home."

Shouts of welcome filled the hall, the noise deafening. Kat drank of her wine. Down the table she saw Sir Luc, his handsome profile slightly shadowed, hiding his look of annoyance.

When it was quiet again, Alex shoved back his chair and stood up. "Sire, I don't know what to say, except . . . I am honored. I shall do my best to make sure that you never regret your words.

"But I must confess," he continued, and then turned and addressed the suddenly rapt crowd, "I have not been as honorable in my actions as husband as I have been in my duty to God and my king."

Gasps resounded throughout the dining hall. Feeling as if she had been hit over the head with a club, Kat raised her dazed gaze to Alex. His eyes held hers in a tight vise that was impossible to escape.

"Kat. To my shame, I failed you. The day we married, I made a sacred vow before God to love, honor, keep and protect you. But in my fear and selfishness, I fled the next day, without thought to what pain my actions might cause you. For that, I am profoundly sorry."

The hall was deathly quiet, except for the roaring of blood in her ears. Even so, she heard the ring of sincerity in Alex's voice. It amazed her that Alex, proud and domineering, would debase himself before the court for her. Pain squeezed her chest and her eyes welled with unshed tears. His apology was too late, though. She was not the same girl he left behind; anger had burned away what little of her heart remained after he rejected her. Nothing could replace the emptiness that resided within her heart. Now all she sought was peace.

King Edward slapped Alex on the back. "Well, Sir Alex, that was a most noble apology. What say you, Cousin, shall you accept this repentant rogue's apology and give him another chance to prove his devotion?"

Kat hesitated. "I accept his apology." She purposely did not address the last part of Edward's question.

But the king laughed jovially, missing the significance. "There, Sir Alex. Your lady has spoken and all is forgiven. 'Tis past time you saw to the begetting of your heirs," he said, turning to smile at Eleanor. "My lady will attest to the joy that children can bring to a marriage." He held out his hand to Queen Eleanor and she smiled adoringly up at her husband. When she put her hand in his, he raised her to stand beside him while her ladies arranged her skirts.

Eleanor, her smile serene, turned to Kat. "Aye, Lady Katherine, I confess there is no greater reward in this life than giving your husband heirs. Indeed, 'tis a duty most pleasurable."

The king laughed. Alex smiled good-naturedly. But Kat

stood like a poker, her fists clenched, barely holding a smile on her face. Duty was the last reason she would ever give birth to a child. Children should be loved and cherished for their own sake, not begotten for the sole purpose of inheritance, or to acquire more wealth, land, and power.

Alex, his smile firmly in place, reached down and caught Kat's hand in his and whispered, "Careful, your anger is giving you away. Relax." Unlike the king, he was not fooled by her grudging acceptance of his apology. She had yet to forgive him and, though she had made a vow to give him a second chance, he knew she would fight him every step of the way.

He unclenched her fist, weaving his fingers through hers. Her hand squeezed tighter at his remark, then relaxed gradually in his grip. Her hand, soft skin and bold strength, felt right in his. He was home at last, and he intended to make Kat see that he was the only man for her. Any other outcome was unthinkable.

The king motioned for the musicians to play and then waved negligently to his court. "Continue on with your merrymaking," he said and retired with his wife to their private quarters.

After the king and queen departed, lords and ladies left the tables, and servants began clearing off the trestle tables so they could break them down and clear the hall for dancing.

Kat turned to him. "I believe I will retire, also. 'Tis been a long and eventful day. I bid you good eve."

Alex halted her. His first thought was that Kat was already reneging on her part of the bargain. Then he saw the slight droop in her shoulders and lavender shadows under her eyes.

He was immediately contrite. "Forgive me. You are weary."

A long black tendril of her hair hung loose from her snood. It grazed her left check enticingly, distracting him. He wanted to wind the silky strand around his finger and tug gently until her lips met his. He contented himself with smoothing it back behind her ear. Grazing the soft skin of her cheek, he felt a subtle tremor.

Alex pulled his gaze back to hers. "Allow me to escort you to our room."

"Verily, you need not escort me," she said. "I would prefer to be alone to my thoughts."

He hesitated, but seeing the fatigue in her eyes he relented. "As you wish."

Unable to resist, Alex raised her hand to his mouth and kissed the underside of her wrist. He nudged the woolen fabric of her sleeve higher. His tongue darted out, and with a light, teasing stroke he licked the delicate skin he exposed. Her breath hitched. At the slight movement, her full breasts rose up against her tight green bodice, enticing him. Then Kat turned and vanished into the crowd.

Chapter 8

"Rose? Who is that dancing with your brother?" Kat asked two evenings later, despite her best intentions to remain indifferent.

She could not quell the disturbing emotion that rose in her breast as she watched the beautiful, flame-haired woman sway seductively towards Alex. Their hands touched for several beats as they turned in a circle. The woman smiled up at him in blatant invitation, and slowly pressed her voluptuous breasts against his chest before they parted.

What a brazen slut, Kat thought, trembling.

Only two days had passed since their agreement was sealed and Alex was already making a fool of her. She refused to acknowledge her part in pushing him away. At supper she had rebuffed all his overtures to start a conversation by answering his questions with stilted responses.

Rosalyn Harcourt, Lady Ayleston, wore a drab gray overtunic, and her beautiful copper hair was completely covered by a wimple and veil—the headdress usually reserved for nuns and older widows. "Her name is Lady Elena Chartres. She is a *friend* of Rand's," Rose responded, her bowed upper lip curled scornfully.

So the redhead was Rand's latest paramour, one of many in a long line of conquests, Kat mused. Brief, meaningless liaisons he conducted because he could not have the woman he loved. Unfortunately, Rand was so adept at hiding his emotions behind the persona of a charming rogue, that she did not think he was even aware of the depth of his feelings. But Kat knew the truth. She read the longing in Rand's eyes whenever he stared at Rose when he thought no one was looking.

It was easy to recognize loneliness in others when one felt it so deeply inside themselves.

Kat just prayed Rand would realize how he felt about Rose before it was too late. No one was more deserving of happiness than her cousin and her dear friend.

Kat fanned her warm face, a bead of perspiration rolled down her temple. The combination of numerous lit iron chandeliers, overcrowded hall, and stale body odor doused by aromatic perfume did naught to improve her disposition.

The music ended in a crescendo, and as the dance required, Alex grabbed his partner's waist and lifted her high in the air. The woman clung to him indecently when he lowered her to the ground. Kat clenched her jaw, and her sharp nails dug into her palms.

At that moment an insidious voice whispered in her ear. "They make a striking couple. Do you not agree, Lady Katherine?"

Kat recognized the weasely voice before she turned. "Sir Stephen, to what do we owe this pleasure?"

Sir Stephen Harcourt was wiry, blond, and below average in stature, so that Kat looked down at him from her superior height. His small, deep-set eyes and pinched mouth were all that kept him from being handsome.

He sneered at her sarcastic tone, undeterred, and nodded towards Alex, who was escorting Lady Elena off the dance floor. "She is quite a beauty and very generous with her favors. Any man would be hard-pressed to resist her. And it looks as if she has chosen your husband to gift next with her generosity."

Lady Elena leaned against Alex and outrageously rubbed her ample breast against his arm. Cold rage pumped through

Kat's veins, her face blank of all emotion. Before she could give Sir Stephen a proper set-down, Rose intervened.

"Why don't you crawl back into whatever hole you slithered from, Stephen," she said, her heart-shaped face contorted with hate. "Your presence is not wanted here. Or better yet, why do you not join Lady Elena, mayhap her generosity will rub off on you. Oh, but I forgot, everyone knows she already refused you her abundant favors. It would seem Lady Elena has *some* standards after all."

Sir Stephen glared at Rose. Though it was not directed at Kat, it made her shiver. Hatred burned in the dark brown depths. "You speak of standards," he said, his lip curled in contempt. "Those are strange words, indeed, coming as they do from a killer."

Rose gasped and turned white as the blood drained from her face. Livid, Kat stepped between Rose and Sir Stephen.

"You little worm, have a care whom you slander," Kat hissed under her breath. "Everyone knows Bertram died when he fell down the stairs in a drunken stupor."

"That is a lie," he said hotly. "Aye, he was drunk, but he was never clumsy. And I know for a fact that Bertram went to his wife's bed that night. As surely as I stand here, somehow Rosalyn had a hand in my cousin's death, and I shall not rest until she pays for her crimes."

Kat straightened to her full height and coldly glared down at the shorter man. "That's Lady Ayleston to you. And if you dare harm Rose in any way, you are a dead man."

Rose shifted to stand beside her. "You need not defend me, Kat. I can take care of myself. Besides, Sir Stephen's accusations are not unknown to me. Despite the fact that the coroner's inquest ruled my husband died by misadventure and a jury concurred, Sir Stephen has never been able to accept the truth. I do believe you have become unhinged in your grief for Bertram, *Cousin.*"

Sir Stephen stepped toward Rose, raised his arm threateningly, and snarled, "You little *bitch*. You will regret—"

Fright flaring in her eyes, Rose recoiled.

Kat, her hand reaching for her dagger, stopped in mid-motion at the male voice that interceded.

"Sir Stephen, do forgive me, but 'tis not fair that you should have a complete monopoly on the two loveliest ladies at court. Ladies," Sir Luc said, nodding to them in greeting, "I hope I'm not interrupting anything."

Kat turned to Sir Luc in surprise at his timely interruption. He looked very handsome in a wine silk tunic, his long, curly mane shimmering like gold in the candlelight. "Nay, Luc, you are not interrupting. As a matter of fact, Sir Stephen was just telling us he is feeling unwell. He regrets he must leave us and retire early," she said, not hiding her contempt.

Sir Stephen glared at Kat, but made a short, stiff bow. Then he turned and marched off, rudely jostling Sir Luc's arm.

Righting himself, Sir Luc said, "What an unpleasant man. What was he saying that made you so upset, Kat? The look on your face was quite fierce." His own face was filled with concern.

"Naught worth repeating. Sir Stephen has always been a sniveling coward, and I have no desire to discuss him further."

"As you say, my dear."

Rose stiffened beside her. "To what do we owe this pleasure, Sir Luc?" she asked.

Her sarcastic question echoed Kat's own words to Sir Stephen earlier. Kat did not understand why Rose disliked Luc. Now that Alex was back, it was understandable that she might be uncomfortable with his presence. But Rose had disliked Luc from the moment they met. Not that her aversion was unique. Rose had a general antipathy of men not of her own family.

"Actually, I was hoping to speak with Kat. In private, if I may?" Luc added, his question directed to Kat. His eyes glowed with appeal, but his smile appeared sad and resigned.

"Absolutely not," Rose blurted.

"Of course," Kat said simultaneously.

Rose looked at her with disbelief. "Kat, you know you do not dare speak to Sir Luc alone. Alex will be furious," she said, ignoring Sir Luc.

"I'm not afraid of Alex. I can do as I please," Kat said, indignant.

"Then at least have a care with your reputation. It will not do to be indiscreet."

"I would never do anything to destroy Kat's reputation, Lady Ayleston," Luc assured her. "I simply wish to speak with her for a moment." He turned to Kat and pointed to the left. "The alcove is in full view of company, yet my words will not be overheard."

"Very well. Why do you not go ahead and await me there. I will meet you anon."

Luc nodded in obvious relief. Raising Kat's hand, he bowed over it and departed.

Kat turned back to her friend and frowned her displeasure. "I don't understand your animosity towards Luc, Rose. He is the injured party in this whole debacle. Would you have me deny him such a small request?"

Rose snorted. "Obviously you will do as you please, Kat. You have ever been stubborn. But remember, I warned you." Her ominous tone rang in Kat's ears as Rose disappeared into the throng.

Kat turned the opposite direction and headed for the alcove. She had no idea what she would say to Sir Luc.

After the initial shock of discovering Alex alive, euphoria had filled her, and Luc had been forgotten. In that brief moment, she easily tossed him aside like refuse from a chamber pot. Naught mattered except that Alex was alive, and he returned to her. But her elation had quickly flickered and died, to be consumed by the conflagration of betrayal's flames.

Never forget, never forgive. Her family's motto was emblazoned on her conscience. Nay, she did not forget, nor forgive.

She could not begin to imagine what Luc must be feeling. Inside, guilt was tearing her apart. Since Alex's return she had been avoiding Luc. There was naught she could say to him to make the situation easier to bear. She'd made a pact with the devil—a marriage bargain that in order for it to succeed had to remain secret. Therefore, until she was free to marry Sir Luc, she dared not give him hope for a future with her.

All of a sudden, a tall knight in black collided with Kat. Catching her from falling, his scabbard got tangled between her legs in the voluminous folds of her dark red skirts. He tugged on his sword, blushing, but merely succeeded in lifting her skirts to reveal her calves. Kat grabbed her skirts and yanked them free. The knight murmured an embarrassed apology and then retreated hastily.

Kat continued around the edge of the room. Up ahead, she spotted Luc. Torchlight shown on his golden head—his regal features drawn and his sensual lips twisted in sorrow. All of a sudden, Alex cut in front of her and she jolted to a stop.

Alex stared at Kat, helpless not to admire how beautiful his wife looked. She wore a wine velvet tunic, embroidered with gold leaves around the neckline and wide cuffs. The deep color contrasted vividly with her coal black, waist-length hair. A ruby-studded girdle draped her waist, emphasizing her tall statuesque body. A barbette and fillet headdress crowned her head.

Which she tilted now at a defiant angle, as proudly as any queen. Alex kissed her hand in a blatant gesture that declared her his possession.

"Kat, I have been looking for you." Alex kept her hand in his.

Kat nodded, her body rigid. "Well, look no more. You have found me. How clever you are."

At his wife's sarcastic wit, Alex smiled, albeit a stiff smile that promised retribution. His gaze alighted on Sir Luc standing in the alcove behind him, and then returned to Kat. A muscle in his jaw twitched. "I am afraid I must interrupt you, my dear. I have a compelling desire to dance with my wife," he said in an even tone, although he was far from calm.

Placing his hand on her lower back, he guided Kat into the

heart of the crowd. Despite the barrier of her clothing, heat seeped into his palm and stimulated other regions.

"Would you not rather dance with Lady Elena?" she snapped.

Startled, Alex looked down at her. "Tell me you are not jealous of Lady Elena?" He smiled, pleased at the notion. "She is a shameless flirt and Rand's lady. I have absolutely no interest in her." Several courtiers noted their passage, their necks craning, no doubt trying to gauge every bodily nuance and facial expression.

"I'm not jealous. Dance with whomever you please."

He smiled, unrepentant. "Good, because it pleases me to dance with my wife. You are adorable when you are jealous, you know."

"And you are insufferable." She frowned, vexed.

"And you are frowning. Smile, my love. We are being watched."

After a slight pause, her lips lifted in a grudging smile. "For the sake of appearances, I shall smile and be all that is agreeable. But do not let it go to your head. 'Tis but an act to keep the bloodthirsty hounds at bay."

Alex threw back his head and laughed at her witticism. Several ladies, startled by his spontaneous gesture, turned and smiled as he passed. Kat merely looked at him as if he had lost his senses, along with four years of his life. Funny, but this made him chuckle again.

"I fear the excitement of your escape and ultimate return has finally caught up with you, Alex. Perhaps you should retire early tonight. After what you have been through, no one would blame you."

"Do I hear a note of concern in your voice, darling?"

"As much as I would be concerned for a lame horse that needs to be put out to pasture, *darling*." She smiled sweetly.

"Ah, Kat, I have missed your wit," he said, and pulled up at the edge of the open area designated for dancing. "Blood-thirsty hounds, indeed." Alex inclined his head towards the curious eyes directed their way. Several courtiers who danced past craned their heads and stared back at them.

"Shall we let the 'hounds' get a whiff of the scent? I would be honored if you granted me a dance. Or would you rather turn tail and take refuge in the garden for a moment's respite?"

The music slowly ended.

"How crass."

"'Twas your analogy. I merely took it up and expounded upon it. Well? Which is it?"

"I'm no coward to turn and run. I accept your *gracious* offer to dance." Kat held out her hand, feeling trapped already. But the alternative was unacceptable. She did not want to be alone with Alex in a dark, secluded garden. She did not trust herself. His heat, his magnetism radiated through layers of material where his hand pressed her lower back. How would she be able to resist him if he kissed her again?

Alex smiled and placed her hand on his arm. A shock of recognition quivered up her arm, but she valiantly ignored it.

"I guess a romantic moonlit stroll in the garden will have to be postponed," he said, and then led her to the center of the hall.

The musicians played a few notes while couples paired up across from each other. To the left of Kat was an older knight with a large paunch. Across from him, next to Alex, was Lady Lynette, damsel-in-waiting to Queen Eleanor. She was a beautiful, petite brunette with an infectious grin, which she turned on Alex.

The music began in earnest. Alex bowed before Kat and held out his hand, she swayed and laid her hand in his.

Then she stared into his eyes, drowning in midnight haze.

The dark depths glinted with some emotion, before dropping to gaze at her bodice, her waist and down her hips. Sizzling heat ignited everywhere his eyes traced, and then swept up into her face, albeit for a different reason. A carnal gleam lit his eyes, his every desire revealed in that one, unguarded glimpse. Alex wanted her. Completely. Unequivocally.

A shiver ran down Kat's spine. Fear? Excitement? Anticipation? Unease, aye, that was what she felt. At least that was what she told herself as Alex guided her flawlessly through the sensual dance.

Kat had eluded him again. One moment he was speaking with Rand and Lady Elena, while keeping a proprietary eye on his wife, who was dancing with her besotted admirers. Then he had looked away briefly at some jest of Elena's and when he turned back, Kat was gone. He had searched for her throughout the palace with no luck, which left only one other place he could think to look.

As he exited the castle, Alex nodded to a black-garbed knight, took the steps down into the courtyard and continued on his way. The moon guided him to the stable, the cool night air bracing. It had ever been Kat's way to seek refuge with her horse when distressed. It surprised him to realize that they were similar in that regard. It made him wonder in what other ways might they be of like mind?

For so long, prior to his wedding, he had bemoaned the marriage pact his parents had made with Kat's father when Alex was just a boy. He had been a virile young man and she was not his ideal of what he wanted in a woman. Not that she ever acted like a young lady. Her father let her roam wild, teaching her skills in arms and educating her as a man, and she had even dressed like one. Alex smiled in remembrance.

Although now he could look back with fondness, at the time he had resented her and the duty he owed his family that bade him enter into a marriage not of his choice. From birth, his father lectured him on the importance of duty, first to God, then to king, and lastly to family. Because he learned the lesson well, he was not able to marry the woman he loved, Lady Lydia St. John.

The vast whitewashed stable loomed up ahead in the moonlight. Not a creature stirred outside. He caught a whiff of wood smoke, straw, and manure on the air. Slowing his pace, he crept on silent feet, wanting the element of surprise should he find Kat. He stopped outside the stable doors, his thoughts returning to the past and Lydia.

He had realized long ago that the only woman he would ever love was lost to him. But it was not memories of Lydia that had kept him sane during the grueling years he suffered in slavery. His homecoming would not be complete until Kat accepted him with her whole heart. Failure was not acceptable, so, shaking himself free of his reverie, Alex entered the vast building without a sound.

The main corridor was long and wide, with stalls on either side. A shorter, narrower walkway intersected the main one so the building had four exits. Several tack rooms—needed to house supplies, equipment and fodder for scores of horses—bordered this smaller aisle.

He had already discovered where Kat quartered her gray mare and was not surprised when he heard a low murmur coming from that direction. He headed straight for Lightning's stall. A beam of moonlight entering from a high, round window lit his path.

Silence now pervaded the stable except the occasional snort and rustling of horses. Alex patted Lightning's head and peered over the closed stall door into the shadows. "Hello there, girl."

He saw a slight movement at the back of the stall, a darker shadow than the rest. "Reveal yourself, Kat. I know you're there."

Kat froze in shock, unable to believe this turn of events. How did Alex know to find her in the stable? And what had warned him of her presence?

Alex opened the stall door. "You may as well come out. I can see you."

This puzzled her, for his back remained to her. She started to take a step forward when a small, shaky voice reached her. "'Tis I, milord. Matthew of Oxford."

Hay shuffled and the dark-haired lad emerged from the back of the stall.

"Matthew of Oxford," Alex said with considerable surprise. "What do you here? I thought you were—never mind, obviously, I was wrong." He chuckled.

Kat nearly sighed with relief, but remained quiet and still. She did not want to alert Alex to her presence behind him near the tack rooms.

"What are you doing with her ladyship's horse? Should you not be about your duties, son?" he asked, his voice gentle and calm.

"Nay, sir. The steward released me from my duties for the eve. Lady Katherine said I might visit her horse whenever I wished," the boy answered, an anxious tremor in his voice.

"Ahh, and you thought to visit the horses before you retire." Alex entered the stall. "I must compliment you on your judge of horseflesh, Matthew. Lightning is a rare breed; she is beautiful, intelligent and spirited." He paused and then said, as though musing to himself, "Just like her mistress," and ran his hand down the mare's graceful neck.

Kat's neck tingled, feeling the caress almost as if he stroked her instead, and warmth spread throughout her. Touched by his unexpected words, she tried to fight the emotion. "Lightning *is* beautiful," Matthew piped up. "But Kat is much prettier."

Alex laughed. "Aye, young Matthew. I must agree with you and bow to your greater wisdom in this matter. But how is it you come to know my lady?" he asked, his tone kind and fatherly.

Her heart turned over. For the first time, she imagined Alex as the father of the child she desperately wanted. As now, he would be strong, yet kind, patient, and caring of the child's needs.

"She rescued me from some mean boys yesterday. She gave me leave to call her Kat," he piped up.

Alex had turned slightly towards Kat. She watched as his smile turned rueful. "'Tis a great compliment that she would entrust the care of her mare to you. She must consider you a very special friend, indeed."

"Are you her special friend, too, my lord?"

Kat held her breath as she waited for his answer.

"We were friends once, long ago. But much has happened since. Even so, I would hope she still counted me as her friend."

Emotion rose in her throat and she pressed a hand to her mouth. Aye, they had been friends once, and antagonists, and finally lovers upon their marriage. Then he had destroyed their chance for happiness by running away. She no longer trusted her judgment where he was concerned, so friendship was out of the question, too.

Matthew peeped up. "Kat said Lightning was a gift from her father-in-law. I wish I had a father-in-law to gift me such a horse."

Alex laughed. "Mayhap someday you will." He grinned as mischievous as a little boy. "Can you keep a secret, Matthew?"

The boy's dark eyes grew wide. "A secret? Aye, sir, I can keep my mouth shut."

"The horse was a gift from me, actually. The moment Lightning was foaled, I knew she was destined for Kat. I thought it best she think the horse was from my father, though."

Kat's heart skipped a beat or two. She did not know what to think. No gift could have pleased her more. Alex *had* cared for her and given her something very precious. She started to step forward, and then caught herself, clutching the wooden wall. A sliver of wood thrust beneath the skin of her thumb and nearly made her gasp out.

Fool, she swore to herself, sucking her sore digit. How could she forget for a single moment the unbearable anguish and despair Alex caused her when he deserted her the day after their marriage? No gift, or his kindness to the boy, could ever make up for his betrayal.

Careful not to make a sound, Kat pushed away from the wall. She took several steps backward, keeping her eye on Alex, when her foot came down on a hard, sharp object.

She cried out, a short yelp of pain quickly cut off. But it was too late.

Alex reached for his sword and peered towards her in the shadows. "Who goes there?"

Not waiting a moment to think, Kat picked up her skirts and ran. She had never been a coward in her life, but every good commander knew when it was time to stand and fight, and when it was time to retreat. So she ran and ran, with no idea where she was heading, her delicate slippers a flimsy barrier as her feet padded over the hard ground. When a sharp pain pierced her side, she clutched it with her hand. But she kept going until, unexpectedly, she found herself in the quiet and secluded Sanctuary Garden.

Short of breath, a hand to her aching side, Kat looked around at the scenery. The garden consisted of sculpted yew hedges above head height, which provided hidden alcoves for private contemplation. That was during the daylight hours. Unfortunately, some of the more base at court met and held illicit assignations here, also. Uncomfortable with the notion she might stumble into an embarrassing situation, she turned to leave.

The dark silhouette of a man rose up from the bench in a corner alcove. Kat gasped. He loomed over her, blocking the exit.

"Who goes there?" she demanded, vaguely aware she mimicked her husband's last words.

Chapter 9

A man stepped out of the shadows, his golden hair shimmering silver in the moonlight.

"God be praised," Kat exclaimed. "You scared me, Luc. But glad I am 'tis you."

He smiled, revealing the dimple in his left cheek. "'Tis glad *I* am you are glad to see me."

"I thought—never mind, 'tis of no import."

She could not explain to Luc that she had thought he was Alex. That Alex had caught her spying and now she was hiding from him. But she was being ridiculous; Luc was already sitting in the garden when she arrived. That thought gave her pause.

"What are you doing here, Luc?"

His gleaming smile turned rueful. "The same as you, I would imagine. I needed a moment alone with my thoughts."

Kat tucked a stray lock of her hair behind her ear. Suddenly, the motion stroked her memory, of the other night when Alex had done the same to her hair—his fingers, his breath, his scent filled her, tantalized her, terrified her.

Nay, be gone, her mind protested against the memory. She would not let Alex destroy her again.

Luc jerked as though he had received a blow and his dimpled

smile faltered. "Forgive me," he said, his gaze hurt. "I shall go forthwith and disturb you no longer as you demand."

God forfend, she thought, *did I say that aloud?*

Kat reached out to stay him, but dropped her arm. "Nay, Luc, you have naught to beg forgiveness for. You misunderstand. I am the one who should go. Alex will not be best pleased if he should learn we were alone."

Sir Luc stepped in her path. "Prithee, my love, do not go yet." His look of yearning was painful to bear. "I know this is awkward for you. But we were interrupted earlier before I had a chance to talk to you about your husband's return."

"Luc, I . . . I have no idea what to say." Kat dropped her gaze to her clenched fingers, unable to look at him any longer.

Sir Luc's fingers brushed her cheek. Startled, her head shot up to meet his stare again.

"It seems we are in accord, as usual," he said, his mouth twisted bitterly. "For I find that no words can begin to express what I am feeling at the moment." He paused, the deep emotion in his golden eyes unguarded. "Although 'tis a sin to think it," he continued in a tortured voice, "I cannot help but wish Alex had died and never returned."

At his impassioned confession, guilt twisted tighter inside Kat. "Nay, Luc. You don't truly mean it."

"Do I not?" he asked doubtfully, as though to himself. He shook his head. "But I did not want to speak to you so that I might unburden my soul. I want to make sure you're all right. It must have been a great shock to you when Sir Alex marched into the chapel very much alive."

Kat paced away and stopped before the bench, then spun back to Luc. The night air suddenly cool, she crossed her arms over her chest and rubbed her upper arms with both hands. "Aye. 'Tis very confusing. I still find it difficult to comprehend that I am not and never have been a widow." Kat took a deep breath. "But what I regret the most is that you have been hurt, Luc," she said, her voice tinged with sorrow.

Sir Luc closed the gap between them and braced his hands

on her shoulders. "I pray you, do not apologize. For no matter that your husband has returned to claim you, I regret not one moment of loving you."

"But you deserve none of this. You have been naught but kind and good to me. 'Tis so unfair."

"Promise me one thing?"

"Of course, if I can."

"Though I would never dare to interfere between you and Sir Alex, I want you to come to me should you ever need aught or are in trouble."

Kat reached out and touched his arm, saying softly, "Thank you, Luc. I appreciate your concern. Your friendship is invaluable to me. Never have you betrayed my trust." Her voice quavered, "I wish—"

Luc drew closer, his gaze intent, a feral gold light in his eyes. "Tell me. What do you wish?"

"Oh, it matters not what I wish now." She shook her head and drew away, aware of the danger being alone with Luc presented. She could not give him false hope until her bargain with Alex was complete and her marriage severed. "I am sorry. I must go."

She made to leave, but Luc caught her arm and pressed close against her. His other hand cupped her cheek and his fervent gaze dipped to her lips. A ripple of unease shot through Kat; she tensed, prepared to draw away.

"Unhand my wife, knave." A primordial growl erupted in the garden and a dark shape charged out of the shadows.

Knocked roughly aside, Kat careened into the bench. Her knee scraped the stone, but she clutched the seat to stop her fall. She turned and saw Alex hovering over Sir Luc, who had landed on the ground. A snarl on his face, Alex pressed his sword against Luc's throat.

Kat jumped between the two men. Her heart pounded erratically. "*Alex*. Put down your sword."

Alex tugged her away and glared at her over his shoulder.

"You dare to command me when I caught you in his arms?" His furious gaze shot back to Sir Luc.

Undeterred, she pressed between them again and forced Alex to meet her gaze. "I was leaving the garden. You must believe me." Beneath her staying hand, his heartbeat was strong and vital, his chest muscles rigid, immovable.

Sir Luc spoke then, his voice stilted. "Sir Alex. She speaks true. When she meant to leave, I stopped her. Don't blame Kat. I am the one at fault."

Alex lifted his lip in a snarl. "Aye, you are." He pressed his sword closer, the tip drawing a bead of blood. "Touch my wife again, and I will kill you. I owe you a debt for saving my life in the Holy Land, but do not challenge me in this."

Luc nodded stiffly. Alex stepped away, sheathing his sword. Kat breathed a sigh of relief and wiped her sweaty palms on her skirts.

When Luc stood up, he tugged his tunic down and turned to Kat. "I humbly beg your pardon, Kat. I should not have put you in a compromising position. I lost my head. Forgive me." He bowed to her stiffly, unsmiling, and left the garden.

Kat watched Luc depart, her jaw clenched. Now that the danger had passed, fury welled up inside her and her face flushed. What right did Alex have to interfere? Overbearing and arrogant, he acted as if he had some say in ordering her life. She could not wait until their bargain was complete and she was finally free of his domineering personality.

"Do not turn your back on me," Alex's voice thundered in the suddenly quiet garden.

Before Kat could turn, Alex gripped her upper arm and yanked her around to face him. His eyes black with rage, he demanded, "I want the truth. Do not lie to me! Did you or did you not encourage him to touch you? To kiss you?"

Kat gasped, startled. "Nay. How can you believe such a thing of me?"

"The man was your lover," he said, incredulous, contempt

blazing in his eyes. "And I caught you in his arms. What else am I to believe?"

She raised her chin in offended pride. "That I am a woman of honor. That I would never forsake my marriage vows and betray you."

"Why?" he shot back. "You despise me. Luc is the man you want to marry. So why should I believe you? Give me one good reason," his voice cut sharp as glass.

"Because I never—"

He gripped her chin and forced her to look him in the eye. "What? What were you going to say?"

"You are mistaken. I meant naught."

He shook her, then wrapped an arm around her and pressed her to his hard, unyielding body. "You lie. Answer me. What were you going to say?" His voice was cold and implacable.

Trapped against his body, Kat stared into eyes that glittered like ice crystals. "Answer me, Kat. Why should I trust you?"

Kat trembled. This was not the same Alex she grew up with. He was a stranger to her now, unpredictable and quite possibly savage. This man scared her, kept her off balance.

"Because I never—" her voice cracked. She licked her lips.

Alex tightened his hold. He cupped her jaw and rubbed his thumb over her lower lip possessively.

A shiver raced down her spine and her breasts swelled, becoming aroused.

"Never what?" he coaxed with a seductive purr, though underneath ran a dangerous current.

"Never slept with Sir Luc," she blurted, her tongue loosened at last.

Stunned, Alex's jaw dropped and his hold slackened. "'S truth? Do you mean it?"

Unable to believe she had spilled the truth, Kat pulled out of his arms and paced away. She inhaled, and then exhaled in an attempt to recover her senses.

Alex's steps sounded behind her in the grass and stopped. His warm breath caressed her nape. "I would advise you to remember that I am yet your husband. Do not lie to me, Kat. Did you or did you not bed Sir Luc?"

Kat spun around to stare up at him. "I did not. Whatever you believe of Sir Luc, he is a gentleman. He would never dishonor me by bedding me without benefit of marriage vows."

His brows drew down, perplexed. "Then why did you not deny it when I accused you of adultery? Why let me believe you and Luc were lovers?"

"Because I was hurt and angry. When you heard the rumors, you did not ask me the validity of such foul lies. You accused me outright of whoring around. The accusation was unjust when *I* have done naught to betray your trust." She refused to tell him the whole truth. That she wanted him to feel the sting of betrayal—even if it was only a small measure of the pain she felt when he abandoned her.

Alex felt his face flush with guilt. He had wronged Kat, again. But his trust had been shattered by years of imprisonment and the actions of a traitor. Against his will, memories invaded—a whip flicked, and a sharp crack resounded in his ears as excruciating pain rippled down his back. Alex flinched with remembered pain.

Kat reached out and placed a gentle hand on his upper arm. "Alex? Are you all right?" she said, distress evident in the soft tone of her voice.

Alex stared down at Kat, her face etched with worry. He latched onto her concern like a man with one foot over death's threshold and recovered his composure.

"I am fine, Kat." How beautiful she looked, with the silver shimmer of moonlight kissing her high cheekbones and full red lips.

"What happened to you while you were imprisoned, Alex? You never speak of it, yet I know—"

He pressed his finger against her lips, stilling the flow of words. The soft, plush feel of them wiped away coherent thought. All he wanted to do was kiss her, paying particular attention to her plump lower lip. Unable to resist, he leaned down, but Kat moved a step back.

"W–was there something you wished to discuss with me?"

"Discuss?" Alex asked, confused.

She canted her head and looked up at him oddly. "You sought me out, so I assume you must have something on your mind. Prithee, discourse away."

She turned and sat down on a bench, her ruby velvet skirt rustling. Folding her hands loosely in her lap, staring up at him with her eyes open wide and expectant, she gave every appearance of waiting patiently for him to 'discourse.'

Having no idea what to say, he hesitated. It had been many years since he was called upon to participate in casual conversation. Indeed, in prison, speaking was forbidden.

He finally sat down beside her, saying, "Need there be something in particular I wish to discuss? Did it not occur to you that I simply enjoy your company?"

Alex scooted closer, so they touched from shoulder to thigh, and took her hand in his. He brought it to his lips and kissed her long, graceful fingers, her scent intoxicating his senses. She smelled exotic, sultry, and mysterious.

"En . . . enjoy my company?" Underneath her nervousness, her tone conveyed confusion, as though she had never heard of such an occupation before.

He smiled at that. Unable to resist touching her golden skin, he feathered his finger along her wrist. It was soft and sleek, and warmth emanated where her pulse jumped beneath his finger. How would she taste?

Lightly, his caress skimmed up her arm beneath her sleeve. When he reached her inner elbow, Alex drew her closer and replaced his finger with his mouth. He pressed his lips against the lavender shadows hidden there, her skin as delicate as papyrus. Then he parted his lips infinitesimally and his tongue stroked her flesh, a slow, teasing caress.

Kat shivered.

He sighed with satisfaction. She tasted of dew and salt, delicious.

Encouraged by her response, he continued his exploration. He kissed her shoulder and then moved higher to her neck. Alex breathed in her jasmine scent, enthralled, and delicately pressed his lips to her exposed throat. A quiet moan escaped Kat and she sucked in her breath, her pulse fluttering like delicate butterfly wings.

His tongue flicked her flesh again. He breathed softly on her moistened neck, whispering, "I have been gone what seems a lifetime. Everyone has changed so much. You have changed so much. Will you not tell me about yourself? I want to know everything."

With an angry jerk, she tore her arm free and lunged up from the bench. Alex stood, too. She whirled to face him and clasped her hands tightly in front of her. Conversely, her voice was quiet, composed. "What, exactly, do you wish to know, Alex? Would you like to know how much your betrayal hurt me? Not to mention the pain you caused your mother and father. Or mayhap you wish to know how damaging your callous actions were to my reputation? How all but a few blamed me for your desertion. Prithee, tell me, where would you like me to begin?"

Although her voice remained steady, Alex sensed her underlying pain and anger. Remorse, razor sharp like the claws of a mighty hawk, sunk into his flesh and tore him apart. Her scathing condemnation was well deserved. He had much to atone for.

"Aye, Kat, I was a bastard for abandoning you. I don't deny it," he said. He would make no excuses for his unpardonable behavior. "How I wish," strong emotion deepened his voice, "I could alter the past and undo the hurt I caused you. Alas, I cannot. But I promise you this, I will do whatever it takes to make it up to you and earn your forgiveness."

She shook her head adamantly. "Nay, you are too late. As you said, so much has changed. I am no longer—"

"Aye, much has changed," Alex interrupted. "*I* have changed, for the better. Older and wiser, I know what I want now. I want you, Kat. You and no other," he said in a soft, entreating voice.

Kat watched Alex advance on her before his words died, his stride long-legged and lazy. Her heart beat faster with fear, even as a primitive thrill raced up her spine. Goosebumps pebbled her skin and her nipples swelled to hard stabbing points.

Bewildered at her reaction, she said the first thing that came to mind to stop his predatory pursuit. "You say you want me, *now*. But we both know you do not love me. You lost your heart long ago to Lady Lydia," she bit out, unable to hide her bitterness.

Alex stopped in his tracks, just inches in front of her. "As you said, that was long ago. In prison, I learned to survive day by day, and the only thing that kept me alive were thoughts of escape, of returning to the bride I left behind."

She smelled the scent of hay and horseflesh that lingered on his skin. "Are you saying that you do not love Lady Lydia anymore?"

"What I am saying is that I'm past regrets. I no longer look back, but forward. And what I see, what I long for, is a life with you."

They were the words she had yearned to hear for so long, but they were too late. As a young girl she had admired Alex above all others; he was so handsome and gallant, kind and honorable. When she began to have the yearnings of a woman grown, her affection for him altered to desire and eventually love. But he rejected her heartfelt offering in the cruelest of ways. She had no desire to fall under his spell again.

Kat stepped away, backing towards the exit. "Mayhap, but without love, you will come to resent me some day. Your yearning will eventually turn to hatred because honor bade you marry me instead of your precious Lady Lydia."

Alex followed in pursuit, his eyes narrowed. "We may not

love one another in the romantic sense, but there are many kinds of love. With time, I believe such deep love will come. Until then, we have something equally powerful between us." He reached out and captured her hand, halting her progress. "Nay, do not deny it, your body tells me otherwise."

The dark blue depths of his gaze roved slowly lower to stare at her breasts. The barrier of her clothing could not hide her desire. Two hard points prodded her bodice. His gaze grew hot, sultry. Kat flushed all over. Her heart pounded harder.

He brought his free hand up and skimmed his knuckles down her cheek and along her throat. With every breath she took, her turgid flesh rubbed against her silk chemise, aggravating her further.

"The harder you try to resist the undeniable attraction between us, the stronger it will become."

She swallowed, her blood pounding thickly. Her arousal proved his words had merit. Could this attraction between them lead to something more, something lasting? Dare she hope it could lead to love some day?

When she realized she was considering opening her heart to love once more, anger surged up inside her. Her temples pounded. She would not be swayed by carnal longings. She tugged her hand free and stepped away from him.

"You speak of lust," she spat, her voice rife with scorn, "but a marriage cannot subsist on that alone. Without love, in time this attraction you speak of will smother and die, and eventually be replaced by resentment and hatred."

He shook his head and captured her gaze. "Nay, I could never hate you, Kat." The glow in his midnight depths was both tender and smoldering.

She crossed her arms and stared at him with disdain. "You believe that now. But don't think I missed how adroitly you avoided the issue of Lady Lydia. You say she is in your past, but she married an old man. Some day she will be free again and you will be tied to a wife you never wanted in the first place. How will you feel then?"

"No one can predict the future, Kat. What is important is how I feel about you. And I do want you. 'Twas not Lydia I thought of for four agonizing years while I was imprisoned."

Kat did not believe him. "That may be so. But I don't doubt you will soon tire of me and seek out other women. If not Lydia, another woman will come along to tempt you into her bed. I refuse to live like that, always wondering who will be the one," her voice cracked.

Alex pressed his fingers to Kat's mouth and stilled her words, her lips cool and silky soft. "Kat, we have a bargain, remember?" Unable to resist, he leaned closer and breathed in her flowery, exotic scent. "Come the feast of St. Barnabas, you can make your decision then whether you wish to reconcile or not. Until that time, I want to say this only once. Lady Lydia was a lifetime ago. Frankly, I am no longer that naïve young man who fell in love with her."

Her lips trembled, stealing his breath away, so that his next words came out in a husky whisper. "I want you to understand, though, that my feelings for you are very complicated. All I know is that I have *never* felt this way about a woman before. Not even Lady Lydia."

Her large, almond-shaped eyes grew wide.

He clutched her face between his hands and held her so she could not look away. His adamant gaze bore into hers. "I know you do not believe me now. But I am a very determined man. My actions shall give truth to my words in the days to come, and I will prove to you that I shall be a faithful and devoted husband."

She blinked as though awakening from a drugged sleep. Tugging his hands from her face with force, she cried out, nearly hysterical, "Must you torment me with the impossible?" Her chest rose with each panting breath. "I have told you no amount of determination on your part is going to change the way I feel about you, Alex. I gave you my heart once and you crushed it." Punctuating her claim, she clenched her hand and pressed it against her heart. "I will never give you a chance to do so again."

A deep growl rumbled in the back of his throat, and he grabbed her around her waist. "Then you wish to renege on your vow?"

"Nay!" she said, her eyes widening, perhaps sensing the danger she was in. "We have a bargain and I intend to abide by it. But you are wasting your time. Naught you say or do is going to change my mind."

Instead of deterring him, her words did the opposite. "I beg to disagree. Despite what you say, you are not immune to me. And I intend to prove it."

Alex crushed Kat against his body. He dipped his head down and captured her mouth, cutting off her startled gasp.

Chapter 10

Alex kissed Kat, the intoxicating scents of the garden mingling with her exotic essence. His mouth moved over hers commandingly, demanding a response. Plump and soft as velvet, her lips seared him. Her heart beat wildly against his chest, the pounding rhythm seeping under his skin like a fever.

Kat, perhaps stunned, did not react at first. But now she began to squirm, trying to escape his embrace. She merely succeeded in enflaming him more. The fever spread rapidly. He grew turgid with a hot, hard ache that needed appeasement. Like a starving animal long deprived of food that is thrown a meaty carcass.

So when she stilled, then arched her lower body away from his, he lifted her against him and took the two steps to the bench. She cried out, but Alex covered her mouth with his. Using his greater strength, he laid her down on the bench without breaking bodily contact.

He nudged her feet apart and lowered his body onto hers. Then Alex moved his hips in a slow circle, grinding his heated shaft against her soft mound. He groaned at the exquisite friction. A soft moan escaped Kat. Exultation made him less cautious and he could not hide his triumph.

"See. You cannot deny you need this, Kat."

It was a stupid blunder.

Breath panting, her eyes blazed. "You arrogant slug. You have not heard a word I said. I will not let you seduce me."

The heel of her hand came up and she shoved hard against his chest, but he was stronger. Her hand slipped off him and he clutched her tighter, continuing his onslaught. Relentless, he slanted his mouth over hers, coaxing her lips apart, while her fists pounded against him, glancing off his back. She fought him for what seemed forever, and then her hands clutched his waist.

She trembled in his arms. Her lips grew pliant. Exhilaration pumped through Alex at the signs of her surrender. He thrust his tongue inside her slack mouth. Her tongue met his, a wild clash of flesh that sent a shudder down his spine.

Moaning, Kat reached up and dug her fingers into his back. She pulled him closer as though she wished to absorb him into her skin. Dueling, thrusting, stroking, their tongues waged battle.

Alex's heart contracted, such strong emotion pumped through him he thought his heart might burst. For the first time since his imprisonment, he felt something other than hate and anger. Kat must have feelings for him too, though locked far away where he could not reach them. Yet. But he had never backed down from a challenge, and he did not intend to start now.

From the first hot penetration of Alex's tongue, Kat knew she was lost. Their mingled breaths were harsh in the hushed silence. The cold bench beneath her might as well be eiderdown, for she felt it not. She swirled her tongue around his, and his shaft blazed a path of fire, igniting an inferno inside her. Hot and moist, her nether lips throbbed. The better part of her concentration resided there, until the cool night air wafted across her chest.

She looked down, her eyes widening with surprise. Unbeknownst to her, Alex had unclasped her brooch and spread the front of her tunic open. She watched as his hand eased one breast free through the slit down her bodice. Alex drew back a little, one arm braced on the seat. He stared down at her bared breast, his gaze rapt. Her nipples puckered, from cold and excitement. The moment suddenly too tense, she brought her arm up to cover her nakedness.

He eased her hand away and bent back over her. "Nay. Do not hide from me, Kat. You are beautiful, beyond beautiful to me." His breath made puffs of air, tickling her flesh where his mouth hovered above her chest. At his soft words, she melted, unable to resist his bold advances.

Slowly, his lips brushed the underside of her breast. A shock of pleasure rippled over her and she gasped. Next his lips skimmed up the plump curve, a slow, teasing caress. She thrust her hips up, writhing against his hard member.

Alex lifted his head, his hot gaze remorseless. "You have no idea how I longed for you. I shall not wait another moment to taste you."

His calloused hand cupped her swollen breast, squeezing her with exquisite pressure, before his lips at last closed around her nipple. Kat moaned. His hot mouth sucked the puckered flesh deep inside. His tongue lapped at the hard point. Excitement shot from her breast straight to her feminine mound like the vibration of a plucked lute string, and she cried out.

Alex looked up, a glint of satisfaction in his eyes.

She wanted him closer. Wanted it hotter, harder. Years deprived of the hot, heady exultation of carnal release made her ravenous. Removing her hands from his back, she clutched his long black hair and tugged his head back to her nipple. He obliged, curling his tongue around it, nipping with his teeth, then sucking once more.

Her hips rose in wild abandon and soft moans expelled from her lungs. She could not look away as he shoved her tunic skirts up to her waist, velvet and silk rustling like a sibilant hiss. A warning she ignored. Air rushed over her sensitized skin. Her legs quivered.

She watched, impatient, shivering with desire while Alex

fumbled with the laces at the waist of his braies. Finally, his shaft sprang free, pale and enormous in the moon's glow. Then he covered her, his body blocking the moon and creating shadow where once was light. Her chest thumped, the wind sighed. Hot, hard flesh nudged her entrance.

"Kat. Oh, God. I swear you will not regret this," he said, his breath tickling her ear.

Regret what? she wondered. Surely he did not think her surrender meant she was ready to reconcile? Then she heard a sound—a soft giggle, followed by a masculine growl.

"Oh, God. Get off me, Alex. Someone is coming." In a panic, she shoved Alex's chest, but he appeared oblivious. "Did you hear me? Alex? Get up," she hissed louder, "someone is coming."

She watched his eyes widen. He jumped up, swearing, and tugged her up by her arm. Her skirts slithered down her legs, but her bodice still gaped open. Frantically, while he tied his braies, she tried to cover herself, cognizant of a moist, sticky trail of desire running down her inner leg.

"Oh, Rand," a woman said in a breathless sigh. "Come along, you stallion. You know how hot I get when you tup me where anyone can stumble upon us. And I have found just the place."

Kat swallowed her gasp when a red-haired woman, her back to them, tugged Rand into the secluded courtyard.

"Elena, I am not sure this is wise, but I am *so damn hard*—"

Rand looked up just then, his jaw dropping. Alex stepped in front of Kat to shield her. She pressed her heated face against his back, shrinking as small as possible.

Alex cleared his throat, tickling her cheek. "I'm afraid you shall have to find some other place, my friend. The garden is already occupied. And I wish to be alone."

Her eyes tightly closed, Kat heard Elena whirl around, her laugh tinkling with joy. "Why, Sir Alex. What a pleasure this is. You must—"

"Come, Elena," Rand interrupted. "Let us leave. Obviously Alex prefers his privacy."

"But . . ."

Listening to the sound of their receding footsteps on the gravel pathway, Kat did not hear Elena's rejoinder.

Finally, Kat peeked around Alex, and saw Rand, his arm around Lady Elena, guiding her out of the hedge opening of the adjoining courtyard.

Kat straightened and ran her hands down her skirts, mortified and unable to look at Alex when he turned around and faced her.

"Kat—"

She held up her hand. "Don't say a word. This was a mistake and shall not happen again. Where's my brooch?"

"Nay, tonight was not a mistake." He picked up her brooch from the ground and handed it to her. "The desire that blazes between us is honest and real and undeniable. If time or distance could not destroy it, do you really think you can continue to deny me forever?"

"You betrayed me, Alex. And I shall never forget that. So, aye, I can and will continue to deny you." She quickly pinned her brooch to her bodice.

He held his arm out. "Come, I will escort you to our chamber."

Her jaw dropped. "What? No more arguments? No more disavowals?"

He shrugged. "Naught more may be gained by arguing this night. You have promised to give me a month to persuade you, and I shall have to be content with that, for now."

Indeed, nothing and no one was going to stand in his way of achieving his ultimate dream. *But it's going to be damned hard,* he thought, *literally.* He pressed his hand against his member, seeking to calm the rigid flesh.

Several days later, wearing only his braies and hose, Alex practiced swordplay with Rand in the field south of the Almonry. His muscles strained with every sword blow. The sun beat down on his back and sweat ran in dirty runnels down his chest.

Though Alex no longer felt his sword arm, sheer stubbornness kept him from giving up. He continued to ward off Rand's blows with his shield and to counterstrike with blunted sword. Then Rand countered with several quick strikes. All Alex could do was evade or deflect the blows. In a moment of inattentiveness, his shield dropped. Rand took advantage and struck down at Alex's unprotected shoulder. In desperation, Alex blocked the strike with the flat of his sword. Sparks flew as their swords slid to the hilt. Rand gave a quick flick of his wrist, catching the cross guard of his sword against Alex's weapon. Pain shot up Alex's arm and his sword spun out of his numb hand.

Out of breath, Alex leaned over and rested his hands on his knees, berating himself for committing such a stupid tactical error. Alex spit on the ground, removing the bitter taste of defeat from his mouth.

Rand retrieved Alex's sword and tossed it to him. "Well done, Alex," he said, clapping him good-naturedly on the back. Alex winced. "You have improved considerably in the last few days. It shall not be long before you are up to your old skill again."

Alex shook his head, disgusted.

"Come, let's have a go again," Rand said.

Alex's squire, Jon, who had arrived at court two days ago, rushed up to them with towels and a bucket of water. He set the bucket aside and handed them each a towel.

Setting his shield and sword aside, Alex wiped the sweat and grime from his face. "Not today. I have other plans." He smiled in anticipation.

"I'm intrigued. What plans have you that could put such a ridiculous smile on your face?" Rand asked, a blond eyebrow quirked.

"Kat and I are going riding."

The squire raised the water bucket. Using the dipper Alex

took a long drink and then passed it to Rand. "You may go, Jon, and leave the bucket over by the bench there." After he did this, Jon collected their shields and practice swords and headed back to the armory.

Unwilling to be late for his rendezvous with Kat, Alex walked back to the bench where he had removed his garments, sword and scabbard earlier. Then he poured the bucket of water over his head and chest. He retrieved another towel and rubbed himself down, wiping off the sweat and dirt.

Rand followed him and rinsed his face off, before he sat on the bench. "Speaking of which, how are things progressing in your campaign to win Kat back?"

Alex shrugged, reluctant to discuss it even with his closest friend. Then he tugged on his sherte and dark blue wool tunic, before buckling his sword belt around his waist.

Undeterred, Rand said, "I admit, I'm curious to know how you convinced my wily cousin to go out riding alone with you?"

Alex smiled, the first genuine smile since his return. "Some secrets must remain between a man and his wife. Suffice it to say, Kat and I have an understanding. 'Tis all you need know."

Rand nodded and stood up. They walked off the practice field together, skirting the open space used for tilting. At that moment a young squire rode full tilt towards the quintain. The end of his lance hit the target off center, then the quintain swung around and hit him in the back. He fell ignobly. The squire got up slowly, spitting dirt and blood from his mouth. His friends watching from the sidelines roared with laughter.

Alex smiled in remembrance. "Were we really ever that young and exuberant?"

They reached the grassy verge along the south transept of Westminster Abbey, stopping in the shadows of its soaring walls.

"Aye," Rand replied quietly. "We could not wait for the day when we would finally earn our spurs. We wanted to go out and fight for justice in the name of God, king and England."

"And for glory," Alex said bitterly. Too late he had learned that glory was a lonely bedfellow. Not to mention extremely fickle.

Just then footsteps approached and a man came around the corner of the transept wall. Of all people, it was Sir Luc de Joinville, head bent and step jaunty. The sun shone down on the top of his golden hair, illuminating the color of bronze.

Alex met Rand's gaze and read the same grim expression he knew was revealed in his own. Taking the initiative, Alex stepped out from the shadowed wall. "Good morrow, Sir Luc." Rand stepped up beside him.

Sir Luc looked up, startled. "Jesu, where did you sprout from?"

Alex gestured back to the open field. "Rand and I were just finished."

"Ahh . . . I am just heading there myself." He paused as though he wanted to say more.

"We shall not keep you, then." Alex nodded.

Luc bowed and carried on towards the practice field.

Alex watched him go, the usual ambivalent feelings towards the man swirling in his breast. Alex was grateful to Luc for saving his life in the Holy Land, even as jealousy consumed him.

Surely Kat does not truly love Sir Luc, Alex thought. How could she be in love with him, and yet respond to Alex as passionately as she did in the garden two nights ago? But it was Luc she wanted to marry.

Alex had befriended him on the long journey to the Holy Land, where they traded humorous stories of their youth around the nightly campfire. Now that Alex thought about it, he remembered many of the stories he told Luc were about Kat. Could it be that Sir Luc became intrigued with Kat all those years ago, forming an attachment for her from a distance, and then sought her out when he returned?

Despite their friendship in the past, Alex did not trust the man. The incident in the garden was proof that Sir Luc still wanted Kat. But how far would the man go to have her? Alex wondered.

So much had changed since that day in the Holy Land when Luc had saved his life. Alex and Sir Luc had been among a contingent of crusader knights who had been returning to Acre when the Mamluk cavalry, garbed in white robes, had swarmed them unexpectedly. The hot, blistering Eastern sun beat down on Alex and glared off his chain mail and helm. Steel clashed, arrows flew and cries of agony filled the air around Alex. Blood from a gash on his neck trickled down inside his sherte, the sensation like a spider crawling over his skin.

A loud pop, followed by a flash of light, spooked Alex's mount, and the animal tossed him to the ground. He landed with a jarring thump, and then rolling to his feet, swung his sword at an attacking Mamluk. He severed the warrior's arm below the elbow and as the infidel cried out in agony, Alex dealt a killing thrust.

Suddenly the skirmish was over, and the attackers retreated, slinking over the rocky hills on their horses to await the next raid. Then from his unprotected side, Alex saw a flash of steel, and knowing it was too late, he turned anyway, raising his shield to deflect the attack. Barely planting his left foot forward, he met the glittering gold eyes of Sir Luc. Alex hesitated in stunned surprise, dropping his shield, leaving him vulnerable. Sir Luc's lethal blade slid past Alex's guard, but Alex felt no pain. A sudden, agonized cry erupted behind Alex and he spun, to see a wild-eyed Saracen glare at him and then crumple to the ground, dead.

Alex had turned his stunned gaze back to the man who had saved his life. Sir Luc had wiped his bloodied steel on the yellow and red braies-like garment of the dead man, then sheathed his sword.

"You are unharmed, Sir Alex?" Shock had held Alex immobile and he had not answered Luc immediately.

"Alex, are you all right?" Luc had repeated.

"Alex, answer me." Rand's insistent voice pulled Alex from his memories.

Alex shook his head. "Aye, I'm fine." The cool spring breeze, so unlike the scorching heat of Palestine, cleared his head as he breathed in the sweet scent of crab apple blossoms.

Rand looked at him with concern, his hand on his shoulder. "You could have fooled me. You appeared to be in a realm far away and none too happy to be there."

Alex laughed without humor at the accuracy of his statement. "'Tis of no import. Come, let us be off. I would not be late and give Kat an excuse to escape my company this afternoon."

When Kat arrived at the stable, she found Alex waiting for her. He emerged from the building's shadow, his gaze soft and admiring. "You look lovely, Kat. That color suits you well."

Kat blushed, unaccountably pleased.

For riding, she wore her usual attire, a dark green wool tunic she had specially designed to allow her to ride astride more comfortably. The skirt was split up the front and back to the knees like a man's surcoate, but the voluminous folds concealed the vertical seams, unless one was looking for them, or until she was mounted on her horse.

"Shall we," he said, gesturing to the groom, who brought out Lightning and Zeus, the big black stallion Alex had commandeered from his father.

The stallion was a rare breed, both proud and stubborn—the irony did not escape her that the same could describe the Beaumont men. Lord Briand was no doubt glad to loan out his favored stallion to his son, in order that the beast got regular exercise while he was laid up in bed with a broken leg.

The groom handed Zeus's reins to Alex then led Lightning to Kat. Kat turned away and without waiting for assistance mounted her mare.

Astride her horse, though she was still modestly covered, the arrangement of her skirts emphasized the long line of her leg and inner thigh area. Alex, his expression arrested, stared at her aghast, and a wicked idea sprang to mind. Taking advantage of his distraction, Kat prodded her horse with her knees and spun her mare around in a complete circle.

"Race you to the road to Kilburn in Hampstead. If I win, you must release me from your company this day. Or do you fear a mere woman can beat you?" Knowing Alex could not resist the challenge, she charged out of the palace gate and onto King Street, her triumphant laughter ringing out behind her.

Alex stared after Kat, stupefied, his mouth agape. He snapped it shut when he realized his quarry had escaped, and with a substantial lead. No way would he let a woman, and especially his wife, beat him in a contest of endurance.

Throwing the reins over Zeus's withers, he vaulted onto his mount, spurred his horse, and shot out after her. His heart pounded with the thrill of the chase, matching the staccato beat of the thundering horse hooves.

Alex saw Kat had already left the highway and headed northwest through the field of St. James. As she approached Spital Street, Kat climbed up the gravel terrace, and then urged her horse faster in a race to cross the road before a rapidly approaching horse-drawn cart. Alex watched, horrified, his heart palpitating. Lightning surged forward at the last moment, coming within five feet of the carthorse. Alex swore, furious. The woman was reckless and willful, a real danger to herself. And he was just the man she needed to rein her in

When he caught up with her, he had a thing or two to say about her atrocious behavior. The odd skirt she wore drew attention to a part of her anatomy he considered his alone.

Conversely, unwilling admiration filled him. One thing he could say about the saucy wench, she certainly made his existence very interesting. She was bold and unpredictable, and he thrived on the challenge she presented.

Alex dug his heels into Zeus and urged him to go faster. The wind, crisp and cool, buffeted his face, making it tingle. His long hair came free from the leather thong and whipped about his face. He laughed again, feeling more alive than he had felt since waking up in that rotting, stinking hole in the ground.

Nay, Alex thought, one could never describe his courtship of his wife as boring.

Chapter 11

Kat soared over a ditch—one of many that bordered the well-drained fields of Westminster—her blood still pounding with exhilaration. She desperately wanted to look back to see how far Alex was behind her, but she did not want to lose the lead she had gained. As she rode through a grove of trees, their dappled shadows washed over her like a cool wave, soothing her over-excited nerves.

Triumphant laughter resounded behind her. Startled, Kat turned her head and cursed. Alex had closed the gap between them to a considerable degree. Only at the halfway point to Hampstead, blood roaring through her ears, Kat snapped the reins and urged her horse faster.

"You shall not win," she hollered back. She would pit her riding skills against any man, confident of her abilities. But Alex was not just any man.

The wind snatched at her plaited hair and full skirts. Zeus's hooves thundered nearer. Her breath hitched with excitement and a laugh of pure joy escaped her. In the distance to the northeast, no more than a mile away, she saw the two-story Norman tower of the Hampstead manor chapel. Straight ahead, in a more northwesterly direction, she headed along Watling Street towards her destination on the outskirts of the manor.

The temptation too great, Kat looked back. Alex, nearly on

her horse's heels, snared her gaze. Unable to look away, she stared, the satisfaction in the glittering depths of his blue eyes holding her as though spellbound. Or so it seemed, for the connection lasted but a beat of her heart before she faced forward again.

"I have you now, Kat. You may as well concede defeat graciously."

Her hands tightened on the reins. Forcing them to relax, she shouted back, "Only when I am dead." *And probably not even then,* she thought.

Alex's laughter floated to her on the air. "You cannot escape me, Kat," he shouted, "although I am enjoying the attempt."

She ignored him. Kat bent forward over Lightning's neck, so close she breathed in the musky scent of horseflesh, and urged her mare into a sprint. "Aye, that's my girl. Just a little farther. Such a brave beauty, you are."

Lightning sprinted down the stretch, her forelegs churning up dirt. Once more Kat dared to look over her shoulder and saw Zeus inch forward, his head coming even with her mare's flanks.

Fifty feet up ahead, a stand of beech trees marked the turnoff to Kilburn Priory.

Reverberating in her ears were the harmonic sounds of shifting saddle leather, hammering horses' hooves, and labored breathing of man and beast.

Thirty feet.

From the corner of her eye she saw Alex and his mount draw alongside her mare, nearly nose to nose. She shivered. She swore she could feel Alex's hot breath on her neck. Tension built between her shoulder blades.

Fifteen feet.

For the first time fear of defeat engulfed her. He would not win! Five feet.

Not much longer, almost there. Three. Two.

Alex and his stallion lunged forward, edged past Lightning by a nose and crossed the intersection before Kat. Cursing fluently, volubly, Kat pulled on Lightning's reins and gradually slowed her mare to a gallop, a cantor, and finally a walk.

Alex turned and sidled up next to her, grabbing the reins to prevent her from escaping. They sat there, breathing heavily, their mounts jostling one another on the shoulder of the road.

His eyes alight with laughter, Alex said, "I see you have grown quite proficient at cursing in my absence. Much more colorful than I remember."

Kat glared at Alex, too disgusted to reply.

A cocky grin spread across his normally austere face, further irritating her. "I won. No matter your devious attempt to get an unfair advantage. What shall be your forfeit?"

Kat bristled. Because she was a woman, her cunning abilities were considered sly and underhanded, but in a man these same traits would be admired as astute and shrewd.

Relaxing her tense shoulders, she stroked her hand down her mare's neck. "I did not cheat. I did no more than any other man would do."

His heavy lidded eyes dropped to her lips, his gaze smoldering. "Despite your attire, you look like no man I have ever seen."

Kat felt her breath stop. Alex was going to kiss her. She read his intent before he dipped his head, his black hair falling in front of his shoulders. Slowly, his sculpted, sensual lips came closer. Closer. Her breath hitched. His nostrils flared. Closer. Desire arced between them, her lips tingling with anticipation. Then he stopped, his mouth inches away from hers. He hovered above her, his breath warm and sweet against her lips. Her anger long forgotten, she wanted to surrender, her need for this man a growing obsession, the masculinity he exuded irresistible.

Indeed, the desire was so strong to surrender everything for a few moments of pleasure—even her pride and self-respect— that Kat suddenly panicked. She raised her hand and shoved Alex away, but in a sudden movement he lunged at her, wrapping both arms around her torso. His chest collided with hers and his forward momentum knocked them off their horses, just as an arrow whizzed past and embedded into a tree trunk with a distinct *thunk* behind them. They landed with a bone jarring thump in the ditch—air whooshed from her lungs and she lay stunned, trying to inhale a deep breath without success.

Untangling his legs from her skirts, her husband grabbed her around the waist, scooped her up as easily as a goose down bolster, and smacked Zeus's rump yelling, "Yaaa." Zeus took off, Lightning following behind. Kat still breathless, Alex half carried, half dragged her into the stand of trees.

Their mounts charged deeper into the trees and disappeared, but Alex pulled her behind the nearest beech. He pressed her face against the trunk, his body covering her back and shielding her body. Air suddenly rushed into her lungs and she gulped each breath greedily.

Her surge of fear from the attack metamorphosed into danger of another kind. A hush descended, not a creature or leaf stirred, except for wisps of her loosened hair where Alex panted against her neck and cheek. Still, against her will, her body reacted to his nearness and her nipples peaked with excitement.

Alex absorbed a ripple of tension going through Kat as he held her close. Despite the danger that stalked them, or perhaps because of it, he could not resist taking just a taste. He kissed the back of her moist neck and cupped her breast, squeezing the lush flesh. Her erect nipple abraded his palm, scorching his tingling flesh. Alex groaned. Kat cursed.

With extreme reluctance he pulled away. "We will continue this later." Peering from behind the tree, he gazed across an open field at a collection of low-lying, dilapidated buildings where the arrow must have come from. "Stay here. I shall return shortly."

Without seeing if she obeyed him, he dashed across the road and into the field, bent low to the ground.

It seemed his enemy had made his first move. Which brought up another possible problem he had not thought of before.

Is Kat a target now because of her connection to me? Alex wondered. Or, had the timing of the attack been purely coincidental?

Kat stopped outside the door of an abandoned cottage Alex had entered and saw him poking around in a pile of rotted wood in one corner. "Did you find aught amiss?"

He spun around, a scowl on his face. "What are you doing here?" he exploded. "I told you not to move." Then he sheathed his sword.

She gave an unladylike snort. "I don't take kindly to commands, *Sir Alex*. And since when have I ever obeyed one of your orders, especially when danger is afoot? Do not expect me to start now."

Tension flared between them as they both remembered the day of their betrothal when an assassin had attacked Alex on Montclair lands. Alex had been furious that day, too, when she rescued him from the murdering whoreson. She shot the man in the arse with an arrow and had no regrets about her actions.

Alex stepped out of the cottage, grabbed her arm and propelled her back towards the road. "You are incorrigible."

"And you are a boor." Kat tugged on her arm as he practically dragged her away. "Alex! Release my arm. You need not haul me about as though I'm a criminal."

He released her and slowed his steps to match her slower pace. "Aye, you are right. I *am* being a boor. Are you hungry?"

Caught off guard by his apology, she responded without thought. "I am fam—" Kat stopped mid-sentence, but not before she realized how neatly he had trapped her.

Alex nodded. "'Tis good I brought a large repast, then. I remember what a great appetite you have." His eyes devoured her, clearly conveying he was not referring to her hunger for food.

Embarrassed, Kat raised her chin. "How would you know

what kind of appetite I have? Perhaps I have changed. You have been gone—"

Alex bent down, wagging a finger in her face. "Ahh . . . Ahh . . . Ahh. We have a bargain, remember?"

She snapped her mouth shut. Alex smiled with devilish pleasure.

Damn. Damn. Damn. Did I leave any out? she wondered. *Oh, aye, DAMNATION!*

"Did you find anything back at the cottage? Who do you think shot the arrow?"

"It was most likely a hungry serf poaching his next meal. He's probably long gone by now. Speaking of which, why do we not find a spot to partake of the repast I packed? I know of a nice private glade not far from here."

When they approached the road, Alex placed two fingers in his mouth and whistled. Not long after, Kat heard their horses approach through the trees. Zeus drew up before them first, followed by her 'loyal' mount. Almost as though in contrition, Lightning nudged her nose against Kat in greeting. She grabbed her mare's reins, unable to blame her for her desertion. It seemed males of any species enjoyed dominating their female counterparts, be they sire or husband.

Alex indicated the horses with a nod of his head. "Shall we?"

Kat shrugged. As if she had a choice.

"Good. I'm famished, too," he said dryly. "Let's be on our way."

He grabbed her waist to lift her onto her mount, but held her suspended in the air. His warm hands penetrated through layers of linen and wool like a brand. "No more tricks, Kat. We are going to have a pleasant ride and then share a meal before we have to return to court. Do I have your promise?"

The heat of him scorched her, his fingers skimming the plush underside of her breasts. "Aye, just put me on my blasted horse!"

Kat nearly sighed aloud when he did as she bid. The man was a temptation the likes of which a nun could not resist. But she must find a way to do so. They kicked their mounts into a trot, Alex leading the way.

Riding along a narrow track, which was the southern boundary of Hampstead manor, Alex pointed up ahead to the woods of Chalcots. "There is a little-used cart track in the woods up ahead beyond the next bend. It will take us to the glade I told you about."

Kat nodded her head in understanding and followed him when he turned right onto an overgrown track and entered Chalcots woods. The trees closely abutted both sides of the track, and forced their horses to walk single file. Kat was perfectly happy with this situation, until she realized she had an unimpeded view of Alex's strong broad back and his long dark hair, which hung down to the top of his shoulders.

She remembered running her fingers through the blue-black strands on their wedding night. Silky and thick, it had brushed her cheeks as he came over her, curtaining her face, giving her the illusion they were the only two people on earth. That she was safe and no harm would ever endanger her as long as they were one.

They were bitter memories now, for she knew it had just been a cruel trick of her imagination. As long as they were married, she would never be safe from heartbreak. She needed stability with a man who wanted her not only for her beauty, but her intelligence and strengths as well. A man who would love her unconditionally for who she was, and not what he wanted her to be.

Alex selfishly thought of only what he wanted and expected her to be obedient to his every command, as though she had not an intelligent thought or was incapable of defending herself. She could never be the kind of woman he wanted. But she had always been different and had long accepted that her unorthodox behavior and beliefs alienated her from her peers.

"You appear lost in your thoughts. Care to share them?"

At his question, Kat gazed around and saw Alex had dismounted. Surrounded by woodland, they stood in a small yard before a stone and wooden structure two stories high. The stone foundation rose six feet high and had shuttered windows on either side of the door. The upper story was of wattle and daub construction. The building looked to be at least a century old, except for a recent addition onto the structure that included a chimney. On the other side of the courtyard, a large, open shed held three stalls.

It looked like a secluded abode for lovers. Kat bristled at his arrogant assumption.

Alex watched Kat study her surroundings, wondering what was going through that facile mind of hers. Then a muscle in her cheek began to twitch and her fists clenched, sure signs of agitation. Alex sighed inwardly, perplexed by what had triggered her hot temper this time. She never kept him guessing for long.

Her beautiful wide eyes blazed down at him. "How dare you bring me here? You assume too much if you think I shall step one foot in there so you can have an intimate setting to seduce me."

Alex held up his hands in innocence. "You misunderstand. I intend no such thing. The lodge is locked and I don't have a key. There's a small dell with a pond just through those trees." He pointed the way.

Before she could rebuff him, he slid his hands around her waist and helped her down. Hands still at her waist, he said, "I can control my base urges if you can."

Although it was faint, she colored prettily.

"See that you do," she said and stepped away. Turning back to the building, no doubt trying to hide her embarrassment, she added, "What manner of dwelling is this anyway? I ride this way nearly every day and never knew it was here."

"'Tis a little-known, old hunting lodge built by the first Plantagenet king, Henry II. Edward came here quite often to hunt in his bachelor years. Though rarely used now, it is kept in readiness whenever the king and queen are in residence at Westminster Palace."

She turned back to face him, her brows raised in question. "You have been here before?"

"Aye, long ago." Alex moved to his horse and removed the leather satchel tied to the back of his saddle. "While I cool down the horses, why do you not find a spot by the pond?" He held out the satchel to Kat. "There is plenty of food in here, along with a blanket and wineskin."

With a grunt, she purloined it from his hands, slung the strap over her shoulder, and spun around. He watched her with appreciative eyes as she stalked off. Her pretty green tunic was cinched at her waist with a braided silver girdle. He had a lot to teach his wife if she thought that being out of doors instead of within four walls would prevent him from seducing her.

Alex seized their horses' reins and guided them to the shed. Anxious to return to Kat as swiftly as he could, he removed the saddles, rubbed their sweaty coats with straw, and gave them cool water. There was no telling what mischief Kat would brew up while unattended.

Chapter 12

Alex quickly finished tending the horses and headed for the pond. When he exited the copse of trees and entered the glade, Kat was sitting on the blanket next to the water's edge, leaning back on her elbows and staring up at the sky. Her glorious black hair, held by a silver circlet and veil, hung loosely down her back and trailed across the grass. She hummed softly, sweetly.

She stopped humming, turning her head at his approach. "I did as you requested," she said, patting the blanket. The wineskin lay next to her hip, but everything else remained packed. Now, why was he suspicious at her sweet tone?

Alex nodded and sat beside her on the blanket, one knee bent up. "I had no idea you could sing. You have a charming voice."

She scrunched up her nose and even that was endearing. His once plain wife was bewitching him. "Nay, I cannot carry a tune, but I can hum a decent melody."

"I have never heard that tune before. Does it have a name?"

She looked at him quickly then turned her head, smiling slightly. Alex was warned immediately. "'Tis naught, really," she said, "just a little tune Sir Luc composed for me. He is a marvelous harp player, by the by."

Alex stiffened and sat up, furious, wanting to throttle her for bringing up Sir Luc. Then he relaxed with effort, knowing she had done it apurpose to bestir his anger.

"Very clever, Kat." She turned to him, her eyes wide with surprise and something else indefinable. "But there is naught you can say or do that will make me angry enough to end this delightful interlude with you. 'Tis nice to be away from the hustle and bustle of court, so you may as well enjoy the outing."

She smiled, shrugging. "Very well. But I don't have to like it. As you know, I was famished," she said, her eyes unblinking. "I hope you don't mind that I ate without you while you settled our horses. I could not resist the delicious smells emanating from the satchel."

Alex grunted and reached for the wine, realizing just then how thirsty he was. But when he picked it up he got his first inkling of unease. Still, he tipped the wineskin back and squeezed it. He took no more than a few swallows when the well ran dry, so to speak. Unable to comprehend what his senses were telling him, incredulous, he squeezed it once more. Not a drop squirted out. Then he heard Kat cough beside him.

Her hand covered her mouth, but she could not prevent a giggle from escaping. "Oh, I forgot to tell you. I had a bit of the wine, too, while I waited for you."

Alex roared with sick comprehension. He tossed the wineskin aside and lunged for the leather satchel. He emptied it on the blanket and found wrapped inside a linen towel all that remained of the feast—one gristly chicken leg, a small chunk of hard bread, and a measly piece of cheese, bruised at that.

Red-faced, he turned on her. Her giggles did little to calm him. "By God, woman," he yelled. "I packed enough to feed the bellies of five grown men. There is no way you could have eaten everything. What have you done with it?"

His stomach growled at that moment, sending Kat into another fit of laughter, tears leaking from her eyes. She sat up, clutching her stomach and gasped out, "Nay, 'tis my . . . prodigious appetite, you see. 'Tis the only thing . . . I am guilty of."

Another rumble sounded, only this time it was the beginnings of laughter at the back of his throat as Alex began to see the humor of the situation. He joined in her laughter, albeit much more restrained, but it felt good after years of having to curtail his voice, to constantly be on his guard to never reveal any kind of emotion.

Stunned at his laughter, she stared at him, her big eyes crystalline silver. She was so enchanting, his stomach clenched with desire.

"Well, it seems you have had a great laugh at my expense. Do you not know how dangerous it is to provoke a hungry beast?"

She chuckled again. "'Twas naught but a harmless jest."

"Mayhap, but I am still famished, with naught left but scraps fit only for the dogs."

"We should return to court, then. I'm sure some winsome kitchen maid will take pity on you and sneak you something from the castle larder." She brushed her hands and made to rise, but Alex was quicker and threw his leg over hers. He straddled her, pinning her thighs beneath him.

"What are you doing?" Kat cried out, trying to buck him off. But her legs were trapped. "Have you gone mad?"

Alex smiled down at Kat. "Mayhap mad for you, but to answer your first question, I'm not ready to leave. I have as yet to dole out your punishment." Her eyes narrowed dangerously. "Nay, punishment seems much too harsh for the crime you committed."

He tapped his finger on his chin. "I know," he said, "I shall demand instead a forfeit of you." Using the pad of his thumb, he traced her lower lip. "I believe a kiss would be fair recompense for you eating my portion of our meal, leaving my appetite unappeased. Besides, you lost our race and I wish to claim my prize."

Her eyes flashing, Kat grabbed his wrist and tugged it away from her mouth. "Never shall I grant you a kiss willingly."

His hand, still held in her grip, moved lower to her chest.

He grazed the back of his knuckles over her left nipple and watched it peak and thrust up against her tunic. Blood rushed downward, and his shaft hardened like a rock. "Mayhap I should just steal one instead." His eyes never left her breast, a clear indication that if he kissed her it would not be on the mouth.

Kat's eyes narrowed and she yanked on his hand. "Whatever you intend, I would not suggest it if you value your manhood."

"Very well," he sighed. "But I shall not let you off so easily. If you will not give me a forfeit, I insist that you be given a penance. And I know exactly what it shall be."

Then he tickled her ribs. Knowing she was extremely ticklish, he tortured her with his fingers as she wiggled, gasping and laughing at once. Her wild laughter startled the birds in the trees into flight, while her struggles succeeded in scooting him up and over her, their loins touching and rubbing against one another. The resulting friction caused his cock to swell larger, and he quivered with need.

Kat took advantage of his distraction and he suddenly found himself on his back beneath her while she tickled him, seeking revenge. Unable to help himself, he laughed, but soon grabbed her hands, stopping her relentless fingers.

She straddled him, her loosened hair cascading down around them like a shimmery waterfall, blocking out the sun. Their hands linked together, Kat gazed down at him, smiling. He tried to keep his desire in check, to proceed slowly, but Kat atop him was temptation incarnate. He stared up into her eyes and slowly rotated his hips, his erection seeking her heat. He found it, stroked it as he lifted his hips and ground against her womanly center once more. Her eyes darkened. She moaned softly.

The odd skirt she wore definitely had its advantages. She straddled him as well as any horse. He released her hands and trailed his right hand slowly down her stomach, giving her time to stop him if she wished. She stiffened, but did not draw away. He cupped her mons through her skirt with his hand

and squeezed. Her eyelids drooped languidly. The tip of her tongue darted out and she licked her lips.

Alex groaned at the sensual gesture, the moist heat of her.

Then he raised his eyes and saw her staring at his lips. His breath caught. She bent closer, her lips hovering just inches above his. She was going to kiss him and he dared not move, afraid of startling her. Her wine-sweetened breath teased his lips, and her soft breasts cushioning his chest were a delicious torment as he waited. She closed the gap, when a drop of water splashed on his forehead, breaking the spell.

They both looked to the sky and saw a bank of dark clouds had moved in unawares. The sky opened up then and a cold spring rain poured down on them.

Kat jumped from his lap, avoiding his eyes and shivering. Alex cursed.

He gathered up their picnic quickly, grabbed Kat's hand and they ran for shelter. He was wet, cold and his clothes sodden by the time they reached the shed. While Alex stood beneath the roof and observed the sky, Kat leaned against the back wall, staring at her feet. Zeus nudged him from behind and Alex considered it a sign.

"There is no predicting how long the storm will last," he said ironically. "I suggest we shelter in the hunting lodge until the storm passes."

She raised her eyes at that, her voice cold. "*You* can wait in the lodge if you like. I'm perfectly comfortable here."

Alex sighed inwardly at the swift change in her attitude. "You may catch the ague if you stay out here in those wet clothes. I believe there are towels inside the lodge and wood for a fire," he said reasonably.

She shook her head. "Perhaps I did not make myself clear. I'm not taking one step from this shed. Besides, you said earlier you have no key."

Alex laughed at her stubbornness. "Very well, have it your way."

Then he scooped her up, threw her over his shoulder and

ran across the courtyard. She screamed in rage, beating him on his back, but his right hand splayed over her buttocks held her secure. He raised his foot, kicked once, then twice, and the door burst open. Once inside, he turned, closed the door firmly behind him and let Kat slide to the floor.

Hot blood pounding, Alex did not immediately release Kat. Instead, he pressed her against the door, and when she opened her mouth to protest, he covered her lips, his mouth hot and hungry as his tongue sought hers. His rampant erection settled against her plump mons, furrowing through the flimsy barrier of wet wool she wore. He searched her warm haven, and the nether lips shielding her entry cradled his cock. Liquid heat scalded him. He growled, his need unbearable.

Thrilled that she did not resist him, that she now stared up at him with dazed eyes, he thrust his swollen member against her mons again and again with slow, teasing strokes. A gasping moan escaped her and she raised her arms, sliding her fingers into his hair. She pulled his head down and kissed him, her tongue thrashing in tandem with his.

Alex's heart expanded and contracted as though about to burst with joy—never before had she initiated any intimacies between them. She ground her hips against him and he appeased her by stroking harder, faster. Her breathy moans and plump flesh held him hostage, enflaming him.

Wanting to give her more, he slid his hand through the seam in front of her skirts and found her hot core. With two fingers he explored the moist folds, rubbing back and forth and side to side, seeking, learning her anew. Her inner lips were thicker, the flesh swollen and wet with desire. Oh, to taste her honeyed flesh.

But that would have to wait. She groaned, thrusting her hips against his invading hand. He moved his fingers down her slick crease, stroking faster. Kat panted wildly, her soft moans driving him to distraction.

After long delicious moments, he added his thumb and pressed against her engorged bud. She cried out loud, her juices bathing his fingers. Alex swallowed her cry with a kiss, then his lips trailed down her neck, nibbling and kissing her, licking the cool rain from her warm, jasmine-scented skin.

He was hot, his cock near to bursting, but he continued with his assault. When at last his finger entered her, her muscles clenched him tightly. Alex gritted his teeth as his cock twitched.

Her head thrashed about. "Alex! Oh, God. I cannot bear it."

"Aye, you can. And so much more." He added a second finger, expanding her, stimulating her flesh.

In and out, his hand pumped between her thighs. With his other hand he cupped her breast, massaging, stroking, teasing, then he dipped his head and closed his mouth over her nipple, the wet wool no barrier to his smoldering lips. He sucked the rigid peak into his mouth and ground his palm against her mound at the same time. The honey-drenched walls of her sheath contracted around his fingers.

He stared down at her in awe and watched as her eyes flew wide, shining brightly. Kat screamed, arching into his hand, her breathless moan shivering across his ear. She shook and trembled, her release beautiful to behold, until she collapsed in his arms. He held her for a long time while she came back to herself, savoring her closeness, pleasure rushing through him that he could please his woman.

At the same time he breathed deeply in and out, willing his arousal to subside. His own denied pleasure was a torment he must bear for the nonce.

Then she pulled back, stiffening in his arms. "Oh, God. What did you do to me?"

He ignored her accusing glare and gently brushed a tendril of hair off her flushed face. "No more than what you wanted."

"Nay. I wanted none of this. No amount of pleasure will ever make up for your betrayal."

"This . . . feeling . . . we have for each other, 'tis more than

lust and you know it. You can feel it, too. Do not deny it." He
touched her heart. "We have a history together, a connection
that is undeniable and if we are ever to go on with our lives,
we owe it to ourselves to explore and discover whatever it is."

When she would have responded, he pressed his lips to
hers. He pulled back and straightening the circlet on her forehead, said, "Say naught yet. All I ask is that you think about
what I've said."

Although he never knew how he did it, he pushed away
from Kat, his cock throbbing painfully. He moved to the cupboard to hunt for drying cloths, leaving a trail of water on the
floor behind him.

"Did you enjoy your ride with Alex today?"

"Huh?" Kat asked, startled.

Later that afternoon in Queen Eleanor's chambers, the
ladies of the court chatted and entertained themselves, waiting for the men to join them before supper. Kat sat with Rose
in an alcove, playing a spirited game of Alquerque.

"How did your outing with Alex go?"

Not immediately answering the question, Kat concentrated
on her next move, although her thoughts were fractured. The
early afternoon spring shower that had come upon her and
Alex had ended as suddenly as it began. They left the hunting
lodge soon after it stopped and returned to court, but she
could not stop thinking about what he had said in the lodge.
His impassioned words had struck a chord.

She felt herself wavering, the ripples of her undoing a
warm imprint on her sensitized skin. Still.

Kat finally made her move, jumping over two of Rose's black
pieces. "We went riding and stopped to have dinner by a pond.
When a shower came up we returned to court." With a noncha-
lant shrug she added, "'Twas rather uneventful, actually."

The lie to her friend felt sour on her tongue, but there were
some truths better left denied.

Even so, Rose looked at her, doubt evident on her face. "I really believe Alex has changed, Kat. Do you not think it is time to give him and your marriage a second chance?"

Kat smiled dryly. "He's your brother. Of course, you believe him. I, on the other hand, cannot find it in my heart to trust him."

Rose looked up from the game, her eyes reproachful. "Aye, he is my brother. But you are my dearest friend and I would say or do naught that would bring you unhappiness."

"Aye, not knowingly. But I would think you of all people would understand my distrust?"

Rose frowned, her light blue eyes darkening with pained memories. "Our situations are completely different, Kat. Alex may have been young and foolish, but he was never cruel. You cannot know what vile acts some men are capable of, or you would never compare Alex to Bertram."

Although Rose never spoke about her brief marriage, Kat had known her friend had been terribly unhappy in her union. But this was the first time she had mentioned Bertram had a cruel streak. She could not imagine what Rose had endured at his hands.

Kat reached across the game board and grabbed her hand, sorely contrite. "You are right. Forgive me, Rose. I should not have brought up unpleasant memories, 'twas thoughtless of me. I'm sorry."

Rose smiled to reveal no harm had been done. "You know I only wish the best for you. You cannot deny, though, that you and Alex have always had this strange and amazing connection. 'Tis as though you are both made of steel, forever clashing and striking sparks off one another whenever you meet. You owe it to yourself to discover the cause and explore whatever underlying feelings you have for each other. If you do not, you will regret it for the rest of your life."

Rose's words eerily echoed Alex's, and Kat could not help wondering. *Is it possible that Alex has true feelings for me? Should she give him a chance to see where this odd courtship* led? Who was she fooling? She had already decided to truly give him the opportunity to prove he wanted a marriage with her based on mutual respect and trust.

What of love, though? Alex claimed to care for her deeply, but Kat would not settle for anything less than love. And what of her feelings for Alex? It was just one of a plethora of issues yet to be resolved. She would give Alex a chance to win her, to prove his desire to have a committed, loving marriage; meanwhile, she needed to explore her own chaotic feelings for Alex.

Still, trust was the key. Her faith in Alex had been destroyed the day he deserted her. And although he returned a wiser man, no doubt due to his horrific experiences in captivity, could she ever trust him again?

Only the coming weeks would reveal the answer to all her questions, but some feeling, warm and soft and expectant, began to creep into her heart. She was startled when she finally recognized the budding, long-dead emotion.

Hope.

Chapter 13

Guilt.

The debilitating emotion roiling around inside Alex since yesterday, making him unable to sleep or concentrate was definitely guilt. His secret search for the traitor was tearing him apart. He could not help feeling that hiding the truth from Kat was going to be the worst mistake of his seven and twenty years. Rather, his second worst mistake. But there was no help for it. To tell her about the assassin and put her in danger was something he refused to do.

"You are awfully quiet this morn, Alex. Kat got your tongue?" Rand, who stood beside him in the crowded reception hall, quipped.

The guards at the entry announced the entrance of yet another lord, one of many returning to court before the opening of Parliament on the morrow. Alex looked at Rand. His smile crooked, he said, "Aye, I suppose that is one way to describe my predicament."

Rand chuckled. "I do not envy you, my friend. Indeed, you are lucky Kat has not ripped out your innards and fed them to the pigs."

She still might when Alex discovered the traitor and the truth came out. After the recent disturbing events, he thought it time to let Rand in on his search, but he had been unable to talk to him alone and away from prying ears at court. Alex wanted someone he could trust to protect Kat when he was unable to. Who better to do so than her own cousin?

Alex looked across the room again, his gaze resting on Kat. She stood with Rose and several other ladies-in-waiting near the queen. She looked delectable in an amber silk tunic and a jeweled snood over her plaited hair. An intricate brooch clasped her bodice closed and her full sleeves tapered down to tight cuffs at her wrists, which were embroidered with green leaves.

She must have felt his stare, because she raised her eyes and unerringly met his gaze. A quiver rippled over his flesh, the attraction instantaneous. Her light eyes flared, glowing with warmth, and sent blood pumping from his heart to his lower extremities in a mad rush. He grew light-headed.

He knew she felt the jolt, too, he saw it in her eyes. But it was more than just lust seizing him. He wanted more from Kat. Wanted to possess her love and admiration and respect, but most of all he wanted her forgiveness. All this he tried to convey with his eyes, then another arrival was announced, breaking the spell. Kat, eyes shocked, glanced at the reception doors. Curious as to her reaction, Alex followed the direction of her gaze.

Alex's mouth dropped open. The crowd around him receded, for there, walking down the center aisle towards the king and queen was the most beautiful woman he had ever seen. And one he never thought to see again. Short, petite, and blond, she exuded an angelic grace rarely found. Her hair was uncovered, the golden waves rippling down her back shimmering like liquid gold, contrasting vividly with the black silk surcoate she wore.

He could not take his eyes off her.

Curtseying to the royal pair, the woman smiled, her expression somehow sweet and sad at the same time.

The king motioned for her to rise. "We bid you welcome and condolences upon the death of your husband."

Alex jerked in surprise. But he supposed he should not be shocked. Lydia's husband was ancient when she married him eight years ago. It also explained her mourning dress.

"I thank you, Sire," she said, surreptitiously wiping something from her eye. A tear. His heart contracted. Lydia must have come to love her husband in the intervening years since she begged Alex to marry her. "He was a good man and I miss him terribly," she said, confirming his thoughts as he watched her exquisite, sculpted lips move.

Then without warning, his heart began to beat out of control as an inexplicable emotion began to take hold in his chest. Bewildered, he tried to concentrate and capture the essence of the feeling bombarding him. *Why do I feel this deep sense of loss and regret?* Alex wondered. When the reason finally dawned on him, astonished disbelief sucked the air from his lungs.

Lord, I have been such a fool, Alex thought.

"'Tis a fine sentiment. But a woman so young and beautiful as you should not remain widowed for long." The king chuckled. "In fact, I am sure there are many gentlemen here today who count you a worthy prize. Eleanor and I welcome your presence at court."

Rand punched his arm. "You may stop gawking like a boy in the throes of his first love."

For the second time that day, Alex was stunned. What, exactly, had Rand read on his face?

Dismissed, Lady Lydia curtsied and disappeared into the crowd.

"I hope you are not going to let that woman make a fool of you again. She has an uncanny knack of arriving at the wrong time."

Kat. Alex turned to her again. She was watching him, her gaze cold. There was no warmth, no smile, no expression. In deliberate rejection, she turned to speak to Rose.

What have I done? Alex wondered desperately. Then he left Rand leaning against the wall and headed for Kat, unsure of the damage he had wrought.

Next to Kat, Rose squeezed her hand, her voice soft. "Prithee, Kat, do not rush to judgment. Alex was very young when Lydia sank her claws into him. That woman is a menace who is clever at hiding her vile nature. Alex will soon see through her disguise."

So Rose had seen all, too. Kat could not say what she felt. Too many emotions clambered inside her, confusing her, numbing her.

But it was not difficult to tell what Alex thought. He had stared at Lydia in fascination, as though she were an angel come down from heaven to grace mere mortals with her goodness. Obviously, he still loved her. Was still awed by her beauty and fragile, ladylike demeanor. She was everything Kat would never be.

And now the woman he loved was free to marry.

Hope. It drained from her like blood from a lethal sword thrust to the heart. She shivered, rubbing her arms. She was cold, so cold. How gullible, how stupid she had been to even dare to hope. She thought she had learned her lesson not to trust Alex, but it seemed her heart had not. At least she had discovered the truth before her feelings for Alex deepened beyond repair. But why, oh why did that statement ring false in her ears?

Damn you, Alex.

Then Rose's eyes flashed with dark emotion as someone nudged Kat's arm. Sidling up beside her, Sir Stephen had returned like a persistent sickness she could not shake, no doubt intending to infect them with his vitriolic poison.

"I do believe this parliamentary session will be quite entertaining. With the arrival of the lovely Lady Lydia at court, I am *so* looking forward to watching events unfold."

"What do you know of Lady Lydia?" Kat said sharply.

He answered in a roundabout way, his voice sly and smug. "Indeed, this reminds me of the time when Lady Lydia made her first appearance at court. If I remember aright, she made quite an impression on the young men at court. And of them all, Sir Alex was her most ardent and devoted suitor."

Ardent sapskull, Kat countered. Aye, she remembered it well, too. At ten and three, Kat had been excited to receive an invitation to attend court during the Christmas festivities that year. It was when King Henry was alive and still ruled. Kat's father had even had a village seamstress make up an appropriate wardrobe for the trip. She had never worn tunic dresses before in her life, preferring instead the more comfortable attire of boys' tunics and hose but, hoping to impress Alex, she had been exceedingly grateful.

It made not a wit of difference when compared to the sophisticated Lady Lydia St. John. Alex was smitten at first sight. And Kat fell far short no matter the comparison. Where Lydia was fair and beautiful, Kat was dark and plain. Where Lydia was curvaceous and mature, Kat was tall, gawky, and had no breasts of which to speak. Lydia was shy and coy and demure and flirtatious all at once. Kat was bold, brash, outspoken, with not a flirtatious bone in her body.

And her unadorned gowns of wool paled in comparison to Lydia's elaborate and costly silk dresses. Indeed, Kat became a figure of fun until Alex's mother took pity on her and altered several of Rose's gowns for her. But naught could change the fact that Alex had fallen hard. Kat was devastated; not even the knowledge that Alex had been the one who kindly warned his mother of the cruel jests about her wardrobe had eased her pain. He had behaved like a lovesick fool over Lydia.

And now, it seemed naught had changed either.

"My, my, look yonder, there is the handsome couple speaking even as we speak of them."

Alex jolted to a stop when Lydia stepped in front of him.

She smiled, her blue eyes shining up at him through her dark lashes. "Dear Alex, what a pleasure to see you. It has been much too long since we last met." Innuendo laced her words.

A rush of heat flooded his face. The last time he saw Lydia, he had taken her innocence at her tearful insistence. Alex hesitated, and then took her outstretched hand. A shock rippled through him as he bowed. *He felt not a thing*—no warmth, no tingling awareness, no aching tenderness—unlike what he felt with just one brush of his wife's hand. Indeed, the hand he held was too pale and too delicate. He preferred the vibrant strength and gold-dusted hands of his indomitable Kat.

Raising his gaze to Lydia in amazement, Alex saw her pleased smile then smoothed his features. "Lady Lydia, I'm glad to see you well. My condolences."

He released Lydia's hand, but she gripped his fingers with a ruthless hold, surprising him. This day was full of surprises. He tugged and he was free. Alex looked to where Kat stood. She was gone. Cursing under his breath, Alex took a step to find Kat. Once more, Lydia stepped in front of him, preventing him from reaching his beloved.

Aye, he finally realized that he loved Kat, that he had loved her for a very long time. But he had not recognized the depth of his feelings before because he had had naught to compare it to except his infatuation with Lydia. That blind, idealized love he once felt in his youth. It was as though he saw Lydia clearly now, realized that he had seen no more than the mirror image Lydia presented; his view distorted by her beauty, never once had he delved deeper below the surface to the inner woman.

In contrast, his love for Kat was no passing fancy. It was volatile, explosive, and exhilarating. Aye, he loved her for so many reasons: for her kindnesses to a young boy cruelly taunted; for her intelligent mind, as cunning as any man's; and for her courage and brave heart, whether she was defying those who scorned her after he had deserted her, or rushing into danger to protect *him* from harm without a care for her own safety.

Aye, he loved his brave, tempestuous, foolhardy wife. And

he had wasted so much precious time. He grieved for those lost years.

Lydia smiled up at him, her celestial blue eyes vapid and empty. Odd, he had never noticed this before. Kat's silvery depths sparked with life, every emotion revealed.

Alex blinked.

Lydia was speaking. ". . . your miraculous return. Prithee? I'm so desperate to hear all the latest court gossip. Since my husband's death I have been so lonely and need some cheering. Unless . . ." Her lower lip quivered. "Unless you have other, more important matters to attend," she beseeched him, a lone tear in her eye.

Unable to refuse a lady, to ignore her tears, Alex nodded. Ostensibly looking for a less conspicuous spot to converse, he searched the crowd for Kat. He did not see her, but caught Rand's eye where he leaned against the wall where Alex had left him. Relieved, he waved and steered Lady Lydia through the crowd towards Rand, even as he felt every eye in the chamber on them.

Upon reflection, he admitted that when Lydia had entered the chamber, her beauty had dazzled him, and all the old feelings came rushing back. But the illusion of love quickly faded. The realization came too late, though. He had not concealed his thoughts and Kat had seen. He winced as he remembered the look in Kat's eyes—one moment they had been warm and expressive, the next they chilled him with their complete absence of emotion. He had never wanted to hurt Kat and suddenly wished time would reverse so he could have those moments back.

Alex stopped before Rand, imploring him with his eyes to rescue him. "Lady Lydia, you remember my friend, Sir Rand Montague, do you not?"

Rand smiled and reached for her hand. Lydia withdrew her arm from Alex's reluctantly.

"Of course," she said, her small smile swift and brief. "How could I forget your charming friend?"

"Indeed, 'tis I who am charmed by your exquisite beauty and grace, as always. Your servant, madam," he bowed deeply.

"Do you mock me, Sir Rand?"

Surprise crossed Rand's face. "Upon my honor, I would never mock a lady."

Lydia's eyes narrowed.

Alex interrupted any reply. "Sir Rand, Lady Lydia was just telling me how she needs cheering. She has had no news from court since her husband's death. I have been here little more than a sennight and I think you would be a much better choice to regale her with court gossip."

"But, Alex," Lydia's soft voice entreated.

While at the same time Rand said, "I would be honored and delighted. I *have* been told I have a unique gift for telling tales."

Alex nearly snorted, but when Rand looped his arm through Lady Lydia's and began to lead her away, he thought better of it.

Rand said to Lydia as he edged them along the crowd to a nearby alcove. "Hmm . . . now where shall I begin? Have you heard the latest scandal about the old reprobate, Lord Stilwell? It seems the very prim and proper wife he acquired so recently was not quite what she seemed." Rand lowered his voice conspiratorially. "Poor Lord Stilwell discovered quite by accident his wife liked . . ."

Lydia thus occupied, Alex scanned the room looking for Kat, his gaze flitting through the crowd in search of her amber surcoate. But she was nowhere in sight. She must have slipped out unnoticed, he thought, cursing his foolishness. He had to find her, somehow make her understand what he had not understood himself. Indeed, he still could not explain his initial reaction upon seeing Lady Lydia; all he knew was that what he once felt for her was not love. Nay, 'twas as if he had been bewitched by Lydia, and as insubstantial as smoke, the spell she cast over him dissipated. She had no more power over him.

And Kat was the one who broke his enchanted sleep. But

was it too late to rectify his mistake? Would Kat even believe him now? He could not wait a moment longer to find out. He began making his way to the reception doors when a man with dark auburn hair blocked his escape.

Thomas de Clare smiled and stepped forward, clasping him heartily and pounding him on the back. "By God, Alex, 'tis good to see you whole and hale." Then he stepped back, shaking his head. "I didn't believe it when Sir Luc told me you were alive."

"Aye, 'tis good to be home." Alex was glad to see his old friend, but he was anxious to be on his way. Still, he did not wish to offend Thomas. Alex had met him soon after Thomas and his brother, Gilbert, the Earl of Gloucester, abandoned Simon de Montfort's rebellion and returned to King Henry's ranks. "I thought you in Ireland. What brings you back?"

"Edward has need of my services in his dispute with the Bishop of Norwich. Once the dispute is settled, I intend to return to Thomond to finish putting down the rebellion there."

"So, Thomas, Sir Luc told you of my return. Did he tell you aught else?"

Thomas crossed his arms over his chest. "If you mean did we speak of his aborted wedding, nay, we did not. 'Tis an awkward business that, I hope, has not caused any difficulty between you two."

Alex replied, his smile grim. "Unfortunately, it can't be helped. I suspect Sir Luc still has aspirations towards Kat. But I shall never give her up." He refused to think about the possibility should Kat demand an annulment at the end of their agreement. Alex had given his vow of honor to do so should he fail to convince her to remain married. And never would he break a sworn oath.

De Clare nodded, then looked over Alex's shoulder. Alex followed his gaze. Rand was speaking to an unsmiling Lady Lydia in the alcove. When Lydia looked up and saw Alex staring, her face transformed. Holding his gaze, her lips turned up in a coy, yet inviting smile.

Where once Lydia's smile had the power to smite him, now it seemed false or contrived. Alex turned back to de Clare, unwilling to give her the wrong impression.

"Obviously, Lady Lydia still has aspirations towards you, too," said Thomas.

"I wouldn't know what Lydia thinks, but should she, any designs she might have of a possible relationship with me are fruitless. I am married now and very content with my bride."

"I'm happy for you, Alex. But I have a feeling her arrival is not happenstance. I hope it shall not complicate matters."

How apropos, Alex thought. 'Matters' certainly just got more complicated. He could blame no one but himself, though. Judging he could leave now without offending de Clare, Alex made his excuses.

"My thanks, Thomas. 'Tis good to see you again," Alex said, bowing.

"'Tis odd, you and Sir Luc have something in common in that regard."

Startled, Alex stopped mid-bow and brought his head up sharply. "To what do you refer?"

His friend's eyes rounded in surprise. "Why, surely you know that Sir Luc cannot abide his stepmother?"

"Stepmother?" Now Alex was truly perplexed.

"Aye. Lady Lydia Joinville."

Taken aback, Alex was sure he misheard Thomas. "Are you saying that Sir Luc's father, Lord Joinville, was the baron Lady Lydia married?"

"Of course. You did not know?"

He had never wanted to know the name of the baron Lydia married and she had never offered it. At the time, to put a face to the man who would spend his nights in Lydia's bed and give her children would have been sheer agony. All Alex had known was the baron she married had been an older man beyond his prime.

Alex shook his head, unable to answer, his thoughts reeling. He tried to sort them out, put each one in perspective.

"Thomas, you mentioned there was discord between Sir Luc and Lady Lydia. Do you know the reason for his animosity?"

Thomas took his arm and pulled him aside to a quiet corner of the room. His voice low, he said, "Rumor has it that Sir Luc never approved of his father's choice of bride. Then one night after father and son had a violent quarrel about her, the old man disowned him. Servants' gossip is that Sir Luc blames Lady Lydia for the estrangement."

Alex bowed again. "I'm grateful to you for this knowledge, Thomas. But I must beg your pardon now. I have something that must needs done and cannot be delayed a moment longer."

"Certes. I shall not hold you up," he said and clasped Alex on the shoulder. "Should you ever need aught, let me know."

Alex thanked him and made his way to the door. When the next arrival was announced, Alex slipped outside while a hundred pairs of thoroughly assessing eyes alighted on the newcomer. He breathed a sigh of relief, glad to escape the hot, crowded chamber. In contrast, the corridor was cool and dark, dark like his thoughts.

"I'm such a dolt, am I," he said to naught but shadows, smacking his palm on his forehead. And for much, much too long a time, he thought. But he intended to rectify his idiocy. Making his way through the corridors, he sighed again; it seemed he was forever in pursuit of his wife.

A fool's errand, perchance?

He shook off the notion like a wet dog after a dip in the river. Doubts were for weak men, doubts clouded the mind and eroded confidence. Nay, he was not a man to lay down his arms and surrender without a fight.

Chapter 14

Taking a deep breath, Kat slid down in the tub of water and immersed her entire body. Liquid heat scorched her, soothing her tense muscles, but naught could melt the cold, pitted knot lodged in her chest.

Cocooned in the water's loving embrace, her knees bent up to her chest, absolute silence blanketed her ears—similar to what an unborn babe must feel inside a mother's womb, Kat imagined. She envied that unborn entity. To be truly innocent and pure, free of pain and sadness and disillusionment.

She stayed under until her lungs burned. Kat surged up off her back to a sitting position, gasping for air and blinking water from her eyes. Aye, water, not a tear, never a tear would she shed for her despicable husband.

Before her a fire crackled in the hearth and she heard her servant bustling about the antechamber on the other side of the screen.

"Jenny, hand me my soap."

A short pause, then Jenny replied, "'Tis on the stool beside ye, milady."

"Aye, of course, I knew that," Kat muttered under her breath. All afternoon she had drifted on an invisible current, treading murky water, too afraid to delve below the surface to the inherent danger hidden beneath, just waiting to suck her under and drown her in misery.

"What shall ye be wearing to supper, milady?"

"I care not. Any old tunic will do."

Silence greeted her. Then Jenny poked her head around the screen, her red braids bright in the fire glow. "Ye do not want to look your best this eve and show up that wicked woman? I thought ye had more pride than that."

Kat grunted at the well-aimed volley. She lifted her leg out of the water and propped her foot on the tub's edge. Not immediately answering, she glared at the delicate arch of her long narrow foot. She wanted to plant it up—

"You may lay out my garnet tunic. Oh . . . and the garnet brooch and my jeweled rings. There, does that please you?"

Jenny chuckled, her green eyes mischievous. "Aye, if you are pleased, I am pleased." Then Jenny marched into the adjacent bedchamber and began rummaging through Kat's chest.

Kat grumbled under her breath. Although she hated Alex for humiliating her, for making her believe even for a short while that he might care for her, she would not let that witch get the better of her. She was *not* taking care with her dress to impress the lying bastard to whom she was shackled, for the nonce.

Lathering her cloth, she caught a subtle whiff of her jasmine, amber, and musk-scented soap. She skimmed the cloth down her leg and then proceeded to do the same with the other one. She finished the rest of her ablutions as quickly as possible, except for her back.

"Jenny, will you scrub my back?" she hollered.

Heat caressed her ear as a familiar, corded bronze hand plucked the soap from her hand. "Here, allow me."

Kat yelped and spun around. It was a mistake, for Alex was kneeling behind her. Their lips brushed—shivery heat raced down her neck and she jerked back in surprise. Alex dropped his gaze. A carnal smile curved his lips and his eyes glittered with desire. She looked down, too, and saw that her nipples, hard as pebbles, jutted above the water lapping at her breasts.

Kat turned around and plunged forward, pressing her chest to her knees. Water splashed over the sides. Unfortunately her back was exposed now. "How dare you intrude on my bath? You have no right. I want you out of here, now!"

Alex chuckled without humor. "I, no more than you, heed well commands. What a grand couple we shall make. What marvelous children we shall conceive and bring forth into this world."

"Never," she declared vehemently, then suddenly remembered something. "Where is Jenny?"

"Jenny?" Alex yelled out cheekily.

"Aye, milord?" the maid responded, her voice hesitant.

"Be gone."

"Stay," Kat countered.

The sound of the door closing reverberated through Kat's rib cage, like a crypt door sealing her to her doom.

"Much better, do you not agree?" Alex purred in her ear.

Nay, I cannot breathe.

Alex swirled the soapy cloth in slow, drugging circles down her back. Fire erupted over her flesh wherever his fingers teased.

Kat stiffened against the onslaught. "Nay, I do not. You have some gall. You humiliated me before the court with your disgusting display over that trollop. Do you really expect me to welcome you as though naught has changed?"

Alex's hand paused. "Nay, but I needs must explain what you saw when Lady Lydia was announced."

Kat stared into the flames. "There is naught to explain. I saw all. You are still in love with her. And I, along with everyone at court, know it!"

Alex leaned forward, his voice insistent. "Kat, I know how it must have looked, but 'tis not what you think. You mistook what you saw."

Kat turned around and swatted his hands away. "This is your defense? Do I understand you aright? What you are saying is that I cannot see with mine own eyes. Cannot see when my husband makes a fool of himself . . . and me." Kat's voice broke. She spun back around, wrapped her arms around her knees and glared into the fire. "I am but a woman, obviously deluded," she said coldly.

"Nay, 'tis not what I meant. Aye, you saw aright my reaction upon seeing Lady Lydia, but 'tis not how I truly feel about her."

"You are unbelievable, Alex. You do not deny you looked upon Lydia as though besotted. Yet you claim you do not feel such for her. And you expect me to believe you? Nay, sir, 'tis you who are deluded."

"I know it sounds implausible, I barely understand it myself. But when Lydia walked into the room, all the old emotions I felt for her came rushing back, then—"

"Silence," Kat cried out, clutching the tub's edge in a death grip. "I don't want to hear this. Get out! Out!" Her voice rose on a screech.

"Nay," he said, clamping his hands down upon her shoulders as though forcing his will into hers. Then he clutched her chin and turned her face to him, a fanatical gleam in his eyes. "I shall not leave until I have had my say. Until I make you understand—"

"Oh, I *understand* perfectly. But I refuse to listen to more of your lies and false words. I shall never trust you. The bargain is off. Lady Lydia is welcome to you."

Alex was crouched down on his haunches, and Kat, maneuvering an arm between them, shoved him. Caught off balance, he flew back into the screen. The screen toppled over and hit the floor with a thunderous crack. Alex landed on his arse atop it with a painful grunt.

Kat jumped out of the tub, plucked a large drying cloth off the stool and hurriedly wrapped it around her torso. Safely swathed in linen from chest to upper thigh, she turned around.

Alex had already regained his feet and stood with his legs spread, hands on his hips. His face was carved with anger, the scar on his chin in stark relief. A low, animal-like growl was her only warning before he dipped his shoulder, grabbed her hips, and flung her over his shoulder like a Viking berzerker.

Kat screamed in outrage, which turned into a squeak when Alex's fingers skimmed up her inner thigh. She squirmed violently to avoid his invading hand, but to no avail.

"In the brief span since my return, you've slapped me and knocked me on my arse. I see now I have been too lenient in allowing you the upper hand. I believe some discipline is in order to prove to you I am not a man with whom to trifle."

"I am no child to be disciplined. Now put me down this instant," she panted.

"Aye, I agree. You are not a child, but all woman . . . a beautiful woman of flesh and blood and passion," he ended hoarsely.

Between her thighs, his fingers threaded through the black curly hair guarding her sheath. He brushed his fingers back and forth again and again, his touch teasing. Her breath hitched at the exquisite torture, stealing her senses and her intended rebuke. Then he tugged the hair gently. Kat moaned.

He delved again, running his fingers along her crease, but not touching flesh, trailing from her buttocks down to her plump bud. Caught up in the exquisite sensations, Kat did not even think to resist. He tugged on the silky hairs once more, setting off ripples of pleasure. Her nether lips swelled, tingling with pent-up longing as she dampened with desire.

"Your dew is sweet upon my fingers, my lady. But 'tis just a taste of what I intend to wring from your lips. I shall give no quarter, and ere I am through, there will be no more talk of ending our bargain."

Kat snarled in disbelief, "You would take me by force?"

Alex laughed. "I shall have no need of force, my dear. You want me. Already your body betrays you. With only a little persuasion on my part, I shall have you writhing in my arms, begging me to take you."

Then she flew through the air, and landed on a soft cloud

of goose feathers, coverlet, and animal furs. Her linen barrier was somehow lost in the scuffle.

Driven by an odd mixture of anger and arousal at his threat, Kat rose to flee. On her hands and knees, she scrabbled away from him, but his hand clutched her ankle and tugged. A startled yelp escaped her. She reached desperately for a carved post, but her hand slipped and clutched only fur as she landed on her stomach.

He dragged her back, the tangled fur beneath her aiding Alex as she slid easily down the bed, exposing the linen sheets underneath. Before she could move, he sprawled on top of her. His hard body, all muscle and heat, pressed her down into the mattress. He grabbed her flailing hands and secured them above her head, effectively imprisoning her.

Her strength sapped, Kat lay unmoving beneath Alex. Harsh breathing, his and hers, resounded like pounding anvils in the aftermath of their tussle. It was not long before she became aware of the pleasurable sensations buffeting her body; underneath her, fur tickled her breasts, quickening her nipples into hard peaks, while above her, Alex's moist breath panted against her neck. And the hard ridge of his arousal prodded her hip.

Charged tension, heavy as a sultry summer day, arced between them.

Her body softened instinctively, and she was immediately horrified by her reaction. Did she have no self-respect? Alex may lust after her, but he was not in love with her. How could she have forgotten so easily that Alex was incapable of ever loving anyone but Lydia? What happened to her resolve to end their marriage and marry Luc, a man who loved and respected her as Alex never could?

Refusing to let her body defeat her, she renewed her struggles.

Chapter 15

Alex's vaunted control had snapped at Kat's stubborn refusal to hear him out. But desperation quickly flared into raging hunger when she thrashed beneath him. His cock slipped into the channel of her buttocks. He groaned. His shaft throbbed and lengthened with each thrust of her body. Up and down, up and down he rode within her erotic embrace, moaning at the exquisite friction.

Needing to do something quickly before he spent like a callow lad, he clutched her wrists in a single grip, raised his lower body a little and swatted her bare bottom twice.

Kat howled in pain and anger. "Hit me again and I shall make you pay. I still wield a dagger with extreme dexterity."

"Then cease your struggles, vixen, unless 'tis your intention to provoke my lust. I shall gladly take you here and now if that is your wish."

Kat stilled and turned her head, gray fur outlining her profile. She spat a wet strand of hair from her lips and Alex gently pulled it away from her face. "What I want is for you to get off me. Why do you not go find Lady Lydia? Whereas I do not appreciate your brutal tactics, I'm sure your whore will."

A brazier in the corner of the chamber illuminated Kat's face and, as Alex gazed down at her bold features and vivid coloring, he was amazed that he had ever admired Lydia's pale, cold beauty. "Ahh . . . I do beg to differ about your predilections, wife. Remember our wedding night?" Kat tensed beneath him. "Though I had to restrain you, I soon had you purring in my arms. This night shall be no different."

Giving her a foretaste of his intentions, Alex drew her earlobe between his teeth, bit gently, and then worried the delicate flesh between his lips. Kat shivered, but her next words came out cool and detached.

"Much is different this night. Lady Lydia is free to marry again and once you get our marriage annulled, so shall I be."

He stiffened, but let the comment pass. He ran his hand over her bottom cheeks, his lips a hairsbreadth from her ear. "I love your rear, Kat," he whispered, his voice a throaty caress. "'Tis nice and firm, with plenty of flesh to hold onto when I thrust deep inside you."

She glared up at him, tugging on her wrists. "You are as arrogant as ever if you think I shall succumb. I saw the way you looked at Lady Lydia. You are a liar and a fool. You deserve each other."

Alex clenched his teeth, his fight to hold his temper in check slipping. "I have told you I do not love Lydia, that 'tis you I want." Now did not seem the right time to tell Kat he finally realized it was she whom he loved. "But it would seem only actions have any merit with you. And I shall not begrudge the undertaking. See how accommodating I am?"

"Accommodating, my arse," she shouted, then spit out the fur that got stuck on her tongue.

He chuckled. "Aye, your arse." Alex sat back on his haunches, drawing her arms down with him. He straddled her thighs and gripped her wrists in one hand behind her lower back. With his right hand he squeezed her bottom cheek, grazing his fingers under the crease where it met her thigh. "The flesh has turned a lovely shade of pink from my punishment. And 'tis hot to the touch. Let me give you some ease."

That said, he bent down and bathed her tender flesh with his tongue, lathing the right globe thoroughly first, then moving to the other one. Her skin was soft, and heat generated from spanking her seared his tongue, enflaming him.

She squirmed beneath him, her breathing more rapid. "By God, 'tis beyond enough. I demand you release me."

Alex looked up, frowning. "I do not respond to commands. My course is set. Now be quiet or I shall gag you."

Her eyes flared silver with rage. "You brute, you would not dare."

"Care to wager on it?" he challenged. He would not do it, but she need not know that.

Kat glared up at Alex in impotence, her head twisted back. He *would* gag her. He was a domineering man who did not like to be thwarted. She turned away and laid her head back down on the bed. She would fight another way. She would just lay unmoving, and when she did not respond to his seduction, he would give up and leave her be. If only she believed she was strong enough to resist.

He shifted and pressed his lips to the nape of her neck, lingering there a moment. Then he kissed and nipped his way down her spine. Reaching her lower back, he began to tease the crease of her derriere. She clamped her lips tight to keep from moaning. Then very slowly, the hot, wet glide of his tongue slithered down and down, poking and prodding the shadowy crevice all the way to the back of her thighs.

Kat trembled. Shivery heat pulsed along her flesh and spread to the moist folds guarding her entry. When he reached an extremely sensitive area, a ragged cry escaped her throat. *Nay, 'twas indecent,* her mind cried.

But she made no denial when he spread her rear cheeks and dipped his tongue back in. He prodded the tight flesh with the tip of his tongue, and eased out, only to return and continue the torture. She squirmed against the furs, moaning as her body quivered uncontrollably. Need overwhelmed her as wave upon wave of tingles battered her nether lips.

Kat choked back a cry of protest when he pulled away, but he was not through. Kissing up her spine, Alex slid his free hand beneath her stomach and cupped her mound, grinding his palm against her in a teasing rhythm. Harder, then softer, he stoked her like a flame. She gasped, arching with unbearable pleasure, begging for more. He answered her silent plea, inserting his middle finger into her feminine channel.

Alex groaned. "Jesu, you are incredibly hot," he said.

He pulled his finger out, only to slip back in deeper with two fingers, penetrating her in a slow, teasing cadence as her pleasure built, her heart raced.

Kat tried to resist, but the pleasure was too intense as need throbbed between her thighs. Panting, feverish, she wanted what only Alex could give her. It was just beyond her reach, but each time she neared that elusive summit, the sensation receded before she could grasp it.

Unable to wait any longer, desperate for release, she ground down on Alex's hand. Groaning in ecstasy, she clutched the furs in her fists, suddenly realizing Alex had released her hands. His hand still pumping between her thighs, Alex leaned over her. Sensuous lips trailed up her neck, licking and sucking a blazing path. She turned her head, seeking a deeper connection. When his lips met hers, she sighed. His tongue plunged between her lips. Kat sought it greedily, her tongue wrapping around his, giving no quarter.

Just then she felt her peak nearing and she pulled her mouth away, moaning.

"Nay, I want to taste your desire on my tongue."

He removed his hand from between her legs, and Kat cried out in protest. But he rolled her onto her back, knelt between her legs, and spread them wide, exposing her glistening flesh to his hot gaze. He stared intently for several beats of her heart. When he looked up at her at last, something she read in his eyes made her feel loved and cherished, but surely it was her imagination, conjured by her own private yearnings.

"You are beautiful beyond words, Kat. I shall have you or no other." A lump lodged in Kat's throat. She wanted to believe him, wanted to believe him so badly it firmed her resolve to resist him one last time. She clutched his shoulders to push him away. But with a fierce gleam in his blue eyes, Alex bent his dark head and placed his mouth upon her wet, throbbing flesh.

With no preliminaries, he thrust his tongue inside her. In that moment she cared not if he loved her or nay. Passion held her in its tense grasp, wiping away all thought, all pride, all common sense. Kat cried out his name, moaning wildly as the pleasure coiled tighter, hotter. Instead of pushing him away, her grip became a plea. She clutched his dark hair and raised her hips to meet his frenzied kiss.

Alex withdrew his tongue from her sheath and lashed her dewy folds, seeking every crevice and hill except where her pleasure centered most. She writhed against his hot, sleek tongue. Until he raised his head and stared at her with a fevered light, his mouth but inches from her wet center. "Do you wish me to stop now?"

Kat shivered as moist air caressed her exposed flesh. When Alex's words finally penetrated her befogged mind, she glared at him and sealed her lips tight. She would die before she asked him for aught.

A ruthless light flared in his eyes. Holding her gaze transfixed, his tongue darted out, light and delicate, to trace around the nugget of flesh at her apex without touching it. She watched, entranced, as he came ever closer, the teasing touch driving her beyond bearing, wanting, nay craving him to end the torture and give her release.

"Shall I stop now?" He rose as if he intended to leave her there wet and throbbing, unsatisfied and wanting.

"Stop!"

"Stop?"

"Nay. Oh God, I don't want you to stop."

With a hoarse groan of satisfaction, Alex cupped her bottom in his strong hands and lifted her hips to his hungry mouth. He clamped his lips around her engorged nubbin and sucked vigorously. Intense desire stabbed her dewy flesh and she thrust up against his relentless mouth, his tongue a raspy caress. He flicked back and forth over the highly aroused bud, the erotic tension tightening beyond bearing as he tormented her with his tongue and lips. Pleasure drew higher, tighter, deeper.

It seemed to go on forever, driving her wild, willing her to promise aught to end the shattering tension. Just when she thought she would never reach fulfillment, Alex pushed his finger deep inside her. He touched a spot so pleasurably sensitive, rippling heat exploded between her thighs. Stars burst before her eyes. She cried out in rapture, her sheath contracting, throbbing. Deep, hot, centered.

Her arms flung wide, she savored every tremor as she stared up at the dark blue canopy above her, its golden embroidered stars still spinning.

Alex was enchanted by her abandonment. He savored every ripple, every quiver of the pink flesh beneath his tongue, her heat and honeyed essence scalding him. Slowly, her contractions abated and her panting breath filled the silence.

Now that he had seen to her satisfaction, the hard arousal pressed taut against his linen undergarments demanded release. Wanted to seek the welcoming haven of Kat's hot, exotic dwelling.

Unable to hold back his raging lust any longer, Alex tore off his tunic. Leaving his sherte on, he reached beneath it and untied the cord encased in the waist of his braies. Kneeling above her, he shoved his braies down to his knees. His erection sprang free, easing some of the pressure. Then he lowered his body in the cradle of Kat's spread thighs.

Hot and heavy, the bulbous head of his cock nudged the entrance of her portal. His movements slow, he rocked back and forth along her slick flesh.

A gravelly moan escaped him. "Oh Jesu, love, I can't wait another moment to have you."

Kat tensed beneath him, but Alex was too blind with lust to notice.

He drew back, ready to plunge into her sheltering depths,

and was startled when she shoved him aside. Kat crawled out from under him with a cry of outrage. But his excitement was too far gone and he could not stop himself even if he wanted to. Did he want to?

Cursing, he rolled onto his back, took his cock in hand and pumped up and down, his pleasure tenfold as Kat watched him at the foot of the bed, her towel shielding her nudity once more. He gazed into her silver eyes, luminous as the moon with some unreadable emotion, and with several frenzied strokes, his hot seed burst free and peppered his stomach.

Kat stared aghast and yet oddly enthralled as Alex caressed his thick shaft until his seed erupted. He was a sorcerer, a practiced seducer, and that she should never forget. Indeed, had he not been moments away from stripping away the last remaining vestiges of her pride and self-respect? Passionate to a fault, she was ashamed that she had relented in her weakness. Tears pooled in her eyes. Was a lifetime of heartache worth a few moments of pleasure?

Using a corner of the bed sheet, Alex wiped off his stomach.

"You disgust me, Alex. Never touch me again. I want you to leave. Now!"

Alex rose from the bed and adjusted his braies, his eyes glaring daggers. "I did not disgust you when you were writhing beneath me and your pleasure drenched my mouth."

Kat gasped, incensed. "You struck me and held me down against my will, forcing your attentions on me. Treating me no better than a whore."

Alex scowled. "Were that true, I would have taken you with no thought to your pleasure. Don't pretend that you did not enjoy the lovemaking we shared."

"You talk of sharing, but what exactly did we share?" Kat answered her own question. "'Twas naught but animal lust. There was no love involved."

Kat held her ground when Alex moved around the bed and stopped inches away from her.

He tenderly stroked her cheek with his thumb, searching

her eyes. "You are wrong, my love," he said, his voice rough with emotion, "I care more for you than you can truly know."

Her resolve slipped at his impassioned words, the tender regard in his gaze. Nay! She *knew* better than to trust him. And she would not let Alex get her hopes up again, only to dash them when he tired of her and returned to his true love, Lady Lydia. *Never forget, never forgive.*

Kat stepped back from Alex and his hand dropped away from her face. "Nay, I don't believe you. You are in love with Lady Lydia. Had I any doubts, your actions in the reception hall proved otherwise. Naught you say can convince me. Just leave me be!"

Shaking with pent-up emotion, she retreated to the outer chamber, opened the portal and waited. Alex stepped out of the bedchamber dressed once again. The crackling fire barely disturbed the seething tension emanating between them as he slowly approached.

He stopped before her, then drove his fingers through her hair and tilted her head up to his burning gaze. "I will leave you. For now. But the bargain still stands. I realized today I do not love Lady Lydia, that my feelings for her were simply a youthful infatuation. What you and I have is so much more real and powerful. I shall not rest until I prove to you Lady Lydia means naught to me."

Tears she valiantly held in check hovered precariously upon her eyelashes, but at his words a teardrop fell and rolled down her cheek. If only he truly meant it. This sentiment only made her angrier. "Nay, you have humiliated me before the court for the last time. I shall never forgive you. I loathe the very sight of you. Just get out!" she croaked.

He nodded stiffly, but instead of leaving, he bent his head down. He was going to kiss her. Kat flinched and turned her face away, but he surprised her with a gentle brush of his lips on her cheek, kissing her tear away. His words barely audible, he said, "I never wanted to hurt you, Kat."

Then he was gone.

Kat wiped her eyes with fisted hands. *Why must Alex continue to torment me? Is it simply a game he refuses to lose, even at the expense of my own suffering? And why do I continue to let him hurt me time and again?*

Deep in thought, she wandered into the bedchamber. Seeing the rumpled bedclothes, self-loathing pummeled her. She moved to the bed and hastily smoothed the covers out, removing all traces of her humiliatingly wanton behavior. All except the incriminating stains on the linens underneath. Kat grimaced. Obviously she would have to change them later before Jenny saw them.

After dropping the damp towel she wore, she pulled on a clean chemise. And not a moment too soon, for Jenny bustled back in the chamber and started up a stream of chatter as she helped Kat dress for supper.

Sir Luc, having settled the last of the household disputes for the night, entered his cramped quarters that adjoined the marshal's office at White Hall. The room was only large enough for a small tester bed to lie lengthwise against the back wall and a chest to the left of the bed near the door. The coals were lit in the brazier stationed in the corner of the room opposite his clothes' chest. He dipped the wick of the candle he carried in the red coals in the brazier. When it blazed to life, he placed the candle in the stand sitting on his chest. Luc sat down with a sigh, dropped his head in his hands and groaned. He rubbed his hands over his face several times, and then shoved his fingers through his hair, pushing it back off his forehead.

With a grunt, he tugged one boot off and then the other. He was so weary, he felt ancient beyond his nine and twenty years of age. He divested himself of the rest of his garments, hung them on the pegs beside the chest, and crawled into bed wearing his sherte. As he laid his head down on the soft pillow he released a sigh, and heard a crackling sound. Perplexed, Luc leaned up on his elbow, frowning and his eyebrows drawn down. When he reached beneath the pillow his fingers grazed parchment. Surprise rippled through him. Wondering who had slipped the message beneath his pillow and when, he seized the parchment and pulled it over by the light of the candle. He immediately recognized the slanted scrawl. His heart pounding, he read the missive.

Dear Friend,
*   Despite recent unforeseen events, proceed with our plan as we agreed. Do not falter, and we shall both have what we desire most in this world.*

It was unsigned. Luc scrunched up the note and tossed it in the brazier. He flopped his head back down on the pillow and watched, frustration gnawing at him. The missive's edges caught flame, browning and curling as it turned to ashes. Would his quest for his heart's desire never end? Disappointment swirled in his breast. He jumped up from the bed and, using the poker, stoked the coals. He had been but a hairsbreadth from solidifying his marriage to Kat when the unthinkable happened. Alex returned after four years in captivity to reclaim his bride.

Luc was torn, though. He truly admired Alex and once considered him a friend. But the man stood between him and the only woman he'd ever loved, leaving him no choice except to find a way to sever their marriage. The only question remained was how far was he willing to go to see Alex destroyed?

Luc clutched the iron poker tighter. It bit into his skin. *I cannot lose her now,* Luc thought feverishly. *Not after coming so close.*

The following day, after the opening ceremonies for Parliament, Alex cantered alongside Rand a goodly distance to the back of a hunting party hastily organized by the king.

"You must see now, Rand, why I have decided to conceal this

knowledge from Kat," Alex said with more confidence than he felt, his voice raised above the pounding of horses' hooves.

Edward, upon learning Queen Eleanor and a group of ladies were out hunting with her greyhounds, decided to join them. Knowing Kat served the queen this afternoon, Alex was more than willing to come along. He glared at the immaculately dressed man riding behind the king. Unfortunately, Sir Luc had joined the party, too, which was no surprise to Alex.

"I'm afraid I have to disagree. You should tell Kat the truth. She deserves to know someone wants you dead."

Alex jerked his gaze back to Rand. "I can't believe what I am hearing. Rand, you of all people know how impulsive and reckless Kat is. Were I to tell her, there is no way I could keep her from muddling into danger in a misguided attempt to help me." Though after last night, Alex thought, she might instead be inclined to aid his enemy in seeing him meet his Maker.

It was a mild, breezy spring day. Freshly scythed grass teased his nostrils as they flew across rolling meadows, the profusion of red and yellow blossoms cheery and reminiscent of home. He lifted his face to the sky, the sunlight like candle glow in comparison to the blazing sun of the Near East.

"You do Kat a grave disservice. She can be a very formidable opponent when someone she loves is threatened."

Alex grinned at Rand. "I, more than any man, am aware of my wife's formidable weapons. Not to mention she is unusually proficient with a dagger and bow and arrow." Then he sobered. "But, if you have not noticed, I'm the last person your cousin loves at the moment."

The pain reflected in Kat's eyes last night returned in a flash. No matter how he swore never to hurt Kat again, it seemed he had done that very thing. Unintentionally, of course, but that did not absolve him from his culpability.

Rand's mouth grimaced in acknowledgement. "Despite your estrangement, Kat still cares for you and would do all in her power to keep you from harm."

"Exactly. Kat gives not a thought to her own safety. Whoever was behind my capture and imprisonment is a very ruthless and determined foe. The villain would not scruple over killing Kat if she interfered in any way."

A gust of wind blew a hank of long gold hair across Rand's face and he shook it off. "Your reasoning is sound, Alex, but—"

"Nay, my friend, naught you say can sway me from this course. No matter the cost, I must protect Kat. I hope one day she will forgive me for lying to her, but I can't worry about that now. I believe Kat's in danger and I need to know if you will help me."

Their horses' hooves thundered on the hard-packed road they crossed and tack jangled as he and Rand prepared to jump the hedgerow bordering the pasture up ahead. Their mounts lunged over the obstacle and landed without misstep, then surged forward rapidly in their excitement.

Rand turned to Alex. "Very well. I think you are making a mistake, but she is not my wife. So why is it you suspect Kat is in danger now?"

Alex explained to Rand how he had been out riding with Kat when an arrow came flying out of nowhere and narrowly missed hitting one of them.

"You checked the arrow shot at you, of course. Were you able to identify it?"

Alex avoided Rand's eyes as heat rose up his neck. It was what any knight worth his salt would do if ambushed. But he had been preoccupied by the exotic scent of his irresistible wife, not to mention her lush curves.

"Nay, everything happened too fast. I dragged Kat behind a tree for cover, made sure she was safely ensconced," Rand raised a mocking eyebrow at that, Alex hastily continued, "then I went in search of the culprit. But I found no evidence of anyone hiding in the buildings."

His voice full of censure, Rand asked, "What did you find when you returned to check the missile?"

Alex cleared his throat and then said defensively, "Kat followed me and I could not very well go back and check the arrow without raising her suspicions."

Rand rolled his hazel eyes in exasperation. "I'm afraid to ask my next obvious question. Instead, why do you not tell me the reason you are convinced it was not an unfortunate hunting accident? You said you saw no other signs of disturbance."

"You have the right of it. But after I returned Kat to court, I went back to check the location where we were ambushed. The arrow was gone."

Coming upon a stream too wide to jump, Alex and Rand slowed their mounts and carefully picked their way through the rocky bed, their horses' hooves splashing up water. Once on the other side, they surged into a canter.

"Very well, Alex. You have convinced me. Do you have any idea who may want you dead?"

"There is one man I suspect. Lord William Calvert. You will remember we had heated words soon after my arrival. He swore long ago to see me pay for killing his son."

"Aye. I do remember. But he has since reconciled with King Edward. Do you have any tangible evidence he is involved?"

"Nay. But I did check with the head groom at the stables. He said he saw Lord Calvert ride out with his hunting bow shortly before Kat and I did the day of the arrow attack. Apparently he returned a couple hours later with no game."

"His behavior could be construed as suspicious, or even coincidental. Mere speculation is not enough. Unfortunately, you need proof."

"Aye. But right now I'm more concerned about Kat's safety. The traitor may use her to get to me."

"I agree. So what is it you would have me do?"

Alex released the pent-up breath he had been holding. "I need your help keeping a watchful eye on Kat. Not all the time, mind you. I don't expect anything to occur at court, too many witnesses. The villain will not want to draw any undue notice to himself."

"Have you a plan in mind?"

Alex nodded. "As Parliament has begun, I cannot keep track of her every move. I have already paid a stable boy to notify me should she leave the safety of Westminster Palace. Remember the lad with bright red hair and freckles?"

"Aye, he retrieved and saddled your horse for the hunt," Rand said, his voice rife with humor.

Alex shrugged, shifting in his saddle. He was embarrassed—it was obvious the boy thought him some kind of hero. "His name is Tim. I'll introduce him to you when we return.

"Unfortunately, much of my time at court I shall be in meetings with the King's Council. If Tim should need to reach me then, I would have him come to you in my stead."

Rand nodded in understanding. "So, when you are thus occupied, you would have me follow Kat and give her my protection. You know 'tis a very difficult position you have placed me in, Alex, spying upon my own cousin."

"Aye, and I do not ask this lightly of you. But no matter how skilled, Kat is just a woman, and would be no match for a determined foe bent on revenge."

"Your plan sounds simple enough, but how do you expect us to spy on Kat without her becoming suspicious?"

"We will simply have to be very clever and make sure she never finds out we are watching her comings and goings."

His lips quirked, Rand looked doubtful. "I shall gladly help you, Alex. But there are no guarantees. And Kat will eventually learn of your deception. What will you do then? Are you prepared for the consequences of your actions?"

Not knowing the answer, Alex was glad when the harmonious blast of hunting horns and hounds baying in the distance reached his ears. The quarry they were hunting was not far away. Alex spurred his horse into a gallop, anxious to catch up with the rest of the men in the hunting party. He had every intention of being at the head of the pack in joining Kat. Never would he allow Sir Luc to steal a march on him.

Never.

Chapter 16

Blast the woman!

Kat frowned at the elegant line of Lady Lydia's back as the running hounds picked up the hare's scent again. No longer in black, Lydia wore a light blue tunic embroidered in gold thread and a matching cloak, giving her the appearance of angelic innocence. But Kat knew differently. The delicate white palfrey the woman rode pranced and preened every bit as much as her mistress.

Usually Kat rode in the forefront of the hunt, but today her heart was not in it. Her curved hunting horn hanging from the baldric—a leather belt strapped diagonally over her shoulder down to her hip and decorated with silver star mounts—remained unused. She would have refused to join the hunting party altogether except for her duty to Queen Eleanor. Besides, she was no coward. It was better to confront an enemy boldly, showing no fear, than to hide and cower in the dark.

But the light brought out all one's imperfections. Compared to Lydia, Kat felt awkward and gauche. Riding upon Lightning only emphasized her large, lumbering frame. Kat's features were too bold and her coloring too dark. Not that she would ever admit in any way how lacking she felt. Lady Lydia was already too full of herself. Although Kat had yet to speak to Lady Lydia, the blond woman kept tossing smug looks of triumph back at her.

Up ahead, when a relay of greyhounds sighted the hare emerging from a hedge, they were released and gave chase after the prey. Horns blew and hounds bayed in excitement as the party of ladies, hounds, and huntsmen surged after them. Horses thundered across open fields. The contest of speed and agility between greyhound and hare was a terrible beauty to behold, accompanied by the melody of the sounds of the hunt. But at last the hare began to lag behind, his ears laid back against his head. A white greyhound closed the gap and brought the hare down, keeping it at bay until the hunters surrounded it in a nearby pasture.

Kat joined the ladies, yet remained distant enough that none noticed her, except one woman. She felt in sympathy with the trapped hare when Lydia left the others and sidled up on Kat's right, their horses nose to rump.

Kat did not see the kill, but the death notes of the horn rang in her ears. Lydia, her back to the other ladies, pursed her mouth in a moue of disgust. "Hunting is quite a barbaric occupation, but I know some abnormal women who enjoy the thrill of it," she said with scorn.

Kat smiled, unperturbed. No one noticed their exchange or could hear them over the excited barking of the dogs in anticipation of their reward. "Aye, Queen Eleanor does love hunting with her hounds. Surely you are not suggesting the queen is barbaric and abnormal?"

Lydia clenched her reins tightly in her hands and her knuckles turned pale. The white mare shifted nervously. "You know full well I was speaking of you, Lady Katherine." In a deceptively even tone she continued. "Why, look at you. What a sad example of womanhood you are, flaunting your legs immodestly in your odd tunic. 'Tis no wonder Alex fled his trap of a marriage. You are too manly for his tastes. Indeed, he did not even bed you before deserting you," Lydia added slyly. "I know the bloody bed sheet was never displayed as proof of consummation."

Kat knew Lydia's game. But she had long learned to conceal her vulnerabilities from prying eyes. "I hate to disappoint you, Lady Lydia," Kat said. Her mocking smile revealed the lie. "But your sources are mistaken. Alex bedded me most thoroughly on our wedding night. Indeed, once was not enough to satisfy him, so he took me over and over again long into the night."

Lydia's eyes spit blue frost. "You lie! I know from experience Alex desires a sophisticated woman with some flesh on her body. He does not want you. And now that I am widowed, he shall be mine. No woman can satisfy him the way I can."

Kat shook her head chidingly. "Do not delude yourself, *Lady* Lydia. Even now his lust for me has not waned. Do you honestly believe I have remained chaste since my husband's return? I really do pity you, Lady Lydia."

Lydia, her mouth twisted in hate, raised her hand as if to strike Kat. Kat tensed, prepared to defend the blow. Instead, Lydia dropped her hand limply and stroked it down the white mare's neck. Her face relaxed and became serenely beautiful once more. "You are the one to be pitied, my lady. You speak of lust, but we both know I am the woman Alex loves. He wanted to marry *me*. But he could not because he was bound by duty to marry you."

Kat laughed in her face. "But he did not marry *you*, did he? No matter your persistent enticements. He could have broken our betrothal if he really wanted to, but obviously your sullied charms were not enough to tempt him away from marriage to *me*."

"Bitch," Lydia hissed under her breath, "you will regret that insult. No matter your brave words, Alex does not love you and never will. A woman can tell when a man loves her. I saw the way he looked at me yesterday, felt his trembling touch. Alex still loves me. And I'm not the only one who noticed. Indeed, gossip is rampant at court that your marriage is doomed, that Alex loves me and intends to leave you for me."

Kat listened as each painful truth gouged her flesh, making her heart bleed, but her pride was a bestial force that kept her head high, her expression free of emotion. Never would she let Lydia know her verbal strikes found a soft, vulnerable target.

Finished boasting, Lydia stared at her with a glow of triumph in her eyes, a reptilian smile upon her face.

Kat smiled down at the smaller woman with a confidence she did not feel and returned Lydia's look with a pleased smirk. "Your conceit is misplaced, Lady Lydia. What you saw was a man amazed to learn that he never *truly* loved you. He was a boy enthralled and fascinated with a beautiful woman who used his naivety for her own selfish ends. But, by all means, you don't have to take my word for it. Indeed, in the days to come, you shall discover for yourself you no longer have any power over Alex. My husband is firmly ensconced in my bed and none of your dubious attractions," Kat's eyes swept Lydia with a look of repugnance, "shall tempt him away from me."

Lydia sputtered in fury, her cold eyes malevolent and promising retribution. She yanked her horse around to leave, and as she did so, she snapped the end of her reins against Lightning's muzzle apurpose.

The mare screamed in pain and reared up, her forelegs flailing. Prepared this time for Lydia to retaliate, Kat clung tightly to her mare, a fast grip on the reins. But Lydia was not as skilled a horsewoman. Unable to control her startled palfrey, she could not escape in time; their mounts bumped and jostled against one another.

Immediately regaining control, Kat took advantage of Lydia's distraction. No one harmed her horse without repercussions. She hooked her long leg under Lydia's left leg, and raising it high, she shoved Lydia in the back. Lydia toppled off the other side of her horse, emitting a piercing shriek. She hit the ground face first. The white mare shambled quickly away, leaving her in the dirt.

Kat's heart thundered loudly in her ears like the pounding of a herd of horses at the swiftness of the attack. Lydia began to wail. Kat stared down at her in disgust, when it suddenly dawned on her that the sound of pounding hooves was real. She looked up, surprised to see a party of men approaching. Her gaze landed on Alex, riding in front beside King Edward.

Alex wore a gold tunic and the sun struck blue sparks off his black hair. But what caught her attention was the thunderous expression on his face. Alex scowled as he took in the scene. Kat was elated. Obviously he had seen Lady Lydia's attack and would at last realize Lydia was a vicious woman unworthy of his love.

Alex had raced like a centaur through a copse of trees so eager to reach Kat, that nearly too late he ducked his head to avoid striking a branch. When he looked up once more, horse and rider surged into the open pasture where the women's hunting party converged. To his horror, his eyes alighted upon Kat just as she struck Lady Lydia in the back and shoved her.

Lydia hit the ground, landing in an ungainly heap. Alex groaned. Spurring his horse faster, he made straight for Kat, unable to believe what he had just seen. She had attacked Lydia without provocation, or so it seemed. Lydia had ever been too ladylike to say an unkind word or do aught antagonistic. But would Kat harm another for no apparent reason? He knew she had a hot temper. Could she have lashed out at Lydia in a jealous fit?

He would withhold judgment until he heard Kat's explanation. Had he not accused her outright of being a whore with disastrous results upon his return? He was wrong then and he would not make the mistake again.

When Alex reined in beside Kat, Lydia moaned in pain. Dragging his gaze from his wife, he jumped off his horse and knelt beside Lydia. "Lydia, are you injured? Tell me where it hurts."

Her voice quavered. "'Tis my knee. I think I twisted it when I hit the ground." She gulped back huge tears in silent misery, but they flowed over her long lashes and down her ivory cheeks. He patted her hand in an attempt to comfort her.

Alex looked up at Kat. "What happened here, Kat?" he asked, his tone neutral.

Kat blinked in surprise. Then she raised her chin in a belligerent manner and aimed an accusatory glare at him, her lips sealed tight. *What is this?* he wondered. Her contemptuous gaze confused him. Why did she not simply answer the question?

Instead, Lydia answered him. "Your lady wife attacked me, Alex. 'Twas so sudden and unprovoked. One moment Lady Katherine and I were speaking. We had quite a pleasant and cordial conversation, actually. I complimented her riding skills and admired her unique tunic. But when I turned back to rejoin the ladies, she knocked me off my horse. I don't understand why she would do such a thing?" Her bottom lip trembled as she looked up at him through lowered lashes, her eyes miserably confused.

Kat grunted.

"Mayhap 'tis my fault." Lydia lowered her eyes in contrition and beseeched Kat. "My lady, if I have ever done aught to offend you, I beg you forgive me."

Kat turned a hateful glare upon Lydia and laughed, the sound harsh and grating. "Bravo, Lady Lydia. 'Tis my turn to commend you," she said sarcastically, "on your excellent mummery skills."

The king and the rest of the party of men reined in just then, no doubt avid for a juicy tidbit of gossip to toss upon the pyre blazing about court already. Alex was not unaware of the delicate situation he had been unavoidably placed in.

Fortunately, Edward waved the men on. "Go on and join the ladies, gentlemen. I shall join you anon."

The men continued on, all except for Rand and Sir Luc. The latter pulled his horse up beside Kat, his expression closed and unreadable. Alex bristled in frustration, torn. He could not leave Lydia lying in the dirt, injured and in pain.

But his concern for Lydia, no matter how innocent, had returned the cold look in Kat's eyes.

Alex wrapped an arm around Lydia and helped her stand up. She cried out, clutching her right knee.

"Can you ride?"

"Nay, 'tis too painful."

King Edward's horse pranced nervously. "Well, since you have things in hand here, Alex, I'm off to see my lady wife." Edward grinned. "I will speak to you back at the palace."

"Sir Luc," Alex snapped. "Why do you just sit there and stare? Come help your stepmother."

Sir Luc recoiled in revulsion. "She is *not* my stepmother."

Alex frowned. "I was led to believe Lady Lydia was married to your father."

Luc nodded reluctantly. "Aye, she was, but she is no step-mother of mine. I claim her not."

"She is still your kin by marriage. I will hand her up to you so you can carry her back to court. She needs to lie down and have her injury tended by a physician."

"Nay, I shall do no such thing."

"By God, man, she is your father's widow, she deserves—"

Lydia leaned against him weakly and moaned in pain, her rose scent cloying. "Prithee, Sir Alex, my knee pains me greatly. You shall not sway Sir Luc with words of the duty he owes me. Ours is an old quarrel. Will you not assist me?"

His gaze shot to Kat and then Sir Luc. He was trapped. "Aye, of course, I shall help you." Damn Sir Luc, no doubt he was enjoying Alex's quandary.

Alex glanced at Kat again, accusation clear in her eyes. If she were innocent, then Lydia lied. But why did she refuse to defend herself, or deny Lydia's accusation? He did not know what to think or believe.

Kat was going to be ill. Alex, concern etched on his face, clasped Lydia's tiny waist in a gentle embrace, his hand dark and masculine against the light blue silk of Lydia's tunic. Nausea churned in Kat's stomach and rose into her throat. Her skin grew clammy and cold. Had those hands that passed Lydia into Rand's arms now, really held her just last night? Held her with amazing strength and extraordinary gentleness, with passion and tenderness?

If Alex truly cared for her as he claimed, he would know that Kat was innocent. Oh, he had not accused her outright, but that he had to ask was proof enough. She refused to defend herself when he could not see the truth before his eyes. Where Lydia was concerned, Alex was blind to her manipulative ways. He thought her a fragile innocent in need of a man's protection and could never conceive her capable of malice or violence. Did they not say love was blind?

When Alex sat on his mount, Rand handed Lydia over to him. Unable to watch the spectacle another moment, Kat turned to Luc. But he was staring oddly at Lydia and Alex, his eyes glittering with some heated emotion she could not interpret.

Then Luc's gaze cleared and he turned to Kat. He smiled, his glance admiring. "The day is much too beautiful to waste, my lady. Shall we join the others and continue the hunt?"

"I would be delighted, Sir Luc."

As they rode back to the hunting party, she averted her gaze from the revolting sight of Lydia in Alex's embrace. She heard Alex call her name, but she ignored him and rode on. Passion had clouded her judgment since Alex's return, but no more. 'Twas past time she remembered that Sir Luc loved her and wished to marry her.

Ever since she lost her mother her fifth summer, all she had ever wanted was to be loved. When she grew older, deep inside Kat feared she was not the type of woman to inspire romantic love. She was too odd and outspoken, too tall and brazen. Men were either intimidated by her or contemptuous of her unladylike behavior.

Then she married Alex and foolishly thought she could make him fall in love with her. She soon discovered her fears were not misplaced when Alex abandoned her after their wedding. With Sir Luc, it would be different. He alone offered her a chance at happiness. He would give her the child she desperately craved, someone to love without fear of rejection. Aye. She would grasp what Sir Luc offered with both hands as though clinging to a steep cliff, knowing he would never let her go to crash below upon the rocky shore of disillusionment.

Alex shifted back in his saddle, trying to create more space between him and Lady Lydia balanced on his lap. But Lydia did not take the hint and clung tighter. The soft flesh of her buttocks pressed back into his groin, her plump breasts cushioned against his chest. He felt the rush of his blood, his flesh lengthening.

Jesu, he was a man after all.

Lydia could have no idea of the unwilling effect her position had on him. Alex had been her first lover and she had married soon after, to a man old enough to be her grandfather. He doubted Lord Joinville had the stamina to do his duty properly and therefore thought Lydia a virtual innocent. But it was no concern of his. He just hoped they reached Westminster Palace soon. He was glad Rand accompanied them. Alex did not want to give Kat any more reason for jealousy.

Alex spurred Zeus faster. He was impatient to finish his duty to Lydia and speak to Kat. He wanted to ask what induced her to commit violence upon a lady. Though Kat was unlike any other lady of his acquaintance, this was not like her. She was stubborn, independent, opinionated, and defiant, but never cruel or vindictive. She was uninterested in ladylike pursuits, the complete opposite, in fact. She rode as well as a man and wore odd riding skirts that revealed more of her legs than he thought decent. Still, he would have no other for wife.

Her exhilarating presence livened his days, lessening the pain of his memories. It was her spirited nature that drew him, challenged him. On the other hand, she needed a strong hand to guide her, to protect her from her impulsive, headstrong ways. And he intended to be the man to do it.

But he felt as if time was rapidly passing him by, the deadline of the bargain drawing nearer and nearer. Lydia's return to court could not have been at a more inopportune time. He simply must find a way to break through Kat's reserve and prove he loved her and not Lydia.

If not, he feared he might be swallowed up by the dark menace of his nightmares, become a brutal savage again. A cold chill ran up his spine. In the deepest part of the night, his demons haunted him, sought to devour his body and spirit. Rotting flesh hung on the specters' skulls, their mummy-like faces distorted. They grinned at him ghoulishly, soulless red-eyed demons that resembled men he had brutally killed with his bare hands to survive.

"Alex?" someone called him from far away.

"Alex, are you well?" Rand's voice penetrated his thoughts.

Slow to reply, Alex turned his head to his friend. "Aye," he lied, "why do you ask?"

Rand studied him with alarm. "All the color leeched from your face of a sudden. You're white as bone."

Lydia shifted in his lap. "Oh pray, Sir Alex, tell me you are not ill." Alex looked down at her. She gazed up at him in concern, her blue eyes searching as she placed her hand on his cheek. "You have no fever. Mayhap 'tis something you ate?"

Alex smiled at her obvious distress. She was really very sweet, but he loved Kat and always would. "You need not worry about me, Lady Lydia. I have had little sleep since my return and I am but fatigued. Likely all I need is a full night's rest."

Lydia's fingernails dug sharply into his back and her eyes narrowed. Then she dropped her eyes demurely from his gaze. Alex could not imagine what he said to perturb her.

Beside him, Rand chuckled. "Aye. I do not doubt it."

Alex realized how his words had been misconstrued and his face flushed. Obviously Lydia's reaction was from embarrassment. He gave Rand a quelling look but, not surprisingly, his friend ignored him, grinning like an unrepentant rogue.

When they reached the crest of the hill they were climbing, Rand pointed. In the distance, Westminster Abbey and the adjoining palace were nestled in a valley along a serpentine bend of the river Thames.

Alex cleared his throat. "It will not be long now, Lady Lydia. When we arrive at the palace, I shall summon your servant and see that someone tends to your injury."

"Thank you, Alex. You are very gallant to help a lady in distress. You were ever kind to me," she said, her voice soft and shy. But when she looked up at him, her lips were tilted in an inviting smile.

With her blond hair, pale skin, and blue eyes, she gave the impression of innocence, but in contrast her lips were full and sensual. In his youth, the dichotomy had driven him mad with lust. Even knowing her a virgin, her mouth had cried to him—kiss me, tear my clothes off and ravish me till I scream in ecstasy.

Now he was unmoved by her beauty. He understood the difference between idolization and real love. Lydia outwardly exuded the model of perfect womanhood. But Alex loved Kat for the woman she was inside, imperfections and all.

He nodded to Lydia and spurred Zeus down the hill.

Chapter 17

Lydia, her face smooth and unmarred by turmoil, lay limply in Alex's arms as he carried her across the courtyard to the double-door entry. But inwardly she seethed in frustration. So the brazen slattern had not been lying. Lydia did not understand how Alex could desire the woman. Lady Katherine was brash and uncouth, her tall mannish form so unlike Lydia's own delicate, though lush and inviting body.

No matter. Lydia was confident Alex would be hers again very soon and do her bidding. She had wanted him the moment she had laid eyes on him all those years ago. Alex had been young, beautiful, heir to a wealthy barony and easily led by his cock. More importantly, he was naïve to the ways of a woman determined to gather wealth the only way available to her: through marriage, whoring, or both.

Unfortunately, her father already sold her to an old, limp man who wanted to impress his friends with a beautiful young wife to hide his 'infirmity.' Lydia was happy enough with the arrangement until she met Alex. The man her father chose, Lord Joinville, had an ample fortune—he also had two sons to provide for. Eventually, she took care of the younger son. But his first-born and heir was too wise to lose his father's affections through any manipulation on her part.

Still, with her talents, early in her marriage she managed to make the old man's withered member hard enough, if not to poke her, for him to achieve gratification. And her manipulations bore fruit, because Lord Joinville assigned a modest fortune in his will to her. Then when the old man lay on his deathbed, his heir filled his ears with evidence of her infidelities. As a result, before he had died he altered her endowment to a pittance. He left her naught but her widow's portion—several small manors that would never support her in the manner to which she had become accustomed.

Alex would not escape her this time. As they approached the residence block, a tall, gray-haired porter opened one of the massive iron-studded doors. Alex strode up the steps and entered the vaulted porch. Beyond the screen was a ground floor hall where the majority of the visitors at Westminster Palace slept rolled up in blankets next to one another like corded wood. On the first and second floors were the more private apartments for the privileged few, along with third floor turret chambers. All were parts of the extensive improvements made to the palace by King Henry, completed only ten years ago.

Alex adjusted his grip, his chest muscles flexing against her breasts. Lydia felt no pleasure in the touch, but she gazed at Alex with adoring eyes and blushed as though embarrassingly aroused.

The gesture was totally wasted on him for he was looking at the porter. "Summon Lady Lydia's manservant. She needs assistance to her chamber."

Lydia frowned. Something was amiss. On the ride here he barely looked at her, was not attentive to her every need. He should be unable to take his eyes off her. She knew he desired her; she had rubbed against him apurpose to incite his lust and had felt his hard arousal.

The servant glanced at Lydia. Alex glanced down at her. "Is aught the matter, Lady Lydia?"

"'Tis just . . . I," she looked down and lowered her voice, "I'm embarrassed to have to tell you this, but my husband left me with little means. I have but one servant, Sara, my faithful maid."

Alex frowned and turned to the porter. "I shall have need of one of your attendants to take the lady to her room."

"Oh nay, Sir Alex. I beg you. Will you not take me? I shall not feel comfortable in a stranger's arms."

"'Tis highly improper for me to be alone with you in your chamber."

Lydia did not respond, just dropped her eyes and bit her lower lip in distress.

The porter spoke up. "My lord, what would you have me do?"

"I will see the lady to her chamber. Summon the physician and Lady Lydia's maid at once and send them directly to her chamber."

The porter bowed and left. Four sets of spiral stairs, cut into each corner of the building, led up to the sleeping quarters.

"You shall have to direct me to your chamber, my lady."

"Third floor, the southwest turret chamber," Lydia replied in a low voice, forcing Alex to dip his head closer to hear her. Alex clutched her tighter and moving past the screen, he turned right for the nearest stairs. His steps echoed like cracks of thunder as he hurried up two flights to the second floor, then he strode down the passage and up a third flight of steps.

He carried her inside the turret chamber and looked around quickly.

"I share the room with two other ladies. But you need not worry you shall compromise me. They won't be back for some time as they are with the queen."

The round chamber was small and sparse; nevertheless, the four-poster bed was luxuriously appointed with furs, red velvet coverlet and bed curtains. The bed lay opposite two narrow shuttered windows that overlooked the river.

Moving to the bed, he knelt on it as he laid her down. His face extremely close to hers, she turned her head and brushed her lips against his mouth deliberately. Alex jerked back and her head and shoulders flopped down on the bed. He stared down at her in consternation.

Lydia blushed and made her eyes widen in innocent appeal. "Oh my, I did not mean . . . I am so embarrassed. You must think me terribly forward."

He looked around awkwardly. "Nay, I would never think such of you. 'Twas an accident. Think no more of it."

Lydia lowered her lids and looked up at him through her eyelashes. "But what if I cannot?"

Alex's eyebrows raised in puzzlement. "Cannot what?"

"Stop thinking of your kiss. I can't stop thinking of you, Alex. How wonderful it felt to be held in your arms the night we made love. And to have your lips on mine once again."

"But 'twas an accident, surely you understand I did not kiss you apurpose?"

"Did you not?" She flashed an enticing smile.

He looked offended. "Nay. I am married now and would not betray my wife."

She sat up, and bracing her hands behind her on the bed, thrust her chest out. "And what about me?" she said softly. "Have you forgotten your vow to me? That day I gave you my innocence? You promised to love me forever." She smiled again. "Now that I am free, we can be together at last."

She took his hand and tugged him. Unresisting, he sat down on the bed beside her.

"Lydia. I don't know what to say."

Pleased at his acquiescence, making her voice tremble, she said, "Tell me you feel the same. Tell me you still love me as much as I love you!"

Alex dropped his gaze and stared down at their joined hands on the bed. Lydia waited, her nerves strung taut in unbearable suspense. Would the man not just say it? How dare he make her stew and wait like a groveling supplicant?

But when he finally looked up, his eyes were not warm and burning with desire, they were grave and apologetic. He removed his hand from under hers. A vein began to throb dully behind her eyes even before he spoke.

"I'm sorry, Lydia. It grieves me to say this, but I do not love you. The time we had together was wonderful. But when I made that vow, I had no idea the path my life would take. We were so young, then, and many years have passed. We are different people now, and naught can change that I am married to Kat."

The dull throb became an annoying ache. "Nay. I do not believe you. You are denying our love because of *her*. She put you up to this. What kind of threat does she hold over you that you would break your vow to *me?*"

A small tear leaked from her eye and she wiped it away angrily. She never cried. Alex stood up and paced around the small confines to the shuttered windows. Then he swung back to her and stood at the foot of the bed.

His dark blue gaze steady, he took a deep breath. "You believe Kat has some sort of hold over me. And you are right." Not waiting for him to finish, Lydia rose off the bed and took several quick steps towards him with her arms outstretched.

He held up his hand to stop her. "You were right about Kat," he continued, his gaze full of pity. "But the only hold she has over me is the love in my heart. I'm sorry, Lydia. I say these things not to be unkind, but so you know that there can never be aught between you and me. In time, I beg you will forgive me for hurting you."

Lydia stood stunned, flabbergasted. Then the rage surged so fast and furious, she felt as though someone stabbed a dagger into her eye. Pain exploded and Lydia cried out. Closing her eyes, all the blood in her head surged to one spot and pounded through a single vessel behind her right eye. Alex caught her as she fell.

"Jesu. Lydia, what is wrong?" Alex said, his voice a distant buzz.

But Lydia remained silent, trying to endure the excruciating pain. The phenomenon was well known to her, but only a few times in her life had it come on so quickly and to such a degree. And she remembered them both very clearly. Her headaches had occurred during times of great distress and disappointment throughout her life. But the first time she felt one this bad was the summer she turned ten and two.

The day she lost her virginity, her innocence, her youth to her beloved Papa.

Lydia heard voices above her, Alex's and a high-pitched male voice, and then she was floating. The mattress enveloped her when Alex laid her on it. But her mind drifted back to the past as the physician examined her.

That had been the worst betrayal of all. She and her handsome father had been extremely close. When her mother died, Lydia and her father were devastated, their shared grief a bond that drew them even closer. It helped that Lydia was a tiny replica of her beauteous mother. Her father showered Lydia with affection and she adored him so much he could do no wrong in her eyes.

Then the changes came upon her; her hips widened, her breasts enlarged considerably and much sooner than other girls her age. That was when her father's embraces changed, became intimate and covert. His hand would caress her face too long, or accidentally brush against her breasts. Then when she did not resist, he grew bolder and cornered her in darkened passageways to caress her breasts and nipples, rubbing them until they tingled. His touches became increasingly more intimate, touching her between her legs, kissing her on the lips.

At first it felt good when he touched her; this was her handsome, adoring father, and surely what he did to her could not be wrong? But deep inside, she knew the truth and the shame mounted after each encounter. Still, he loved her, he called her his precious little girl, said she was a good girl for letting her Papa touch her. After nearly a year of this, one night he came to her bedchamber.

A noise woke her and she was afraid. Then she saw him and her terror began in earnest. He stared down at her unsteadily. Then he groped for the bed and tripped, landing beside her on the bed. He was *naked.* She recoiled at the large ugly snake extended straight out below his belly, but he was too strong. He grabbed her, crawled on top of her, and poked that thing inside her, ripping her apart. She screamed, begged him to stop, but he hushed her. He slurred his words, promising to hurry and calling her Lyla, his beloved. When it was over, he rolled off her and fell asleep like an exhausted puppy.

For the next two years the routine varied little. He came to her chamber smelling of stale ale, proceeded to rape her, called out his dead wife's name, and then promptly fell asleep beside her. Until she began taking lovers of her own. One night he came to her bed and found her fornicating with a strapping, handsome villein. 'Twas the first time he ever looked at her with shame.

She had been extremely hurt by it, but at the same time she had wanted to kill him for making her the way she was. But from that day forward she held all the control. She manipulated men to her advantage using carnal favors to get what she wanted. And none had ever denied her, except . . .

You have betrayed me for the last time, Alex, Lydia vowed. *If I cannot have you, I guarantee that she-witch never will. I shall destroy your marriage and deny you that which you desire most. And unlike you, I do not break my vows.*

Alex paced on the landing outside Lydia's chamber, waiting for news from the king's physician. It was silent in the darkened stairwell except for his footfalls. He thought back on that moment when she had cried out in pain and collapsed. He had knelt on the floor with her in his arms and brushed back her hair to stare aghast at her paler-than-death complexion. He called her name over and over, but she did not respond. Then the physician entered the room, his expression appalled and scandalized. But Alex had quickly explained what happened and left her to the man's examination.

It was his fault. Alex did not mean to hurt her, but there

was naught he could do to blunt the pain. He could not give her false hope and, therefore, had decided to be completely honest about his feelings.

Alex's eyes widened and he stopped pacing abruptly. In all the emotional turmoil, it just dawned on him that Lydia walked on her injured leg without any difficulty. How could that be, unless . . . ?

Alex dropped his head into his hands and groaned aloud. Lydia had faked her injury. She had manipulated the situation to get him alone. He could see things all too clearly now. And it made him wonder how many other times, in his youthful blindness, had she duped him?

Looking back, he remembered how besotted he had been with Lydia's beauty and sweetness from the moment they met. The attraction mutual, over the course of the summer they snuck away many times to kiss and fondle one another, though they never committed the ultimate act of love. Lydia was already betrothed to another and Alex was intended for Kat. Lydia wanted them to elope, but in the end she understood that he could not dishonor his family or Kat by breaking his informal betrothal.

Then the night before Lydia left court to go to her groom's home and marry, she came to his bed. She wanted Alex to make love to her, claimed she loved him and wanted him to be the one to whom she gifted her virginity. She was so sweet and shyly embarrassed by her request, he could not deny her. Besides, he was young and virile and wanted her desperately.

Now he hardly recognized himself in that naïve, idealistic youth. Afterward, Lydia had tearfully drawn from him an oath to love her forever. He remembered now he had been reluctant to make such a promise. He knew it would not change the fact that their love could never be. But at the time he truly believed Lydia was the only woman he would ever love, and he could deny her naught when she cried.

Of course, he now regretted making that vow. It allowed Lydia to cling to hope they would reunite one day and start anew as though the intervening years never occurred. But people changed, matured, grew wiser. His own experiences melded him into a stronger individual. So he could look back and see how, blinded by what he thought was love, he let Lydia influence him against his better judgment.

Lydia's chamber opened and the doctor stepped out, wiping his hands on a cloth. He was tall, gaunt, and stoop-shouldered, but his eyes were dark and penetrating.

Alex frowned with worry. "Will Lady Lydia be all right?"

The man's lips dipped down in consternation. "And who are you to the young lady?"

Alex raised an eyebrow. "A friend, concerned for her well-being."

The man nodded. "Well, then. You shall be glad to hear the lady has suffered no permanent damage. Her knee is sore and tender to the touch, but there is no swelling or bruising. And I have given her a potion for her headache. If she stays off her leg for a full day as I directed, by tomorrow she should be feeling better."

It was just as Alex suspected. The evidence from his own observation, along with the lack of any bruising or swelling proved Lydia had faked her knee injury. Although he would never know to what extremes she manipulated him in the past, her pain at his rejection had not been contrived. She truly cared for him and he regretted hurting her.

But a shield had been removed from his eyes and his heart was leading him in a different direction. 'Twas fated the day he escaped. When God gave him a second chance to seize his true destiny. Kat.

Alex found Kat, or rather heard her when he entered the queen's solar later that afternoon. Her full-throated laughter rang out over the chatter of the room's occupants, drawing him to a back corner of the room. Alex smiled at her exuberance.

Not shy was she, he thought. She exuded confidence. Kat appeared in a gap between several people who stood near her.

She wore a buttery yellow surcoate over a green tunic, and sat on a carved wooden bench, a chessboard before her. Her long black hair hung down her back and was held back by a gold circlet and white veil. A big grin on her face, she picked up her black knight and cried 'check' as she moved it into position. Alex could not see her partner, but masculine laughter rang out in response. The grating sound revealed the source. He jabbed his sword hilt against his side to keep from shoving people out of his way to reach Kat and beating Sir Luc senseless.

Then Alex saw him. The man's golden curls were perfectly groomed and brushed his broad shoulders. Sir Luc smiled at Kat in mock chagrin. "I do not know how you convinced me to play chess with you. I have never beaten you. Not once."

Kat smiled, her glance warm. "Don't feel so bad, Luc. 'Tis a rare man who can beat me at chess."

Alex bristled at the easy familiarity between them and rudely interrupted. "You were speaking of me, my love?"

Startled, Kat looked up. Her thick, elegantly arched brows dipped in disdain above her gray glare. "Pardon?"

"You said 'tis a rare man who can beat you. I agree and charge that I am your man to beat you . . . at chess. Care to wager on it?"

"Nay. Luc and I have not finished playing." She looked down at the chess pieces as though contemplating her next move.

Alex bent down and placed his hand on her right shoulder, then with his left hand he moved her knight to checkmate Luc's king. His lips brushed her ear as he whispered, "Your game is over."

Kat jerked away and pressed her back against the wall. "Aye, I agree. I am through playing games. You will pardon me if—"

Alex smiled, but his patience had elapsed. He would not argue with Kat in front of Sir Luc. Knowing she would be unwilling to cause a scene, he hooked his arm through hers and tugged her up from the bench. Sir Luc, straddling the opposite bench, rose up as though he intended to intervene.

Alex warned him with a fierce look. "Sir Luc, pardon us. I wish to speak with my *wife*. Alone."

After a short pause, his expression bleak, the knight bowed and returned to his seat.

Naught was private at court. Alex was aware all along of the interest of those near enough to hear their exchange. For that reason, he smiled and nodded at acquaintances as he led Kat sedately through the chamber and out the door past the guards. The moment they were alone in the corridor, her pleasant expression disappeared and she jerked her arm free.

Crossing her arms, she glared at him. The sconce's flames flickered over her high cheekbones and long, slender nose. And her gray eyes glowed silver. "I am going nowhere with you, Alex. State your business and be gone. I intend to return to the chamber anon."

"What I wish to discuss is not for public consumption."

"Well, I don't care what you want. I'm going back inside." She turned and reached for the latch, but Alex grabbed her arm and spun her around.

He held her pressed to his body and lowered his voice. "We have a bargain, you and I. Until that time elapses, you are bound to spend time in my company, at the time of my choosing, as long as it does not conflict with your duties to the queen. Now are you going to come with me willingly? Or must I resort to force?"

It was too much. The hurt rage Kat bottled up since Alex rode off with Lydia that afternoon exploded with frightening force. One instant Kat was held immobile against his powerful body, the next she drew her dagger from her boot and pressed the lethal blade against his belly.

Alex tensed and his blue eyes darkened the color of midnight. "What do you think you are doing?" he growled beneath his breath.

She pressed the dagger closer. "Release me. Now."

Alex swore low and long. "Have you lost your wits? What do you intend to do with that thing? Are you prepared to use it?"

Kat dug the blade into his tender flesh. "Aye. Care to test me?"

He did not respond, just glared down at her impotently.

"Now release my arm and back up, slowly." When he did, she said, "Turn around and put your hands behind your back."

Alex obeyed, though with a fierce scowl. "What are you going to do? Someone can come upon us at any moment."

"Since you are so fond of using your superior strength to get your way, I believe 'tis time you see how it feels to be powerless and at the mercy of another.

"Now, walk. No sudden moves, mind you."

"Where are we going?"

Kat kept a safe distance behind him, prepared should he decide to attack. "Oh, I merely wish to give you some time to contemplate the error of your ways. Mayhap next time you shall consider the consequences of your bullying."

She stared at the back of his head—the light from the hall sconces struck his black hair with blue sparks, enthralling her.

"Aye, consequences. Just be prepared. You shall have a few of your own to contend with after the doing of this deed. I shall see to it." His voice vibrated with lethal promise.

Kat shivered involuntarily. "Turn right, here. Slowly!" They turned down a narrow passageway rarely used by guests. At the end was a cupboard for the personal linens of the king and queen. As lady-in-waiting, Kat carried one of the keys to the small room on her girdle. Lady Lynette, who had the other key, would get quite a surprise when she opened it to retrieve sheets to make the royal beds later that evening.

"Stop. There is a door on the right." Kat pressed the dagger against his back. "Stick your face against the wall beside it." Kat retrieved her key with her left hand, unlocked the door and shoved it open. She backed up and ordered him inside.

But quicker than she could blink, he spun around and

grabbed her wrist in a hard grip. Fire shot through her wrist bone. She screamed and dropped the dagger. Spinning her so her back was to his chest, Alex covered her mouth with his other hand and dragged her into the cupboard.

She kicked and flailed about, her fist hit him in the head, and her foot connected with a knee. Alex cursed. He tried to imprison her arms, but desperation lent her powerful motivation; she wiggled about like an eel and slipped his net again and again. The momentum of her struggles slammed him into the shelves stocked with linens, which scattered to pile upon the floor.

"Damn it, you little spitfire. Cease fighting me and I will release you." Kat did not trust him and continued her struggles.

In answer, Alex shoved her down on the pile of linens, muffling her curses. Then he collapsed on top of her, a hot ridge of flesh prodding her hip. She lay there stunned and disbelieving, unable to move. How had he so handily turned the tables on her? So close to achieving her goal, she had not counted on becoming ensnared in her own trap.

Chapter 18

While Kat and Alex were occupied in the linen closet, another secret, more sinister conversation was taking place.

"I see you are making some progress," said the first of two men.

Luc shrugged at his companion's comment. "'Tis not a difficult task."

The first man laughed evilly. "Indeed. I, too, have made some progress in our endeavor. But, unlike me, you don't appear pleased with our success."

"I just . . . I am having doubts about my part in this affair."

"Why these sudden doubts?" the first man asked angrily. "Need I must remind you of what you will gain when our plan succeeds?"

"Nay, 'tis all I can think about," Luc said, impassioned.

"Then hold the course, and you shall have everything you desire."

"I know. I'm just weary of the enterprise."

The first man's face contorted swiftly, becoming ugly. "You are weary?" he spat, grabbing Luc's tunic, his face red, "You fool. I have waited and plotted for too long for you to back out now. This is only the beginning of my plans for revenge. Certes, and I will *not* let you destroy everything because you have suddenly found your conscience."

"Get your hands off me," Luc said and shoved the other away like a dirty peasant. Luc smoothed the wrinkles in his silk tunic. "I have no intention of backing out of the plan. But just do not expect me to take pleasure in what we do. I am doing this for her, and only for her—so we can be together at last."

Luc listened as the blond man spoke of revenge, disgusted by the vermin standing before him, but more so with himself. He had once been an honorable man. But his obsession with one woman had changed all that.

The cupboard was incredibly dark inside. Kat's senses became very acute as Alex's heavy weight pressed her into her bed of linens. His warm breath panted in her ear. The linen nap chapping her cheek, she inhaled his masculine scent of sandalwood and sweat.

"You are the most stubborn, wayward, hot-headed—"

"I thank you for the compliment. Now release me, you big ox."

"So now you wish to be cooperative?"

She shivered at the silken caress of his lips against her ear. "Nay. I want naught to do with you. Except for you to get off me. I cannot breathe."

She was astounded when Alex rolled off her and plopped down on his back beside her. Suspicious of his easy compliance, she turned over onto her back, cradling her throbbing wrist on her chest, and braced for some sort of trick. Though tender, her wrist was not injured and as moments passed she began to relax.

Alex shifted onto his side and with infinite gentleness he lifted her hand off her chest. The movement was not awkward, and she marveled at his unerring perception. She could not see her own hand in the dark. He kissed her sore wrist, surprising her. "Does it hurt too terribly? Forgive me, Kat. I did not mean to hurt you."

She was hot. A bead of sweat rolled down her temple and

their breaths intermingled. The dark created an intimacy that felt much too comfortable for Kat's peace of mind.

She pulled her hand free. "What *do* you intend, then?"

"Pardon?"

"What do you intend to do with me now? What new scheme have you devised to bend me to your will?"

Kat heard Alex shrug. "I merely want to speak with you."

"Nay. I do not trust your sudden change in attitude. I threatened you with a dagger and was going to lock you in the cupboard. 'Tis unlike you not to retaliate."

"Aye, 'tis true, but something you said changed my mind."

"It did?" she asked in a bewildered voice.

"You said you wished me to know 'how it feels to be powerless and at the mercy of another.' But I, of all people, understand how it feels to be powerless. My captors taught me that lesson most thoroughly. For that reason, I should have realized how my behavior made you feel. That I did not, shames me."

Kat grimaced as it finally sunk in what she had been about to do. Alex had suffered years of imprisonment and she had planned to lock him in a dark, confined space for several hours. No wonder he had struck her with such force. Since he kept his pain well hidden behind a stoic façade, she tended to forget the invisible scars he must carry around with him every day. She would never know to what extent his captivity had altered him.

Kat cleared her throat nervously. "Now I must apologize. I didn't think how my actions might cause you distress. You always appear so strong, I forget how much you must have suffered."

Though he did not respond, Alex exhaled a deep breath. Tension rippled across her flesh. His hand brushed hers at her side. Unnerved, she sat up to rise, but he caught her hand.

"Wait a moment, if you would. I wish to speak to you about a matter of utmost importance."

"Can it not wait until later? We should leave before someone discovers us in the linen cupboard. I need to dress for supper."

"Nay. It can't wait. I need to know what happened out there today on the hunt. 'Tis imperative you tell me your version of events."

Kat jerked her hand free and stood up, planting her hands on her hips. Alex rose, too. "Why? I need not defend my actions to you. Nor would it matter, you are too besotted with Lydia to ever believe she would deceive you."

"So you contend that she lied to me?"

"Aye . . . nay . . . what I mean is that I shall not defend myself to a man who believes me capable of malicious intent. How do you think it makes me feel knowing you believe Lydia can do no wrong, while you believe such of me? Give me one reason why I should trust you."

"I know I have given you no reason to trust me in the past, Kat, but I know you would harm no one unless provoked. Also, I believe Lydia lied to me. Long have I been blind, but now the veil has been lifted and I can see more clearly."

Although she did not see him move, whisper-soft fingers caressed her jaw. She sensed his overpowering presence in the light touch, his irregular breathing, his masculine scent that filled her nostrils. Kat tried to resist the growing attraction, but the compelling intimacy of the moment held her in thrall.

His coaxing voice reached out to her in the dark. "Will you not tell me the truth?"

Think of it as a test, she thought desperately. If he did not believe her, Kat would know once and for all whether Lydia still held Alex in her spell. But what if he did believe her? Free of Lydia's corrupting influence, might Alex come to love her someday?

Her decision made, she nodded and stepped back. Away from his disturbing touch.

"Kat?"

"During the hunt, I kept myself apart from the rest of the ladies. When we stopped at the clearing, Lydia approached me. She did strike up a conversation, but she immediately proceeded to insult me and I responded in kind." Kat colored, remembering her licentious boasts. "Lydia became incensed. When she spun her horse around to rejoin the ladies, she purposely snapped her reins against Lightning's muzzle. I believe she intended my mare to bolt or throw me, thus humiliating me in the process. But I was expecting her to retaliate, and easily brought Lightning under control."

"And that was when you pushed her."

"Aye. I was furious. I can withstand her insults, but no one harms my horse!"

Alex closed the gap between them. Kat bumped into the door behind her, stepping on something hard and flat.

He leaned down, his breath an airy caress. "My fierce lady warrior," Alex rasped, the words a compliment. Warmth unfurled inside her and spread its wings like a bird in flight. Her heart soared.

His warm, sensual lips covered hers, and her mouth parted without hesitation. Their tongues entwined, exploring one another with agonizing thoroughness. Kisses soft and coaxing one moment, fierce the next. Alex clutched her tighter, a ragged groan torn from his throat.

The brooch that closed the neck of her tunic must have fallen off, for his hand slipped through the opening. His fingers swept across the upper curve of her breast, teasing and taunting her. She melted against the door, her reservations forgotten in the heat of the moment.

Then his calloused hand cupped her breast. He squeezed the heavy weight, brushing his fingers over the distended tip. She moaned and arched up into his caress, pressing her enflamed nipple against his palm, craving relief. Alex groaned in satisfaction, his lips blazing a moist path down her bared throat—an offering freely given—then trailing lower still.

He raised her breast up to his seeking mouth, while his other hand clutched her rear and pressed her against his hot, hard member. Kat sucked in a deep breath, waiting in anticipation, feeling each beat of her heart as he came ever closer, until . . . hot breath bathed her erect bud.

Someone shoved on the door behind her.

Kat nearly gasped, but Alex covered her lips with his fingers. "Shh." He braced his hands on the door as it was jarred more forcefully. Angry grumbling came from outside, then retreating footsteps. Kat expelled her held breath.

They had come so close to being discovered in a linen cupboard. How humiliating that would have been. Kat stepped away from Alex. Her hand shook when she brushed back a stray wisp of hair that came free from her veil. She had nearly succumbed to passion, but no matter how thrilling Alex's lovemaking, she could not let herself get carried away.

But a part of her that wanted to love and be loved in return wondered: What if Alex truly regretted his abandonment of her years ago? What if he did love her and wished to be a devoted husband? Could she let go of her dream so easily?

"We should be away." Alex opened the door to peer out.

Light speared the interior of the room, illuminating the linens scattered across the floor. Amid them she found her brooch and pinned it to her bodice. When she turned to Alex at last, he held her dagger in his hand. Flipping it over, he handed it to her hilt first, his brow quirked in self-mockery. Her eyes wide, she took it and sheathed it inside her boot.

Alex held his hand out to her palm up, his blue gaze expectant. She hesitated for one moment, before she placed her hand in his. Then without a word they exited the linen strewn cupboard together.

After supper, Kat entered her apartments and made for the bedchamber, the glow from the fire lighting her way.

"Care to share a cup of claret with me before you retire?"

Kat turned to Alex, surprised. Usually she was long asleep before he retired to their chambers. He sat in the shadows at the table along the wall opposite the fire. A flagon of wine at his elbow, the chessboard was set up before him as though he had been playing someone.

Kat crossed her arms, one eyebrow raised. "What are you doing sitting in the dark, Alex? Surely you are not playing chess?"

Alex shrugged. His chest muscles flexed beneath the linen sherte he wore, the fabric straining with the movement. "To keep my mind occupied while in prison, I played chess against myself. I did not have the implements to do so and instead visualized the moves. So I am accustomed to playing in the dark."

That explained his unerring perception in the pitch-black cupboard earlier today. But Kat was disturbed by his glib reference to his horrific ordeal. His eyes held hers, dark and compelling.

Kat hesitated. She did not trust herself alone with Alex. The walls she had built around her heart were weakening, softening towards him, the pull of his magnetism a powerful force. But this was the perfect opportunity to learn more about his time in captivity. Every time she questioned him, he found a way to provoke her and avoid delving into his painful memories.

"What happened to you, Alex? In prison, I mean. You say you want to be a true husband. But you refuse to confide in me."

Alex shoved his chair back, the legs scraping loudly, and stood up. The shrill sound echoed in his ears like the cries of the tortured souls who had lived and died Saracen captives. His memories were painfully near the surface this eve; he feared what he would reveal.

But this time he could not ignore the hurt in her voice. "Why, Kat? Why is it so important for you to know what happened to me? Can you not leave well enough alone?"

Her eyes held naught but compassion. "I'm your wife. I need to know what happened to you, Alex. Your experience in prison is a part of you I know naught about. And mayhap in the telling, I can share your pain and ease the burden of your memories."

Choked with emotion, Alex could not speak at first. He had betrayed this woman in the most despicable way, but she still found it in her heart to try to comfort him and ease his pain. He was grateful God had given him this second chance. And prayed Kat would forgive him in time.

Clearing his throat, Alex began. She listened in grim silence while he told her of his attack and subsequent imprisonment. He left out any mention of Scarface. He told her how after he was released from the oubliette, he was one of many Christian slaves who by day drudged away hauling rock quarried from a defensive ditch around their prison fortress, and then at night were returned to their cells, until the next day dawned.

"In order to prevent an uprising or escape, we were not allowed to speak our own tongues. We could only speak the Kipchak language of the ruling Mamluks. And, of course, few could speak it. Still, when I first arrived, I tried to explain to the guards that I was a knight and could pay ransom. But all attempts were met with floggings.

"From dawn to dusk we carried the quarried building stones to various sites on the castle ward. There was always a wall to be repaired or a tower to be constructed. The work was relentless and grueling, and guards whipped any laborer who moved at a slack pace. Only the strongest survived the backbreaking toil and many just fell dead where they stood from heat and hunger."

He moved jerkily to stand before the fireplace and braced his clenched fist against the stone hood above. Images of dead men flashed across his vision as he stared into the flames.

His voice low, tortured, he continued. "Overworked and underfed, the men died slow and torturous deaths, while their bodies withered away leaving naught but bone and little flesh.

"Corpses were stripped naked and tossed one upon another in mass graves. The task carried out by prison burial details. No prisoner escaped this duty."

He looked down at his hands and rubbed them, trying to remove the stain of blood from the men he killed with his bare hands. "One day, another prisoner and I were burying two Frank prisoners in the village below the castle. My cellmate was gravely ill and the guard, Asad, kept swearing at him to pick up the pace." Alex shook his head as images of that day flashed before his eyes. "Finally, he fell down, too feeble to get up and Asad—" his voice broke with emotion. "Asad jumped off his horse, ran him through with his sword, and shoved him in the grave with the other prisoners. It happened so fast. I couldn't do anything, I couldn't—"

There was no escape for Alex—Richard's skeletal face, his sightless eyes stared up at him in reproach. Something brushed his shoulder. Alex shuddered, whirling around violently.

"Kat." She stood beside him, her wide-eyed gaze quickly shuttered. Alex exhaled. "I beg your pardon, you startled me."

He clutched his shaking hands behind his back.

Then Kat did something totally unexpected. She took a hesitant step, closing the gap between them, and slid her arms around his back.

Alex hesitated. Then he groaned and clutched her to him tightly. He buried his lips in her hair and breathed in her intoxicating jasmine scent. "Asad just laughed and ordered me to finish the burial. I didn't even think. I smashed my shovel in his laughing face, grabbed his sword and killed the other guard before he could react. With both guards dead, and less than thirty miles from the nearest port, I seized the chance to escape. Wearing the robe and turban I stripped from Asad, I stole their horses and intended to ride for the coast. But my legs were fettered, so I snuck into the shop of the village blacksmith and cut the chains free. When I reached the port of Tortosa, I caught a Venetian merchant ship bound for Cypress."

"I am so sorry," her voice rumbled against his chest. "It must have been horrible. I cannot begin to imagine the suffering you endured."

The heat of her breath penetrated his sherte, warming his heart. Amazingly, he did feel better for the telling. Her strength and caring flowed into him, making his heart soar. Surely she could hear it thumping a wild staccato. Her hands ran up and down his back and he squeezed her tighter—she felt so perfect in his arms.

He kissed the top of her head then leaned back a little. Placing his palms on either side of her face, he lifted her gaze up to his. His thumbs smoothed over her sculpted cheekbones, her golden skin tantalizingly soft. But it was her eyes, damp with unshed tears that held him spellbound.

"Prithee, do not fret on my account. 'Tis over now, and I am exactly where I wish to be. In your arms."

Crystal tears clung to her dark lashes. Unable to resist, he bent down and kissed her eyes, her nose and cheeks. "You are beautiful beyond belief, Kat. And I do not mean just your outer beauty. Your kind heart and selflessness move me."

Alex stared at his wife, trying to read the thoughts going through her head. She looked breathtakingly beautiful standing there, shy and uncertain and nervous as a new bride. His groin tightened; his skin tingled. How was he going to keep his hands off of her?

He needed her much more than she knew. He needed her spirit and her laughter and her compassion, the way she savored every experience to the fullest. But more importantly, once given, her love would at last bring him the peace he sought.

Kat stepped back and patted her tunic skirts. Then she shocked him completely when she grabbed the bottom of her skirts, pulled them up her long legs, over her chest and off her head. Next, she pulled the jeweled snood out of her hair. Shaking her head, the black shimmering mass fell wildly about her shoulders. Just as boldly, she removed the last barrier, her chemise, and stood proudly naked before him except for her hose and slippers.

"Kat?"

"Hush. Do not say a word," her throaty voice demanded of him.

Alex gazed at Kat in amazement. She was absolutely beautiful, with her hair slightly mussed, her silvery eyes feral and her cheeks flushed with desire. He reached out to her, but she shook her head, biting her plump lower lip. Christ, she was starting to get skittish and was about to bolt.

Before he could think of something to say to change her mind, she turned and entered the bedchamber. Holding the velvet curtain in her hand, she looked back at him, her gaze hot. "Are you coming?" The curtain dropped behind her, swishing like the sway of her deliciously dimpled derriere.

He was so *coming.*

Chapter 19

Alex strode into the bedchamber, his gaze unerringly finding Kat at the foot of the huge canopy bed in the middle of the room. It was dark, but the brazier's lit coals illuminated her shapely body with a shimmer of gold. His heart skipped a beat and then began beating double time.

Grabbing her hand, he pulled her into his embrace and kissed her, his mouth hard and demanding. She clung to his arms and returned the kiss, shoving her tongue against his as he probed deep into her mouth. The melting kiss went on and on. Until she tore herself from his arms and stepped back. The back of her knees hit the bed.

God, what a woman she is. Alex savored the tall, svelte beauty of his wife's stunning body. No longer the slender, budding virgin he took to bed on their wedding night, Kat was full-breasted. Her amazing height showing to advantage her perfectly proportioned breasts, narrow waist, lovely rounded hips, and long legs.

He ran his gaze up her legs now, admiring her firm thighs, from riding no doubt, then higher to stare at the lush black curls guarding her entry. Alex groaned. Blood surged hard and fast to his groin, making his erection ache. It thrust upward against his stomach and grazed his navel beneath his linen braies, seeking freedom.

Her eyes aglow, Kat dropped to her knees, shoved up his shirt, and began unlacing the points of his hose. Her fingers were quick and nimble at her task. His shirt clung irritatingly to his sensitized skin. Alex hurriedly tugged it over his head and tossed it on the floor just as she drew his braies and hose down.

His shaft sprang free and Kat licked her lips. Half groan, half growl escaped him. Her hot breath wafted across his stomach, nearly driving him to his knees. But he continued to stand and stepped out of his undergarments with her assistance.

When he would have reached down to help her up, she shook her head again. "Just look. Feel," she said, her voice low and seductive.

She proceeded to wrap her hand around his thick flesh and explore the length of him, squeezing and then releasing him. He inhaled sharply at the unbearable pleasure. Soon she added her other hand, searching between his legs, shaping and rubbing his ballocks. His flesh tightened in ecstasy at her dual caress, untutored though it was.

Eyes closed, he was wondering how much longer he could control himself when her wet tongue stroked his length. His cock jerked. He opened his eyes and watched as she licked the drop of moisture that seeped from the tip.

Groaning, he clutched her hair and tipped her face up to him. "Kat, what are you doing? You don't have to do this."

"I'm tasting you as you did me. Do you not like it?"

"Of course. I am a man, am I not?"

She laughed, the seductive sound shooting straight to his heart and lower still. "Then why are you complaining?"

Not waiting for his reply, she dipped her head and this time took him completely inside her hot mouth. "Oh God," he cried out. Why *was* he complaining? Alex gave over to the sensation, guiding her in her endeavors, showing her how he liked it, while he held firmly onto whatever command of himself he retained.

Kat reveled in her newfound daring; for once she was in

control. Experimenting, she used her tongue and lips and teeth, alternately licking and sucking his member. She must be doing it aright, for clutching her shoulders, he began arching into her mouth, probing deeper, his excited groans filling the cool room.

But Alex was not the only one aroused. She dug her fingers into his firm flanks, marveling at the wicked feel of his erect flesh in her mouth, her own essence slicking her entry, ready for his possession. As though he read her thoughts, Alex pulled away abruptly and tugged her to her feet. His eyes burning into hers, he lifted her behind her thighs and spread them as he laid her down on the bed. Thrilled at his loss of restraint, Kat hooked her arms around his shoulders and wrapped her legs around his waist. Her moist center throbbing, she pressed against his upthrust shaft.

Obliging her, Alex drove inside with one quick thrust. Kat cried out in pain and ecstasy and wonderment.

Alex stilled. "Christ, Kat, did I hurt you?"

"Nay." Her joy at the feel of him inside her overrode any discomfort. To prove she was all right, she wiggled her hips, moaning at the exquisite feel of him inside her.

Alex groaned. "Oh God, Kat, you feel incredible," he said, staring into her eyes. His admission embarrassed her and she closed her eyes. "Look at me, Kat. I want you to feel you can say or do aught that gives you pleasure when we are private. I want no deception between us."

Kat raised her gaze to his and held it. "Aye, you are right." Then she smiled boldly, unwilling to give him the edge. "So what are you waiting for?"

What am *I waiting for?*

Alex returned her smile and pulled out of her slowly to the very tip, then plunged in deep. Kat cried out, wide-eyed. Her heat scorched him, squeezed him to the point of pain. She dropped her hands to the mattress and clutched the bedclothes beside her hips.

Their bodies joined, her hips draped on the edge of the

bed, Alex stood up over her. He stared at the beautiful wanton sprawled on the bed smiling seductively up at him, their black groin hair merging as one where he was buried to the hilt.

Then he unclasped her legs from his waist and hooked them over his shoulders. Impossibly, he slid in deeper. She moaned softly, mingling with his ragged groan. Clutching her hips for purchase, he lunged into her quivering flesh again. He began a slow cadence, but with his pleasure too long delayed, her hot depths pulling him back in, he soon forgot finesse. Driving into her again and again, he spiraled out of control, releasing the wildness that had been building up with each carnal encounter.

He was afraid his savagery might scare her, but she went wild, raising her hips clear off the bed to meet each of his downward strokes, their flesh slapping like waves upon the shore. It was as if the tide had at last been released and there was no stopping it ever again; the untamed, primitive rhythm of their coupling was more exciting than any practiced seduction.

He tried to wait for her before he took his own pleasure, but her panting moans and erotic cries drove him over the edge.

"Look at me, Kat."

She opened her eyes, their glittering silver hue glazed with excitement. He held them captive, pumping uncontrollably inside her. Then her tight passage squeezed him like a fist, unmanning him. His seed surged into his cock, his flesh aching and tingling with the fullness. "Come with me, Kat. Now!"

He shouted out as his essence exploded inside her. Simultaneously, her honey-drenched muscles contracted tightly around his shaft again and again, drawing out his pleasure. He watched her eyes widen, elated to hear her excited cries mingle with his groans of satisfaction.

"Oh God, oh God," Kat cried out as her flesh throbbed and her honey flowed, the little contractions inside her milking his seed into her womb. She felt its hot spurt, while enticing ripples of pleasure seared her flesh. Then his jerking movements subsided and he collapsed on top of her.

Smiling in satisfaction, her heartbeat slowly returning to normal, Kat dropped her hands to his sweaty buttocks and caressed him, enjoying the supple, muscular flesh. Alex's lips clung to hers in benediction as he skimmed his hand down her side slowly, brushing her outer breast. Then he rolled off her, his relaxed shaft slipping free, and turned onto his side so they were face to face. He grasped her right hand in his and weaved his fingers through hers.

She raised her eyes to his. The black of his pupils nearly engulfed his eyes, leaving only a narrow ring of blue.

He smiled, pleased. "That was amazing, Kat."

She swallowed, pleased at his compliment, but . . .

"Just because we—"

Tenderly, he brushed a strand of her hair from her cheek. "I know."

"And it does not mean I have—"

"Of course, I would never assume aught of you."

Hope? Aye. Assume? Never.

She continued. "It just means I have certain needs. That I indulged them, you should not infer I wish to reconcile with you. I need more time."

Certain needs? Alex wondered if she had no more feeling for him than an eager mare for a willing stallion.

Certain needs? Kat wondered where that idea sprang from and then decided to brave it out. "So long as you understand that, we may continue as we are."

"As we are?" he growled. "I take that to mean we shall continue satisfying our mutual needs together, till such time as our bargain is fulfilled."

"Aye, you understand it aright." She frowned, unsure whether he was angry or aroused.

I just hope I have not made a huge tactical error, she thought.

Alex rolled over on top of her and spread her thighs, his gaze feral, dominant, ruthless.

Kat gasped in surprise. "What are you doing?" she squeaked

out. "Oh my." Such inadequate words for such an impressive specimen of maleness, for Alex was hard again.

"Indeed, my needs are great. And I don't intend to waste a moment of the time remaining to us."

With one exquisite stroke, he drove inside her. Kat cried out, the pleasure intense. It was as if a great dam burst inside her and her passion, released after a long dormant winter, could no longer be checked. He kissed her, their hips moving in a wild frenzy, their panting breaths filling their cozy bower in the curtained bed. Their hearts one beat.

When the explosion came it was swift, merciless, shaking Kat to the core. But her last thought as she drifted off to sleep was how wonderful she felt wrapped in Alex's strong arms.

Alex woke the following morning feeling content for the first time in a very long while. He lay in a clean sweet-smelling, soft feather mattress as rosy light shimmered through an opening in the bed curtains. But his contentment stemmed from Kat. Soft and warm, she snuggled up against his backside. When she pressed her lips to a thick scar on the back of his shoulder, he stiffened and turned to face her.

"You need not be exposed to such ugliness."

Her gaze softened with tenderness. "Your scars, like your memories, are a part of you, Alex. I don't want you to keep any part of you hidden from me."

She smiled and rolled on top of him. Her hair cascaded over him as she bent down and kissed his nipple below the round puckered scar on his shoulder. He groaned, even as guilt reared once again.

"If I am to commit to our marriage, there can be no lies between us, nor deception. I want an open and honest relationship, where you can tell me anything."

Her smile turned wicked and she reached around behind her and grabbed his cock. Squeezing him gently, she slid her hand up and down his shaft in a languid motion. Heat exploded, he grew erect. A deep moan escaped him and he surged up into her hand with a sharp thrust.

Kat released him and shimmied down his body. She spread his thighs, knelt between them, and then skimmed her fingernails down his chest, over his stomach and into the curls at his groin. Teasing him, she combed through the curls and tugged. Her eyes glittered, and she clasped his cock in her hand. Hot breath seared his flesh. Then she licked the scar that sliced down through his groin hair. His body shuddered.

Suddenly, she raised her gaze and held his, all teasing gone. "So now is the time to tell me. Is there anything else you need to confess about your disappearance, or aught else?"

Alex swore, blocking out the guilt that roiled inside him. Naught had changed—a dangerous traitor sought his death. And the stakes were even higher now. The man had threatened Kat. If Kat were to learn the truth, she would not rest until the traitor was caught.

His gut clenched. He would die if anything happened to his brave, beautiful wife. So he drowned out his nagging conscience the only way he knew how. Alex tugged Kat up into his arms, rolled on top of her, and then wedged his hips between her spread thighs.

His bulbous head nudged her entrance. She was wet, creamy.

"Nay. There is naught else to tell you." He closed his eyes and kissed her, a hard, desperate kiss, even as he drew back and thrust inside her tight sheath. A moan of ecstasy burst from his lips, mingling with her soft cry of pleasure. Alex pumped inside her, frenzied, until her damp inner-muscles squeezed his cock dry, their cries ricocheting inside their sultry curtained bower.

A sennight later, the atmosphere of the riders on the busy thoroughfare was jovial as they traveled to a village west of Westminster to go to the market faire. Except for Rand and

Alex, who rode behind Kat and Rose. They spoke in hushed tones, the ladies blissfully ignorant of what they discussed.

Reluctantly drawing his gaze away from his wife, Alex looked over at Rand. The not unpleasant cacophony of the jingle of tack, the beat of horses' hooves, the hum of conversation and the creak of wooden wheels on packed dirt ensured their voices could not be overheard.

"I spoke with King Edward. His trap has snared Scarface. One of the king's scouts sent word that Scarface is in route to England as we speak. That means Scarface is unaware I am alive or he'd be suspicious."

Rand watched Alex, troubled. "On what pretense did Edward lure him to England?"

"He believes the king needs his services, a special mission that requires his unique skills and utmost secrecy." His smile twisted into a parody of a grin. "But when he arrives on our shores, he shall be sorely surprised when the king's men clap him in irons and escort him to the Tower instead. It shall not be long now before Scarface names the man who hired him."

"When shall he arrive?" Rand asked, his concern for Alex growing. The hate distorting his friend's handsome face was something to behold. Although a renowned knight, Alex had never taken any joy in killing as long as Rand had known him. Alex saw it as his sacred duty to God and king. But Rand hardly recognized the hate-filled man beside him.

"He should arrive in a sennight, mayhap more," Alex said.

Then, as though the conversation never occurred, Alex swung his gaze to Rand's, eyes shining with expectancy. "Well, my friend, shall we catch up with our ladies?" He laughed, deep and rich. "It would seem in their excitement they have pulled ahead of us." Alex spurred his horse forward.

Rand smiled and followed after him, his fear for Alex concealed as he pondered the swift mercurial change he witnessed. The sudden switch from stark malice to undiluted happiness was disturbing, not only because it was so uncharacteristic, but also that it was so easily done. Alex repressed the hate as though it did not exist and Rand wondered where he buried the debilitating emotion.

Rand knew from personal experience how hate could warp and fester body and soul, like poison. And that animosity eventually spilled over to harm others around you as well.

Rand's father had bitterly resented his marriage to his second wife. Rand's mother had descended from Plantagenet royalty, albeit the illegitimate side. And even though she came with a rich dowry that amply filled the depleted coffers of the Montague estates, Rand's father was an overly vain, proud man who thought Lady Claire socially inferior to him. But at old Lord Montague's insistence, he married her. After years of ridicule from his peers, his father's resentment turned to hatred. And when Rand and his younger twin sister had been born, his hatred found a new target.

Rand vowed never to allow his father's antipathy to infect him. For hate in its extreme personified evil, and if it was not released, one day it would rise up and consume you. He prayed Alex learned that lessen sooner rather than later. Before his rancor became more important than aught else, even his love for Kat.

Chapter 20

From atop her horse, Kat gazed at the colorful tents, waving flags, and faire stalls on the village green in the center of the market town. The gaiety of the crowds was a contagion one did not wish to stave off. Alex grasped her waist and lifted her off Lightning. Their bodies touched—breasts, loins, and thighs—as he slid her to the ground. She felt every nuance, his heat and hardness, her blood pounding thick and sluggish.

Since the night they made love, her relationship with Alex had taken an odd turn. In public, they were civil and circumspect in their behavior, making sure not to engage in any expression of physical intimacy. Then, in the darkest hours of the night, he slipped into their bed and into her body, rousing her from sleep. No carnal act was forbidden as he tutored her in pleasure, their illicit couplings thoroughly wicked, yet wildly exciting.

Now her body craved constant stimulation. Craved pleasure, the kind only Alex could give her.

"What would you like to do first?" his voice rumbled low, erotic. She barely noticed when a young boy led their horses away.

"Huh?"

He smiled, wolfish, as though he wished to devour her. "The faire awaits, madam. What is your desire? Hungry? Or shall we start with the amusements? Or is it more to your pleasure to visit the merchant stalls?"

A vein beat at the pulse of her throat, her voice thick as she spoke. "I *am* hungry, but should we not ask Rand and Rose, first?" Kat glanced around, but saw no sign of them.

"Gone. It would seem they have left us to our own devices. Come. I, too, hunger and yonder is a baker's stall." Hooking his left arm through hers, he led her to the field not fifty yards away, where a smiling, corpulent man wearing a flour-covered apron stood behind his stall.

When it was their turn, they bought a feast for two and found a crab apple tree a goodly distance away from the crowd. Alex settled her there beneath its spreading canopy of pale pink flowers before going to another stall that sold ale. Kat leaned back against the tree trunk and impatient as usual, sank her teeth into hot bread glazed with honey. The flavor of yeast, honey, and almonds exploded in her mouth. Honey dribbled over her fingers and she licked them one by one.

Bold, unhesitant footsteps approached. She looked up and found Alex staring, his gaze riveted on her lips and sticky fingers. His eyes sizzled, reminding her of when he pleasured her and her own honeyed essence coated his fingers and mouth. A low, dull throb pounded through her veins and spread downward to exquisitely sensitive areas.

Slowly, his smile turned rueful and his eyes filled with laughter. "I see you could not wait until I returned to start eating. *Again*. At least you have not disposed of my portion this time," he teased. "I believe we are making progress." Alex handed her a wooden mug of ale, sat down beside her, and propped his left arm on his bent knee.

"Just do not make me angry and your food supply will be safe," Kat teased, falling into the easy camaraderie.

"Why not? I must admit I enjoy riling you. With your flashing silver eyes and flushed cheeks glowing," he raised his hand to her face and trailed his fingers down the curve of her cheek and jaw, "all that passion raised to the surface, you are beautiful beyond words." His thumb joined the caress, smoothing over her full bottom lip.

The surface of her skin throbbed where his fingers traced. Kat bit her lip and turned her head to stare at the crowds moving among the tents and stalls. At a striped red and green tent, a group of boys laughed and teased their friends as they played a game tossing rings over wooden stakes.

Alex handed her a hot pie. "Here, Kat. Eat up. We have a lot of ground to cover if we wish to see all the faire has to offer."

Kat tucked into her food with relish, a combination of hunger and excitement over partaking in the faire's amusements. They ate in silence. Besides a beef pie and honey bread, she consumed half the loaf of bread, an apple-filled pastry, and another filled with jam, and then washed it all down with ale. Full and replete, Kat leaned back against the rough bark of the tree with a loud sigh.

Alex laughed and leaned forward, blocking the sun from her face while the petals fluttered in the tree above them. She stilled, her breath leaving her as he neared. Suddenly, his smile sobered and using his thumb, he wiped the corner of her lip. "You missed something," his voice roughened. Then, without releasing her gaze, he sucked his thumb between his lips. His eyes darkened to molten midnight. "Hmm . . . raspberry."

Kat's heart dropped at the sensual gesture. Entranced by his wicked smile, she did not realize that same hand trailed up her leg and under her skirt, until he brushed bare skin above her garter.

Kat pulled back in shock but to no avail; the tree behind her prevented escape while Alex loosely clasped her leg. He skimmed his hand along her inner thigh, bold fingers feathering over the sensitive surface. She gasped. "You are mad, Alex. Remove your hand. We are in public where all and sundry may observe us."

She turned her head sharply and gazed out over the crowd, fear of discovery mingling with excitement. It sparked along her skin, ratcheting the tension as she searched faces, praying none looked their way. Still, his hand rode higher, a finger's breadth from her moist heat. Her chest rose and fell in agitation.

"Have no fear. You are situated such, with the tree guarding you on one side and my body shielding you on the other, that none can see what I do."

She returned her gaze to Alex. "'Tis not the point. What you do is indecent. Should only be shared in the privacy of our chambers. Not in bold daylight, in the middle of a field. Before an audience of strangers!"

"Tell me you don't like it and I shall stop."

His thumb, gloriously wet from his mouth, surged up inside her, deep, penetrating. "Ahh . . ." the moan escaped her. Biting her lip, she glared at him. "You do not play fair."

He smiled with wicked knowledge. "You do not want me to play fair, darling. You revel in wickedness as much as I." Demonstrating, he rotated his thumb inside her. Kat bit back a groan and he smiled in satisfaction. "So why not just sit back, relax, and enjoy it."

Relax? Now she knew he was mad. Without preamble, he withdrew his thumb and ran it down her slick channel. His thumb smoothed back up her swollen folds, then flicked and massaged the gem nestled at the top. The flesh filled with blood, throbbing, and her stomach quivered. Desire slicked her thighs. All the while Alex held her gaze. Blue embers sparked in his eyes, conveying his pleasure at her physical response and his own painful excitement.

His fingers plunged inside her, setting up a bold rhythm, flaying her senses, heating her blood. She held her breath, trying to appear as if naught more stimulating than conversation enthralled her. But a trickle of sweat rolled down her cleavage, her skin flushed with desire, and her heart beat like a drum against her chest.

Her left hand lay in her lap, her fingers curled as though to hold onto her sanity. The empty cup fell from her other hand and rolled over. In the distance the sounds of children laughing, a crowd applauding, faded as she fell into a carnal void where only pleasure existed.

Kat gasped.

She felt it coming, the tang of ale on her tongue. Kat clutched a clump of grass to keep her hips from surging up into his marauding fingers.

Felt the mad rush of desire. To reach the summit. Plunge over into the dark abyss.

It was coming. Aye. Just a little closer it neared.

Higher.

Higher. Breathing. Faster.

Higher.

Panting, unable to catch breath. It was there. The edge.

Coming.

Closer. Higher.

Fingers deeper.

Coming. The edge.

Oh God. Help me.

Her inner muscles contracted, and she soared over the abyss. Bucking into his hand, shoving his fingers deeper.

With her eyes open, she stared into his midnight depths. A swift gush of desire drenched his hand and her thighs, feminine muscles quivering, shaking, weeping. Spent.

Kat slumped against the tree, dazed. A pale pink petal drifted down and landed in her lap.

"God, you are amazing, Kat." Alex's eyes burned with unfulfilled desire, but with exquisite gentleness, he wiped the corner of her eye with his finger.

She blinked, realizing a tear fell. The sounds of the faire returned in a loud crescendo, like a sudden call to battle, destroying their pleasurable idyll. Kat reddened, cursing her waywardness and lapse of control. She did not like the power Alex had over her body.

Sitting up, back stiff, she brushed out her skirts, refusing to look at him. She was afraid that when the time came to make the right choice, lust would win out. But she would not let it. She needed to keep reminding herself passion faded. What really mattered was who would make the best husband and father of her future children.

"Kat?"

He shifted beside her then cupped her jaw, forcing her to meet his intense blue gaze. "I didn't intend for that to happen. But I am not sorry. I will *not* apologize for an honest expression of my love for you. You were just sitting there, looking so lovely, a smear of fruit on your delectable lips and I," Alex shrugged, ". . . I could not help myself."

Love. Kat stared, trying to probe his gaze, sure she heard wrong. Then Alex looked away and the moment was gone. Smiling, he helped her to her feet and hooked his arm through hers. "I promised you a day of amusement, my lady. And I always keep my promises. So, what would you like to do first? Your pleasure awaits."

For the first time, Kat felt on more stable ground, for Alex had made a most revealing comment. To a man, love was often confused with desire, but, more importantly, Alex also said, "I could not help myself." So, obviously, he too lacked control over his desire for her.

Could it be Alex was coming to love her? If so, she must do whatever it took to protect her heart. Aye. She would never make the mistake of falling in love with Alex ever again. The pain was just too unbearable. But that did not mean he could not fall in love with her.

Alex took great pleasure watching Kat as they browsed the merchant stalls. She was attracted to bold, vivid colors and touched everything. They stood now at a silk merchant's stall, and as if he was not hard enough, Alex watched as she ran her hand over rich silks, brocades and velvets. Glad he was that the day was still cool and his mantle covered his embarrassment.

He was also glad Kat had missed his little slip earlier. He was not yet ready to reveal to Kat that he was in love with her.

For one thing, she still did not trust him and would not believe him, and another was that it would be disastrous if he confessed he loved her and then learned she could never return his love. It was a weakness he did not want exposed and he despised weakness. He had to be strong; never again would he be at the mercy of another, stripped of dignity and honor and pride.

Slinging his arm around Kat, he guided her towards the sound of a rowdy crowd a short distance away from the tents. People hovered closely together to view some spectacle, making it impossible for him to see what the attraction was. However, Alex heard the shouts and cheers as bets were called out on the outcome of some sport. "What do you suppose is going on over there?" he wondered aloud.

Kat glanced up at him and grinned, excited, a curious light igniting her eyes. "I was wondering the same thing. Shall we find out?"

By mutual accord they shoved their way to the front of the crowd, but before they made it the sounds of growling mastiffs reached Alex's ears. He cursed under his breath. Although his view was still blocked, he was sure now of what *sport* drew the crowd. Kat's shoulders stiffened beneath his arm, and he realized she, too, understood the significance of the dogs. But it was too late to turn back as the crowd closed in and they were propelled forward.

Jostled, Alex tightened his hold on Kat and elbowed aside the stocky man who swayed drunkenly against him. The man grumbled and glared up at him. Alex was surprised to discover it was Lord Calvert, his face twisted in hatred. Alex placed his hand on his sword, holding the man's stare until the oaf stumbled away, cursing.

No sooner had he left than the space opened up in front of Alex, revealing the underground stone foundations of a long abandoned round tower. It held a huge brown bear, its hind leg tied to a stake in the center of the makeshift bear pit. Wounds covered the bear's face and body—gashes, new ones red and open and raw, along with older, healed wounds. And one of his ears was missing.

Kat gasped, the sound quickly drowned out amidst the shouts of bettors calling for the death or victory of the bear. Off to the side, two men conversed near a set of steps dug into the earth. The steps led down to a locked door and entrance of the bear pit. Wearing a green felt hat, the younger man held the leashes of three large mastiffs. He nodded at the older man, the ward of the bear, who turned and walked down the steps.

Kat looked up at Alex, tears of anger in her eyes. "That poor bear. Tied to a stake and set upon by mastiffs trained to go for the bear's throat and kill him. Bear baiting! 'Tis such a cruel sport, I despise it."

While Kat had been speaking, the bear ward unlocked the door.

The mastiffs and bear were both trained to kill. Bears were brutally mistreated, specifically to make them extremely vicious and, therefore, more entertaining to watch.

Grim, Alex nodded. "Aye, there is naught sporting in pitting two courageous animals against one another for entertainment. Come, let us go, there is an opening over here."

The dogs were released and their excited barks filled the air. The crowd roared its approval, shouting out encouragement to their chosen victor as though the animals could understand. Pulling Kat close against his chest, Alex used his free hand to clear a path. Angry shouts followed him, but died away as the disgruntled spectators quickly turned back, unwilling to miss the fight.

The bear roared, and in morbid fascination, Alex looked back. He watched as a huge paw swiped out, flaying the lead mastiff aside. The other dogs were on the bear the next moment and Alex turned away, unable to watch the senseless carnage.

He led Kat away as more people hastened past them and headed for the bear pit, anxious not to miss the bloody sport. Among them a group of boys, young pages from the palace, darted past, whooping and hollering. One of them waved, a pleasant-faced boy with black hair.

"Good day, Lady Katherine, Sir Alex," he cried out.

"'Tis young Matthew of Oxford," Kat said, startled.

"Aye, so it is." Alex led Kat off the straw-covered pathway and into the shade between a small patched tent and colorful stall. Once hidden in the shadows, he placed his hands on her waist in a loose embrace.

She looked up at him, her hands on his chest, eyes haunted. "'Tis shameful to treat animals so cruelly. We should do something for that poor creature."

"I agree. Unfortunately, there is not much we can do. The bear is too dangerous to release, now that he has been indoctrinated by mistreatment and violence. The only other choice is to liberate him from his owner and keep him caged, though treated kindly. But even then another bear would just take its place because of the great demand for such sport."

"Such brutal sports should be outlawed, then," she said, incensed.

Tenderhearted was his warrior woman, the paradox an irresistible puzzle he wished to unravel.

Her almond-shaped eyes were large and wide. Alex stared into their quicksilver depths, drowning, unable to resist her pull. "Aye, but I am afraid that will never happen," he said slowly. She must have read his desire, for she inhaled swiftly a heartbeat before he dipped his head.

He stroked his thumb over her lower lip, coaxing her lips apart, and then he closed his mouth over hers. She raked her fingers slowly up his chest and locked them behind his neck. Her tongue met his and he groaned, her fingers tangling in his hair, drawing him deeper into the kiss. She pressed her hips into him, and his erection, which had finally abated, surged up to prod her shadowed delta.

Jesu, she knew how to drive him insane. He wanted to throw her down right here on the grass and drive inside her hot sheath. Or take her from behind standing up. He would not stop until he exploded, spilling his seed deep inside her fertile depths.

He wanted to make her mad with desire, too. Drive her to the brink over and over till she begged him for release. Bind her to him forever so she would never look to another to fulfill her needs. He alone would give her children, hearth, and board.

"Uhhrum." Someone clearing his throat startled Alex.

Kat jerked away, her face turning pink. But Alex kept his arm around her waist.

Rand, who stood next to Rose, grinned at them from ear to ear while Rose's wide-eyed blue gaze darted away in embarrassment.

"Cousin," Rand said, nodding to Kat, his solemn tone at odds with his laughing hazel eyes.

"Don't 'Cousin' me, you fool. Have you never seen a man kissing a woman before?" Kat flounced away from Alex and hooked her arm through Rose's.

"Come, Rose. I saw a fortuneteller back by the baker's stall and have a mind to see what my future holds."

Arm and arm, they strode off.

"Kat, don't get too far ahead," Alex hollered. "I don't want to lose you in this crowd."

Kat waved nonchalantly and continued on.

Chapter 21

Alex and Rand followed in the ladies' wake. Casually glancing at the various stalls and fairegoers as though unconcerned, Alex kept his gaze on Kat up ahead.

Although there had been no trouble since the arrow attack, he was constantly on guard and would be until the villain was caught. Indeed, a part of him had been consciously alert to his surroundings all day, except during the passionate interlude with Kat under the tree. He groaned. And the kiss by the tents.

The woman was fast becoming a temptation he could not resist. But resist her he would. Until the traitor was apprehended, the need to be vigilant was imperative, or the consequences could be deadly.

For a moment Alex lost sight of Kat when several people crowded past him. Then her distinctive black-haired head bobbed into view. He breathed a sigh of relief and quickened his pace. But his relief was short-lived. Suddenly, when another pathway merged into his, a group of tri-color-dressed dancers burst onto the pathway. They weaved in and out among the spectators, urging them to participate. The young couple walking in front of Alex was swiftly pulled into the dance and spun around and around.

Meanwhile, Kat drew farther away. Alex panicked, sweat broke out on his forehead and he began to push his way through the revelers. Then some woman grabbed his hand and tugged him into the dance, down the wrong pathway.

Alex twisted his head around. When his gaze met Rand's, Alex shouted, "Follow Kat. Don't lose her!" Rand nodded and continued on.

Alex ripped free of the hold, but he had been dragged ten feet down the path and had to backtrack. At the intersection, he relaxed upon seeing Rose and Rand heading towards him. His gaze moved beyond them, seeking Kat, when Rose's insistent voice drew his attention back to her.

"Alex. I'm sorry. I got separated from Kat in the crowd somehow. And she's not at the fortuneteller's tent."

Alex grabbed her arm and shook her. "How could you lose her?"

Rose winced with pain. "Ouch! You're hurting me, Alex."

Rand immediately came to her defense and clamped his hand down on Alex's arm. "Let go of her arm, Alex. This is not helping the situation."

But Alex was not thinking very clearly and gripped her harder in his fear.

All of a sudden, a woman's terrified scream rose above the noise of the crowd. It came from the direction of the bear pit; a chill premonition shimmied down his spine. He released his sister and took off running.

He ran faster than he had ever run in his life, terror clawing his stomach at what he would find when he reached the bear pit. His heart pumped wildly. He hollered for people to get out of his way, shoving them aside in his haste, knocking anyone over who did not move fast enough. When he reached the bear pit, he saw several others who had rushed to the clearing pointing with cries of shock and disbelief, their fear palpable.

Alex's heart clawed up his throat, he could not breathe. An image, a vision, flashed in his head, of Kat lying in a pool of her own blood, her flesh gored by huge bloody claw marks.

Nay, he refused to believe Kat was hurt, or dead; he would not let fear consume him. He charged into the growing crowd.

The huge lump in his throat suddenly dropped to his stomach. Kat was not hurt, but she had crawled out onto one of the pikes driven into the earth over the pit. The pikes were embedded every five feet, meeting in the center like slices of a pie, acting as a makeshift roof.

It was a courageous, though foolhardy, risk she took. For young Matthew had crawled out onto one of the spikes, and hanging by two hands into the pit, was dangerously within reach of the bear chained to the tall stake in the center. While the animal growled and pawed ineffectually at the young intruder, Kat hugged the spike and reached out to Matthew. She hollered for him to grab her hand, but the lad was too terrified to let go and reach out.

Kat was persistent, though, and inched farther out on the spike. Leaning over, her perch precarious, she stretched her hand out to the boy. The little fool, she was going to get herself and Matthew killed. Unwilling to startle Kat, Alex quietly stepped over the rope surrounding the pit and proceeded to crawl out onto the neighboring pike. Unlike Kat, he sat down on the rounded post, his hands balancing his weight in front of him as he scooted forward.

Alex watched Kat reach out again, farther this time, encouraging the frightened boy in a soothing, but confident tone. "Come, Matthew. Take my hand. You are very brave. I know you can do it. Just grab my hand and I will pull you up."

Alex inhaled sharply. If either of them fell, they would surely be mauled to death. Frustration and fear gnawed at him. He could not just grab Kat and thrust her away from the danger as he wished. Nor command her to back away and let him rescue Matthew. He could only watch and plan as he came ever closer.

Just as Alex reached her, Matthew let go and reached out for her extended hand. Kat caught his wrist and held tight, but Matthew panicked and tugged hard on her arm. She teetered on the pike, her body slipping sideways away from Alex. Her face red and dripping with sweat, she struggled valiantly. Matthew cried out. Then Kat lost her perch and she and the boy plummeted into the dark pit.

Alex roared in agony and disbelief. Feral instinct surged up inside him and in one simultaneous motion he swung his leg over the pike, withdrew his sword and jumped down into the pit. He landed on his feet and fell to one knee, his sword hand stopping his fall. A huge furred claw swung out directly for his head. Alex lunged back and the bear's curved claws passed his cheek, missing him by inches. So close a current of air swept his face and the putrid smell of the bear filled his nostrils.

His heart beat as though it would burst from his chest. Alex swung his sword at the bear, distracting the predator from the pair who had landed with a sickening thump nearby. Staying well out of the creature's lethal range, Alex jabbed and slashed at the larger bear while moving around and away from Kat and Matthew huddled on the ground.

The gambit worked, for his blows annoyed the bear like a pesky bee. The animal followed Alex, roaring in frustration and batting at the sword with his paw. The bear's chain clanked loudly, the rank smell of his hot breath too close for comfort.

Keeping his attention on the bear, Alex yelled, "Kat, are you hurt?"

He heard a groan and then her voice emerged as a croak. "Alex?"

"Aye, 'tis me. Are you all right? Are you able to move?"

"I believe so."

"While I distract this brute, I need you and Matthew to move to the back of the pit out of the bear's range."

"Kat?" Alex called out when she did not respond.

"Matthew is unconscious. I'll have to drag him."

Alex listened as Kat grunted, dragging Matthew away.

"'Tis done. We are safe. The bear cannot reach us here."

When Alex finally backed off, he heard another roar,

but this time it was a roar of approval from the crowd. Alex thought cynically, *I wonder what my chances were with the odds makers*. Then he forgot everything and raced to Kat's side.

She knelt beside Matthew, but when he approached, she jumped up and into his arms. Kat clung to him tightly, shaking. For his part, Alex squeezed her as though he would never let her go, their hearts pounding against one another as a single entity.

Reassured of her safety, he placed his palms on either side of her face and tipped her head back to look at her. "Praise God you are all right. For a moment I thought I'd lost you."

He brushed her loose hair back, her relief shining in her face. "I too thought . . ." Kat gulped and then continued. "What are you doing here, Alex? *How* did you come to be here? I don't understand."

Now that the danger was over, Alex's anger surged to the fore. He gripped her shoulders in a tight vise. "Aye, I know, you little fool! You would have been dead had I not come upon this travesty."

Kat's eyes blazed up at him, but he interrupted her before she opened her mouth. "Nay. We can discuss this later at a more opportune time."

He knelt down beside Matthew and checked the boy's limbs for broken bones. Kat knelt, too, and cradled Matthew's head in her lap.

Her troubled eyes met Alex's. "I feel a large bump on the back of his head."

Alex nodded. "The blow to his head must have knocked him unconscious. I can find naught else wrong with him." He tapped the boy's face, trying to rouse him. "Matthew? Can you hear me? Wake up."

The boy groaned, his eyelids flickering several times before he opened them. His pupils were unfocused. "My lord? What are you . . . ? Where am I?"

"Do you not remember?"

Matthew closed his eyes, his brow puckered. "The dare. The boys dared me to climb out over the bear pit. But I fell. Lady Kat tried to—" His eyes flew open. "Lady Kat. Where is Lady Kat?" he cried out, trying to raise his head.

"Hush now. I am safe, Matthew," Kat said, smoothing back the sweat-matted hair on his forehead. "We are all safe. You may thank Sir Alex for his brave rescue." She looked up at Alex then, her smile brilliant.

Alex's heart thumped, pride filling him at her praise. "Can you rise without assistance, Matthew? We're still in the pit. I don't know about you, but I have no wish to further my acquaintance with Sir Surly Bear."

Matthew smiled. "Aye, my lord, I need no help." Even so, Alex and Kat stood up and helped him rise. Though shaken, the boy was fine.

Alex looked around. The bear had quieted and settled down on his hindquarters against the pole. On the other side of the pit, the iron door remained locked. "Where is that blasted bear ward?"

"Aye, 'tis strange indeed," Kat said, her expression perplexed.

"Well, I do not intend to wait for that fat idiot to let us out of here." Alex stared at the stone wall before him, gauging its height. "The wall looks to be about twelve feet high. I can lift you both onto my shoulders so you can reach the top. Someone above can pull you out."

"Alex, Kat, you both all right?"

Alex shaded his eyes and gazed up at the top of the pit. Rand peered down from the edge, Rose beside him, fear etching her face.

"Aye, Rand. We're unharmed. But I need your help. I'm going to lift Kat and the boy onto my shoulders, and I want you to pull them up and out of the pit."

"Of course. Whenever you're ready."

"Be careful, Alex," Rose's voice quavered.

Alex nodded and turned to Kat.

"You go first, then Matthew. I want him to see how easily 'tis done."

"But what about you? How will you get out?" she asked, her expression unsure.

Alex withdrew his dagger, and using the pointed tip, gouged a hole in the mortar between two stones about waist high and another shoulder high. "I shall use this for a toehold and handhold. Then Rand can reach down and help me up."

He hollered above and Rand stuck his head over the precipice, ready to assist them. Alex knelt down on one knee so Kat could use his other knee as a step. He assisted her onto his shoulders and stood up. "Are you ready?"

"Ready." He held very still while she stood up straight above him. When she released his hands, he gripped her ankles. A few moments later her weight lifted from him, dirt and grass scrabbling down the wall as Rand pulled her out.

The bear had been silent and resting, but suddenly he became agitated, roaming the width of his chain back and forth, growling and tugging on it.

Alex looked at Matthew, who had remained very silent for some time now. "Are you ready, son?"

But the boy was staring at the disturbed bear. Alex grabbed his shoulders and turned Matthew so he faced him and not the animal. "The bear is chained and cannot harm us, so there is naught you need to fear."

Matthew gulped, nodding.

"Do you trust me?"

The boy nodded more vigorously.

"Good. You have naught to worry about."

The bear became more restless, the chain clanking with great force as he tugged and pawed violently at the iron ring attached to his hind leg.

"Alex?" Kat hollered down, her voice troubled.

"We're ready," he hollered back, his tone confident. Then he turned to Matthew and kneeling, he helped the boy climb onto his shoulders.

After he was lifted out, Kat poked her head over the edge of the pit. "Matthew is safe." Her gaze strayed nervously to the bear. "Hurry, Alex. Get out of there."

He looked over his shoulder. The bear's agitation had not abated. Indeed, he seemed enraged now. Not twelve feet away, the bear tipped his head up and roared at him, tugging desperately on his chain. Alex felt like roaring back, but he had had enough of confined, dark spaces. Flipping the right side of his mantle over his back, he turned and put his foot in the makeshift foothold.

Kat, unnerved by the bear's odd behavior, knelt on the ground, leaning over the dark precipice while she waited for Alex to climb up.

Beside her, Rand wrapped his arm around her and squeezed once, saying, "Don't worry. He is going to be all right. This will be all over soon," before he drew away.

When Alex lifted his foot and stepped up, for some reason Kat raised her head. She stared in stunned horror as the bear ripped free of his shackle and charged Alex.

She screamed. "Alex. Behind you." The bear roared, drowning out her cry.

She watched as Alex jumped, tucked his body into a ball and rolled over several times on the ground, his sword clanking against the packed earth. Barely evading the bear's charge, he sprang to his feet and withdrew his sword. Steel raised, he backed away, but the bear attacked swiftly. His huge paw swung out and Alex lunged to the right, slashing the bear's chest as he did. Suddenly, Alex stumbled. Kat cried out as a collective gasp rose up behind her. Alex quickly recovered, putting the center pole between him and the bear to impede its attack. The crowd cheered.

The brown bear stood up on its hind legs and roared, using its height to intimidate his rival. Her heart pounding, Kat reached for her dagger, then cursed. For once she had not brought her dagger, just when she needed it most.

She reached for Rand's sword, ordering, "Give me your sword. Alex needs my help."

His hand clamped down on hers as she clutched his sword handle. "Nay. You will only distract him. He needs all his concentration to escape the bear. Watch and see."

The bear charged then, and Alex dodged to the left, keeping the pole a barrier between them and striking out with his sword to keep it at bay. The bear attacked twice more while Kat watched on helplessly, her heart about to burst with the strain, fear clutched in her throat.

The combatants faced one another on opposite sides of the pit, the bear bleeding profusely. Kat watched, appalled, when Alex ripped the pin from his mantle and removed the voluminous green wool from his back. On her knees, she clutched the grass in her fist. Alex spread his cape open before him and moved slowly towards the center of the pit.

When the bear came at him once more, Alex flung his mantle over the beast's head. Blinded, its sense of smell hampered, the animal stopped in its tracks and began shaking the fabric away. Alex ran past him and towards Kat. "Here. Catch."

Instinctively, Kat reached out, caught his sword and tossed it on the ground beside her.

She turned back and grabbed Alex's outstretched hand. Rand grabbed his other hand and they tugged him up with all their strength. Alex's black head emerged, followed by the rest of his considerably heavy body. He crawled forward and collapsed face down. Kat flopped down beside him, her face looking to heaven as she tried to catch her breath.

"That was a close call, my friend," Rand said.

Breathing easier, Kat turned to Alex. "Do you fare well, Alex?"

He did not answer, nor move either she realized.

Alarmed, she rolled onto her knees and shook his shoulder. "Alex? Answer me!"

She looked up at Rand. His gaze was fearful. "Help me roll

him over." She pushed on Alex's right shoulder while Rand tugged. "Careful!"

At last, they rolled Alex onto his back.

"Jesu," Kat cursed. She crossed her chest, but not because of her blasphemous verbal slip. A pool of blood saturated the grass next to Alex. Her gaze moved to him. Alex's tunic was slashed open. Five claw marks ran down his left shoulder and upper chest, blood oozing from his gouged flesh. Rose began to cry loudly.

Chapter 22

"Will he live?"

Kat, her hands trembling, stared down at Alex on their bed. His chest and left shoulder were swathed in bandages, while light from the brazier and wall sconces flickered over his pale, still body. He had not regained consciousness yet. Indeed, he had not awoken when he was carried to the cart and placed in it, nor on the long interminable drive back to the palace as she cradled his head in her lap. Nor while the king's physician treated his wound as she, Rand, and Rose watched on anxiously.

Closing a leather bag containing his instruments, powders, and glass vials of medicine, the gaunt physician turned to her, his brown eyes probing. "Though the wound is not extremely deep, he has lost a large amount of blood. And there is always the risk his wound will fester. But I have stopped the bleeding, which is good."

Kat grimaced. She had some experience in treating wounds so the physician had merely confirmed what she already knew, but she had wanted reassurance.

The older man left instructions for preparing the poultice. "You will have to keep a close eye on him over the next few days. Change his dressings thrice a day and check his wound.

Let me know if it begins to fester or his condition worsens. The king has asked me to personally oversee his recovery."

Rose harrumphed after he left. "You would think that man believed he alone knew how to care for wounds. 'Tis women who have long treated and nursed their men's injuries."

Kat sat down on the bed beside Alex and brushed his hair off his dirt-begrimed forehead. He was warm to the touch, though not overly so. "I doubt the man intended to cast aspersions on your healing abilities, Rose."

Rand smiled at Rose. "Well, I, for one, value your skills most highly, Rosie. The leg wound I incurred on Crusade never healed properly till you took me under your care. I shall forever be indebted to you."

Her round cheeks flushed at his compliment, but her gaze darted away from direct eye contact with him. "You may thank Mother. She taught me everything I know."

Rand bowed, acknowledging her subtle rebuff. "Next I see her, you may be sure I shall compliment her on her teaching skills. Now, if you will pardon me? There is something I need to attend to. I will return soon to check on Alex." He nodded to them and departed.

Kat retrieved a linen cloth from the table beside the bed. Dipping it into the basin of cool water, she wrung it out and began to wipe the dirt and sweat from Alex's face and neck. His face was pale and lined with pain even in sleep, the creases beside his mouth and on his forehead pronounced.

Rose sat down on the other side of the bed and took Alex's hand in hers. She gazed down at him, a frown upon her face. "I know what you are thinking, Kat. But Rand knows I despise that name. Ever since I was a young girl, the man has constantly tried to nettle me one way or another."

"I wonder why that is?" Kat asked.

But Rose missed her tone, shrugging. "Alex was so brave today. After all he has been through, I cannot believe he was nearly killed by a bear."

"Aye, 'tis strange," Kat murmured, remembering another

close call, when she and Alex had almost been struck by an arrow.

A knock on the entry door interrupted her thoughts. Rose left to answer it and returned a moment later. "I must go to the queen. She is most anxious to learn of Alex's condition. I will send Jenny to the kitchens to get more water and bandages, and everything you need to prepare the poultices." She stood at the side of the bed and looked down at Alex lying so drawn and pale. "My brother is not going to die! He has just been returned to us and we shall see him through this difficult time together, Kat."

Aye. God willing.

Then Rose leaned down and kissed Alex on his forehead. "I will return as soon as I can."

After Rose left, Kat opened the shutters and tossed the bloody water out. She kept the shutters open for a moment to air out the stuffy room. Once she poured fresh water into the basin, Kat returned to the bed, drawing Alex's bedcovering down to his waist. His upper chest and left shoulder were bound in bandages, but his bare arms and lower torso were coated with dried sweat and blood.

She started cleansing his arms and hands first. Then rinsing the cloth, she gently rubbed the blood from his stomach, and lower, where it had congealed in the hair on his groin.

Kat bit her lip as images of Alex flashed before her—Alex fearlessly jumping into the pit, drawing the bear's deadly wrath onto him. Without a thought for his own life, he had come to her and Matthew's rescue, giving them time to escape. And not once, but twice, it nearly cost him his life. She had felt so helpless as she watched Alex battle the bear, unable to aid him, knowing not what to do.

She dropped the cloth into the bloody water and stared at Alex. Reaching out, she gently laid her hand on his chest. His heartbeat was slow and steady, his chest barely rising and falling. But he lived.

Her hand trailed down his stomach next, feeling every

indention, his sleek skin, so soft and resilient. A sob escaped and Kat pressed her fist to her mouth. If only it were truly so. That Alex was resilient enough to stave off contagion and recover completely.

Covering his chest with the sheet again, she rose and closed the shutters, tossed a few coals into the brazier, and pulled up a stool to the side of the bed. When she sat down, she reached for his hand and held it tight. And began to pray that Alex would be all right. That he would soon wake so she could tell him how deeply she still cared for him.

Rose was exhausted and sat down in the hall's darkened alcove to catch her breath. The moon high, she had just relieved Kat for a spell and was returning to her pallet in the queen's apartments. Two whole days had passed since Alex was attacked. Kat had assumed most of the burden of Alex's care, refusing to leave his side. But Rose had had very little sleep, either. She was worried about her brother. His wound was healing nicely, but fever had set in.

Deep in thought, she nearly missed the quiet, furtive steps of the man who passed where she sat. But something about his sneaky behavior caught her attention. She held very still, unwilling to alert him to her presence, when suddenly, moonlight from a high round window shone on his blond hair. She recognized him immediately.

She waited until he started up the spiral stairs before she got up and followed him. 'Twas the same wing as Kat and Alex's chambers, although on the opposite end. She did not trust the man, knew he was up to some mischief and she intended to discover what it was. She lifted her skirts and strode quietly up the steps in his wake.

He continued up the third flight, surprising her. She stopped on the landing below and waited, unsure what she should do next. Then a scratching sound echoed down the stairwell. Soon a door opened from above and a woman purred a warm throaty welcome. Revulsion roiled through Rose, for she recognized the woman's voice and tone all too well.

"Are we alone?" Sir Stephen asked Lady Lydia.

Rose strained to hear the whispered response. "Aye, darling. I bribed my bed mates to find other accommodations for the night." Then the door shut and Rose slumped against the central post.

Memories she had spent the last three years trying to put behind her came hurling back to haunt her. Sickened to her stomach, cold sweat dripped down her forehead as she fought them off. She told herself she had naught more to fear. But she knew she lied. Rose stood up and wiped her eyes. She had a beautiful son she loved, who needed her protection from his greedy, grasping cousin. And secrets from her past that if discovered, could destroy everything.

Lydia, after her initial passionate embrace, moved to the bedside table and poured Stephen some wine. *The fool.* Stephen always let his passion overrule his ambition. He had no idea she despised his touch; he thought her offering of wine a gracious gesture. Lydia smiled in satisfaction.

Of course, Sir Stephen believed her smile was for him. After taking a drink, he set his wine down and pulled her into his arms. She kissed him and let him fondle her breasts for a brief interval, then shoved him down on the bed. Capturing his hungry gaze, she pulled her sheer chemise slowly up her thighs and hips, hesitating before she revealed her golden delta.

"Drink up, darling. The wine will strengthen your blood. You shall need the extra fortitude for what I have in mind this night."

Stephen gulped in anticipation, grabbed his wine chalice from the bedside table and drank till his cup was empty. Rewarding him, she slipped the chemise off. She stood boldly before him, naked except for her slippers and hose, the glow from the brazier gilding her body. His eyes glazed over and he reached out, groping for her breasts, but she shoved him back again.

"Christ, Lydia. I must have you now. 'Tis been too long since we last met like this."

"You know the rules. Do not touch me unless I tell you to." Her lips curled up in a seductive smile. "The anticipation will heighten our pleasure and you shall be thankful in the end."

Stephen groaned and leaned back on his elbows, waiting.

She raised her left foot, exposing her pink petals, and pressed it against his chest. "Remove my hose."

His eyes trained between her legs, his fingers fumbled when he removed her slipper, then garter.

Lydia purred, "Now, I would hear what you have learned of Alex's condition."

Occupied peeling her hose down, he answered by rote. "Sir Alex was wounded on the chest by the bear, but the wound appears to be healing. 'Tis the high fever he has contracted that may do him in."

Lydia frowned, annoyed at the thought that he might die. She wanted Alex to suffer for his betrayal, but a quick death was not what she had planned. The fool had fallen in love with his pathetic wife, and she wanted him to feel the pain of that love being ripped away. Either at the hands of his wife's death or . . . she had another plan that might achieve the goal of tearing the lovers apart.

"Your plan was too risky the other day. It depended too deeply on circumstances and luck. We must be very careful now to avoid suspicion."

Stephen became surly. "I *was* very careful. You can be sure there are no witnesses to attest to my involvement."

"What of the bear ward?"

Stephen smiled, his close-set brown eyes empty. "I have taken care of him."

"Good." She raised her right leg and he removed the other slipper and hose. Next, she stood back and cupped her breasts, drawing his eyes to their large dusky crowns. "Remove your clothes," she commanded. She lifted her breasts up and squeezed them together. With her thumb and forefinger she squeezed and plucked her nipples to stinging hard points.

Stephen's eyes never left her as he stripped off his tunic and undergarments in haste.

She propped her foot on the bed, giving him a view of the moist, tender flesh. "You may have a taste now."

He groaned, grabbed her hips and buried his face between her legs. His manhood rose up hardened and erect.

"Are you sure Sir Luc has no idea of my involvement in your schemes?"

Sir Stephen drew back, blinking, his eyes unfocused. The drug she slipped into his wine was working; she had to hurry if she were to accomplish all she wanted this night. She crawled on top of the bed and straddled him, rubbing her dampened delta over his semi-erect member.

"Stephen?"

He stirred again. "Aye, Sir Luc has no idea of our plans, or my relationship with you. He is a convenient pawn. His obsession with the woman blinds him to all else."

Lydia smiled a secret smile. "Good. He must never know or he could ruin everything."

His patience at a limit, he growled, "Now, Lydia. I cannot wait a mom' mo'," his last words were garbled, but he grabbed her hips and she rose on her knees. Wanting the disgusting experience to end quickly, she took him inside her and plunged down. His hips heaved up several times and in a matter of moments, he spilled his seed with a guttural groan. He collapsed on the bed, his eyelids fluttering closed.

The belladonna finally took effect and he fell asleep. She rolled off of him and left the bed to the sound of his snores, then washed the sticky filth from her body. If she had her way, she would not copulate with him at all. But she did not want him to wake up with no memory of bedding her and become suspicious.

Feeling extremely unsatisfied, she knew she would have to

give relief to the flesh she aroused earlier if she were to get any rest this night. First, however, she had to come up with a foolproof plan to achieve her revenge should Alex recover. Sir Stephen was right about one thing. Sir Luc *was* a convenient pawn. So now, she needed to decide how best to use him to her advantage without his knowledge of her involvement.

Hot, Kat had stripped down to her chemise. Alex's fever had not abated. Indeed, it had worsened early this morning. Or yesterday morning, rather; now it was after matins.

Rose had returned from speaking with the queen three nights ago and prepared an infusion of henbane to help Alex sleep through the pain when he awakened. Since his fever set in, though, Kat had given him infusions of feverfew and yarrow, when he would cooperate. In and out of consciousness, there were times he thrashed about, rambling unintelligibly.

Now that he was restful for the moment, Kat bathed Alex in an attempt to cool his body and bring down his fever. She had performed the task numerous times, but 'twas not an onerous one. Try as she might to remain indifferent, she could not help but admire his masculine physique. He had a splendid body, his arm and leg muscles superbly built, a masterpiece of muscle, skin, and bone.

After rinsing the cloth in cool water again, she bathed around his manhood and drew the cloth down both his legs. The only sounds in the room were the rasp of the cloth and Alex's uneven breathing.

Kat repeated the process over his whole body once more and then prepared a poultice for his wound. Using a pestle and mortar, she ground the dried comfrey leaves Jenny had brought from the kitchen into a fine paste. Doing the same with the yarrow, Kat added honey to the mixture and spread the cool poultice onto his wound to help heal it and soothe the pain.

It was a struggle to lift him and wrap the bandages around his chest, but she did. Panting lightly, she drew back to examine her work and arched her lower back, stretching her aching muscles. A hair came loose from her braid and she tucked it back in.

Idle for the nonce, Kat had time to think, to allow fear to invade her against her will.

So she began to tidy up the room as best she could; she tossed the dirty bandages into the antechamber for Jenny to retrieve, threw out the dirty water, cleaned the mortar and pestle, and poured fresh water into the basin. Then she made sure the shutters were secure before she climbed into bed beside Alex, although she knew she would be unable to sleep.

She laid her head on the pillow next to Alex, her worried gaze intent on his flushed face, but moments later her eyelids began to droop.

Kat jerked, realizing she had fallen asleep and that something or someone woke her. Lying as still as possible, she listened for any sign of an intruder as she groped under her pillow for her dagger. Of course, it could be Jenny or Rose or Rand, but ever since the bear attacked Alex, she had been uneasy for some reason.

She heard it again, a loud bang. Kat sighed—it was simply a shutter blown open by a brisk breeze. Going to the window, she looked out at the sky as dawn gleamed. Dark clouds were brewing on the horizon and another gust whipped her loosened hair back off her face.

It felt wonderful, but she closed the shutter and returned to check on Alex. She pressed her palm against his forehead. He was burning up. His fever had spiked while she was sleeping, and she noticed now he had tossed off his covers.

Without warning, Alex grabbed her hand and flung it away violently, snarling, "Don't touch me or I will kill you." His eyes were pitch black and he looked not at her, but through her. Her heart thundered.

It was the first time any of his ranting made sense. He dropped his head back to the pillow and began to mumble incoherently once more, the pain of his nightmares etched in the creases of his forehead and around his mouth.

His burst of anger frightened her, and she hesitated over what to do next. But when she caught a few of his words, she drew closer. He was demanding his sword. "Give me my sword. I need my sword. Protect her. Must protect her."

Kat gasped. "Who, Alex? Who must you protect?"

His head shifted back and forth as if he searched the room, but his eyes were unfocused. "Where is my sword?" he bellowed, too weak to rise.

"You shall have your sword. When you tell me who you must protect."

He mumbled some more then said quite clearly, "Kat. Danger. Must save her."

Kat sighed with relief, afraid for a brief moment that it was Lydia for whom he was concerned. She stroked his fevered forehead and whispered, "Rest, Alex. I'm safe now. You saved me. Do you hear me? I am safe. And you are going to recover. I swear it."

Chapter 23

It had been five and a half days since Alex contracted his fever. Kat was exhausted; sweat dripped down her back, her eyes burned and her back ached. But she was determined to see Alex defeat his fever. So, when Jenny brought her a midday repast, although not hungry, at her maid's gentle scolding she had eaten a few bites to keep up her strength.

Now, a flash of lightning illuminated the chamber through the partially closed shutters.

Alex's wound was healing, the red puckered skin knitting nicely together, and she continued to change his dressing three times a day. His high fever was a different matter. It seemed as though she had been trying to rid him of it forever. Preparing infusions to reduce the fever, forcing him to drink whenever he woke disoriented from his delirium, cooling him down with cool clothes. It was a continuous cycle that kept her mind too busy to think, or despair.

Alex stared at her now, his eyes blurry with fever, barely cognizant. Supporting him under his shoulders, she held a cup to his mouth. "I need you to drink, Alex."

Instead, he nuzzled his face between the swells of her breasts and groaned. He was incorrigible. Even delirious, he was bent on seduction. Shifting him away, she placed the cup to his lips. "Drink. And then you can play all you want," she lied.

She did not know if he comprehended her, but he drank the infusion of pennyroyal when she tipped the cup again. Since the dangerously high fever had not abated, this morning Rose decided to treat him with the herb to induce sweating. The situation was dire. If his fever did not break soon it could kill him. The next hours were critical.

"Enough." He shoved her away with his injured arm. The cup flew out of her hand, the remaining contents spattering her shift. "Jesu', my arm," he cried out. Metal clanging, the cup hit the wooden floor.

Kat jumped up and pulled the wet bodice from her chest. Alex grabbed her arm, squeezing it painfully, and tugged her to him. "What did you do to my shoulder?" He snarled in her face.

Careful not to hurt him, knowing he was not in his right mind, Kat pressed Alex down on the bed gently and wrenched free.

His energy spent, the air whooshed out of his chest. Shaking his head from side to side, Alex struggled against an imaginary foe. "You cannot kill me. I am going to kill you first," he swore.

Kat sat back on the cushioned window seat, shaken and bewildered. As the afternoon progressed, when not exhausted senseless, Alex continued to rant and rave against his captors as his fever raged higher. His ramblings were mostly indistinct, until he hollered for someone called Sir Richard.

There was a restless pause then Alex roared, an agonized wail of grief that pierced Kat's heart. "You killed him. You killed Sir Richard. I shall see you in hell!" Gasping for breath, Alex's head fell back to the pillow and rolled to the side.

Kat jumped up, shaking with fear. She leaned over Alex and pressed her ear to his chest. She detected a weak, but steady heartbeat. A sigh of relief escaped her.

Kneeling down beside the bed, Kat dropped her forehead on the mattress, haunted by Alex's grief. She breathed in and out deeply, trying to calm her rapidly beating heart. Who was

Sir Richard? How had Alex known him? Had the man been incarcerated with Alex in the Saracen fortress?

She pounded the bed with her fist. "You will not die, Alex! You will not die!" she swore into the bed linens, her shout muffled. She remained there until her knees began to ache, then she got up and crawled into bed beside him.

When he calmed much later that evening, she tried to dose him again as the abbey bells rang the hour of compline. After lifting Alex behind his shoulders, Kat forced several drinks down his throat, but the rest dribbled down his chin.

Frustrated, she shoved his dull, matted black hair off his forehead, and then eased his shoulders back down on the bed. She turned to the bedside table, rinsed a cloth in the basin and ran it over his face. The motion was automatic now.

Alex grabbed her hand suddenly and Kat gasped.

Bleary and streaked red, his eyes held hers wonderingly. "Kat?"

Kat sighed in pure relief. "Aye. 'Tis me, Alex."

"I am not dreaming? I escaped prison and have returned home to you?"

Tears welled up in her eyes. "Aye, Alex. You are home at last."

With a sigh, his eyes closed.

But Kat could not rejoice yet. For just as suddenly as he had roused clear and aware for a few moments, virulent chills set in and Alex began to shake violently.

Alex was in hell. His body blazed like a bonfire in the hot Eastern sun as he labored. Bending down near the precipice of the fifty-foot deep, rock-cut ditch, Alex grunted as he and Richard hoisted another heavy stone block and carted it over rocky terrain. His back ached with the strain, the pace from dawn to dusk relentless. When they approached the tower under construction, they put down their burden where the master mason indicated. Sweat dripped into Alex's eyes, stinging them. Unable to see, he stopped a moment to rub his eyes.

A mistake. The guard's whip snapped; it licked a burning path across his shoulder and chest. Alex gritted his teeth in excruciating pain, tamping down his fury and hate. Otherwise he would grab the master mason's chisel and drive it through the guard's skull. His will to survive was stronger than his rage.

The next he remembered, he was hurtled into his dark cell for the night and began shivering with cold. Except for the disbursement of the evening rations—stale bread and a thick sticky grain dish—Alex was left in peace for the night to dream of escape. Holding out his bowl through the iron bars, he waited till a veiled female servant came to his cell. She spooned gruel into his bowl and pulled a bit of bread from the sack hanging from a strap on her shoulder.

Suddenly the robed slave metamorphosed into Kat. She was standing in a bedchamber before a washstand wearing only a shift and looking over her shoulder at him. She appeared weary, her expression fearful. Then she turned away and removed her shift. He was burning up, his shoulder throbbed poker-hot, but the sight of Kat naked was like a drink of water to a man lost in the middle of the Syrian Desert.

He watched transfixed as she began to wash her body with a wet cloth she wrung out in a basin. She ran it down her neck and around one breast, which plumped back up when she removed the cloth. Alex groaned, the sight of her naked body undoing him. He knew 'twas just a dream, one of many he conjured in prison to keep him from going mad, but it seemed so real.

Alex groaned again, the torment unbearable. He tried to move, tried to reach out to her, but he could not budge a muscle. He was so hot, could barely breathe. Then he remembered she was in danger and he tried harder to reach her. He had to save her, had to protect her. But suddenly Kat disappeared and he was back in prison surrounded by guards.

Naaay!

The Mamluk guards jumped Alex and held him down, one of them sitting on top of him as they tried to subdue him. Alex cried out in anguish, clawing and fighting them like a man possessed as they lashed him with their whips. Kat was in danger because of *him*. And he would reach her even if he died trying.

But pain shot though his chest and shoulder, making it difficult. He was growing weaker, sweat pouring down his face, when he heard Kat's voice pleading with him to stop struggling or he would reopen his wound. In disbelief, he breathed in the exotic scent of her perfume. He was dreaming! Or was he?

Blearily, Alex opened his eyes. Stunned, he realized he was in a dark room, a soft mattress beneath him. But he was more amazed to discover Kat straddled on top of him, with her hair in disarray and her chemise riding up her hips. Her bodice gaped open, giving him a delicious eyeful of the slopes of her upper breasts.

He remembered everything.

Kat stared at him, blinking. "You are awake."

Alex chuckled, his voice scratchy. "Aye, I am awake."

Her silver eyes glimmered with tears. "You are sweating."

"Aye, sweating."

Surprising him, she leaned down and began kissing his moist face wherever she could reach. "Your fever has broken. You're going to live."

He did feel much cooler, but certain parts were just starting to heat up. His member hardened and lengthened, not even the pain in his chest could detract his attention from it. With his right hand, he reached over and touched the bulky bandages, remembering the precise moment when the bear clawed him.

"Your wound is healing well. 'Tis the fever we were worried about. You were injured over a sennight ago."

"A sennight!" Limply, he raised his hand and brushed her hair back over her shoulder. "And is this normally how you greet a sick man who has just recovered?" he asked, looking down at where she sat on him, a peek of her black curls vivid against her white shift. Kat looked too and blushed furiously.

He gasped in mock shock. "Surely you did not intend to take advantage of me in my weakened state." He *was* weak, achy, and in pain, but he had never felt more alive either.

"Oh . . . you devil." She slapped his good shoulder. "Of course I did not. You were delirious. I had to hold you down so you wouldn't reopen your wound." She began to scramble off him, but he wrapped his good arm around her waist and halted her. The blunt head of his erection prodded her moist center.

Kat gasped in shock. "What are you doing? Alex, release me."

"Pray, do not leave yet. I was not chastising you on your unusual nursing habits. In fact, you have done a remarkable job of lifting my spirits." He chuckled. "I believe I remember hearing you say that if I drank that nasty concoction you would let me play all I want?"

Kat sputtered. "Are you mad? You are weak, injured, and barely recovered from fever. I will not have your relapse on my conscience."

She scrambled off the bed on his good side, her shift dropping back down to her ankles.

Alex chuckled. "I believe it just might be worth it. A relapse, I mean," he said.

"Well, that certainly is not going to happen. Indeed," Kat said, as she bustled about straightening the covers over him. "I intend to see that you recover completely. Foremost, I imagine you will need to remain in bed a sennight or more."

"A sennight?" Alex barked, and then began coughing.

Kat came to his side, helped prop him up with pillows behind his back, then poured a cup of water and held it to his lips.

He took several drinks, the aches in his body making their presence known. He was extremely weak and his head throbbed painfully along with his shoulder.

"Aye, a sennight at the least. 'Tis imperative you get plenty of rest and sustenance. And there shall certainly be none of . . .of . . . well, you know what I mean," she ended, blushing. "Eventually we shall have you up and about at full strength."

Before he could utter a word, Kat left him to find Rose and the sustenance of which she spoke.

Chapter 24

Later that afternoon Alex woke slowly, immediately sensing someone's presence in the room.

"You're looking much better."

Opening his eyes, he could just barely make out Rand in the shadows of the cushioned window alcove. Rand got up, pulled a stool next to the bed and sat down in the light of the bedside lamp.

"'Tis amazing what some rest and nourishment can do to revive an injured man." After propping the pillows against the headboard, Alex reclined. "Are you alone?"

"Aye. Rose let me in and has returned to her duties. And Kat is fast asleep on a pallet in the antechamber."

Alex frowned. After Kat had returned to their chamber this morning, bringing him some measly broth to eat, she had insisted on making up the pallet in the other room. She did not want to disturb him or accidentally aggravate his wound while she slept. But he would have preferred her comforting presence beside him.

"Tell me, have you seen young Matthew of Oxford since the attack? How does he fare after his brush with death?"

Rand chuckled. "You know how boys are, all bravado and beating chests. It appears he has become quite notorious with the ladies at court, who all wish to hear of the attack firsthand."

He paused. "Actually, the attack is what I wish to speak to you about."

Alex's heart lurched, excited by Rand's tone. "Why? Did you discover something about the traitor who hired Scarface to get rid of me in the Holy Land?"

"Aye. Knowing your imprisonment was no random act, and your belief that Kat may be in danger, too, I was suspicious of this latest attack. So I returned to the village to investigate."

"Did you have a chance to question the bear ward?"

"Nay. 'Tis difficult to question a dead man."

"Dead!" Alex said in disbelief. Then his shoulders sagged in disappointment. "How did he die?"

"The villagers discovered his body floating in a stream near the outskirts of the village. They believe he must have slipped and hit his head on a rock, then fell in the stream where he drowned."

"How convenient," Alex said in disgust.

"Aye, and it gets worse." Rand leaned forward, shadows in his eyes. "I checked the bear pit and discovered someone had deliberately tampered with the chain. One of the large links was cut through part way, by an axe most likely."

"And the one person we could get answers from is dead. Damn the man!" Alex choked out, his fist clenched as though gripping his sword. Then he began to cough.

In the other room, Kat moved hurriedly back to her pallet, laid down and closed her eyes. Feigning sleep, she relaxed, breathing deep and even. The curtains rustled and Rand's gaze bore into her. Moments passed in excruciating torment as the tension drew out. A film of sweat broke out over her body. Then Rand dropped the curtain and the stool scraped the floor as he sat once more.

Rand and Alex began speaking again in low whispers, but she had heard more than enough.

Alex's attack and subsequent imprisonment had been no random act? Flabbergasted, Kat felt her mind flood with questions. Who could possibly want Alex dead? And why?

Who was this Scarface who attacked him? And finally, how did Alex intend to discover the person behind the plot?

Then a moment from her past returned—the day in the woods at Montclair when three men attacked Alex. Afterward, two villains had lain dead, but one great hulking brute escaped. Though not without a souvenir from Alex's sword, a slashed face. Could this be the unknown Scarface he spoke of? Were the two events related in some way?

The more she thought about it, the angrier she became.

Alex was searching for an unknown traitor and apparently did not think Kat important enough to confide in her. Not only did he not confide in her, he lied to her the morning after they made love for the first time since his return. She specifically asked Alex if there was anything else about his imprisonment he had not told her about. She had asked for honesty in their marriage, but all Alex was capable of were lies and distrust. Even more damaging was the knowledge that Alex had known she was in danger and did not see fit to inform her. How was she to protect herself if she did not know her life was threatened? And why?

Two things she knew for certain, though. One, Alex did not trust her, never would. And two, she could never accept a marriage with Alex on those terms. When their agreement expired, she would ask Alex to annul their marriage. But could she marry Sir Luc once she was free? For no matter Alex's betrayal, no matter his inability to love her, she was still in love with her husband.

At this last realization, tears slowly slid from her eyes. Kat crushed her fist to her mouth to still the sob rising in the back of her throat.

When Rand left, Alex turned his mind to several problems that were nagging him.

Despite his injury, he had no intention of remaining in bed for a sennight as Kat wished. His injury and resulting fever had cost him precious time in seducing his wife. The feast of St. Barnabas, the day their marriage pact expired, was only a sennight away. He needed to get back on his feet soon, for he feared he had not yet convinced Kat to forgive his betrayal. Aye, she desired him, but emotionally she continued to keep him at a distance.

Neither could he afford to lie abed when he had a dangerous enemy out there who wanted him dead, an enemy who had threatened Kat, too. Alex could feel how close he was to discovering the man's identity by the desperation of the last attempt on his life.

He had no proof of the culprit's involvement, but it had the mark of his ingenuity. At first glance, both Alex's imprisonment and the bear's attack appeared to be random incidents. But what the assassin did not know was that Alex had recovered his stolen dagger as proof of the man's guilt, along with the name of his scarred accomplice.

And that was another reason why he needed to recover quickly. Besides the fact he had no idea when the next attack would occur, Scarface would be arriving any day. Alex closed his eyes, dreaming of Scarface in his power, the taste of revenge burning in his mouth. Alex's face was going to be the last thing the mercenary ever saw if he did not confess who hired him. No one harmed Kat and survived to tell of it.

In the deep of the night, Kat stared down at Alex lying pale and gaunt beneath the covers. His breathing was deep and even. Earlier she had given him a sleeping draught to help him rest. She moved to the large chest along the wall. Alex had put a leather satchel containing his personal belongings in it the day after they began sharing a bed.

Alex had deceived her, again. What a nightmare, a nightmare that kept repeating itself.

She pulled the satchel out and rummaging through it— hose, tunics, a comb, razor—she tossed them aside in her search for more evidence. When, suddenly, at the bottom of the leather bag her hand grazed cold hard steel.

She pulled out the dagger and gasped, unable to believe her eyes. The sheath was adorned with raised double spirals punctuated with garnet enamel. The handle was quite simple in contrast, except for a ruby on the pommel. The Beaumont dagger, the dagger that was stolen from Alex the day he was attacked in the Holy Land. It glittered brightly in the glow of the hanging bedside lamp.

Finding the dagger only raised more questions. How did Alex come to be in possession of his missing dagger? When did he discover it? And how long had he suspected his captivity was not a random act? She was pretty sure he had to have known since before his arrival at court. But how did the Beaumont dagger figure into the equation? she wondered. If only Alex would trust her enough to confide in her.

She unsheathed the dagger and tested the steel blade with her finger. The Latin inscription on the blade below the crossguard read: *Ad mortem fidelis,* Faithful till death. A bitter laugh escaped Kat, and her finger slipped on the blade. The sharp point pricked her finger. "Ouch," she cried out. She sucked the bead of blood, infinitely sad and disillusioned. How ironic that the Beaumont family motto claimed the one ideal she wished Alex would profess to her.

Slowly, Kat put the items back in the bag and returned it to the chest where she found it. Alex moaned. Kat spun around, her heart racing. Alex kicked at his covers, though he remained blessedly asleep. Breathing a sigh of relief, she left the bedchamber, her hand pressed against her aching heart.

Alex stood in a wooden tub and scrubbed his body with jerky motions. Beside him, his squire handed him a bucket of cold water. Alex poured it over his shoulders, the water sluicing down his body and into the tub. St. Barnabas' feast was two days away and his courtship of his wife had not progressed as he wished.

The chamber door creaked open, interrupting his ruminations, then his wife walked around the screen with a tray of food in her hands. Her gray eyes wide, a cry of dismay escaped her lips.

"What are you doing, Alex?"

He smiled wickedly. "Just what it looks like, wife," he said, indicating his naked body with a flourish of his hand.

Kat blushed, and then harrumphed. After she placed the tray on the table, she turned to him, hands on her hips. "What are you doing out of bed? It has only been four days since your fever broke. You need bed rest." She turned on his hapless squire, who had stood frozen beside Alex during the terse exchange. "Jon, how could you allow this?"

Alex took pity on the poor man. "That will be all, Jon. My wife will attend me now."

After handing him the drying cloth, Jon beat a retreat. Alex stepped from the tub, the air cool upon his wet body, and began drying off. Once done, he wrapped the cloth around his hips and approached Kat, placing his hands on her shoulders.

"I am fine, Kat. You need not worry about me. I feel much better today." He bent down and kissed her on the lips. She stiffened, but otherwise did not move. "Now what is that delicious smell coming from the bowl?" he asked and sat down in the larger chair to eat.

Kat sat down in the other chair. "Very well, but I insist you not leave this room. 'Tis foolish to overdo before you are completely mended."

Alex took several bites of the savory venison pottage, steeling himself for the explosion ahead. "I'm afraid that is impossible."

"Pardon?" She drew her eyes away from his lips.

He would have smiled, but frustration gnawed at him. Kat had barely spoken two words to him or acknowledged him these last few days. To make matters worse, Scarface had been ensnared in King Edward's trap and Edward had summoned Alex to the Tower. It was the moment Alex had been anxiously awaiting, but the timing was abominable.

"The king has summoned me to attend him at the Tower. I must leave for London as soon as I am dressed."

Kat stared at him in disbelief. "Surely you jest?"

"Nay. I jest not."

She jumped up from her seat and thumped her fist on the table. "That is ludicrous. You are injured and cannot be expected to traipse about the countryside on the king's whim. Send him word that you cannot attend him till you are better."

Alex finished his pottage and stood up. "Kings do not have whims, Kat. You know I can't disobey his summons."

Alex strode into the other chamber and began pulling on his braies and a pair of hose. His shoulder throbbed slightly, but he could move his arm well enough to dress without disturbing the healing flesh.

Kat entered the room behind him, opened her clothes' chest and searched through it. She retrieved her dagger and dropped the lid. Pulling up her skirts, she propped her foot on the chest and strapped her dagger to her thigh.

He stared at the hint of shadowed flesh exposed, distracted for a moment before her intent registered. "What do you think you are doing?" He regretted the words the moment he spoke. "Never mind. Obviously you have retrieved your dagger. But what do you intend to do now?" he asked, although he already had a sneaking suspicion.

She looked at him as if he were an idiot. "If you must meet with the king, I am going with you." Then she moved to the table beside the bed and retrieved linen bandages. "Raise your arms." He obeyed, bemused. While she began wrapping a linen strip around his chest, he wondered how best to forbid her to accompany him.

* * *

Kat followed Alex to the stable, trying to reason with him. She had threatened to follow him on her own if he refused to let her accompany him. In turn, he promised that if she followed him, he would have her escorted back under the king's guard. Threats were getting her nowhere so she decided to change tactics.

"Who is Sir Richard?"

Alex stopped abruptly in front of her and spun around, his expression forbidding. "Where did you hear his name?"

"You spoke of him when you were delirious with fever."

He stiffened, his gaze wary. "He was an English knight I befriended. We shared a cell in prison."

"What happened to him?"

"He's dead," he said, his voice guilt-ridden and his eyes shadowed with pain. "Murdered." Then his dark blue gaze pierced hers as he asked stiffly, "Did I say aught else while I was senseless?"

"Nay. But I know there is something you are keeping from me. What does Edward want with you at the Tower? And why now, when you have yet to recover from your injury? I'm not a fool, Alex. What are you hiding? Tell me," she implored.

Kat waited, her eyes begging him, giving him every opportunity to tell her the truth. She watched the struggle in his eyes. He wanted to tell her the truth, to confess everything. Then he blinked and the midnight depths she implored became blank and unreadable.

"I have no time for this now, Kat. I have to go. I dare not make King Edward wait any longer." Alex turned sharply away and mounted his horse with Jon's assistance.

Kat nearly staggered.

His abrupt dismissal crushed her heart, the weight of despair unbearable. She could not breathe for the pain. She had asked for honesty in their marriage, but Alex was shutting her out of his life, again. She knew now he would never trust in her ability, her judgment. Without trust, there could be no marriage. She needed more than he could give. She needed his acceptance. His faith and trust to share everything with her, even his troubles and burdens whatever the circumstances. And she refused to beg for a morsel of his trust.

On his mount, Alex closed the distance between them and leaned down in his saddle. He clutched her head between his two large palms and held her gaze. "I *must* go. We will speak when I return."

No matter that she had told herself she hated Alex, would never forgive him his betrayal, she had lied to herself. She had never stopped loving him and never would. But sometimes love was not enough.

Then he dipped his head and kissed her. She kissed him back, her lips clinging to his, putting all her love and forlorn misery into the kiss. A kiss of farewell, although he did not know it. He drew back, spun Zeus around, and rode off for London accompanied by a small contingent of King Edward's men.

Kat stared after him in defeat, her heart shattered. *I love you, Alex. Why can't you love me in return?* A tear slowly rolled down her cheek. She tried to contain it, but her emotions were so volatile she knew any moment they would erupt into a violent cataclysm. She had to get away, flee before anyone witnessed her emotional destruction.

Blind instinct drove her to the only source she could count on when stricken by turmoil and tribulation. Forgotten were any thoughts of imminent danger. Escape was all she thought of.

Lightning pounded down the road, Kat clinging tightly to her back. A sob choked Kat. She did not hold it back this time and let it rip free from her lips. Sobs racked her body. The wind whipped her hair loose around her face like a whirlwind and tears coursed down her cheeks in a torrent. So she did not see the downed two-wheel cart blocking the narrow road until it was too late.

Kat gave the reins a sharp tug. Lightning reared up, whinnying wildly. Though Kat clung tightly by her knees, she began slipping sideways. Preoccupied with controlling her horse, she did not see the two men rush out of the trees towards her. A massive hand grabbed her wrist and yanked her off her horse. She slammed into the hard-packed road, wrenching her hip. Pain flared and she cried out, then a heavy weight landed on top of her.

Crushed beneath her attacker and unable to breathe, she heard the man's voice waft through her stunned consciousness. "I gots her, Ralph. Ye see to the beast."

Her cheek was mashed into the dirt, but Kat saw a man with a jagged knife wound over his left eye grab Lightning's reins and bring the mare under control. Kat struggled beneath her captor but it was futile. He soon had her hands bound with rope behind her back. He grabbed her hair and jerked her face up. Pain seared her scalp and, against her will, a yelp escaped her lips.

She glared up at him in rage. "I shall make you regret accosting me. What do you want?"

But the bastard just laughed. He was big and bald and had black eyes that were devoid of emotion. Then his eyes flared with lewd interest.

An evil grin spread across his face and he shifted his gaze to his partner. "This be the one, Ralph. She be a beauty alright, 'er husband did not lie. He said her eyes were the color of pewter, like what the fancy drink from. Spirited, too." He looked back down at her. "I like that in me woman," he said, grinding his aroused flesh against her bottom.

Kat recoiled, her stomach churning at his foul touch. And what did he mean by 'her husband'?

"What do you intend? If you harm me, my husband will hunt you down and kill you."

He grabbed her tied wrists and yanked her up onto her feet. Pain ripped through her arm sockets. She bit her lip to keep from crying out, refusing to show fear before these villainous scum.

"Who do ye think paid me and Ralph?" He laughed evilly. "*Yer husband* wants ye dead now ye have served your usefulness."

She turned her head and spit in his face. "You lie."

He struck her and split her bottom lip. The metallic taste of blood filled her mouth.

"Do 'at again and I can make things mighty unpleasant for ye," his voice low and sinister.

Kat spat blood from her mouth, vowing to make him pay for his assault.

The man with one eye was wiry and of average height, and had remained silent during the exchange. Now he shuffled his feet. "We should not dally, Stan. 'Er 'usband said make it quick like."

"Aye. 'e paid us to kill her. No reason we can't have us some fun, first, 'ey, Ralph. Let's go."

One Eye just shrugged. "What 'bout the cart?"

"Leave it. We 'ead for camp. I 'ave more urgent doings to attend." Stan squeezed Kat's breast. She cringed from his touch, shuddering with disgust. Laughing, he grabbed her arm and dragged her into the trees. His partner, leading Lightning, took up the rear.

Kat gulped down her panic as she entered the dense woods of Kilburn. She ignored the wrenching pain of her abused body and concentrated on escape. Although she had her dagger, it was useless with her hands tied behind her back. She needed to find a way to get them to untie her. Once free, she could use the dagger. The element of surprise would give her an advantage, which she intended to use with lethal precision.

Back at Westminster Palace, a silk-clad arm reached out from the shadows and yanked Sir Luc into a deserted narrow hall. He reached for his dagger but hesitated at the sibilant whisper. "'Tis me."

His eyes widened in surprise. "What are you doing?" he hissed. "You know we should not meet like this."

"We have a plan, remember?"

Grimacing, Luc darted a nervous glance over his shoulder. "Aye. We do. 'Tis well we meet. I have been meaning to speak to you about our alliance."

"It shall have to wait. I set into motion a trap for Lady Katherine. If you wish to rescue her, you had best go after her now."

"What are you talking about? Surely you jest?"

"Nay. My men have been waiting to ambush her on the road to Kilburn for several days now. And I just saw her ride out heading that way. She is so predictable in her habits." A wave of scorn emanated from the speaker.

"My God, Lydia," he said, grabbing her arms and shaking her. "What have you done? This is not as we planned. If she is harmed in any way—"

Lydia shook free, hissing, "If you hurry, she will not be harmed. I paid them to frighten her, to reveal that Sir Alex is behind the attack. It will drive her into your arms, as we have long wanted. I shall have my revenge." Her tone suddenly turned seductive and she pressed up against him, wrapping her arms around his neck. "And we can be together at last."

She ground her loins against him and he hardened. He began to weaken, then saw her eyes gleam with triumph. Disgusted with himself, Luc shoved her away. "Nay. I wanted naught to do with your plans for revenge. All I ever wanted was you. But I see now you can never love anyone. And I have no one to blame but myself." Luc turned to go after Kat, saying over his shoulder, "You better pray Kat is all right. I have decided to confess everything to Kat and Sir Alex. I shall no longer be a party to your revenge."

With his back turned to Lydia, he did not see the glitter of hatred in her cold blue eyes.

Chapter 25

Moisture dripped down the moldy walls on the ground floor of the White Tower and rats scrabbled into dark crevices as Alex and King Edward advanced down the corridor. His shoulders tense and breathing heavily, Alex was unnerved by the tight, dark confines. But he would let naught get in the way of his mission. Before long, they stopped in front of an ironbound door that led down to the dungeon.

"Open the door," the king ordered the larger of the two grim-faced yeoman warders who accompanied them. The second warder held a lighted torch. The first man removed a key from his belt and unlocked the door. As it creaked open, the stench of excrement and piss bombarded Alex's nostrils. The all-too-familiar smell nearly made him stagger back. Instead, he squared his shoulders and followed Edward down the steep spiral stairs, the torch-carrying warder leading the way.

When they reached the bottom, the guard lit the rushlights in the wall bracket. Light flared inside the chamber, casting eerie shadows around the cavernous room. A row of wooden columns supported the roof, and it was on one of these that Alex saw the prisoner hanging from a hook by his manacled wrists. He was naked except for a loincloth, while his long, lank dark hair shielded his face.

The prisoner did not stir when Alex approached him, so Alex

grabbed the man's hair and jerked his head back to study his face. Bruises covered his right cheek and his left eye was swollen shut, although both eyes remained closed during the inspection. A long, curved scar ran down the mercenary's cheek from the outer corner of his left eye, to his protruding chin. Alex recognized him instantly. A surge of icy hot fury unfurled inside him.

"Is he the one?" King Edward asked from behind Alex.

"Aye." Alex dropped Scarface's head. "Tie him to the stakes," he ordered the warder, his voice coldly calm. His gaze briefly settled upon a pile of heavy stones stacked nearby.

The warder looked to Edward for confirmation.

"Do as he says. Sir Alex shall direct the interrogation." Edward turned to Alex, saying, "I will be in my chambers when you're finished. As soon as you have the traitor's name, I'll order his arrest."

Alex watched Edward retreat up the spiral stairs and exit the miasmic chamber. The door closed with an ominous thud. Alex shuddered, but whipped an iron grip back over his emotions. He would not falter now.

The warder placed the torch in the nearest iron bracket. Alex, his gaze cold and pitiless, watched as the bigger guard supported the prisoner beneath his shoulder while the other guard grabbed the chain off the hook. Scarface was an unusually large man and his body slumped, causing the warder to stagger.

In a sudden flurry of movement, Scarface grabbed the warder's dagger and stabbed both guards in the chest before they could react. One guard dropped dead, the other fell to the ground clutching his stomach and moaning as he bled profusely. Alex already had his dagger drawn and was ready for Scarface.

The villain smiled in recognition. "So we meet again, Sir Alex. Did you have a pleasant stay in prison? I only wish it had lasted longer."

"I could ask you the same. You shall never escape here

alive. Though I might let you live . . . if you give me the name of the traitor who hired you."

"Nay, I believe I shall take my chances. It would appear you have been injured." He pointed at Alex's chest with the stolen dagger.

Alex looked down and saw a spot of blood seeping through his sherte. Scarface, his dagger raised beside his head, stabbed downward at Alex's chest. Having feigned his distraction, Alex quickly blocked Scarface's forearm with the outer edge of his left hand and then rolled his hand to grasp the mercenary's arm in a hold. A blaze of pain ripped through his wounded chest. Scarface was caught off balance and tried to wrap the chain around Alex's arm. His strength dwindling, Alex thrust his dagger from below; the blade slid deep between the mercenary's ribs and entered his chest.

"Who hired you to kill me?" Alex asked urgently. "Give me his name."

Blood gurgled from Scarface's mouth. "Go. To. Hell."

"Was it Lord Calvert?"

The villain's eyes widened, but otherwise he remained silent. Was that acknowledgement?

Alex shoved the blade deeper. "The man who hired you. Give me his name!"

"Grave . . . with me." Scarface laughed long and shrill. Suddenly, he coughed, choking on his own blood. It spewed from his mouth and splattered Alex's white sherte. Then his black gaze grew vacant and he fell to the ground dead.

"Nay," Alex howled. He grabbed Scarface and shook him. "Answer me, give me his name! I want a name!" he raged, his face flushed. He swore the bastard smiled up at him in evil satisfaction. To come this far and fail, it could not be. Alex jumped to his feet and paced away. He checked the second guard and saw he was dead, too.

This is all my fault, Alex thought, pressing the heels of his palms against his temples. He had been careless, and now two men were dead because of him. At a loss, he stared at the

bloody weapon in his hand. His entire plan had hinged on
Scarface's interrogation, on prying from him the name of
the man who hired him. But that idea was as dead as the mercenary, the traitor still free to wreck havoc. And the only remaining person who could identify him was now dead.

"Damn you," Alex roared and kicked the instrument of all
his woes. "I hope you are burning in Hell."

At the same time Alex was despairing at the White Tower,
Kat struggled to get free of the rope binding her wrists.
Dragged into the Kilburn woods a good distance, they reached
the outlaws' camp in a small, secluded clearing.

Looking around, it appeared they had camped out here
for a few days. Several coney pelts were piled up next to an
ash-filled fire pit in the middle of the clearing, the animals no
doubt poached from the neighboring warren in Hampstead.
On either side of the fire were two makeshift shelters.

"What do you intend to do to me?"

The leader, Stan, shoved her. "Sit an close yer yap. I devel-
oped me a thirst."

Kat stumbled and fell, landing hard on her bruised hip.
Pain shot down her thigh and she hissed. Then she scooted
upright onto a rotted log before the fire pit, her scowl ignored.

Rooting around in one of the shelters, Stan hollered,
"Where's me ale, Ralph?"

One Eye, meanwhile, tied Lightning's reins to a tree near
two other horses. Both looked scraggly and maltreated and
were probably stolen.

With a grunt, Stan crawled back out of the shelter. Wineskin in hand, he sat down across from Kat and guzzled his
ale, his lewd eyes never leaving her. One Eye joined them and
sat down next to Stan.

Kat discreetly twisted and pulled on her wrists tied behind
her back, but the rope burned and scraped her skin without
loosening the knot at all. So she tried another tactic.

"I have to use the necessary."

The fat leader grunted. "As ye can see, *me ladee*, this ain't no palace. Do ye see a fancy garderobe to piss in here?" he asked sarcastically.

"Yonder trees shall do just fine for me. Or would you have me relieve myself here?" Her lip curled in disgust. "Might spoil your fun, though."

Stan jumped up, grabbed her bodice and yanked. Startled, Kat cried out. The silk ripped, exposing her cleavage. "Ye 'ave a smart mouth for a ladee," Stan snarled. He groped her breast with one hand and his crotch with the other. "I shall be 'appy to stuff it full to keep it shut."

She cringed away from him. Gulping back tears, she cursed her wayward mouth. But she cursed him more for making her feel humiliated and ashamed. Then he shoved her and she fell back off the log. It hurt, but he was no longer touching her. She started to roll over in an attempt to stand when One Eye clutched her arm and tugged her up.

"Take 'er into the trees, Ralph. Be quick about it. I fancy a good drubbin' in her hot pus."

As One Eye escorted her into the trees, Kat glared over her shoulder at Stan. He stared at her with a gloating smile. She was going to wipe that smug smile from the fat bastard's mouth.

Kat pushed past One Eye, surreptitiously searching for a rock or tree limb. The quickest and surest way to dispatch him would be to slit his throat, but Kat wanted him alive for questioning. She prayed she would find what she needed, and nearly gasped when she saw a rock the size of a horseshoe next to a beech tree five feet before her.

She stepped over it, and stopped so it was concealed beneath her skirts where One Eye could not see it.

"Do yer business, lady. I'll be waitin' near that tree." He pointed.

"I cannot do my business with my hands tied." She presented her hands to him, hoping he would not argue.

He hesitated.

She looked over her shoulder at him, her eyes wide. "Surely you don't fear me? How can I escape? I'm just a woman."

He grunted. His undamaged eye held a warning. "Don't try to flee. You cannot escape me," he said before he untied her hands.

"Nay. I shall not run," she said honestly, rubbing her red, raw wrists.

He turned and took up a position by an elm tree not far away, his back to her to give her privacy. He was not the smartest mongrel in the pack. Which was what she counted on.

Quietly, Kat picked up the rock and approached him from behind. With a solid hard strike, she bashed it against the back of his skull. Groaning, he dropped like a stone.

Needing to hurry before Stan became suspicious, she checked to make sure One Eye was alive, then grabbed his arms and tugged with all her strength. She grunted, pulling him up so his back was propped against the tree. Next, she found the rope where the ruffian dropped it and tied his wrists together around the tree trunk. Finally, she retrieved his dagger and tested the knot to make sure it was secure.

Hurriedly, she crept back to the clearing and peered at Stan from behind a tree. He was grumbling under his breath and pacing back and forth with the wineskin in his hand. Then the bald outlaw stopped in his tracks and took a swig of ale.

Kat stepped out of the trees, and in one smooth movement drew her arm back and then forward, releasing One Eye's dagger from the tip of her fingers. Turning end over end, it flew past Stan's head and embedded in the tree ten feet behind him.

Stan jumped with a screech, sloshing ale down his tunic. Shocked and sputtering, he stared at her.

Withdrawing her own dagger, she pointed the blade below his waist and mocked, "It appears you have had an accident."

He looked down at his wet crotch. "Mouthy bitch," he replied, tossing the wineskin aside. He withdrew a dagger from his wide leather belt. "I'm gonna enjoy slittin' your throat," he said, then peered nervously over her shoulder.

Laughter bubbled up from her chest. "I am afraid your friend is in no position to help you. 'Tis just you and me." Kat closed the distance between them though she remained out of striking range.

His deep-set black eyes jerked back to her. "I'm not 'fraid of ye," he growled.

"Good. It will make this so much quicker."

Kat took the measure of her opponent as they circled each other. While Stan held his dagger near his ear in a reverse grip, Kat held her dagger at her waist near her hip, the blade extended forward.

Stan struck first with a downward stab of his forearm to her chest. But Kat was ready. She clutched both ends of her dagger and used it as a shield to deflect Stan's forearm. As Kat pushed his dagger arm to the right, her left hand slid from her blade and clutched his arm before he could withdraw and strike again. Sweat broke out on her forehead and Stan's rank odor burned her nostrils. She thrust her dagger at Stan's stomach, but he pivoted backward on his right foot, barely avoiding a direct blow. He backed away, a red slash on his side where the blade nicked him.

Stan clutched his side, stunned, blood oozing between his fingers. "No wonder yer 'usband paid me to kill ye. Yer unnatural."

"You are a liar. My husband would never harm me."

More cautious now, he circled her, gauging an opening. He had brute strength on his side, but she was quick and clever.

"Who really paid you to kill me?" she countered

He shook his head in mock pity, sighing. "I told ye. Yer 'usband, me ladee."

Kat circled to her left, watching, waiting. "If my husband really hired you, describe him."

"Tall. Black hair and blue eyes." He smiled insolently at her. "The face of a man liked by the ladees."

"I don't believe you."

In a single fluid movement, Kat reversed her grip on the

dagger so her thumb was by the pommel, and thrust the blade at Stan's neck. But he caught her wrist and using his greater strength, trapped her arm under his armpit in a strong hold. Kat, drenched in sweat and propelled face down, grunted as she strained to hold onto her dagger and escape the trap. She saw her opening.

Stan made a fatal mistake when he placed his feet behind her body. Kat swung her left leg back in front of Stan's feet, and lifting his weight over her hip she flipped him onto his back. Stan landed with a painful grunt. Kat knelt down and planted her knee on his chest, then stabbed him in the shoulder twice in rapid succession.

A sudden shout and a horse charging through the trees distracted Kat. The outlaw jumped up and limped for the horses, clutching his bleeding shoulder.

Sir Luc bolted into the clearing on his bay horse and pulled to a halt beside her. His gold eyes wide with fear, he bounded to the ground and grasped her shoulders taking in her disheveled appearance before gathering her in his arms.

The outlaw had untied Lightning's reins, but her faithful mare reared and kicked her legs. Stan jumped back quickly and veered towards one of the other horses.

At the commotion Luc released her. "He's getting away." He looked torn between following in pursuit and making sure she was all right.

Stan managed to untie the reins, climb up awkwardly onto the horse's back and disappear into the trees.

Kat clutched Luc's arm. "Leave him. We can send some of Edward's men after him when we return to the castle. He won't make it far with his injuries."

"What of you? Did he harm you?" His voice frantic, his gaze searched her for any sign of injury. Her lip was bruised and bloody, and her body ached terribly, but she was all right. "He hit you," he said, his voice dangerously low. He skimmed his fingers lightly over the swollen flesh. ·

"Aye, but I am fine otherwise."

Recalling Stan's vile hands on her breasts, she shuddered.

As though he read her mind his eyes dropped to her torn bodice, his eyes furious. "My God, Kat." He pulled her into his arms and held her tight. "Are you sure you're all right? If he harmed you, in any way, I shall hunt him down and kill him."

"Nay, I am unharmed," she said, her voice muffled against his chest. "Just shaken."

"If aught had happened to you . . . I would never forgive myself." His voice shook.

Kat pulled out of his arms. "Don't blame yourself, Luc. 'Tis naught you could have done to prevent it. I should not have ridden out unattended."

He shook his head about to reply, but she suddenly thought of something, her brows drawn down in confusion. "Luc, what are you doing here? How did you find me?"

His eyes darted away from her probing gaze. "I knew you rode out this way and I followed you. When I saw the downed cart and discovered signs of a recent ambush, I followed the trail into the woods."

"I'm glad you did. I don't know what would have happened if you did not arrive when you did," Kat said, though she had had matters well in hand.

"Prithee, Kat, I beg you. I do not deserve your praise. Verily, just the opposite." He looked up at last with a shame-filled gaze.

Kat frowned, confused once more. "What in the world are you talking about, Luc?"

"Tell me what happened. What did that man want?"

Puzzled at the switch in topics, Kat told Luc of her attack. How she had escaped. That the other outlaw still remained tied up in the trees and unconscious.

"Luc. It was Alex. They said he hired them to kill me." No matter how hard she tried to deny it, pain and anguish seeped out in her voice.

Luc shook his golden head and turned his back to her. "And you believed them?"

"Not at first. But the leader described who hired him in

vivid detail. He described Alex exactly. And what would the man have to gain by lying? So, aye, I believe Alex hired those men to get rid of me." Embittered, disillusioned, her shoulders slumped.

When Luc turned back to her his mouth was drawn down, deep lines bracketing his mouth. He appeared remorseful, despondent. "I have a confession, Kat. I have not been completely truthful with you."

Kat immediately became alert. Then Lightning neighed and approached her. "Come. I want to leave this place. We can talk as we ride. Someone will need to send the sheriff to retrieve the outlaws." Her hip aching, she needed Luc's assistance to mount her horse.

Once on his bay, Luc sidled up beside her. "Kat, I must speak. I cannot wait a moment longer. The guilt and shame are tearing me apart."

She laid her hand gently on his arm. "Luc. What nonsense is this? I can't believe you could ever do aught to be ashamed of."

He shook his head and spoke quickly, as if afraid he would not be able to get it all out. "Nay, your trust in me is misplaced. I'm a fraud. My desire to marry you has been a ruse from the very beginning. When she came to me with the plan over a year ago, I loved her so much I would have done anything for her. I did it for her, you see." His eyes begged her to understand.

Kat recoiled and stared at him in mute shock, even as everything began to make terrible sense. A woman scorned, revenge upon those she blamed for her disappointment, a woman who used and manipulated people. Men especially.

Although she knew of whom he spoke, Kat asked anyway. "Who put you up to such a cruel and deceitful thing?"

"Lady Lydia."

"What was her plan? And what did she hope to gain?"

"She promised if I married you, it would prove to her that I love her, and she and I would be together at last. She felt hurt and betrayed when Alex asked her to marry him, took her virginity, then spurned her. And she blamed you as well."

"That's a lie. Alex would never do such a thing. He is an honorable man. He would never have asked Lydia to marry him. He was as good as betrothed to me when they met." Even as she uttered the words, she realized the truth. That Alex was an honorable man and would never stoop to murder.

Bitterness etched Luc's forehead and turned down lips. "This I believe. Now. But I loved Lydia. I believed her lies for so long." He continued. "I'm ashamed to say my collusion did not end when Alex returned from captivity. I knew Lydia would not be satisfied until your marriage was destroyed utterly for all time and I have been working to cause dissention between you and Alex ever since. Then after her arrival at court, Lydia sent me a message telling me to proceed as we had planned."

"And if her plan had succeeded?"

Luc could no longer look her in the eyes and dropped his gaze. "Her revenge would be complete. She would have succeeded in destroying your marriage to Alex and humiliating you in the process."

"Why did you do it? I thought you were estranged from Lydia?"

He met her gaze once more, his golden eyes infinitely sad and defeated. "I have always loved her. Since the day she arrived to marry my father. I was mad with jealousy thinking of her with him. Until she confessed she loved me, too. After that we became lovers. Then one night my father discovered Lydia and me in bed together. To protect her, I made it appear Lydia was unwilling. That's the real reason why my father disowned me. And I have kept up the pretense ever since."

"You said you did it so you and Lydia could be together. But that would be rather difficult as she was married to your father."

"Aye, but my father was old, and as he was ailing these last two years, I knew he was not long for this earth."

Kat could surmise the rest. No doubt Lydia had planned, once Kat married Sir Luc, to be Sir Luc's mistress. The

Church would never have given the lovers a dispensation to marry because they were related via marriage through a direct descendant's line. Besides, Lydia need not marry the man, Luc was besotted with her and would have done anything she wished. And Lydia would have reveled in humiliating Kat by bedding her husband, and flaunting her sorcery over Sir Luc. But obviously something had changed.

Lightning shifted nervously beneath Kat. She clutched her reins tighter. "Why are you telling me this now, Luc?"

"Because I have come to care for you as a friend. And I realize now Lydia never loved me. I suspect she craftily arranged for my father to discover her and me in bed together, then manipulated my love for her to gain revenge. I know it does not absolve me of my guilt, but I never intended it to go so far. Believe it or not, I used to be an honorable man before I met Lydia," he said, his lips twisted in a bitter expression. "But there is more, I need to tell you the rest. Lydia—"

A familiar whooshing sound hummed in the air a moment before Luc's confession abruptly ended. He shouted and clutched his side. His eyes wide from shock, he stared down at the arrow protruding from his stomach, while blood trickled through his fingers. Then he slowly slumped over his horse.

Held immobile by surprise, Kat jerked her gaze up. The cold, calculating perusal of the man across from her caused a shiver to race down her spine. Not to mention the arrow pointed directly at her.

Chapter 26

Alex rode through the palace gate, slid off Zeus and tossed the reins to his squire, Jon. His shoulder throbbed, but he ignored it and strode purposely to the nearest palace entrance. He desperately wished to see Kat. He needed to tell her of Scarface, of his failed attempt to discover the man responsible for his captivity. Long had he wanted to confide in her, knowing she would understand his need for vengeance. But fear had kept him silent.

Now it might be too late. He could not forget the look on her face this afternoon when she beseeched him to tell her the truth, or her devastation when he turned away. Having kept his suspicions secret, it was as if he had betrayed her all over again. He should have trusted her from the beginning, but he had taken a vow to protect her, and duty had been ingrained into his blood and bone and sinew. Still, he should have found a way to be honest and protect her at the same time.

Upon entering the palace's darkened structure, he searched the ground floor first, checking the dining hall and chapels. Next he glanced into their chambers upstairs. Seeing no sign of her, he headed for the queen's solar where the ladies often entertained at court.

Fear had also kept him silent in regard to his true feelings for his wife. He had wanted to be sure she loved him before he confessed he had fallen in love with her. But he had wounded

Kat deeply when he deserted her after their wedding, so he knew the next step was up to him. He must risk his own heart if he was ever to find the happiness he sought.

His thoughts were interrupted when he rounded the corner to the solar and collided with another. A soft, feminine gasp alerted him to the woman's identity. Alex groaned inwardly. Light from a sconce shone on her golden hair like a halo, though her eyes remained in shadow.

"I beg your pardon, Lady Lydia. If you will excuse me?" He made to step around her but she reached out and clutched his sleeve.

She smiled, a stingy lift of her lips. "Are you looking for your lady wife, perchance?"

Alex stiffened. It was difficult to interpret her tone but he got the feeling she was gloating, a spider stringing him along her web into a deadly trap. How could he ever have been fooled by her coy, innocent act? "I am. So if you will excuse me?"

"I know where you can find her, Sir Alex."

Though he was unwilling to ask aught of her, he was curious. "And how come you to know my wife's whereabouts?" he asked suspiciously.

"I was in the garden this morning when I accidentally overheard a very illicit, private conversation. Can you imagine my dismay?"

Alex glared down at her. "Nay, I cannot. Nor can I imagine what that has to do with my wife?"

She gazed at him pityingly. "I'm so sorry, Alex. But it appears the woman you are so besotted with is not worthy of your love."

His jaw clenched. "Lydia," he growled, "explain yourself."

"Very well." She sighed. "The conversation I overheard was between Lady Katherine and Sir Luc. They were making plans to meet at some hunting lodge for an assignation. Then shortly after you left the palace, I saw her ride out, Sir Luc fast behind her. If I were you I would check the lodge. Do you know of it?"

He grabbed her shoulders in a tight grip. "You are lying, Lady Lydia. My wife is no whore."

She squirmed to be free and he released her. Then she shrugged as though unconcerned. "I guess there is only one way for you to find out. But I can understand why you would not want to learn the truth. Good day, Sir Alex."

Lydia left him staring at the gray stone walls in disbelief. Swiftly, memories of the last few days assaulted him one after another like fiery missiles slung from a trebuchet. Beginning with the day he had awakened from delirium and had discovered his wife on top of him, her hot center open and vulnerable to invasion. Kat had wanted him as much as he wanted her. But he was in no condition to make love to her.

Later, when she had returned from the kitchens with nourishment, she had tended to his needs most attentively. Then everything changed that evening after Rand had visited him. She became distant and cold. And no persuasion on his part could get her to tell him what was troubling her.

Now Kat, if he were to believe Lydia, had cuckolded him with the man she nearly married. The man Alex loathed for no other reason than jealousy. Nay, he would not believe Kat capable of such duplicity. But a niggling doubt festered and grew, compelling him to seek out the truth no matter the cost.

Alex rushed back to his chamber, dug the Beaumont dagger out of the chest, and tucked it inside his wide leather belt. When he exited the palace, he dashed across the courtyard and into the stable. Kat's mare was not in its stall. Neither was Luc's bay gelding. But there could be some other reason for Luc to have taken his horse. So Alex sought out the lad he had paid to keep an eye on Kat.

Alex found Tim replenishing the hay in one of the stalls' mangers, and pulled the boy aside so none could overhear. "Did you see my wife ride out today after I left the palace?"

The lad's eyes widened with fear. "I, um, I don't know, Sir Alex."

"What do you mean . . . ?" Alex's voice grew louder. He

paused, constricted the rage growing inside him and lowered his voice. "What do you mean you don't know? I paid you to get word to me or my friend if my wife left the castle grounds on horse."

Tim gulped and shuffled to his other foot. "Aye, sir, you did. But the head groom sent me on an errand to the tanner. I did not see your lady leave."

Alex cursed.

Fear lit the boy's eyes. "Did I do wrong, milord?"

"Nay. 'Tis not your fault. But mayhap you can still help me. Can you tell me who has ridden out since your return?"

The lad took off his cap wringing it in his hands. "Not many, Sir Alex. A small party of ladies traveled to London town. And Sir Randall, Sir Connaught and Lord Calvert rode out to the hunt."

Alex reached out and clutched Tim's shoulder. "Can you remember aught else?"

The boy dropped his gaze. "I wish I could help you, milord, but . . ." he broke off, then his wide-eyed gaze shot up again, "Oh . . . wait, I just remembered something."

Alex nearly shook him. "Go on."

"When I returned from the tanner, one of the lads was complaining because Sir Luc boxed his ears for being too slow saddling his mount. His lordship was in a mighty hurry and finished saddling his gelding himself. He's not returned yet."

His last hope that Lydia had lied shattered at the mention of that one name. Alex slammed his fist into the wall. "Get my saddle." Then he turned on his spurs and went to the stall holding Zeus.

He opened the door, pulled a lead rope over the black's head and led him out into the yard. Sensing Alex's anger, Zeus sidled away from him. Alex relaxed, breathing deeply, and ran his hand down the stallion's neck. "Easy boy. I know you've earned a rest. But I need you for one more mission."

Impatient, Alex watched as the lad saddled his horse. He would have tacked his mount himself, but the range of his injured arm was limited. Alex paced back and forth, restless, feeling caged. The demons he worked long and hard to bury clamored and clawed to dig their way free. Their claws scraped beneath his skin, undermining his iron control, while a tic at his temple pulsed with each rapid beat of his heart.

He was going to kill Sir Luc. But first he was going to sever his cock and shove it down his throat. And his darling wife. . . .

Jon jogged into the courtyard from the direction of the household barracks. "Is aught amiss, my lord?"

Alex mounted his horse, groaning beneath his breath from the pain. "Nay. Naught I cannot handle on my own."

The squire's eyes widened when he saw the Beaumont dagger at Alex's waist. "My lord, wait—"

But Alex rode away without a backward glance.

Kat tried to rouse from the murky shadows, but total awareness was beyond her reach. Her skull reverberated with a pounding ache and a heavy weight upon her eyelids prevented her from opening them. Her battered and bruised body throbbed painfully.

A tug on her skirts alerted her to the danger; cloth ripped, cold steel grazed her calf. Her heart beat wildly as panic flooded her. She tried to kick out, but her ankles were bound tightly together. Her head began to pound louder. Then someone cursed, grabbed her hands together in front of her and bound her wrists. As darkness pushed her under again, she recognized the sound of hoofbeats approaching.

The next she woke her mind was clearer, though her head ached and her swollen lip throbbed. She dared not move and alert her abductor that she was awake. After the fiend had shot Sir Luc, he had ordered her to get off her mare and to turn around. Then everything went black. He must have knocked her out, but where was she now?

Kat vaguely remembered being lifted into a cart and then her body being painfully jostled over rough terrain. She slowly cracked her eyelids open to ascertain her whereabouts. And almost gasped as her gaze landed on Sir Luc. He lay deathly pale beside her in bed, his breathing shallow and labored. The coverlet was pulled up to his bare chest. They were at the hunting lodge. She remembered the bed vividly from the time her and Alex had rendezvoused here during the rain.

Why had Sir Stephen brought them here? she wondered. If he meant to kill them why go to the bother of bringing them to the lodge? Which led her to question why he intended them ill in the first place?

Then she remembered the hoofbeats she heard earlier.

Her fear escalated and she searched deeper into the shadows. She gasped aloud this time. Alex sat slumped in a chair beside the bed, his chin resting on his chest. He was trussed to the chair, the rope looped several times around his chest, feet, and hands.

Then the significance of her and Luc in bed together finally registered. Oh God. Alex. Alex was his target. A bead of sweat popped out on Kat's temple. All along Sir Stephen had been the traitor Alex sought. But what could the man possibly have against him? It made no sense.

A light flared, growing larger and brighter as Sir Stephen approached the bed. "Good. You are awake. We can proceed now."

The glow of the lamp shone on Alex, revealing a trail of blood down his temple. But he was alive or he would not be tied to a chair.

"W–what have you done to Alex?"

He smiled with a satisfied leer. "Just a blow to his head. He will wake with a headache. Never fear, I shall give you one last chance to speak to him before I kill you."

She glared up at him. "You shall not get away with this. The king knows you are responsible for Alex's disappearance in the Holy Land. That you hired Scarface to do the job," Kat bluffed.

His close-set weaselly eyes revealed his surprise. "You lie," he hissed. "If that were so I would be in the Tower right now."

"Dare you take the chance I lie?"

"I don't believe you. But if what you say is true, then I have naught to lose by killing you, do I?"

His boots rang on the floorboards as he stomped away. He strode back to the table behind Alex and placed the lamp on it. Sweat dribbled down her neck as she tested her bonds beneath the coverlet. Her feet were tied together, as were her wrists, but she was not restricted in any other way.

Relief flooded her, for Sir Stephen had not discovered her dagger strapped to her thigh. With a little maneuvering, she could retrieve it and cut free of her bonds.

Shuffling footsteps were the only sound in the stuffy darkened lodge. Sir Stephen reached down and picked up a bucket, then threw the contents over Alex's head.

Icy water slapped Alex in the face, bringing him around. He shook his soaked head and a jabbing pain seared his skull. He groaned. Blinded by a bright light, he blinked several times. A man's form took shape as the light dimmed. Alex looked up at the gloating countenance of Sir Stephen. His first thought—what has the bastard done to Kat? Alex surged up, furious. The chair legs scraped the floor beneath him, but tied to the chair he was unable to get up.

He strained against the ropes, his face flushed with exertion. "By God. What have you done to Kat? If you have harmed her—"

"I am here, Alex. Unharmed, but bound same as you."

Alex stared into the shadows, he could see little except the outline of the bed. Sir Stephen moved to the other side of the bed and lighted a hanging cresset lamp. Light shone down on Kat, her hair was disheveled and fear glazed her eyes. Alex had never been more relieved to see his wife. Or scared for her life.

"Kat. Thank God. Are you all right?"

"Aye, but Sir Luc is seriously wounded. Sir Stephen gut-shot him with an arrow."

Alex followed her gaze and narrowed his eyes upon Sir Luc, who lay beside her in bed, his face pale and covered in the sheen of sweat.

"They look cozy do they not? Such a handsome couple," Sir Stephen mocked. Alex's second thought—he had discovered the traitor at last.

"Go to hell, you spineless bastard," Kat spit out.

Sir Stephen took a threatening step towards Kat, his face contorted in hatred. Alex drew Sir Stephen's attention away from his imprudent wife.

"You shall pay for your transgressions, Sir Stephen. Unless . . . Release us now and I shall ask the king to go leniently with you."

Sir Stephen returned to stand before him, gloating. "Nay. I think not. With you dead, I shall have everything I ever wanted."

Alex shook his head. "You make no sense. What could you possibly gain with my death?"

"Revenge, for one. Your sister murdered my cousin," he snarled. "Bertram was the only person who ever loved me, who treated me with respect. And I want her to suffer, as I have suffered, for the rest of her life."

"Nay. You are wrong. My sister could not kill anyone."

Stephen shoved his face in Alex's and swore, "I have a witness who says otherwise." Spittle splattered Alex's face.

"Then why did he not come forward when your cousin died?"

Stephen spun around, stalked to the post at the foot of the bed and gripped it with his hand. He stared down pensively at Sir Luc lying still and as pale as bone. "*She* feared the repercussions of doing so. But it matters not anymore. I shall deal with your sister in my own way."

Alex kept him talking, hoping to discover a way to break free, but the situation looked hopeless. "Whether my sister was responsible or not, your cousin died two years ago." Alex glanced at Kat uneasily. "That does not explain why you hired Sir Hugo Krieger to attack me in the Holy Land." At Sir Stephen's surprised look, Alex continued. "Aye. The king has Scarface in custody at the Tower. The mercenary admitted to me just this day that you hired him to capture me and sell me to the Mamluks. The king has ordered your arrest and even now his men are searching for you."

Sir Stephen smiled, his expression smug. "You're bluffing. Your wife tried the same trick on me. But she could not possibly know Sir Hugo confessed if he just admitted it to you. I think you both lie."

Surprised at this revelation, Alex glanced at Kat. She held his gaze steadily. Suddenly her recent mood shift made sense. Somehow she had learned about Scarface. That Alex had been lying to her for some while.

But Alex had no time to continue speculating. "Yet I notice you do not deny you hired Scarface. I have yet to understand why, though. What motive could make you do such a thing?"

Sir Stephen laughed gleefully. "Exactly. It's brilliant. No one will suspect me of your demise. For what reason could I wish you dead?"

Surprisingly, it was Kat who enlightened Alex. Her gaze meeting his confused one, she explained. "He has an accomplice."

Of course, Alex thought. He should have realized it sooner, but he had been completely absorbed in discovering a way to escape Stephen's deadly trap.

"Lady Lydia," Alex breathed the words.

He glanced at Kat again. "When I returned to the palace looking for you, I ran into Lady Lydia. She said she overheard you and Sir Luc making plans to meet at the hunting lodge. I didn't believe her at first, but—" Alex shook is head with regret. "Obviously it was a trick and she has been behind the attacks all along."

She gave him an enigmatic smile, though slightly strained. "Indeed. *Hell hath no fury like a woman scorned.*"

Chapter 27

Sir Stephen stopped laughing and turned to Kat. "How did you discover my involvement with Lady Lydia?"

Alex was curious to know that question, too.

Though Sir Stephen asked the question, Kat did not move her gaze from Alex. "Sir Luc," she replied, her lips down turned in a bitter smile, "confessed to me that he had intended to marry me under false pretenses. Luc said Lydia concocted the whole scheme to revenge herself on you and me because she hated you for refusing to marry her."

Alex dug his fingers into the chair's armrests. "But why would Luc agree to such a plan? I thought he despised his step-mother."

A bark of bitter laughter burst from her lips. "Just the opposite. Luc was in love with her and she convinced him that if he did this for her, they could finally be together. With Luc's revelation, I realized Lydia was the missing link that connected Scarface's first attack on you before we were married, and your captivity in Syria. 'Twas a simple matter of deduction that she manipulated Sir Stephen, too." Kat's gaze moved to Stephen. "What I do not know is why you agreed to the plot."

Alex stared at his clever wife in amazement.

Could it be so simple? he wondered. Looking back it made so much sense. As Kat mentioned, it explained the mercenary's first attack on him the day of his betrothal to Kat. Lady Lydia must have put the plot into motion after Alex refused to marry her. When the first attempt failed, she bided her time and waited for another opportunity.

A loud crash splintered the silence. Stephen had kicked the bucket across the room and it now lay smashed on the rush-covered floor, his face twisted in evil menace. "Lady Lydia was not using me. No one uses me. Sir Luc was *my* pawn."

Kat turned her gaze on Sir Stephen, her voice mocking. "Lydia enjoys manipulating men. If you think back I think you will agree. *You* and Sir Luc were her pawns. And I would guess there is no evidence to tie her to any crime. Am I right, Sir Stephen?"

Hate distorted the blond man's features. "Goddamn deceiving bitch. It was my cousin Bertram. Lydia and he were lovers. At her behest, he hired a mercenary to get rid of you. But Bertram sent me to the Continent to hire him. So there is no evidence that can point to Lydia as the instigator."

Stephen grew more agitated, murmuring under his breath as he paced before the bed. Alex, needing to keep him talking, but unwilling to provoke him, spoke in a neutral tone. "Then I unexpectedly returned from the dead."

Sir Stephen spun around and snarled, "You should have died in prison!" He grabbed Alex by the throat and squeezed, cutting off his air passage. Alex choked, his face reddening as he tried to inhale air into his lungs. Spots danced before his eyes, his body jerking with the force to breathe. He heard Kat scream, then the pressure lessened and Stephen stepped back. "But it would seem you are a hard man to kill."

Alex sucked in deep breaths of precious air. The man's emotional imbalance, shifting from rage to satisfaction in the blink of an eye disturbed Alex. At any moment his rage could push him over the edge of madness. He needed to keep Sir Stephen calm, distracted.

"And when I returned?" Alex choked out, his throat scratchy.

Stephen's gaze glittered black with hatred. "I decided to take matters into my own hands when you returned. Originally I hired the mercenary at Bertram and Lydia's behest, but now I want revenge for his murder. When Lady Lydia arrived at court, together we began to plot your demise." He turned and stared at Kat slyly. "'Twas Lydia who arranged today's roadside attack on you. You and Luc fell neatly into her trap." Stephen sneered, his maniacal laugh grating.

Alex swung his gaze to his wife. Kat was attacked today? Upon closer inspection, he noticed the bruising on her cheek and lip. In the shadowed canopy bed it was unnoticeable at first. Fury welled up inside him. His fists clenched, he strained against his bonds.

Kat gazed at Sir Stephen in contempt. "I was not the only one Lydia manipulated. You had no idea Lydia and Luc were lovers. That she plotted behind your back with him."

"Nay. The bitch lied to me. Nor did Sir Luc seek to enlighten me, either."

Alex jerked in surprise. "Do you mean that Sir Luc was involved with your plot, too?"

"Aye." The blond man smiled in evil satisfaction. "I approached Sir Luc after you returned to England. I realized I could use him to stir up trouble between you and your wife. You see, he thought my goal was to destroy your marriage." Then he frowned, remembering Luc's ulterior motive. "But at the time I thought he was doing it to win Lady Katherine, not Lydia."

Alex shifted in his chair. The ropes binding his wrists, which he had been working to loosen while distracting Sir Stephen, slackened a little. On the bed he heard Kat moving about quietly and wondered what she was about. But he dared not look her way.

"So you used Sir Luc to cause trouble between Kat and me. Was Luc involved in the plot to kill me? Did he have aught to do with the arrow attack in the woods, or the bear attack at the faire?"

Cruel satisfaction gleamed in Stephen's eyes. "Nay. The

fool. He had no idea I had anything to do with your captivity, or my attempts to kill you. He is a weak man and I could not trust him with all my plans. And obviously I was right because he could not even keep his mouth shut about his association with Lady Lydia." Stephen glowered at Kat. "But enough of this," he said, slashing his hand in the air.

Panic assailed Alex. His hands were still bound and he had yet to form a plan to escape and save Kat. "Wait. You said revenge was only one motive. What other reason could you possibly have to want me dead?"

Stephen grinned. "Land and power, of course. With you dead and your father another victim of a freak accident, I'm sure then King Edward will give me wardship of my nephew. Young children are so vulnerable, what with illnesses and accidents. A shame, really."

"Never. I shall see you dead," Alex swore.

Sir Stephen, his eyes glittering with madness, fingered the Beaumont dagger at his waist. "You are in no position to stop me. I'm the one in control. Do you not wish to know what I have planned for your deaths?"

Kat spoke up, shifting in the bed. "Sir Stephen. Do you really expect that you can kill us and get away with it? King Edward will hunt you down till you are captured or dead."

Sir Stephen ignored her. He paced to the end of the bed, withdrawing the jeweled dagger and digging the tip into the flesh of his palm. "My plan is brilliant." He cackled. "Sir Alex, having discovered his lady wife fornicating with her lover, went on a murderous rampage and brutally stabbed the lovers to death." Alex exchanged a fearful look with Kat. Sir Stephen spoke as though they were already dead. "When Sir Alex realized what he had done, he committed suicide in despair. They say his body was found floating in the Thames. How sad. How tragic."

Alex jerked in his chair, sweat beading his forehead as panic overwhelmed him. "You shall not get away with this,

Stephen. King Edward will never believe that story, no matter the evidence you concoct."

Stephen moved closer to Kat, his gaze unblinking, emotionless. "On the contrary. He may be suspicious, but there will be no proof of foul play. The court will revel at the salacious nature of the killings and be all too willing to believe the tale."

Then he held the dagger up to the glow of the lamp. "After all, Sir Alex's dagger was discovered with the bodies to lend credence to his crimes."

Alex began to struggle in his chair, his heart hammering. Kat stared up at Sir Stephen with a feverish intensity, the light refracting off the jeweled-pommel splashing red across her drawn face. "You have always been a coward, Sir Stephen. Release me and fight me like a man!" Alex yelled desperately.

Despair flooding him, Alex twisted and tugged as hard as he could on the ropes. His flesh was raw and slippery with blood. He pulled so hard that the chair scraped the floorboards as it dragged across the floor.

Alex looked up and caught Kat's gaze, all the love he felt for her shining in his eyes. Then he stared aghast as Sir Stephen raised the dagger high and plunged the knife down at her chest.

Kat screamed. Alex howled her name and his chair toppled over with the force of his rage. He landed close to the bed, the oak monstrosity blocking his view. Pain shot up his arms. But it was naught compared to the pain that reverberated through him at the sickening plunge of the dagger into Kat's flesh. A death gurgle rattled, followed by silence, except for Alex's harsh breathing.

His heart was ripped from his body with Kat's last breath. Numb, shock whispered through his body like a cold artic blast. He had fought for so long and hard that the fight left him at last. Without Kat, he had no reason to live. Sir Stephen could do with him what he would.

Then he heard a strange sound he could not identify and the ruffling of the bedcovers. Slowly, Sir Stephen came around the bed. Alex looked up, his eyes bleak, uncaring what was in store for him. But he received another shock. It was Kat who stared down at him, her bodice ripped and her black hair hanging wildly about her pale face. Her eyes were unfocused, an odd light glowing within them, and her bloodied dagger dangled from her fingers.

"My God, Kat. I thought you were de—" Emotion clogged his throat.

Kat, her legs shaking, fell to her knees before Alex. With her bloody dagger she cut through the ropes around Alex's wrists. Her emotions were a tangle of guilt, horror, satisfaction and—oddly—understanding. Sir Stephen had loved his cousin to such a degree he was willing to kill for him. And in the end, that single-minded devotion drove him to madness.

As she sawed through the ropes with the blade, her hand began to tremble. She saw again Stephen's eyes bright with madness, the blade plunging down towards her, only moments after she had retrieved her own dagger.

"Easy, my love. You are alive. We both are, because of you. Stephen can never hurt anyone again."

His voice, soft and sure, enabled her to gather her composure. Her body shuddered once and she continued slicing through the rope around his ankles.

"How did you do it? I thought Stephen had . . ." He shook his head as though unable to complete the thought. "How?"

Her mouth twisted in an ironic smile. "While you kept him occupied talking, I was able to retrieve my dagger from under my skirts. He couldn't see me clutching it under the coverlet and when he went to stab me I drove it into his heart. He died instantly."

Once free, Alex rose to his feet and pulled her into his arms. Dropping the dagger, she went willingly and snuggled close to his chest, savoring his warmth, his masculine scent, and his strong arms around her. But it was a temporary balm.

Alex pulled back and stared down at her, she read the light of admiration in his cobalt gaze. "Kat, you are the most amazing woman I have ever met. I don't know what I would have done without you."

Was that the remnants of dried tears she saw on his cheeks?

He gently rubbed her swollen lip with the pad of his thumb. "Are you all right? Did they hurt you?"

She shook her head. "Have no fear, Alex. I shall be fine. 'Tis just a couple of bruises. The villains Lydia hired to attack me had no time to do any further damage. One man escaped, but not far from here his accomplice is tied up in the woods of Kilburn."

Rage glittered in his eyes. "I will see Lydia pay for hurting you."

Then a ragged groan escaped him and he pulled her into his embrace. Surrendering for the nonce, she melted into him, her breasts pillowing his warm chest. She wrapped her arms around his neck and raised her mouth to his. A soft moan beckoned him. Alex answered the call and kissed her, his lips tender, soothing her abused flesh. With a lick of his tongue, warmth salved her split lip.

His hand slid inside her torn bodice and kneaded her breast. Still tender from Stan's foul touch, she flinched and jerked away. She could not look at Alex.

"Kat. What is wrong? Did I hurt you?"

She shook her head and turned away. Her gaze landed on Sir Luc. Good Lord. How could she be so thoughtless? She moved to Sir Luc's side and pulled back the coverlet, ignoring the body slumped face down on the other side of the bed.

Sir Luc's tunic and sherte had been removed, but his braies and hose remained. She leaned over and discovered him still alive, barely. His breath was shallow and erratic. Then she checked his wound. Low and on the left side, an arrow with the fletching broken off protruded from Luc's stomach. A pool of congealed blood saturated the linen sheet beneath him.

"How is Sir Luc?" Kat looked up at Alex's query. He stood opposite her and had turned Sir Stephen over. Blood soaked the dead man's tunic where she stabbed him, his face a grimace of surprise. Alex's eyes held hers tenderly.

Kat turned her attention to Luc again. "He has lost a large amount of blood. He needs care immediately. You will have to ride to the palace to fetch the physician."

Alex nodded reluctantly. "Will you be all right alone here while I am gone?" He pried his dagger from Sir Stephen's clenched fingers, retrieved the enameled-sheath and returned the sheathed dagger to his waist.

"You needn't worry about me. I shall be fine."

"Need aught else before I leave?"

She looked up at him once more. "I can manage, but . . . Prithee, take that foul offal and remove him from the lodge."

"Of course." Alex came around and took her hand in his. Her palm was sweaty. "After I arrange for Sir Luc's care and see that Lady Lydia and the villains who attacked you are detained, there are things we need to discuss."

Kat nodded, but she had already made her decision. This day's events had merely reinforced her belief that ending her marriage was the right choice. Alex smiled gently and hugged her one last time. Then while he dragged the corpse from the lodge, she busied herself with starting a fire to boil water.

Chapter 28

"You have been avoiding me."

Two days later, Alex tracked Kat down in their chamber. She sat in the stone window embrasure beneath the opened shutters writing a letter. Her hair was unbound and she wore an azure tunic with yellow embroidered flowers on the rounded neck and flared cuffs. Sunshine illuminated her, giving her an ethereal quality that made her appear otherworldly.

She surprised him when she did not deny the accusation. "And?" Kat shrugged without looking at him, then dipped her quill in ink and continued writing. *Scratch, scratch, scratch.*

He spread his legs and fisted his hands on his hips. "And? That is all you have to say? You have been staying at the lodge for the last two days nursing Sir Luc, causing scurrilous talk with your behavior and you have naught to say in your defense?" Alex grimaced. It was not how he had intended to start this long overdue conversation.

She snapped her head around and glared at him. "Why should I? I have naught I'm ashamed of which needs defending," she said pointedly.

Scratch, scratch, scratch.

Alex tugged on his tunic and cleared his voice gruffly. "Ahh . . . I understand what this is about now. When I mentioned we had matters to discuss, 'tis one of the things I wished to address."

"And that would be?" *Scratch, scratch, scratch.*

Alex gritted his teeth. Obviously she was not going to make this easy for him. "You know what I am referring to, Kat."

Kat placed the quill aside, capped the inkwell and turned to him. "Aye, but I would hear it from your own lips. No more lies or evasions," her voice implacable.

Alex paced away. He felt incapable of proceeding, unsure how to begin as Kat stared daggers at him. Though he had imagined what he would say a hundred times, his suddenly dry tongue stuck to the roof of his mouth. The month he had been given to woo Kat had concluded and the time had come to learn her decision.

But first, he had some explaining to do. He wavered with indecision. He realized now his reason for deceiving Kat had been shortsighted. By keeping his secret, Alex had done the very thing he had wanted to prevent. He had put Kat in danger. And there was no defense he could give to justify his actions.

So clumsily, he blurted the first thing that came to mind. "Kat, I love you."

"I see," she said, her voice much too calm given the nature of his declaration.

"Did you hear what I said?"

She perused what she had written on parchment and then sanded it.

"Kat!" He moved to stand over her. "To whom are you writing?" he asked suspiciously. "What is so important that you cannot do me the courtesy of giving me your undivided attention?"

After placing ink and quill in her writing box, she set it down. Then Kat unfolded her legs from the window seat, stood up and brushed past him, her scent a sensual lure that distracted his senses. She whirled to face him and handed him the letter without comment. Eyeing her curiously, he read the neat, no-nonsense script. It was a letter to her steward at Montclair informing the man of her imminent arrival.

Alex crunched up the letter and tossed it out the window. Kat squeaked in protest. "When were you going to discuss this with me?"

Kat moved away and flounced down on the bed, crossing her arms. "That was a childish thing to do."

"Answer me, Kat."

She sniffed. "Though I need no longer give account to you, I had planned on informing you before I left."

"So you were running away." It was a statement.

She stiffened, offended. "Nay. Our bargain is at an end and my return home is overdue. I fulfilled my obligations of the bargain, now I expect you to do the same and see that our marriage is annulled."

Alex spun away and scrubbed a hand down his face. "So, as easy as that you have made your decision?"

Kat jumped up and clenched her skirts in her hands. "How dare you, you arrogant son of a bitch. I resent that. Naught about us or my decision has been easy."

"Then you admit you care for me?"

"Of course I do. But you lied to me, Alex, and put my life at risk. So how can I ever trust you?"

Alex clutched the bedpost, his knuckles straining. "I admit I should have told you about the traitor. But I did it to protect you!"

"Protect me?" Kat strode forward and poked her finger into his chest. "I was attacked by two outlaws and nearly raped, then bound again by Sir Stephen and almost stabbed. Had I not my dagger, we would both be dead."

Alex could not argue with such sound reasoning. He had been in the wrong. He had let his obsession for finding the traitor cloud his judgment, and in the process he endangered Kat. And that he could not forgive. At least the two outlaws had been caught and confessed that Lydia had hired them. Lydia was bound for a convent on a barren island in the north. And as soon as Sir Luc recovered, he would be dismissed from the king's service and banished from court, likely forever.

Alex turned to Kat. "I'm still confused how you learned about the traitor I sought?"

Her dark eyebrows drawn into a frown, Kat explained. "The day you recovered from your fever, I overheard you speaking to Rand about the traitor. At the mention of Scarface, I reasoned that the attack on you the day of our betrothal and the subsequent attack in the Holy Land were connected somehow. Then later I searched your belongings and found your dagger." She shrugged.

"Very clever. I always admired that about you."

Her eyebrows rose in disbelief. "I find that unbelievable considering you treat me as though I am an infant in need of mollycoddling."

"I do not treat you like an infant, but as my wife. I love you, Kat. You cannot expect me to stand by and watch while you're in danger. I have taken a vow to protect the helpless—"

Silver eyes flashed. "Arrrgh . . . When will you learn that I am not helpless." Her arms shot down beside her hips, her hands fisted. "Have I not proven to you again and again I am perfectly capable of protecting myself?"

"I'm sorry. 'Twas a poor choice of words, of course you are not helpless. I realize I should have been forthcoming and never kept secrets from you. Have you never done something you later regretted but at the time did for what you thought honorable reasons? Can you not forgive me for being so blind?"

She turned her back on him and wiped her cheek impatiently with her hand, her voice riddled with pain. "I'm sorry, Alex, but I cannot. You have betrayed me for the last time. I want an annulment."

Alex stared at Kat's stiff back in disbelief. He had never been at such a loss before. Command had always come easily to him. But neither had the outcome of a skirmish been more vitally important to his survival. Though he knew her pain was genuine, Alex hurt, too, and he inadvertently reverted to anger.

"And what will you do when an annulment is granted? Marry Sir Luc if he survives? Oh, but I forgot, he is in love with his stepmother. He was just using you so he could fornicate with his mistress." He flung the words at her like barbs, cold mockery evident in his tone.

Kat gasped and spun on him. "'Tis a cruel thing to say, Alex. How could you?"

In that moment, Alex hated her. Hated her for being so stubborn. Hated her for being so proud, so unforgiving. Mostly, he hated her for making him fall in love with her. But even as she stood before him, her face flushed, her silvery eyes condemning, a surge of excitement quickened his phallus.

"*Mayhap* because I'm not feeling very *kind* at the moment." He growled.

His gaze dropped to linger on her full bosom, which rose and fell in agitation, then lowered to her narrow waist and flaring hips. Lush hips made to harbor his hedonistic thrusts despite her denials.

Hate, anger and lust rose up and toppled him over the edge. Fierce possession blazed.

Kat saw the moment his simmering anger turned to hot lust. His eyes darkened to pitch and dropped to ogle her heaving breasts.

He released the bedpost and slowly stalked her. "Indeed. Kindness is far from my mind. You want to sever our marriage? Fine. But not before I demonstrate how much you crave my cock between those hot thighs of yours."

Instead of feeling disgust at his crude words, Kat's heart raced and her thighs quivered in anticipation. With each step Alex took, her resolve weakened. She could not seem to summon up any resistance. This would be the last time she would ever experience the amazing closeness they shared during lovemaking. The one time she could forget the past betrayals. Her disappointments. The life of loneliness she saw stretching before her.

Finally, he stopped before her, his gaze a torrid caress. Heat and hunger emanated from his body in sultry waves, reaching out to her like a primal beast in the forest calling its mate. Her breasts swelled and throbbed, blood pounding, her nipples prodded her silk chemise.

Then he raised his lustful gaze to her face, his satisfied devil-grin splashing her cheeks with the heat of embarrassment.

"You may deny that you want me, but your eyes do not lie. Your body does not lie." His voice was a dark silken taunt.

Without preamble, Alex kissed her. He took her in his arms and crushed her to his chest, his mouth a tempest as lightning struck her fevered flesh. Kat clutched Alex's back, her tongue stroking his in perfect tandem. Her nipples prodded his hard chest and she quivered in sweet torment.

"You were made for me, Kat. Deny it to yourself, but not to me." He pressed his erection against her, prodding her moist delta and causing a hot tingling.

Just as suddenly, Alex stepped back. He grabbed the hanging end of her girdle and yanked it free from the buckle. It went *thunk* to the floor. Next he removed her gown. Not to be outdone, Kat reached for Alex's tunic and tugged it over his head. They quickly divested themselves of their garments in a frenzy to touch skin to skin.

When they were both naked, Alex bent and took her nipple into his mouth. She emitted a low cry. In the same breath, the sound altered to a blissful sigh as he stroked her nipple with the rasp of his tongue, once, twice, and thrice. Then he drew her breast deep into his mouth, sucking and releasing, sucking and releasing the rigid point.

Heat shot to her feminine delta, igniting a molten flame. She pressed her lower body to his and ungulated against him trying to get closer. But she would never be close enough. She needed the oblivion of penetration where her mind did not trump her heart, needed a sweet memory to savor wherever life took her.

Alex murmured in approval, his husky voice thrilling her.

Then he surprised her when he spun her around and wrapped her hands around the bedpost.

Standing behind her, Alex saw the bewildered look on Kat's face as she peered at him over her shoulder. *She is so innocent,* he thought.

"Hang on," he said and cupped his palms under her full breasts, weighing, measuring and squeezing the exquisitely soft flesh. Next he worried the fiery tips with thumb and forefinger. Kat moaned, trying to twist around to face him. But he shoved her legs further apart with his knee and he stepped between her spread thighs.

"Alex, w—what are you—"

He kissed her upturned face hard, his tongue thrusting deep as his manhood soon would. The hot pounding of his blood filled him to bursting.

He released her lips. "You trust me in this, at least, do you not?" he asked, his breath harsh with excitement.

Kat nodded without hesitation. "Aye, Alex. I need you inside me. Now!"

She surprised him this time when her hand reached back, closed over his shaft and drew him to her entry. The passionate response nearly unmanned him, his need spiraling out of control. So poised at her entry, he dipped his knees and drove up into her in one smooth stroke. Their groans mingled as her wet sheath sucked him inexorably upward. When he reached the hilt, Alex hissed like a hot steel blade plunged into water.

"Oh God, this is wicked," she cried, her voice ragged. "We shall surely burn in Hell."

"Nay, we shall burn in ecstasy." To demonstrate he rotated his hips.

Kat whimpered. The sensation of Alex inside her, stretching her, was still new and strange, but the pleasure was like nothing she had ever experienced before. With him inside her, his arms wrapped tenderly around her, she no longer felt alone, abandoned. And though she knew she should be appalled to be taken in such a primitive fashion, her secret feminine side that wanted to be dominated found it supremely provocative.

Then he began to move inside her, guiding her hips back and forth, teaching her the primordial rhythm. She took it up and pushed her hips back to meet him. He drove into her again and again, his thrusts hard, savage, making her wild.

With each plunge, pleasure spiked deep inside her, spreading rapidly, their flesh slapping in frenzied abandon. Sweat from his body dripped onto her back.

He moaned in her ear. "Aye, my feisty kitten, that's it, move with me." He attached his lips to her earlobe and sucked.

Their strokes became hard and uncontrollable. His teeth nipped her vulnerable neck, only to soothe it with a swipe of his tongue. A shiver of pleasure raced down her spine, raising goose bumps in its wake.

"Mmmm," he murmured, "you are delectable. I shall never forget your taste."

His hand pressed against her quivering stomach, she clutched the bedpost tighter, arching her back wantonly as he plunged deep inside her. Faster. Harder. In that moment all thought was obliterated. Her sheath tightened around his marble-hard shaft, a silken torment as he rammed into her with jarring force.

"Alex . . . Oh God. Ahhh . . . Ahhh . . . Ahhrgh," she screamed, unable to hold back her wild moans. Heat and desire surged through her body like a mighty tide, her moist folds pulsing and throbbing unbearably.

Kat's screams carried Alex over desire's precipice. Her inner muscles contracted around him. Squeeze and release. Squeeze and release. Alex convulsed excitedly, shouting in satisfaction as pleasure erupted and his seed flooded her.

He came and came, her steamy vortex sucking him dry till he was spent, weak, and shaken by the aftermath.

But when her legs collapsed he had enough presence of mind to support Kat with one arm. His own legs shaky, he drew her onto the bed and settled in beside her. He wrapped his arms around her, their panting breaths harsh in the intimate confines of the curtained canopy bed.

Kat did not feel him drape her on the bed. Or brush her hair back from her moist brow tenderly. Or hold her close against him as their heartbeats slowly returned to normal. Her senses were still reeling and overwhelmed. She tried to keep her eyes open, but exhausted, emotionally and physically, she fell into blessed sleep.

Chapter 29

Kat opened her eyes. Alex stared down at her. Lying on his side next to her, his head propped on one hand, he stroked her temple with his left hand. She must have fallen asleep. She looked down, wary and embarrassed, clasping her hands on top of the coverlet that covered her.

The musky scent of their lust perfumed the air inside the curtained bed.

"Your pardon. I did not mean to fall asleep."

Alex chuckled. "I am hardly offended."

Kat sat up abruptly and then screeched when the sheet dropped. She grabbed it and clutched it to her breasts. "You need not boast. I have had very little sleep what with nursing you then Sir Luc—"

Alex jumped out of the bed and spun on her, his handsome face furious to behold. Against her will, her gaze dropped to stare at his *still* hard member jutting up heavenward, threatening. "You need not mention that scurrilous bastard. Are you not angry that he betrayed you? He was Lydia's lover. He was going to marry you under false pretences because of his obsession with the conniving bitch," he swore, his eyes filled with wrath.

His accusations infuriated her. Clutching the sheet to her chest, Kat scrambled out of the bed and wrapped the linen around her to shield her nudity. They stared at one another across the chasm of the bed. She knew her eyes blazed as bright as his. "You are a hypocrite, Sir Alex. *You* were Lady Lydia's lover. *You* married me under deception."

Alex raised his chin defiantly and punched the bedpost with his clenched fist. "That may be true, but the circumstances are completely different and you know it. Sir Luc pretended to love you to get you to marry him, so he could whore with Lady Lydia behind your back. So why do you not hate the bastard as you hate me?"

When she did not answer he stormed around the bed, his face twisted in fury. She did not move a muscle, standing her ground, prepared to give no quarter. It was a decision she came to regret. Alex grabbed her shoulders and shoved her against the bedpost, trapping her. The carvings dug into her back as he shook her. "Answer me. If you do not, I shall personally see we are bound together forever. No matter my vow to annul our marriage."

Kat gasped. "You would not break a sworn vow. Your honor means more to you than your life. Than even me!" Her voice cracked with the pain of betrayal.

"Answer me!" he roared.

Fear made her blurt, "Because I do not love him, you fool. I never have!" she cried.

Kat gasped at her unbidden revelation. Alex's eyes widened when he caught the significance of her words.

He plopped down on the chest at the foot of the bed, holding her gaze. "You love me," his voice a mixture of hope, wonder, and disbelief.

"Nay, I hate you." Kat heard the desperation in her voice.

His eyes sparked with deep emotion, with love. "'Tis too late, my love. You cannot undo the words."

A tight grip on the sheets, she shuffled away. "It changes naught. I still want an annulment."

He stood, his eyes narrowed. "So you can forgive only those you do not love? Is that what you are saying?" his voice vibrated dangerously.

She glared. "I expected more from you."

"That is your problem, Kat. You expect those around you to be perfect. You give your loyalty unswervingly to those you love and woe to anyone who fails you. Long ago you built up this heroic image of me in your mind that never existed. I am no legendary King Arthur. I am just a man, nothing more. An imperfect, fallible man who made unwise decisions that caused harm to the woman he loves."

She shook her hair back off her face and jabbed her hand out pointing a finger at him. "You shall not turn this on me, Alex. Are you going to fulfill your sworn oath and have the marriage annulled as you agreed?" She stubbornly refused to listen to him and open her heart to rejection again. It hurt too damn much.

Alex quickly shuttered his expression, concealing all emotion except anger. "By God, Kat, you are a hard, unforgiving woman."

A brief wail of pain escaped her lips as she clutched her chest. It felt as though he plunged a hot stake through her heart. All her life, all she ever wanted was to be loved. But always, the people who were supposed to love her most had failed her. Suddenly, his cruel words opened a rift and years of heartache and despair that she kept hidden from everyone lest she be pitied spewed forth.

"Unfair! If I am a hard woman, 'tis because I have had to be. Everyone I have ever loved has abandoned me!"

"What are you talking about, Kat? I have no intention of abandoning you. 'Tis you who wish to sever our marriage."

"First my mother abandoned me, then my father. I had no family left, so when you and I married, I thought if I could just make you love me I would not be so alone anymore and we could start a family of our own. But you left me, too," she whispered in misery, her shoulders sagging in defeat.

Kat did not resist when Alex tugged her into his arms. "Oh Kat, I have been such a fool. Aye, I left you, but part of me was running away from the deep feelings I had come to have for you. I was afraid, never having felt aught like it before, not even for Lady Lydia. That was why I snuck away like a thief. It did not take me long to realize that running away was a mistake. But by then it was too late to turn back."

Tears rolled down Kat's face as Alex held her pressed to his chest. His admission eased the hard ache she had carried around in her heart for as long as she could remember. Since her mother died giving birth to a stillborn, much-desired heir.

After her mother had had several miscarriages, the midwife told her parents that if she ever carried a baby to full term she could die. But despite the warning, her mother desperately wanted a boy. Kat, a girl, was not enough to make her mother happy. Kat had never forgotten that, and feelings of inadequacy tormented her through her whole life.

Then when her mother died, Kat and her father grew closer. She became the boy he never had. Then her father died, too. And she did not know where she belonged anymore.

Kat pulled out of his arms and gave him her back.

"I love you, Kat. I believe you are the strongest, bravest, most courageous woman I know. Except when it comes to your heart. I gave you up once and hurt you badly. But I promise I will never hurt you again. Can you not find it inside you to forgive me? To trust me with your heart and give me a second chance?"

Kat was forlorn. Alex was right. She was afraid. Only cowards could not confront their fears and triumph over them. She despised cowardice. Alex was a good man who made mistakes and asked that she forgive him. On her part, she loved him and knew he truly regretted hurting her. How could she not put her trust in Alex when he would brave death to protect her? He proved that to her when he nearly died saving her and Matthew from the bear.

And Lady Lydia no longer stood in the way. Alex was free of the woman's manipulative influence. Even before he learned Lydia was the traitor, he had recognized that his love for her had been a youth's infatuation. That day in the linen cupboard, he had believed Kat's word over Lydia's lies.

But was she brave enough to entrust her heart to Alex?

"If I have to beg, I will," he said grimly.

At the rustling sound behind her, she twisted around. Alex knelt before her and raised the linen material pooling around her feet. She watched in horror as Alex bent over and kissed the hem.

She jerked the sheet from his hands. "Get up, Alex. You look ridiculous. You need not beg. It will not change my decision."

He ignored her and took her hand in his. His bold blue gaze shone with emotion, with a tenderness that made her tremble. "I beg your forgiveness for deserting you after our marriage. I beg you let me love you for all the days we have left on this earth. I cannot promise I shall not die. Only God has that power. But I have had a glimpse of Heaven here on earth with you and I swear I shall never abandon you again."

"Alex—"

He kissed her hand. "I beg you be my partner in marriage, my confidant, my conscience and my protector. And grant me the same right to protect you when you are in need. I am naught without you, Kat. Can you forgive me?"

"Aye, you fool. I forgive you. Now prithee, stand up, begging does not become you." Alex appeared so startled Kat nearly laughed.

"You forgive me?"

She nodded gravely.

He did not move, but remained kneeling. "You forgive me, but what of your heart? The choice is yours to make. Would you have me as your husband to love and honor from this day forward, till death parts us?"

Kat threw up her arms, frowning. "You are insufferable. Aye, I choose you. Now I beg *you*, rise."

Alex rose onto his feet, his blue eyes wide and stunned. "Do you mean it? Verily?"

Kat grinned. Her heart felt as though it would float away. For too long she allowed fear to get a grip on her heart and in the way of her happiness. Alex loved her and she loved him.

If they never lost sight of that, any other troubles that arose in future they could face together.

"Verily. I do. You were right. 'Twas fear holding me back, though I hate to admit it," she confessed ruefully. "But I shall not let it dominate my life anymore. I love you, Alex. I always have and always will."

Alex pulled her into his arms, clutched her face between his warm palms and stared down at her with a passionate intensity. "I must be dreaming. Tell me you love me again." His eyes shone with an odd combination of fear, disbelief, and hope.

She licked her suddenly dry lips, her heart pumping rapidly in her chest. "I love you, Alex. I want naught more than to share my life with you at Montclair and if the Lord wills it, have a passel of babies to fill the castle with laughter."

Alex grinned with wicked promise. "A passel of babies? I love this woman," he shouted. He wrapped his uninjured arm around her hips, lifted her up in the air and spun around, the sheet trailing behind her. Kat giggled above him, her hands braced on his shoulders. But she did not fear he would let her fall.

"Aye, a whole castle full."

Slowly, Alex slid Kat down his naked torso. It was enough to make a man explode. Instead, he felt a grin spread from ear to ear. "I want to have little girls just like you—bold and beautiful, with black hair and silver eyes. I shall teach them how to hunt and ride and fish and swim. And wield a dagger, of course," he said, a devilish gleam in his eyes. His wife blushed adorably.

This is the happiest moment of my life, Alex thought. With Kat by his side he could achieve anything.

Kat planted her hands on her hips. Her eyes sparkled. "And what of using the bow and arrow?"

"My girls shall be the best marksmen in the entire shire, nay, the country."

"Markswomen. We shall start a new trend. And what if we have boys?"

"You shall teach them. But first we must begin procreating at every opportunity if you want a large family." He whipped the sheet off Kat.

Kat pressed her hand on her bare belly. "Who knows?" she said in wonder, "I may be with child even now."

Alex's heart jolted at her words. A buzz sounded in his ears, his vision spun, right before his knees buckled beneath him. Luckily, he fell forward and landed on the bed, unconscious, shock at the possibility of impending fatherhood too much.

Kat watched, amazed, as Alex fainted. The notion that such a brave, strong man like Alex, a man she had thought invulnerable, feared becoming a father, endeared him to her as naught else could. She crawled up on the bed next to him and gently brushed back his hair from his moist forehead.

Breathing in his enticing manly scent, she kissed his cheek. And uttered a whispered caress. "I love this man."

More by Bestselling Author
Fern Michaels

__About Face	0-8217-7020-9	$7.99US/$10.99CAN
__Wish List	0-8217-7363-1	$7.50US/$10.50CAN
__Picture Perfect	0-8217-7588-X	$7.99US/$10.99CAN
__Vegas Heat	0-8217-7668-1	$7.99US/$10.99CAN
__Finders Keepers	0-8217-7669-X	$7.99US/$10.99CAN
__Dear Emily	0-8217-7670-3	$7.99US/$10.99CAN
__Sara's Song	0-8217-7671-1	$7.99US/$10.99CAN
__Vegas Sunrise	0-8217-7672-X	$7.99US/$10.99CAN
__Yesterday	0-8217-7678-9	$7.99US/$10.99CAN
__Celebration	0-8217-7679-7	$7.99US/$10.99CAN
__Payback	0-8217-7876-5	$6.99US/$9.99CAN
__Vendetta	0-8217-7877-3	$6.99US/$9.99CAN
__The Jury	0-8217-7878-1	$6.99US/$9.99CAN
__Sweet Revenge	0-8217-7879-X	$6.99US/$9.99CAN
__Lethal Justice	0-8217-7880-3	$6.99US/$9.99CAN
__Free Fall	0-8217-7881-1	$6.99US/$9.99CAN
__Fool Me Once	0-8217-8071-9	$7.99US/$10.99CAN
__Vegas Rich	0-8217-8112-X	$7.99US/$10.99CAN
__Hide and Seek	1-4201-0184-6	$6.99US/$9.99CAN
__Hokus Pokus	1-4201-0185-4	$6.99US/$9.99CAN
__Fast Track	1-4201-0186-2	$6.99US/$9.99CAN
__Collateral Damage	1-4201-0187-0	$6.99US/$9.99CAN
__Final Justice	1-4201-0188-9	$6.99US/$9.99CAN

Available Wherever Books Are Sold!
Check out our website at **www.kensingtonbooks.com**